NRDS

SEASON 1

* National Recently Deceased Services

JP RINDFLEISCH IX
JEFF ELKINS

For all of those who die with unfinished business, those they leave behind, and the weirdos who have to deal with all of them.

Contents

Introduction

This book was written as a serial. Chapters were written as contained weekly episodes from Autumn 2021 to Winter 2022. We are excited to have them all together, in their original serial form, in this season one volume of NRDS.

One

High Strung

"T HIS GHOST KILLED TWO of our agents, and we're just gonna stand here with our dicks in our hands?" the spunky agent with a high ponytail said.

Buck ignored her, shifting his weight from his right leg to his left as he looked past the bright sodium streetlights to apartment 1097.

"I say we just charge in and take this bastard down," one of the younger agents declared. The kid looked barely out of high school, with a wisp of peach fuzz on his baby face. He looked especially young standing next to the guy built like a tank with tattoos streaming up his neck.

Buck hoped something would happen soon. His sixty-one-year-old knees couldn't stand here much longer, and the five NRDS agents crowding behind him only added to his discomfort. They all wore the same crisp black and white suit too, which clashed with his well-worn brown one. Even the briefcases they held looked brand new compared to his older model. Newbie NRDS, always dressed to impress.

"Come on, chief. There's six of us and one of it. We can take it," Tattoo Neck agreed.

"We wait on Buck," Agent Rodgers said. She was a tall Black woman with a shaved head and a gold nose ring. She was their team leader, and the only one who seemed to know what she was doing. The National Recently Deceased Services was smart to make her a team leader, Buck thought.

"What are we waiting for, Buck?" Baby Face whined.

Buck sighed and loosened the tie around his neck.

"Come on, chief. This old timer here is going to have us standing out here all night," Tattoo Neck complained.

"We wait on Buck," Rodgers said.

A car rolled past them, paying them no notice. Even in downtown Chicago, this backstreet was quiet at two in the morning. A light flickered in the apartment.

"Did you see that! That was it, right? Let's go!" Number Five said, his eyes never leaving the apartment window.

Buck considered the light. "Could just be the daughter getting a glass of water."

"Or it could be killing someone else," Tattoo Neck countered.

"Anyone know what level this is?" Buck asked.

"I know it killed agents White and Anderson," Ponytail blurted out. The rest mumbled in agreement.

"So, no?" Buck pushed.

Their mumbles quieted.

"None of you," Buck said, looking each one of the junior agents in the eye, "no one has any idea what we are walking into?" And with a sigh, he returned to watching the apartment.

"Doesn't matter. We can take it," Tattoo Neck spoke up.

"What's your name, agent?" Buck asked without looking back.

"Anthony Ramirez. Third generation, two-year agent with twenty-one hostile catches," Ramirez bragged.

"Two years in? That's about where the rest of you are too, huh?" Buck asked.

There was a murmured response.

"Why, then, are you all so eager to join White and Anderson? You have some kind of third-gen death wish?"

"No. I mean, no sir," Ramirez said, looking down at the ground.

Rodgers raised a hand. "The main office sent Buck to us because he's a legend. You all know his stats. Over three-thousand hostile catches. Over forty years in the agency. And I know we've all heard about the Night of Twenty-Five, or the South Shore Stampede, or the Morgan Park Massacre? I mean, guys, this is Buck Hampton. This man here is in the manual, right?"

The team murmured in agreement.

"So, as much as we all want to charge in there, maybe we give Buck a little respect and wait for his call. Got it?"

"Yes, Captain," the team mumbled in agreement.

"Great. Now stay focused. Because tonight, we're going to take this son-of-a-bitch down," Rodgers said.

Buck sighed. Hearing his stats only brought back terrible memories and reminded him how old he was.

Another car rolled by, and Buck looked at his watch. Two thirty-four.

"The last agents went in around two-thirty. We lost contact shortly after. If the pattern holds, it'll be any second now." Rodgers stated the facts she knew he already knew.

Buck agreed. He squeezed his silver, standard-issue badge and looked back up at the apartment, squinting.

"Look, look" he heard Baby Face shout. What first looked like a trick of the light slowly congealed into a green haze forming in the kitchen window.

"It's happening!" Ponytail confirmed. Frost built at the edges, yet the windows nearby were untouched.

"Green glow. Ice formation." Rodgers confirmed.

"We've got Level 4 confirmation." Ramirez choked.

"Let's move!" Rodgers ordered. Her four team members raced across the street in a manic rush, swinging their briefcases wildly as they ran.

Buck shook his head as he sauntered behind them and laughed when their charge was ground to a halt when two of the agents both tried to enter the revolving door at the same time.

They wedged themselves into the small triangle of a space by meticulously side-stepping into the building. Buck quietly waited his turn as each agent anxiously pushed through the door.

By the time Buck made his way into the lobby, Rodgers was holding the door to the stairs open, shouting, "Let's move!" as her team raced through the opening.

Watching them go, Buck walked to the elevator and pressed the "up" button. The doors opened, and he casually stepped inside.

Journey played softly through the elevator speaker, and Buck quietly hummed along as he rode the car to the tenth floor and checked his phone.

There was a message from his husband. "Remember, dear. Inexperience is not the fault of the young. It's their connection to wonder." Buck snorted a laugh and stuffed his phone back in his pocket. His husband always knew the best motivational quote to send him.

He arrived in the tenth-floor hallway a few seconds before the team burst through the stairway door. "Let's go, agents," Buck said as he waved them to follow him. He walked in silence down the hall as the team stalked behind him.

As they approached the door of apartment 1097, Rodgers asked, "Should we break it down?"

Buck shot her a glare and said, "No." Knocking, he called, "Landlord. Gas leak. Open up."

When there was no answer, he banged and yelled again, "Ms. Parker! Ms. Parker! It's the landlord! Open up!"

Rodgers whispered nervously, "Get ready to breach, men. Ramirez, I want you kicking it down. Lee and Thompson, you are the first two through! Briefcases and stun guns ready!"

Buck sighed, shook his head, and pulled a paperclip and a pocketknife out of his jacket. He straightened the paperclip and then bent it slightly at the end. Pushing the blade of the knife into the bottom of the lock, he turned it gently until he felt resistance.

Keeping pressure on the knife, he pushed the paperclip into the top of the lock and pushed the pins of the lock up one at a time. As the fifth pin released, his knife turned, and the door came open. Closing the knife and putting it back in his jacket pocket, Buck called into the dark apartment, "Hello? Ms. Parker? Gas leak? Anyone home?" When no answer came, he crept through the door into the stillness.

The front living space was only big enough for a couch, coffee table, and TV stand. Buck whispered, "Clear it," and the other agents fanned out, examining every nook and cranny of the room, their tasers at the ready.

Past the living room was a kitchen only wide enough for two people to stand in. There was no sign of the green mist he'd seen from the sidewalk outside, so Buck continued down the hall to the bathroom. The door was cracked open, so he peered inside, but it was empty.

He turned to look back at the team when something caught his eye.

"Slowly!" Buck instructed Ramirez as he caught sight of the elderly woman. "We don't want to startle her."

She stood still as a statue, in a faded white nightgown. Her head was cocked to the left at an impossible angle, and her eyes were wide with a soft green glow.

"Level four possession." Ramirez whispered.

"Badges up and tasers at the ready!" Rodgers yelled from behind Buck as the retrofitted tasers of several agents came to life with a hum.

At the sound, the woman gave a low, ragged growl before twitching her head and taking a step forward. Buck spotted the green glow around her, and he held up a hand.

"No! Wait!" Buck yelled.

The elderly woman bent her head in the other direction and smiled. She mimicked his movement, raising her hand, revealing fingernails that had been filed to razor-sharp points. Her voice sounded like several screeching out all at once. "No! Wait!"

"Something's not right," Buck said, taking a step back.

"This is for White and Anderson!" yelled Ramirez.

"We got this!" yelled Lee.

The elderly woman smiled wider, cracked lips pulling back to reveal filed dentures. Her head flopped to the left as she took another step forward.

"Wait! Just wait!" Buck yelled.

"Buck! Get out of the way and let us tase her!" Rodgers yelled.

Buck squinted at the old woman, squeezing his badge tight in his hands. Then he saw it. "The daughter," he whispered, pointing to the fishing-line-thin strand of light streaming off the elderly woman's wrist into the darkness of the ceiling.

"On my count, deploy your cases," Rodgers commanded, understanding Buck's plan as the old woman took another step forward as she mimicked Buck's actions and the echoing voices called out "The daughter."

"One."

Buck took a step closer and raised his briefcase.

"One," the voices mocked.

"Two."

He popped open the case with one swift motion, filling the hall with bright light and unveiling another woman, younger, paler, with ravenous eyes, peering down from the corner.

"Two." The voices cheered, thinking they'd won.

"As far as you can. Three!" Rodgers screamed, and five briefcases flew past his own and landed under the younger woman on the ceiling. The extra lights revealed hundreds of strings of green mist tied around the elderly woman, tracing back to her daughter.

"No!" the voices echoed.

The spirit daughter hissed as the light surrounded her and yanked her downward.

The team held their breath, willing the spirit to go quickly.

The elderly woman collapsed to the ground, the green strings receding.

The team leaned forward, silently pleading with the spirit to move on.

The spirit screamed and howled, resisting the light. She clawed at the ceiling, leaving behind deep gashes, but the light didn't loosen its grip on her.

No one moved, the silence deafening the apartment.

Finally, as if in slow motion, the young woman fell free from the wall and into the briefcase.

"Yes!" Ponytail shot a fist into the air as the case slammed shut, leaving them all in darkness again.

Baby Face and Jitters jumped forward, closing the cases one by one with massive smiles on their faces, returning the apartment to darkness. Ponytail and Ramirez flipped the light switches, casting the room in iridescent light before pulling on a pair of rubber gloves and grabbing cleaning supplies from under the sink.

"Good thing you were here. I'd hate to think how many more she'd have killed using the old woman like that," Rodgers said.

"You've got a good team here. They're a little green, but they'll grow out of it." Buck muttered under his breath while the other agents clapped and celebrated the victory.

Walking to the woman lying on the floor, Buck checked for a pulse. "Looks like Ms. Parker and her daughter have both been dead for some time. You'll probably find the daughter's body in the bedroom. Get it cleaned up and make sure you file the right paperwork."

"I'll go look," Baby Face volunteered.

"Photos first," Rodgers reminded him. She turned to Buck and made a "get out of here" motion with her head before heading down the hallway to the bedroom.

Buck yawned as he rode the elevator back down. He mumbled to himself, "I'm getting too old for this."

The chilly night wind brushed against his face, giving him a jolt of unwanted energy as he tried to remember in which direction he'd parked his car. He stifled a yawn, contemplating if he wanted to make the long drive home or just hit up the nearest motel when his phone rang. Hoping it was Gerry, he answered without checking the number. "This is Buck."

"Buck. It's Martin. You bagged it. Never a doubt." Buck's manager said on the other end of the line, his words popping through the phone.

"Yeah, boss. Got it."

"Good job. As always. It take anyone?"

"Everyone's fine." Buck stifled another yawn, wishing Martin would skip the recap and get to the point.

"Good to hear. Good to hear. Hey, I'm sorry to call so late. But something's come up."

"Another job?"

"Gerry loves new places. Right?"

Buck sighed. "You got any details?"

8

"Comes straight from DC. Marked urgent."

"How urgent?"

"I'm in the office. Filing the paperwork. There's been reports of odd flare-ups. Spirits left and right."

Buck waited, knowing there was more. Martin wouldn't call in the middle of the night after a hostile capture for a flare-up.

"DC thinks someone is behind it. They want you to find the source. There's a new office opening. Use it as your cover."

"Where are we going this time?"

"Gerry's going to love it, Buck. Great little town called New Richmond."

"Where in the fuck is New Richmond?"

Two

Dead End Job

T HE BOXY BLACK OLDSMOBILE Cutlass cruised down South Knowles Street, one-story shops passing by in a blur. Ethan looked down at his phone and attempted to open the new puzzle game his sister had downloaded, but a quick turn caused the device to slip from his hands and fall between the seat and the door.

As he fished for it, Buck, the older man behind the wheel said, "Sit up. We're almost here."

Ethan could touch the corner of the device with his finger, but he couldn't get a hold of it. Pushing closer to it, he said, "So, um. I heard you were transferred here."

"Month ago," Buck said, expressionless.

"Got it!" Ethan said as he pinched the phone with two fingers and drew it out.

"You're on the clock. Act like it," Buck said without taking his eyes off the road.

"Cool. Cool, cool, cool," Ethan said, stuffing the phone into the inside pocket of his suit coat.

A moment of silence passed as Ethan watched the buildings of downtown New Richmond turn into countryside. Adjusting his tie, he considered taking off his jacket. He'd purchased the suit from the Salvation

Army two days ago and had only this morning discovered it was a touch too small.

Breaking the silence, he asked, "Do you like it?"

"Like what?"

"Being transferred?"

Buck shrugged, keeping his eyes on the road.

"So, um. Did you, like, have to move here? Or do you just commute in during the week?"

"We moved," Buck said.

"Cool. Cool," Ethan said with a forced smile and nod.

They rode in silence again. Ethan watched more one-story shops and small houses whiz by. Already feeling like a child riding next to an angry parent, he fought back the urge to ask, "How much longer?"

"New Richmond's a pretty good place to live. I mean, I like it. I don't really know anything else though. I've been here my whole life. Grew up over in Clear Lake. Go Warriors!" Ethan said with a fist pump.

Buck didn't respond.

Ethan laughed to himself. "That was my high school mascot. Clear Lake High Warriors. It was cool. I could have gone to college. I had a scholarship and everything. But, you know. It didn't really work out. Anyway, if you need the hook up, I know all the good stops to eat. I can show you around, if you want. You know, since you're new in town and all."

Buck kept his eyes on the road, his hands at 10 and 2.

Ethan scrambled in his mind for something else to say. "Did, um. Did you go to college somewhere?"

Buck nodded. "Long time ago."

"Cool. Cool," Ethan said with another nod and smile. "I'll probably go someday. I don't know. Getting this job has got me pretty pumped, though. I mean, it's not what I thought I'd be doing. When I took that government service test, I was thinking I'd, like, be at the Post Office or something. I didn't even know National Recently Deceased Services was a thing."

Buck sighed.

"I mean, last week I was bagging groceries and mopping floors at the Walmart outside of town. This has to be better than that, right?"

"Hmm," Buck grunted as he gave another shrug.

"I mean, I won't be cleaning poop off toilets at least. I feel like that was the bottom. Nowhere to go but up, you know?"

"Sure, kid."

Ethan looked down at the floorboard. The car was pristine, as if it had been vacuumed that morning. His car was never this clean. Looking up again and flashing Buck another smile, he added, "I mean, I've only been on the job for thirty minutes, and I'm already on a ride-along. That's way better in my book."

Talking about Walmart made Ethan think about the smell of the cleaning fluid in the mop bucket. He could feel its sting in his nose. Even though his old boss had told him it was fine, he was sure it was giving him cancer. Shaking his head, and taking a deep breath, he asked, "What are we doing today anyway? Is this like a house call or something?"

"Only way to explain what we do is to show you," Buck said as he slowed the car.

Turning left, he pulled into the parking lot of an old red-brick church. The sign out front read "St. Patrick's Episcopal Church." The building was little more than a few big rooms with steep roofs and a steeple with a small statue of their patron saint overlooking everyone who entered. Ethan wondered if they had bells that chimed every hour. He loved the sound of chimes. "Do we work with a lot of churches? I'd imagine we help with funeral rites or something?" he asked.

"No. You got your badge?" Buck asked as he parked the car and put the keys in his pocket.

"Yep. Got it right here," Ethan said as he leaned forward to remove the leather wallet he'd been handed this morning from his back pocket.

Opening his coat, Buck pointed to how his badge was tucked into his inner pocket. "Put it here."

"Oh. Okay. That makes sense. This way I won't drop it," Ethan said as he rushed to follow Buck's instructions by moving his phone to his front pocket and then his wallet inside his coat.

"Get the briefcase," Buck said as he and Ethan stepped out of the car.

Opening the back door, Ethan retrieved the black leather briefcase from the backseat. "Should there be something in it? I checked earlier and it's empty, but I didn't want to say anything."

Buck opened the door to the backseat and picked up a clipboard full of forms. He stood and made eye contact with Ethan over the roof of the car. "You didn't read the manual, did you?"

"What? Come on. I read it. I know the case is supposed to be empty. Of course it's empty, duh. Because we're like, going to put stuff in it."

Buck snorted a laugh and started toward the church.

"So, like, part of the manual that confused me was, like, how we figure out where to find the stuff that goes in the case," Ethan said as he chased after him.

Buck talked as he walked. "Alright, kid. Rules. First, never leave the car without the badge and briefcase. Second, never come alone. Third, don't let the deceased touch the badge or the briefcase. And fourth. Until you've been trained, don't talk. Got it?" Buck asked.

"Yep. Keep my mouth shut. Got it," Ethan said with a smile.

"Good," Buck said as he walked past the church's front door toward the side of the building.

Once they had rounded the corner, Ethan spotted the cemetery next to the church. It only contained a couple hundred graves and was surrounded by a small stone wall. Two men leaned against the far corner. The first was older and in a tan suit Ethan was sure was more out of date than the Salvation Army special he was wearing. The second man was younger and wore a green army uniform like soldiers wore in World War II movies. "Take a look at those guys. It's like a costume party, right?" Ethan quipped with a laugh.

Buck took hold of the iron gate, pulled it open, and explained, "Herschel and Charlie are scheduled for weekly stop-bys. They've been Class Ones since the fifties."

"Class Ones?" Ethan asked, confused.

"In that manual you read," Buck said, looking at Ethan.

"Well, I mean, you know, it's big. I don't really remember everything in it. Like, I didn't memorize it or anything."

"Page seventy-eight. Top of the page. Classification system. Memorize it."

"Okay, page seventy-eight. Got it. Page seventy-eight."

Walking toward the two men, Buck nodded and said, "Herschel. Charlie."

Herschel, the older of the two, nodded back. The one in uniform smiled, stepped forward, and said, "Hey, Buck. Man, it's good to see you. Beautiful weather, right? I saw in the paper that you guys have an opening in the office. You think I might—"

Buck interrupted by clicking his pen and beginning to scribble notes on the top form of his clipboard. "We've already got one BOB in service It'll be a while before we get approval to dig up another. This is just a routine check-in."

"Who's the new kid?" Herschel asked.

"Ethan Malik. First day, so be nice," Buck said.

Remaining against the wall, Herschel offered a slight smile, but Charlie stepped forward and said, "It's a pleasure to meet you. My name is Charlie Clementine."

"Nice to meet you too," Ethan said, extending his hand. Charlie returned the gesture, but rather than shaking hands like Ethan had done a thousand times before, cold air tore through Ethan's knuckles and made them ache as his hand passed through Charlie's. Taking a step back, Ethan exclaimed, "What the hell!"

Herschel laughed. "He really is new."

"It's crazy, right?" Charlie said as he waved his hand back and forth through Ethan's. Ethan pulled his hand back after a moment, opening and closing it to get the circulation flowing again. "Go ahead. Put your arm in me. I know you want to. Promise, it doesn't hurt," he added, puffing out his chest.

Ethan looked at Buck, who was still focused on his form, and then stuck his hand into Charlie's chest. Seeing what should be solid flesh swirl like dust in the wind, Ethan recoiled. "Whoa," he said as he did it again. That time, Charlie's face turned a funny color, and he backed away, dry heaving.

"Sorry. I didn't mean to—"

Herschel let out a roaring laugh and pulled Charlie back against the wall. "Guess old Charlie here doesn't know his own limits."

Charlie coughed out a laugh and looked at Ethan. "Too much phasing makes ya woozy."

"I'm sorry. I didn't know," Ethan offered.

"Don't worry about it. You're handling this a lot better than I would have when I was your age. If you'd told me that, after I died, I'd end up floating around a graveyard for seventy years, I'd have lost my mind."

Crossing his arms, Herschel said, "If you told me I had to spend seventy years with this moron, I would have willed myself to live forever."

Charlie looked at Ethan, shook his head, and said, "He's just kidding."

"No, I'm not," Herschel said.

Charlie nodded knowingly. "He's hysterical, right? You gotta love him."

The immediate shock passing and the weight of everything falling on him, Ethan took a step back and stared at the pair, his head cocked and his mouth hanging open.

"You broke the new kid," Herschel said with a laugh.

Looking up from his form, Buck said, "Alright, gentlemen. Let's get into it. How are you feeling today? Have there been any surges or fears of escalation in your condition?"

"Same as always," Herschel said.

"I feel great. Fit as a fiddle," Charlie said.

Not looking up from the form he was filling out, Buck said, "Any disturbances in your immediate area?"

"No," Herschel said.

Charlie waved his hand in front of Ethan's face and asked, "Is he alright? Ethan? You doing okay?"

"He'll be fine," Buck said.

"Close your mouth, kid. You might catch a bee in there," Herschel said.

Ethan took a deep breath and looked around, focusing on nothing in particular. "So. Are you, like . . ."

"Dead," Herschel said.

Charlie shook his head in disapproval. "He didn't read the manual, did he? Probably didn't even look close at the job description."

"Leave the kid alone," Herschel said.

"What? I'm just saying that it can be a shock. One minute you think people die and go to heaven and then the next you learn some of us are still hanging around." Stepping closer to Ethan, Charlie raised his voice to say, "We are ghosts. Herschel and me. Ghosts."

"Spirits," Buck corrected.

Taking a step back again, Charlie said, "Ethan. I died in '51 during the Battle of Heartbreak Ridge. I took mortar fire while I was trying to take a hill. At least, that's what they said at my funeral. I don't really remember. Herschel here died in '42."

"Leave me out of this foolishness," Herschel said.

"Heart attack. Left behind a wife and two kids. She's buried over there. But I'm not sure about his kids. They're not here, and he won't tell me."

Frantically looking around, Ethan began reading the names on the surrounding tombstones. "Herschel Blake? That's you. Right there. That's your grave," Ethan exclaimed.

"Keep up, kid," Herschel said.

Tapping his pen on his clipboard, Buck said, "Have you thought of anything that might keep you from transitioning?"

"No," Herschel said.

Looking at the sky, Charlie sighed and said, "I don't know. I don't think so. I've been thinking a lot about my mom and how I didn't get to say goodbye to her."

"He's fine too. Next question," Herschel said.

"Do you have any information for me about your surrounding community that might be helpful to our organization's mission?" Buck said.

"Okay. So . . ." Charlie said, moving his hands like he was about to start an important story.

Holding his hand up, Buck said, "Information that will be helpful to our organization's mission."

Charlie raised his hands in defensiveness. "Buck. Come on. I'm not here to waste your time. I've got actual stuff this week."

"You may want to take a seat, kid. He can go on for a while," Herschel said to Ethan.

Ignoring him, Charlie pressed on. "This week, Martha—she's the priest. She's really sweet, but in way over her head with this congregation. Anyway, she's been getting regular visits from Anthony Parker. He's the used car salesman. He's got a shop over on Deere Drive."

"The one with the busted sign," Ethan offered.

"That's him!" Charlie exclaimed.

"Ony's Garage," Ethan said with a grin.

"I don't know how that place stays open. There are never any cars there. Not enough to pay the bills anyway," Charlie said.

Buck pointed his pen at Ethan and said, "Don't encourage him." Then pointing the pen at Charlie, he said, "Get to the point."

Charlie nodded. "I'll sum up. So, Anthony. He's been coming by to see Martha regularly. And I think it is more than pastoral care visits, if you know what I mean. So, for a few nights this week I followed her home. She lives right up the street over there, so it isn't much of a walk. And guess what?"

"What?" Ethan said.

"Seriously," Herschel complained.

"He brought her dinner. And flowers. Which, I think you know, means they are definitely courting," Charlie said, folding his arms over his chest.

Scribbling notes on the form, Buck said, "Thank you for the intel. I'll log it in our files."

"There's more," Charlie said with a sly grin.

"No. We have enough for now." Buck finished up his notes on the form and clipped his pen to the board.

NRDS: NATIONAL RECENTLY DECEASED SERVICES

Kicking at the dirt, which wasn't responding to his boot, Charlie said, "Alright. Well, next week then."

"See you next week," Herschel said with a wave.

"It was, um, really great to meet you both." Ethan waved before turning to catch up with Buck, who was already on his way back to the car.

"Come by anytime," Charlie called.

"We'll be here," Herschel yelled.

As they reached the car, Ethan caught Buck's eye and said, "Um. We talk to dead people? That's what we do."

"Read the manual, kid," Buck said with a smile.

Three

An Office Full of NRDS

E THAN RUBBED HIS EYES and cracked open another can of Bang Energy. Beside him, Buck pecked away at the keyboard, as he had been doing for the past hour, one key clicking at a time.

His eyes couldn't take it anymore, and the urge to ban this man from ever using a keyboard again was palpable. Ethan leaned back, looking up to the ceiling. "Do we need to file everything they said?"

Buck just kept pecking away at the keyboard, his eyes glued to the screen. "Yep."

Click. Click. Click.

Ethan took another swig of his energy drink, noting how stained the ceiling tiles were in this building. He figured a government agency could have at least purchased something nicer than the second floor of the oldest building in the entire town.

"But she kept going on and on about her son adopting that damn cat. How can this help?" Ethan asked.

Buck turned, his chair squeaking the entire time as he turned. "We report everything."

Ethan stifled a yawn and gestured to the screen. "But how does this matter? How is this going to get her a step closer to going into the afterlife?"

"You don't see it?" Buck sighed, shaking his head.

"No, I don't. We've been at it three hours past our shift, and I don't know what good it will do."

Buck turned back, looking over the screen before he started. "She resents her son for not marrying and giving her grandkids before she died. Him getting a cat means, to her, that he's given up on dating. Completing this psych evaluation and submitting it to central will grant us permission to interview the son and mediate if necessary. The manual, if you'd read it, would have told you she showed signs of progression into Class Two, so we need to act promptly."

Ethan eyed the manual sitting pristinely on his desk across the room, untouched. "Come on, the thing is like five hundred pages."

A voice sounded behind Ethan. "It's five hundred and forty-seven pages to be exact. Thirty-two articles to memorize."

Ethan nearly jumped out of his seat. He didn't even know how long Alexus had been there. By the looks of it, from her half-eaten sandwich and empty mug of coffee, it had been longer than he thought.

One thing Ethan had learned quickly was to leave Alexus alone. She came in, did her job, and got out of there. She left no room for chitchat. He barely even noticed she was there, let alone talked to her, until now.

Ethan figured now was as good a time as any to see if she really was impervious to conversation. "Memorize? So, you're telling me you know the whole manual, every single article, by heart?"

"It's not that hard. What else is there to do in this town?" Alexus said, backing away from her monitor and swiveling around in her chair to face him.

Ethan smirked. "I don't know, I figured you were the type to hit up the Wild Badger when you're not here."

"Who says I'm not? Can't a girl do both, or is that too much for you small-town folk?"

Buck nudged Ethan's ribs and grinned. "Why don't you try her, greenhorn? Maybe you'll learn something."

"Yeah, sure, why not? Maybe I will." Ethan said.

He stood and crossed the room, picking up his book and cracking it open. It really cracked too, that crack of a book used for the first time. He leaned against his desk and held it up with two hands. "Ok, Pop quiz. Uh, here. Article eleven."

Alexus's eyes glazed over, and she looked to the wall behind Ethan. "Article Eleven. In the event that a Class One entity becomes unsettled, file form 11.B.72A within twenty-four hours. Follow up with the entity every seventy-two hours until a new class determination is established and verified with one other NRDS Agent."

She shifted her gaze back to Ethan and smirked. "Want me to continue to each of the proceeding sections?"

"Um, no. That was . . . word for word. How do you just know all that? What, you have a super brain or something?" Ethan said, staring at her wide-eyed.

Alexus turned back to her computer, waking it and staring back at her files. "It's called reading the manual and doing my job. Maybe you should try it."

"Aww, quit giving him a hard time." Buck said.

She paused and darted a look at Buck. "You're supposed to sign off on his training within two months of hiring, else you both get more paperwork to file. On top of that, you'll bring all our numbers down."

Ethan pushed off his desk and tossed the manual onto his desk. "Wait. We'll have more paperwork for not finishing paperwork? Is that all we do?"

"If Brenda in Regulatory had her way, yeah." Buck said, taking a massive swig of coffee.

Alexus eyed her own mug of coffee and stood. "What else have you been making this rookie do?"

Buck stuck out his mug to Alexus and shook it. She huffed and rolled her eyes before grabbing his empty mug while he said, "It's the captain. Has him reviewing the obits."

"So, she's got him on grunt work. How do they expect us to do anything with no staff?" she said, crossing the room and picking up the carafe of questionably aged coffee.

Buck grabbed the mug of cold, blackened liquid that was once known as coffee and chugged. He wiped his face and cleared his throat. "Secretary will be in later this week. She should pick up the slack that . . . oh, no."

The door to the stairwell opened, and in came two people. One was River, a curly haired hippy that hadn't seen a pair of scissors in years nor seemed to care how baggy his suit was. He was the fourth and final local agent of NRDS, carrying a small old leather bag, not much bigger than a purse, with him as he passed through the doors.

Beside River was an older man, thin with graying brown hair and large, black-rimmed glasses, carrying a Tupperware bowl. Ethan couldn't place the man, but he looked so familiar.

River's voice cut through the silence, ". . . and you bake it, just like normal."

"Won't it smell bad though?" The man holding the large Tupperware container said.

River smirked, glancing over at Buck before shaking his head. "Nah, man. Just pick a pan and open some windows. Make sure you infuse your butter long enough, but don't burn it."

"Ger, what are you doing taking baking advice from this delinquent?" Buck said, crossing the room and butting between the two, planting a kiss on the man's cheek.

The light clicked in Ethan's head, and he looked over to Buck's desk. The only picture at his desk was of two younger men, smiling back at the camera, one was Buck, and the other Ger.

"You know I can't smoke the stuff, Bucky bear. Lungs can't take it. So why not get some advice from someone more experienced?" Ger asked.

Buck pointed his thumb back at River. "But him? I can't even trust him to get a pizza order right."

River slapped a hand on Buck's back and said, "Cheer up, pops. I'd never give poor advice to your better half. Especially if he wants to explore the boundaries of consciousness. He's in safe hands, man."

"You know I could report you." Buck said, shrugging off the hand.

"Nah, man, I got my card last week. Doctor agreed, looks like I have glaucoma."

Alexus hopped up and ran over to Ger, eyeing the Tupperware. "Don't be such a buzzkill, Buck. Hi, Ger, how are you—"

"Me? A buzzkill? Why am I the buzzkill?" Buck said.

Alexus looked at River and winked. "What else should we do in this small-ass town? Brood and complain?"

Ger opened the lid, wafting up a scent of cinnamon and vanilla as cupcakes with a towering dollop of frosting sat inside. "Yeah, Bucky, come over to the dark side. We've got cupcakes . . . and brownies."

Buck reached a hand into the Tupperware and inspected it. "You shouldn't be wasting your time baking for these . . . delinquents. The doc said you need to rest."

Ger stepped past Buck, lifting the collection of cupcakes to Alexus. "All I've been doing is rest. If I can't be useful, I'm going to lose my mind. So, eat your damn cupcake and be happy, k?"

River, now the proud owner of two cupcakes, tossed the leather bag on his desk and plopped in his chair. "Aww, you two are the cutest."

I hate you." Buck huffed.

Ethan grabbed a cupcake decorated in a copper glitter while Ger smiled up at him. "Name's Gerry. You're the newbie, right? Is this guy treating you alright? Or do I need to teach him a lesson or two?"

"He's . . . uh. He's been great." Ethan said, darting his eyes away from Buck's glare.

Ger patted Ethan's cheek. "Aw, well that's a lie if I've ever seen one."

Alexus unraveled her cupcake and began picking off chunks with her fingers and popping them into her mouth. "Ignore him. Your husband has more patience than I do."

A loud laugh boomed out of River. "At least he gives the kid a chance. I'm sure you'd leave him the first chance you got."

Alexus shot him a glare, but Ger cleared his throat before she could chime in. "Right. Well, I didn't mean to cause drama. I'm sure you all have some reports to work on. I just want to drop off some of these with Mel."

He moved faster than Ethan thought he could, scuttling off into the captain's office before Buck stopped him.

"That man is going to get me fired, or promoted, and I don't want either," Buck said.

River leaned back in his chair, licking off the frosting remains of his devoured cupcake and resting his muddy feet on Buck's desk. "Well, you're never going to guess what I ran into."

"Feet. Off my desk." Buck said, swatting at River's feet.

Ethan leaned forward and asked, "What was it? A poltergeist?"

"Ha, funny. No, it was—"

The lights above Ethan flickered, and the hum of the computer behind him deadened.

Alexus slapped the side of her computer and turned, eyeing the bag on River's desk. "Dammit Bob! You better fucking stop or I'm going to bury your stupid bag of bones in the middle of the Mississippi." She then glared up at River. "You better get your fucking ghost under control."

River pulled his badge out of his pocket and pointed it at Alexus. "He's not my ghost, I just carry him around because no one else wants to."

"Gonna to tell us, or what?" Buck asked.

River's eyes focused on the space between him and Buck. "What? Yeah. No. Fine. He wants to tell you all."

Buck and Alexus got the hint immediately, pulling out their badges and focusing on the space between them and River. Ethan . . . took a moment. Then raced to his desk and wrapped his fingers around the badge.

A large man dressed in tactical gear materialized in the middle of the office, shouting. ". . . bootlegging operation that got forty of them KIA. Got a Class Three tying up some Class Zeros stuck in a loop. We need to saddle up and get eyes on the target before someone ends up in a meat wagon. Then—"

"We need to mark the manor next to Saint Anne's. Double up and detain the Class Three." Buck said.

Alexus shook her head. "I am not working double time. That's his jurisdiction. Rounding up Class Zeros is just going to knock into my percentage."

A woman, shorter than anyone else in the office even with a haphazard bun holding up her dark brown hair, threw open the door to the captain's office.

Melissa wore a form-fitting gray pantsuit and wide, black-framed glasses as she stepped out of her office. She had a cup of coffee, black with no sugar, in one hand and the badge in the other. "Bob, could you be any louder? I can hear you through the walls."

"Seriously, my name is not Bob! It's—"

Alexus hopped up from her desk and stood in front of "Bob." "Boss, I'm three trips away from making a hat trick for the month. I can't let a couple of bootlegger Class Zeroes screw up my cases."

"It won't. You and Buck will pick up on the other cemeteries on River's route until he finishes cleaning this up. None of his charges are ready to transition, so just check in on them once this week and they should be fine." Melissa said.

Buck cleared his throat. "And the rookie? I've now got River's cases on top of my own. I don't have time to train him."

Ethan perked up, looking between Buck and Melissa. "I can go out into the field and help River. Class Zeroes are easy, right?"

Melissa nodded. "They are. Sure, why not? You'll go with River and Bob. Guide the Class Zeros out of the house and back to the cemetery. Follow River's orders. If things get hairy, get the hell out."

Bob waited until it was silent, then took in a deep breath. "Will you all stop calling me Bob? I'm more than the just a bag of bones. My name is—"

Melissa cut in again. "Make sure the Zeroes settle, then you can float to whichever agent is out on the field. They are not training you. You are just shadowing them. River, detain the unsettled and clean up the mess. I'll expect a full report in two weeks."

River tossed his badge on his desk and smiled up at Ethan. "Nice. I always wanted a partner."

Bob turned to River, waving his arms wildly at River's unflinching face. "And I've been dying for a buddy that might actually listen for a change."

Four

Spooky Business

THE CAR FILLED WITH smoke from River's cigar-sized, hand-rolled joint. Ethan coughed, tugging against his tight gray suit as he waved the fumes of River's exhale away. "Hey. You mind blowing that out the window?"

River pulled back his tangled mess of curly brown hair and dropped his head as if his neck had no muscles. He eyed Ethan over the top of his sunglasses, his glossy eyes a deep shade of red. "What's that, bro?"

Ethan rolled down his window while keeping his eyes on the road. "I'm not looking to get hot boxed with you. Could you blow out the window?"

"Ah, yeah, man. No worries. Sorry about that." River laughed as he rolled down the passenger side window and let out another massive exhale.

"Reprobate," Bob said from the backseat, his bald Black head blocking most of what Ethan could see in the rearview mirror.

Taking another long drag, River said, "So, how'd they hook you in? You one of them horror freaks? Steven King fan? Or are you just a ghost groupie? Usually, I can spot 'em a mile away."

"Me? No. I mean, they offered me this job after I signed up for one of those government placement tests. Didn't really know this was a thing. I've heard of NRDS but didn't really know what you guys did. Seems cool, though."

River exhaled out the window again. "It is cool, but dude. I've seen some crazy shit."

"Left at the corner," Bob commanded.

"Thanks. I got it. I grew up here, remember?" Ethan replied.

"He still backseat driving?" River asked with a grin.

"You're a disgrace to the badge," Bob barked.

Ethan looked in the rearview mirror to see Bob's nasty stare at River. "You can't hear him?"

River took another long drag, then coughed hard, throwing his head between his legs. Between gasps, he said, "Nah. I tossed my badge on the floor. Don't want to hear directions from a guy who failed his driving test three times."

Bob cracked his knuckles and eyed River. "He's lucky he can't hear me, else I'd—"

"Wait, you failed your driving test?" Ethan asked.

"Yeah," Bob said, his glare shifting to Ethan in the rearview mirror.

"But you were a mechanic for the military?"

"Yeah, and?"

"Do you know how to drive?"

River let out a loud laugh. "Oh, you're in for it now."

Ethan didn't think ghosts' faces could turn so red, but the color coming off Bob was terrifying. Then he let out a slow, controlled breath and pinched the bridge of his nose. "When you both die, I'm going to spend a decade kicking your asses."

"Woah, hey! I just asked a question. Don't wrap me into whatever beef you've got with River."

River leaned back and looked at the ceiling of the car. "Ah. We've reached the decade of ass kicking then?"

Ethan raised an eyebrow. "How d'you know?"

"We're together a lot." River reached into the backseat and pulled on the leather bag, patting it and shifting the bones inside.

"Third house on the left," Bob barked.

Ethan slowed down the car and shot a glance at the bag of bones River held. "So, how d'you become Bob's handler? That's what you are, right?"

River took off his sunglasses, sat up, and stared at Ethan. "Man, I'm not his handler. I'm an agent, and so is Bob. We're partners."

Bob scoffed.

"Sorry. I didn't mean—"

"Nah, dude, it's fine. Just don't want you getting the wrong impression." River said as he put his sunglasses back on and leaned back in the chair again.

Ethan pulled the car up in front of an old white two-story Victorian house.

The path leading up to the wrap-around porch was slowly being consumed by unmowed grass. No light came from the tall and looming windows, even though the curtains weren't drawn.

His gaze rose past the second floor and locked on to the topmost window. A little tower was built out from the attic, and even though it was just as dark as the others, he felt the eyes on him. A chill tore through his spine, and his gaze remained locked on the window.

Something was in that attic, something that every core in his being told him to run from.

Bob jumped from the backseat without opening the door, and a flit of green passed Ethan's gaze, screaming, "On your feet!" He sprinted over the lawn at full speed, as if he had just stepped off a boat at Normandy.

River stretched and cracked his knuckles. He took his time, bending down and picking up his badge, dusting it off. He nodded toward Bob and grinned. "Watch this."

Ethan looked out the window as Bob, wearing his military uniform, seemed to run straight into an invisible wall. He stumbled back, landing on his ass, and became engulfed by the overgrown grass.

Ethan turned back to River for answers. He held up the brown leather bag, shaking the bones inside. "Never gets old."

Ethan looked back toward the invisible wall. "Wait. What the hell was that?"

Bob attempted to recover by rolling back up on his feet, only to stumble again before regaining his footing. He looked left and right, then waved them on. "Come on! Quit goofing off and move your ass!"

River chuckled as he pushed the car door open and stepped out, straightening his loose black suit. "He's on a leash. Can't get a hundred-and-fifty feet from his bones."

Bob reached the edge of the invisible barrier, pushing up against it. "Come on, wet rags. Move your asses. The enemy has the upper hand."

Ethan hopped out of the car, straightening his tie, and opened the back door. He pulled an old black leather briefcase from the back, the silvery lock clasps shining in the moonlight.

Bob slipped against the invisible barrier and shouted, "Let's burn rubber! The mission doesn't wait for you, beatniks!"

Sauntering behind Ethan, River yawned and stretched. "Chill, dude. Can you just relax for once?"

"I'll relax when I buy the farm!" With the barrier slipping forward, Bob raced halfway up the stairs to the home before stopping again.

Ethan tilted his head at Bob and said, "Buy the farm? You mean dead? But you are—"

Interrupting him, Bob screamed, "No time for chit-chat, maggot! Move! Move! Move!"

"You see what I have to live with," River called as he took a final drag of his joint and flicked the remnant of the blunt into the grass.

Bounding the rest of the way up the stairs, Bob crossed the porch and pressed his back against the double front doors.

Looking left, then right, then at River, he nodded and screamed, "GOING IN!" Pivoting on his left foot, he turned and gave the front door a forceful kick with his right heel.

Instead of the door shattering from the blow, Bob's foot passed right through, and he disappeared to the other side. "I'M IN! COVERING!" he screamed from inside the house.

"Seriously, dude. He does this every frickin' time," River said as he leaped past Ethan on the stairs, slipping a key into the lock and swinging the door open.

River turned and saw the look on Ethan's face. "Owners went away for the week. Things got a little hairy. Gave us the key so we could take care of it."

Ethan nodded and stepped through the door and into the foyer.

Stale, musty air hit Ethan's nostrils, and he gagged. He put his hand over his mouth, hoping that would somehow lessen the pungent odor. He found the light switch and flicked it on. A dull light, almost too dim to be useful, came to life above him.

Cobwebs lined the corners of the ceiling, and a thick layer of dust coated the credenza and banister of the red-carpeted stairway. To his left was a formal sitting room whose furniture was covered in beige drape cloth. The hallway in front of him, lined with portraits and low-hanging light fixtures, flanked the stairway, leading to what Ethan figured was the kitchen.

"I thought you said people lived here?"

River popped his head in and looked around. "Yeah. Didn't look like this when I came by before."

Before he turned and looked at River, he spotted three people in the living room to his right. An older woman with silvery hair tied up in a tight bun and a long gray dress sat on a worn mustard-yellow valor couch with a curved back. She looked mournfully at the floor as a younger man and woman packed boxes around her.

The man, wearing a white T-shirt and jeans, looked to be a few years older than Ethan, well-toned, with close-cropped brown hair and a beard to match. The woman looked to be around the same age, her blond hair tied back in a loose bun, matching the man in clothing choice.

"Oh, hey. Sorry for disturbing you. My partner here said you all were away for the week." Ethan said, stepping toward them.

Grabbing him by the arm, River whispered, "Don't. Not until Bob tells us more."

Ethan looked at River for a second. When his eyes traveled back to the living room, the people were gone. "Wait, they were just—"

Then the three in the living room flickered back into place, and the man looked up from his box. "Did you get her blanket from upstairs? I don't want her getting cold."

"I think I put it in that box over there. Mom, are we forgetting anything?" the younger woman responded.

Still looking at the ground, the older woman said, "You two are so sweet. You don't need to do all this for me."

The man sighed, looked back down into the box, and said, "Mom. They're going to be here any minute, and we don't want you to forget anything."

"It's fine. Don't worry yourself," the older woman said, waving him off without looking at him.

Then they flickered away again into nothingness, leaving the room empty.

Ethan looked at River and asked, "What's going on?"

River smiled. "Trippy, right?"

They flickered back, and the younger man looked up from his box and asked, "Did you get her blanket from upstairs? I don't want her getting cold."

"I think I put it in that box over there. Mom, are we forgetting anything?" the younger woman responded.

Still looking at the ground, the older woman said, "You two are so sweet. You don't need to do all this for me."

The man sighed, looked back down into the box, and said, "Mom. They're going to be here any minute and we don't want you to forget anything."

"It's fine. Don't worry yourself," the older woman said, waving him off without looking at him.

Ethan's mouth fell open, and he looked back at River. "What? How?"

"Dude, bro. You gotta read the manual." River laughed.

"Sure, yeah, I get that. But that doesn't help me now. What am I looking at?" Ethan said as the drama in the living room played out for a third time.

Before River could answer, Bob rushed down the stairs and barked, "Three Class Zeros in a loop in the living room. One Class Three roaming upstairs. New kid, lead the Zeroes out. We'll handle the Three upstairs."

"Wait? What? How do I—" Ethan asked.

"Let's light it up, maggots! MOVE! MOVE! MOVE!" Bob screamed as he raced back up the stairs.

Ethan turned to River, his heart beating heavy in his ears. "Wait, hold on. I don't know what I'm supposed to do."

A loud crash rang out from upstairs, jostling dust free from the ceiling to rain down on them as the house shook. The Class Zeros paused from their loop to look up at the ceiling.

Bob's voice screamed from upstairs, "CASE! I NEED THE CASE!"

River rolled his eyes and looked up the stairs. "Fine! Jeez, dude! I'm coming!"

He pointed at the briefcase in Ethan's hand. "I'm gonna need that. Just deal with these three while we contain the one upstairs, alright?"

"Deal with them? How? What does that even mean?"

Another loud crash rang from upstairs, and the three Zeros in the living room shook. Their faces shifted and changed. The youthful face of the man became bloodied for a moment before flickering back into the old self. The younger woman's eyes glazed over, a pale dull gray that Ethan had to turn from. The elderly woman rotted in place before snapping back into her astute self.

Bob's voice rang from upstairs. "IF HE GOES FOUR AND POSSESSES YOUR ASS, I WILL NOT HESITATE TO BUG OUT AND WAIT FOR REINFORCEMENTS!"

"WHATEVER HAPPENED TO NEVER LEAVE A MAN BEHIND?" River screamed up the stairs.

"THAT—"

Another loud crash, and what sounded like breaking glass.

"ONLY APPLIES—"

A crash and a thump that knocked a few portraits off the wall.

"TO REAL MEN!" Bob retorted.

River started up the stairs, leaving Ethan behind with the three flickering Zeros.

A lump formed in his throat as their bloodied and rotted faces turned toward him, their eyes shining like ravenous zombies.

"I . . . What do I do?"

Five

Stuck on Repeat

"I . . . What do I do?" Ethan asked.

His eyes looked back at the Class Zeroes, who'd looked like blood-thirsty zombies a moment before. He sighed as his eyes ran over a group of three spirits looking through boxes.

The crashing sounds continued upstairs as Bob and the Class Three spirit wrestled.

River stopped halfway up the stairs, briefcase in hand. With his tangled mess of curly brown hair and the oversized suit, he looked more like a kid playing dress up than anything else. "Okay, crash course. Zeros aren't dangerous. Just walk into their loop and lead them back to the cemetery down the street. Find their headstones, get them to stand over their grave, and voilà, they'll settle back into their bones."

He turned and continued up the stairs.

Ethan's heartbeat thrummed in his head as he pulled at his tie for air that his tight gray suit wasn't willing to give. "Wait, how am I supposed to get into their loop?"

"Just dive in, rookie. You got this," River called as he rounded down the hallway at the top of the stairs.

Another crash, and Ethan thought he saw something fly by the top of the stairs. Bob's voice raced past, shouting, "WE'VE GOT A LIVE ONE!"

Ethan looked back into the living room.

The man in the living room looked up from his box and asked, "Did you get her blanket from upstairs? I don't want her getting cold."

"I think I put it in that box over there. Mom, are we forgetting anything?" the younger woman responded.

Still looking at the ground, the older woman said, "You two are so sweet. You don't need to do all this for me."

The man sighed, looked back down into the box, and said, "Mom. They're going to be here any minute, and we don't want you to forget anything."

"Don't worry yourself. It's fine," the older woman said, waving him off without looking at him.

Ethan shook his shoulders and rubbed his hands, psyching himself up as he whispered, "Okay, get into the loop. Get into the loop."

The man in the living room looked up from his box again and asked, "Did you get her blanket from upstairs? I don't want her getting cold."

The younger woman responded, "I think I put it in that box over there. Mom, are we forgetting anything?"

Still looking at the ground, the older woman said, "You two are so sweet. You don't need to do all this for me."

The man sighed and again looked back down into the box. "Mom. They're going to be here any minute, and we don't want you to forget anything."

"Don't worry yourself. It's fine," the older woman said, waving him off without looking at him.

Ethan straightened his tie and took a deep breath as he stepped into the room. "Hi. Um. Did someone call for a car?"

The man looked up from his box and asked, "Are you from the home?"

The young woman looked to Ethan as well and said, "Oh, perfect. So, there's five boxes in the kitchen. And then these two here."

Biting his lip, Ethan replied, "Um. Yeah. I'm from the home."

The man smiled and said, "Great. Mom. Are you ready?"

Not looking up, the older woman shook her head and said, "Oh. I don't know."

The man put his hands on his hips and said, "Mom. We talked about this."

"I know. I know. But, see. I don't think I want to go," the older woman said.

The younger woman rubbed her temple as if a sudden headache had come on. "Ma, don't do this. You don't know how much convincing it took to get your son here."

The man paced, running a hand through his close-cropped brown hair. "Mom, you've got to go."

There was a crack in the old woman's voice when she said, "But. But this is my home."

"Jesus. Mom. Do you want to have another episode again? There won't be anyone here next time. Do you want that?" the man exclaimed. Ethan noted the tears welling up in the man's eyes before he turned away and looked out the window.

The younger woman sighed. "It's going to be okay, Mom."

"Mom. We've talked about this. You agreed this was the right thing to do," the man said.

The older woman still didn't look up, clenching her hand at the side of her dress. "But. It's just . . . the memories here. I don't want to forget. If I stay here . . . This was our home."

The spirits flickered around Ethan. The man vanished from the window and reappeared at the box and said, "Did you get her blanket from upstairs? I don't want her getting cold."

The younger woman looked into her own box and said, "I think I put it in the box over there. Mom, are we forgetting anything?"

Watching the loop restart, Ethan's heart raced. "Um. I've got the car out front when you're ready to leave?" he offered.

The man smiled and said, "Great. Mom. Are you ready?"

Not looking up, the older woman shook her head and said, "Oh. I don't know."

"I'm a part of the new loop," Ethan said to himself.

The man put his hands on his hips and said, "Mom. We talked about this."

Ethan raced across the room, hoping to stop the next loop, and knelt next to the old woman's chair. "So, uh. This house is gorgeous. I bet you've, um, had a lot of memories here, yeah?" he asked in desperation.

The old woman looked up from the floor and met Ethan's gaze, nodding. She motioned to the younger man and said, "He grew up here. Right over there is where he broke my favorite lamp."

The man grabbed at his beard and let out a sigh. "And you're still talking about it. That was decades ago, Ma. This is what I'm talking about. She won't let anything go."

The younger woman stepped away from her box and moved to the younger man. "It's okay, dear," she said as she rubbed his back.

There was another loud bang from upstairs, and River screamed, "DAMMIT!"

"HE'S ON THE MOVE! EVASIVE MANEUVERS!" Bob screamed.

"ON YOUR LEFT!" River screamed.

Ethan looked at the three spirits. Their expressions flickered and shifted, turning back into their horrific selves.

Blood poured from a wound across the man's head, spilling onto the floor while he stood still, his eyes locked on Ethan.

Ethan took in a slow breath and looked at the woman, half rotted on the couch. "Leaving your home is hard."

In an instant, they all reverted into the loop. Ethan wiped his sweaty palms on his pants while the old woman picked at the cuticles. "I just love it here. All my kids were born here."

The man paced. "Mom. We had to sell. Your treatments are more important. We talked about this. You can't stay."

Still looking down, the old woman said, "Maybe we could talk to them and get them to hold off for a while. I know it was double or nothing, but I just want a little more time."

Still bending down to her eyeline, Ethan smiled. "It's hard to leave, but the place we're going to is really nice. You'll make new memories, and your kids can come and visit you whenever you want."

The old woman shrugged and said, "Billy's the only one still in town. Estell moved to Michigan. And Sammy's all the way down in Texas."

"You know, we've got many people just like you there. So, if you come with me, your kids can come visit and you don't have to be alone when they're off doing their own thing."

The old woman looked up, and Ethan felt a surge of hope. She said, "I'll need to watch my shows. Every day at eleven. I can't miss Oprah. Or Ellen."

Ethan stood and said, "We never miss an episode. Why don't you come and try it? If you don't like it, maybe we can talk about you coming back."

The old woman looked down again and sighed. "Okay. I'll give it a few days."

From upstairs, Bob yelled, "ON YOUR SIX! ON YOUR SIX!"

"COME ON! STAND STILL!" River screamed.

Ethan smiled and tried to maintain eye contact with the older woman. "Just a few days," he reassured her.

For a moment, she flickered, her eyes shriveled into nothingness and her body covered in rot. Then she snapped back and smiled. "Alright then."

The man came to her side and helped the old woman stand.

"Let's go. My car is right out front," Ethan said, motioning to the door.

As the three spirits followed him out, the younger man caught his eye and said, "Thank you."

Ethan took a deep breath, shrugged, and said, "This is my job."

He held the door open for the old woman, making sure all three spirits got in the car before he got in and started the engine. "It's just a few blocks," he said as the engine came to life.

"It was a magnificent house," the old woman said from the backseat.

The man took her hand and said, "It was, Ma."

As they pulled into the road, the younger woman said, "We didn't want to sell. We wanted her to stay there forever."

"Oh, yeah?" Ethan checked in the rearview mirror to make sure the spirits were still there.

"With her health, and then the offer, we didn't have a choice," the younger woman said.

"They said if we didn't sell, they'd just claim it by eminent domain. We needed the money after they diagnosed her," the man said from the backseat.

"We'd have her move in with us, but our place is so small. It's only a one bedroom," the younger woman explained.

"I just don't know why they wanted my house so much," the old woman said.

"I know, Mom. I'm so sorry," the man said.

Ethan bit his lip, wondering if he should just let the topic lie, but the nagging in his gut had started, and he knew he wouldn't be able to leave it alone. He kept his eye on the spirits in the rearview as he asked, "Do you know why they wanted your property?"

"They've been buying up the entire town," the man said.

"I heard they're planning to sell everything off to some Silicon Valley types looking to build some big tech firm," the younger woman said.

"Did Doreen tell you that? Those are just rumors. If that were really happening, they would have said something in the news. They're probably just putting up new condos or something," the younger man said.

"Well, here we are," Ethan said as he passed by St. Mary's school and spotted the entrance to the cemetery. The sprawling cemetery sat at the bend in the road, with several hundred graves stretching to the tree line with room for a few hundred more.

The younger woman stared out the window and said, "We'll get out here and walk the rest of the way."

"Thanks for the ride," the man said as he got out of the car.

"You're a very nice young man." The old woman reached out and patted Ethan's shoulder. A cool chill passed through him, and she smiled. She then opened the car door and followed her son.

Ethan jumped out of the car and walked behind the three spirits as they wove their way through the graves. The spirits came to a stop in front of a set of headstones. They paused, looked at each other, and held hands.

A blinding light emanated from where they were standing, forcing Ethan to cover his eyes. When he looked back, the spirits had vanished.

"Woah," he whispered to himself. Slowly, he approached the graves and read the inscriptions on the headstones.

Ester Ruben
Loving Mother of Three
October 24, 1941 to December 15, 2019

William Ruben
May 13, 1977 to April 4, 2020

Becky Ann Ruben
January 5, 1979 to April 4, 2020

Ethan took his phone out of his pocket and snapped a picture of the headstones before heading back to the car to pick up Bob and River.

Six

M is For . . .

O N THE THIRD ATTEMPT of his alarm sounding, Ethan garnered enough energy to roll out of bed. After picking up his one suit where it lay in a pile on the floor, he gave the jacket a quick sniff and shrugged. A week of wear was nothing a little deodorant couldn't cover up.

He raced down the stairs, catching the sweet scent of maple that hovered in the air. Not the fake cheapo brand stuff, the genuine stuff that once you have you can never go back. Skipping the last few steps, he hopped into the kitchen, planted a kiss on the slightly plump elderly woman with curlers still in her long gray hair, and said, "Morning, Granny." Looking to the table where his younger sister was devouring her breakfast, he added, "Morning, Ellie."

His grandmother turned and smiled, wiping batter off her hands. "Pancakes are coming off the griddle. They ain't going to be good cold, so you better hurry."

Ethan eyed the browning cakes on the griddle and sighed with longing. Reaching for the bag of sourdough bread, he said, "Thanks, but uh . . . I think I better just grab toast and go."

Swatting the bag out of his hand with her spatula, she said, "You will not. I can't have my grandson out in public looking like skin and bones. It's bad enough you ain't washed that suit yet. What will the neighbors think?"

Ethan flexed his biceps. He teased, "Skin and bones? You see these guns right here?"

Rosemary swatted his belly, making an audible thwack with the spatula before shooting him a glare, "Barely anything there. Your granddad would be disappointed in me, starving his precious grandson."

"I said I'd grab toast."

"Toast is a side dish. Sit and eat some of this before your sister devours the whole plate."

Ethan ducked out of the way and turned, eyeing his sister Ellie. Her hair was a tousled mess of brunette that looked like a bird had made a home, and her clothes were muddier than usual. She stabbed another pancake from the center plate and dropped it onto hers, drenching it in syrup. "I am a growing girl." She was the definition of junior high tom boy; he worried for the safety of any boy that took an interest in her.

Granny passed by Ethan, scooping up the empty plate at the table and filling it with more pancakes from the griddle. "That's right, but if you get sick again, then how are you going to enjoy lunch? I promised I'd make it today."

"You mean . . . mac and cheese?" El asked, dropping her fork as she stared wide-eyed at her grandmother.

Ethan rolled his eyes, sitting down at the end of the table and tossing a pancake onto his plate.

His grandmother crossed the room, pouring on more pancake batter onto the griddle. "Of course. With little hotdogs and ketchup."

"You two ruin perfectly made mac and cheese," Ethan said, stabbing his fork into a syrup-doused pancake.

Ellie rolled her eyes and rested her hands on her hips. "Ugh, men. They just don't get it. Am I right Grandma?"

"That's absolutely right, sweetie. Men are the devil. You keep reminding yourself of that."

"Hey. I'm feeling attacked," Ethan quipped with a laugh.

His grandmother pulled up a chair and joined them at the table. Picking up a mug of coffee and taking a sip before smiling at Ellie, she said, "Oh, calm down. Just a little girl's talk."

"I'm just saying. Hotdogs and ketchup don't belong in mac and cheese. Now, throw in some bacon and croutons . . ."

"That's gross," Ellie said, sticking out her tongue.

Granny tutted her tongue. "No faces at the table, dear. Now Ethan, any chance you'll swing by Oakland Cemetery this morning?"

"I'm not really in charge of where I go yet."

"That's where we buried Mable. You remember. Go and check on her for me. See if she is still around. Tell her I said hello."

Ethan leaned back in his seat, rubbing the back of his neck. "It doesn't work like that. I'm still training. I just kind of do what they tell me."

Granny sipped her coffee and stole a bite from his plate. "When you see her, tell her I got her plants after the funeral. And that Doris took her cats. She'll want to know that Mr. Westminster Tabby is okay."

Ethan shook his head. "But Granny, it doesn't work like—"

"Now, here I go making you pancakes and trying to take care of you. I didn't want to get up early to do all this mixing and cooking, but I know they're your favorite, so I did it, and in return you're going to sit here and tell your poor old grandma no?"

"I just wanted to have toast," Ethan mumbled.

"And turn into some frail boy? What would my bridge club say about me?"

Ethan rolled his eyes and pushed himself up from the table. "Fine, but if I get fired, you're helping me find a new job."

As Ethan pulled his car into the parking lot, he glanced at the clock and a pit formed in his stomach. He was already running behind, and Oakland Cemetery wasn't exactly on the way to the office. He hoped he didn't see any spirits. Maybe he'd just be able to duck in and out.

"Ok, ok. East corner," he mumbled while fishing around for his badge in his pockets. Hustling down the gravel path, he passed through the brick entrance into the graveyard and up past the pines. Quiet and still. So far, so good.

The cool metal wrapped around his fingers, and a woman appeared inches away from his face. "May I help you?"

Ethan stumbled back, falling on his ass while taking in the elderly woman with the gray streak in her hair and piercing light blue eyes. His heart pounded in his chest, but he muttered, "M . . . Mable?"

"Depends on who's asking? You one of those agents?"

Ethan stood, brushing the pine needles off his suit, and squeezing the badge tight. "No. Well, yes. But It's me. Ethan. Rosemary's grandson. Remember me?"

Mable crossed her arms and laughed. "Little Ethan? I haven't seen you since you were yay high. You look all skin and bones. Does your grandmother not feed you?"

"It's just a fast metabolism. Granny asked me to come out and check on you."

Mable turned, gesturing to him to follow. "I see you have a badge. Same as the boy who keeps smoking next to my garden."

"Yes, ma'am. Took a placement exam, the agency was building a remote location in town, turns out they needed a local, so here I am."

"Ah, well, like I told him and that big oaf he carries around, I'm not interested."

"Not interested in what?" Ethan asked, pausing in his tracks.

Mable stopped in front of an old building, the only one in the graveyard, and turned. "Any of it. Ratting out my neighbors. Moving on. I'm just fine right here. So go on back to your little office and don't worry about me. I'm good."

"No. I'm not here for any of that. I mean, I could be. But I'm here because Granny wanted to see how you were doing."

Mable laughed again. "Well, you can tell her I'm still here and still stubborn as a sleepy bull."

Ethan kicked at the gravel with the tip of his shoe. "Is there anything I can do to help? Like, do you need to make amends with anyone or anything?"

"Now, I told you I was good. I've got a good job here. It keeps me busy."

"A job?" Ethan asked.

In the distance, the bell at the catholic church up the hill began to gong, sounding that it was eight o'clock. With it, a surge of three children raced through the graveyard.

Mable wagged a finger and called after them, "Now slow down. No running on people's graves. Respect, please." Turning to Ethan, she said, "You see what I'm dealing with here."

Ethan's mouth hung open, and his heart ached at the sight of the young kids. Each seemed to be dressed from a different time period. They laughed and darted around, tagging each other, and calling, "You're it."

"They're dead?" Ethan asked, a knot forming in his throat.

"No. I'm a ghost nanny to live children that just happen to be transparent. Of course they're dead," Mable said.

"But. But they're just kids," Ethan stammered.

"Children die too, Ethan. Now close your mouth. Gawking doesn't help anyone."

Ethan followed her instructions and swallowed. He could feel tears building behind his eyes. "I just. I didn't think about. You know. Kids?"

Mable laughed again. "Oh, Lord. If your grandfather saw all these emotions pouring out of you, he'd have your head. Life ain't fair, son. You of all people should know that. It wasn't fair that your parents died in that car wreck. It wasn't fair that your grandfather had a weak heart. And it wasn't fair that I was murdered. Life ain't fair."

Ethan locked eyes with Mable, and his mouth fell open again. "Wait, what? Murder? Someone murdered you?"

"You really think I had a heart attack? Please. I was in my prime."

Truth was, he hadn't really paid attention when Mable died. Old people die. That's just what happens.

"Excuse me now. I've got to get this mess under control," Mable said, clapping her hands together. Laughing, the four children stopped their tag game, jogged over, and formed a line behind her. Looking at them with a warm sternness, Mable said, "Alright now. You all know that eight o'clock is time for lessons. I don't like having to call you all over here."

"Sorry, Miss Mable," the four children all said with a grin.

"You're holding school?" Ethan blurted out, confusion and pity replacing the sorrow he'd felt for the kids.

Mable shot him a silencing glare she'd mastered during her thirty-eight years of teaching high school math. "Idle hands lead to mischief, living or dead."

"But," Ethan started, unsure what objection he could actually raise.

"Now children. This is a new agent. His name is Mister Ethan."

"Hello, Mister Ethan," the children said in unison.

"He's here to help you move on. If you think of anything that might be holding you here, I want you to tell him," Mable instructed.

"I'm not really here for that today," Ethan interjected.

"Shush-shush," Mable said, waving him off.

A boy Ethan thought might be seven or eight raised his hand and said, "Miss Mable. I was thinking about something last night."

Looking at Ethan, Mable explained, "This is Dylan. He's new. Buried last week. Big funeral. Very sad."

Seeing the boy in his Sunday finest, a knot formed back in Ethan's throat. "Hey, Dylan. I'm Ethan. What can I do for you?"

The boy looked at the ground and kicked at the dirt as he explained. "So, um. My dog. His name is Tiger because he's kind of orange. Well, really my mom says he's brown. But I think he's orange. And he likes to run and jump on stuff. Like a Tiger."

"How can Mister Ethan help you with Tiger, Sweetie?" Mable asked.

"Well. I was just kind of thinking about him last night. Because my dad didn't really like him because he pooped on the floor a lot."

The other children giggled, and it made Dylan smile as he continued, "And my dad always said that he was going to give him away if he did it again. I just kind of want to know if he's okay. I just, you know. He's a good dog. So, I just want to know if my dad, like . . . just if he's okay."

"I'll check on him for you," Ethan said with a smile.

"Really? Thanks, Mister Ethan," Dylan said with a grin.

"Anyone else?" Mable asked the kids.

They all shook their heads "no" and a few giggled again.

"Okay then. Everyone say goodbye to Mister Ethan. He's going to go check on Tiger. And he's going to tell that delinquent coworker of his to stop smoking in my garden. Because why, children?"

"Because only morons smoke pot," the youngest child said with a smile.

"That's right. Only morons smoke pot. You all need to remember that. Now, say goodbye to Mister Ethan."

"Bye, Mister Ethan," all the kids called.

Remembering, Ethan asked, "Oh. Wait. Is there anything you want to tell my Granny?"

"Like I said. I'm good here. You come back and see us next week, alright? And don't you forget about Tiger. We need to get these kids out of here," Mable said.

"I'll try," Ethan said with a nod.

Seven

Ready For My Close-Up

E THAN BURST THROUGH THE office door, gasping after his race up the stairs. Buck looked up from his computer monitor and said, "You're late."

He passed by the newly installed secretary's desk. The woman who sat behind it, Doris, was somewhere in her mid 50s and wore a pink jogging suit with a blond bob cut that screamed she was trying too hard.

She didn't even glance up as he passed, too focused holding up her phone to an unflattering angle while angrily tapping the phone with her acrylic nails to get a selfie.

He placed his backpack on the table and straightened his tie, looking around the office and hoping someone else was running late too.

Unfortunately, Buck was busy filling out a form on his computer, River was rearranging the briefcases on the wall to find space for one of the outgoing captures, Melissa was in her office leaning back in her chair on her phone, and Bob was pacing back and forth, ready for action.

Ethan looked back at the exit, noticing a new guy sitting in one of the waiting chairs behind the front door. The forty-something Latin-looking man in a blue polo with a quality dad bod held his phone up like he was filming the room.

Ethan looked back over at Buck. "Yeah. Um. Sorry about that. I had to take care of something before I got in."

Bob barked in reply, "You listen here, bullet catcher. Personal matters are for personal time. You are on company time now, private."

"Yes, Sergeant Bob."

Bob's face turned red. "Not you too! My name's not Bob, it's—"

Ethan turned to the receptionist and spotted a basket of muffins sitting on the desk. "Morning, Doris. These for everyone?"

Doris pushed the basket toward him and said, "They sure are. Trevor brought them in."

"Trevor?" Ethan asked, nodding to the forty-something Latin looking guy who was still holding his camera up.

"The new hire's not even an agent. A real dud if you ask me," Bob scoffed.

"Trevor is my new social media assistant," Doris said while posing for the camera.

With a mouth full of chocolate chip muffin, Ethan said, "Nice to meet you."

Trevor grinned and replied, "Nice to meet you too. Would you mind introducing yourself to everyone watching at home?"

Ethan nearly choked on his muffin. "Wait, people are watching?"

Doris smiled at the camera, and on cue, Trevor focused on her. "This is Ethan, our most recent agent on the team, and a local. He's the guy who hasn't read the manual."

Ethan turned away from them and looked out into the office. "I bet she hasn't read the manual. Since when do we need a social media person?"

"We don't," Alexus said from behind Ethan, causing him to drop the remains of his muffin on the floor.

Ethan grabbed his chest. "Jesus Christ! Way to creep up on me."

Bob stopped in his tracks and rounded on Ethan, wagging a finger in his face. "Do not take the Good Lord's name in vain, you motherfucker!"

"Sir, yes, sir. Sorry about that."

"Oh, Ethan's taken the Lord's name in vain. Betcha Bob is reaming him out. Dude hasn't grown out of the 50s. He needs to lighten up." River haphazardly stuffed a briefcase onto the shelf for outgoing containment and walked back to his desk.

Peering over the camera, Trevor raised his eyebrow and asked, "Um. Excuse me. Who's Bob?"

Doris laughed and said, "Don't worry about it, dear. We can't see him."

"Can't see him? Is he invisible or something?" Trevor asked, panning over to Doris again.

"I'll explain later," Doris said with a wink.

"No. You won't," Buck said, eyes still on the computer.

"Later," Doris whispered to Trevor.

Ethan shook his head and looked over Buck's shoulder. "So, um. I think I need to fill out a form."

"What'd you do this time, rookie?" Alexus said as she propped her feet up on her desk.

River snapped his fingers at Trevor until the camera was pointed at him. "We fill out forms for everything. There's even one to record when you take a dump."

"And you're the only one of us who had to fill it out 'cause you were on 'probation,'" Alexus said, tossing her badge up in the air.

Looking up from the camera again, Trevor asked, "Wait, really?"

"No," Buck said.

River kicked up his legs on his desk and leaned back in his chair. "Actually Buck-o, it's form F39-2 of the Probationary Records Log, Section D. And because they always wanted me to go into excruciating detail of my bathroom habits, I had to file a request for the addendum, F39-2 Section D-2."

Trevor chuckled. "Ugh, that sounds terrible."

"Don't encourage the moron. It's like feeding the monkeys," Bob snapped.

Ethan looked at Bob and shrugged. "I don't think he can hear you."

Bob looked at Ethan and rolled his eyes. "Oh really? And why do you think that is?"

"Um. Because you're dead?" Ethan said.

"Wait? Dead? Who's dead?" Trevor said, whipping the camera over to Ethan.

Bob threw his hands in the air and looked at Buck, shouting, "Come on, honcho. Seriously, this is what you bring onto our team?"

"I don't pick 'em," Buck said, clicking through his form.

Melissa stepped out of her office and rested a hand on her hip. "Good morning, everyone. How is my wonderful team doing today? Good to see you all made it in. Oh, and who do we have here?"

Without putting down the phone, Trevor waved and said, "Hi. I'm Trevor. It's my first day."

Doris rose from her desk and grabbed the basket of muffins, holding them out for Melissa. "Morning, boss. Did you see these? Trevor brought them."

Melissa grabbed a muffin and picked at the top. "First day? I don't remember signing off on any new hires."

"Good. Now mama-san can finally sort the mess out. We don't need someone waving a camera in here all day." Bob laughed.

"Jesus. I can sense him, even without the badge. Ugh, calm down dude." River complained.

Bob crossed the room and hovered over River's face. "You're worthless and I hate you."

"So, you're the boss? Nice to finally meet you," Trevor said.

Doris turned and wagged a finger at him "No, I'm your boss. She's my boss."

Buck stood, put on his suit jacket, and announced, "Coffee break."

Trevor perked up and aimed his camera at Buck. "Oh, can I come with? I love coffee. The cafe down the street has anything you can think of. Mochas, lattes. They even have this little—"

"No." Buck walked past him without another word.

Melissa picked off a blueberry and popped it into her mouth, eyeing Trevor. "So, I ask again. First day?"

Doris placed the basket back on her desk and stepped in front of Melissa. "You remember when you said I needed to take on more responsibility if I wanted to grow in this company?"

"I suppose that rings a bell," Melissa said.

"And you remember how you said we should have a bigger social media presence?"

"That sounds like something I'd say," Melissa nodded.

Doris nodded along with Melissa and added, "And do you remember the requisition form 739 that I asked you to sign?"

Melissa took in a breath and looked at the ceiling. "Where is this going? No, I don't remember that specific form. I sign a ton of them all day. Yesterday I lost count after reaching form three-hundred and twenty-seven."

"This agency makes no sense." Bob laughed again.

"I've seen you sign things you don't even need to. I handed you a napkin for your coffee, and you signed that." Alexus pitched in with a grin.

"Yeah, I bet you'd sign my ass in the bathroom if you had a chance." River said with his eyes still closed.

"Ugh, degenerate," Bob scoffed.

Melissa glared at River, then looked past Doris to the camera. "For the record, I do not go into the men's room. Nor would I sign any of my staff's asses."

Doris cleared her throat and motioned to Trevor. "Well, after you signed form 739, I had the authorization to requisition Trevor here. He's my new part-time social media assistant."

Melissa shook her head and said, "Oh, no. I would remember filling out that form. I'd never—"

"I've got the copy here," Doris interrupted as she reached toward her desk, snatched a form, and passed it to Melissa.

Melissa took the form and brought it close to her face, eyes tracing back and forth. "I see my signature, but how do I know someone didn't forge this?"

Doris stared at Melissa, wide-eyed. "Hopefully you aren't accusing me! I'd worked this job for twenty years down in DC before I trekked my way into the Northwoods. I have gone, and will always go, through the proper channels."

River laughed. "Trevor. How could you? Breaking in and forging Melissa's signature so you can get yourself a job, here at the armpit of government agencies. Then, to top it off, you bring in delicious muffins on your first day? Shame. Shame on you."

"Hey, sanitation has to be the armpit. We're like . . . the appendix," Alexus said.

Opening his eyes and sitting up, River said, "As if. Do you know how much they get paid to ride around on a truck all day?"

"How much?" Alexus asked.

River leaned back in his chair again and closed his eyes. "I don't know. But it's gotta be more than us."

Folding the form into a little square, Melissa said, "Well, Trevor, you seem like a very nice person. But I didn't sign this. You have to go. It's not personal. But, you're fired."

"You can't do that," Alexus said with a grin.

Melissa turned to look at Alexus. "And who is the boss here?"

Alexus shrugged. "I'm just saying. That paperwork is already filed. You've got to file at least a 739-I and a HR943-72B."

"And that will only get you scheduled to talk with HR at the main office." Doris added.

"Then there's the HR113-24 performance improvement plan. Which I think has at least one new addendum if you want to fire them within a certain period of their starting date," Alexus said.

Doris shot a grin at Alexus. "That's right. And before you can fire someone, there needs to be a six-step review on one of the HR forms. I can't remember which one, but it's like fifty pages."

"HR237 Parts A through K." Alexus said.

River sat up again and looked at the camera Trevor was still using to stream the office. "Don't worry, Trev. Can I call you Trev? It's super hard to fire us. I've been trying to get them to fire me. One time I even blew up an office microwave by putting a can of Coke in there. Didn't even get written up because they said it was a harmless prank. I think the boss just didn't want to file the paperwork."

"You are the absolute worst thing this office offers," Bob said.

Returning to his nap position, River added, "And tell Bob my badge is in the drawer."

Ethan smiled and said, "Hey Bob, his badge is in the drawer."

Bob pointed a finger at Ethan. "I thought I was going to like you."

Melissa crossed her arms. "What's a little more paperwork? I'm the boss, and I can fire anyone I want."

Buck pushed open the door, a hot cup of coffee steaming in his hand. "No, you can't."

Doris turned to her desk and flipped open to a page in her manual that she had tagged. "According to the manual, you can only terminate a direct report. The form you signed made Trevor my direct report. And I need to approve the request for termination."

"But you could fire Doris and then fire the new guy," Alexus said.

Doris shot Alexus a glare, and Alexus stared right back, taking a bite out of her muffin.

"We'll see about that," Melissa said. Pointing at Trevor, she added, "Don't go anywhere. I'm going to make a few calls."

Trevor gulped.

Buck sat back down at his desk and eyed Ethan. "You starting work or what? You needed a form, right?"

Ethan blinked a few times, the memory of this morning coming back to him. "Yeah. I, uh, met a new spirit? I think I'm supposed to record it, right?"

"You met a new spirit? Where?" Alexus asked, taking her feet off the desk and leaning forward.

Noticing that everyone was staring at him, Ethan felt a sudden twinge of fear. "Oakland Cemetery?" he offered.

"What were you doing at my cemetery?" River asked.

"Idiot, never go alone. It's in the manual," Alexus declared.

"You probably didn't even have a briefcase with you, did you? Stupid maggot," Bob said.

Ethan looked down at the carpet. "Well, it was just a quick check. My grandmother sort of made me. I checked on an old friend. Mable."

"Don't go blaming your grandma, dude. Not cool." River said.

"Yeah, I agree," Alexus said, shaking her head.

"I expect more, yard bird." Bob said.

"And Mable is the new spirit?" Buck asked, clicking through several forms on his computer.

River shook his head. "I already reported her. Retired teacher. Mean. Doesn't want me talking to anyone there."

"No, not her. There was this kid there. His name was Dylan. I think. He wanted help with finding his dog," Ethan stammered.

"You think? The manual has a list of questions you are required to ask during the first interview." Alexus laughed.

"And, my grandma's friend, Mable. She said this weird thing about being murdered?" Ethan offered.

"Dammit, kid." Buck sighed, clicking through the program to pull up another form on his desktop.

"You seriously need to read the manual," River said.

"I'm sorry. I didn't mean to mess things up," Ethan said.

"Look, we don't go alone because you don't know what you're going to find. And never go without a briefcase. What if you had walked into a Class Three or Four? You'd be screwed," Alexus explained.

"I won't do it again," Ethan said.

"Alright, pull up a chair and let's go through what happened," Buck said.

"I need to fill out forms for this?" Ethan asked.

River laughed. "You said the word murder, dude. Got way more out of her than me. You're gonna be filling out forms for days."

"Get comfortable, bullet catcher," Bob said.

Ethan scooted his chair across the room and next to Buck. "Where do we start?"

"Right here. Used to have to do all this by hand and make copies, but now it is all online," Buck said.

Putting the phone down for the first time, Trevor waved his hand to get the room's attention. "Hey, um. Yeah. Excuse me. So, am I hearing this right? You all actually think you can see ghosts?"

Bob laughed.

"Just keep the damn camera off," Buck said.

"I'll explain at lunch, dear," Doris said.

Trevor nodded in reply and then sank into his chair.

All Work and No Play

E THAN LEANED BACK IN his chair, flexing his hand and yawning. "So, that was it, right? We're done. No more forms?"

Pulling a form off the printer and handing it to Ethan for his signature and date, Buck chuckled. "No. You still have eight more to go."

"Eight more? Come on. We've been doing this all day." Ethan reached for his mug and hopped out of his chair, seeking his tenth refill of the day.

River laughed. "Should have thought of that before you went all Lone Ranger. We've got procedures for a reason dude."

"Stupid. Really stupid, beatnik," Bob quipped.

Ethan poured the remaining contents of the coffee pot into his mug. He looked around the office as he slipped the pot back under the maker, hoping no one else noticed. "I didn't do it on purpose. I didn't know."

Bob pouted and mimicked Ethan's voice. "I didn't know."

River leaned back from his monitor and waved his hands in the air. "Crazy, it's like we don't have a manual for how to do our jobs or something."

"Maybe if you read it, you'd have less paperwork," Buck said, collating the forms and stapling them, tossing them onto an ever-growing tower of paper.

A rattle sounded from the back corner of the office, and Ethan jumped.

"Relax, rookie," Buck said.

"What was that?" Ethan asked, looking to the wall past the printers where a shelving unit full of briefcases stood.

"Would you believe me if I said it was probably . . . a ghost? Ooooo," River said, holding his face in his hands.

"Just ignore it, get back to work," Buck said.

Ethan leaned further to get a better look at the wall. A case on the second shelf was vibrating back and forth. "So, that's just normal, then?" he asked.

Buck shrugged, standing and picking up his coffee mug. "They try to get out sometimes."

"Wait. What?" Ethan exclaimed.

"Chill out, dude. The locks usually hold," River said.

Buck crossed the room and pulled the carafe from the coffeemaker. "Hey! Who took the last of the coffee? Ethan?"

Ethan slid his mug across the desk and looked away from Buck, looking at River instead. "Usually?"

"You're in for it, rookie." Buck said, dumping out the old coffee grounds while glaring at Ethan.

"Just don't touch the cases, and everything will be fine," River said.

"But what are we supposed to do if one of them gets out?" Ethan asked.

"Pursue and detain," Bob commanded.

Buck leaned against the counter and crossed his arms as the coffee poured into the carafe. "They don't get out. They just try from time to time."

River leaned back in his chair and said, "You ever hear about that newbie in DC? He had to go into Containment for something, and a Class Five shook their case loose. Heard it was pretty gruesome."

Ethan swallowed, looked at the vibrating case again, and asked, "What happened?"

"Not true. Don't listen to him," Buck said.

River rolled out from behind his desk and over to Ethan. "The Five tore and ate the newbie's face clean off."

"Really?" Ethan asked, his eyes darting back to the vibrating case.

"No," Buck said.

River rolled his chair to block Buck and got face to face with Ethan. "But the rookie didn't die. Oh, no. He just lived the rest of his life with no face. That old fart can say it didn't happen all he wants, but I met him at the annual conference in Seattle a few years ago. His face looked like someone had burned it right off."

Ethan swallowed. "A Five can't really do that, can it?"

"Don't listen to him. He's pulling your leg," Buck said.

"But, seriously, though. They can't get out? Right?" Ethan asked.

"Dammit, maggot. I keep losing faith in you every time you open your mouth," Bob said.

River laughed. "Look at you. You're terrified. I'm just playing with you, man. Class Fives don't eat your face. They just possess you and drain your essence."

"Drain my essence?" Ethan asked.

River rolled away, back to his desk. "Life force, soul, chi, whatever you want to call it."

Buck shook his head, pouring his coffee and crossing the room back to his desk. "Enough. The cases are secure. Don't touch them and they'll be fine."

"But will the Class Five drain my essence? I don't want it to do that." Ethan asked.

"Kid, this is the last time I'm going to tell you. Read the manual," Buck said.

Ethan grabbed the manual from his desk and cracked it open on his lap, flipping through the pages. "I will. I promise."

"Even I don't believe you, short round." Bob laughed.

Looking back at the computer, River rubbed his eyes and asked, "Why is it that Alexus gets a half day and we are all stuck here in the office after hours? Anyone else getting hungry? I could use a break, you know?"

Buck took a sip of his coffee and nodded. "Why not? I could eat." He grabbed the stack of papers and dropped them in the overflowing box outside Melissa's office.

"What are you thinking? Indian?" River asked.

"No," Buck said.

Ethan perked up. "Well, there's a great burger place just down the street. They put a fried egg on the top. It's amazing."

"I like burgers," Buck said.

"I would push River onto a landmine for a burger," Bob said.

River ignored Bob and nodded. "They got a solid fry game?"

"Fried cheese curds are where it's at, but yeah, they have a beer cheese they pour over top of their fries," Ethan said.

River's eyes grew wide, and he gulped. "Then what are we doing waiting here? Let's go. What's it called?"

Ethan stood and grabbed his suit jacket off the back of the chair. "Shorty's. Just take a right out the front and it's two blocks down. Can't miss it."

River looked at Ethan and raised an eyebrow. "Woah, where are you going?"

"Shorty's? With you guys?" Ethan said.

Buck looked at River and laughed. "You've still got forms to fill out."

Bob stood at attention, listing off the forms Ethan still had to do. "R-78 for the unauthorized approaching of a graveyard without a briefcase, S-62 for the use of a standard issue badge during off hours, and E-9—"

"E-9's my favorite," River said.

"What's the E-9?" Ethan asked.

"The customary 'Please don't fire me' form," Buck said with a smile.

"Can't I do those after we eat?"

"No," Buck said as he walked to the door. "I'm sure Alexus won't notice if you swipe one of her bars."

"Oh, she'll notice. Just blame it on Buck. I'll think about you as I eat those cheese fries though." River said, rubbing his belly as he followed Buck.

"No. Guys. Come on, really?" Ethan pleaded.

Ducking back into the office, River said, "Oh, mind keeping an eye on Bob? Since you're probably about to do an all-nighter, anyway."

"Oh yes. The wet rag and I will stand guard over the office. Zombie job. Finally," Bob said with a grin.

"Great. Thanks." River headed back out the door, leaving Ethan and Bob alone in the office.

Ethan settled back into his work, filling out forms. He nearly jumped out of his seat when the briefcase rattled on the shelf again, this time rattling the bookcase against the wall.

"Haha, didn't know you were enlisted in the Crybaby Division." Bob muttered.

"You know, you could be nicer." Ethan pulled the next form up on the computer. He squinted, his eyes aching from staring at the screen all day. Pinching them shut, he rubbed them with his palm.

Talking in a child's voice, Bob retorted, "Aw. I'm so sorry. Did I hurt your wittle feewings?"

"Shut up," Ethan said as he tried to focus on the first question of the form. "What does this even mean? Coordinates and classification of charnel grounds?"

Bob crossed the room to look over Ethan's shoulder. "It means where is the graveyard, dumbass."

"How am I supposed to know the coordinates?"

"You use the goggles, moron."

"Goggles?"

"You know. That map thing on the intern net."

"You mean, Google and internet?"

"Don't talk down to me, maggot. Just fill out the forms on your own then if you're going to be rude."

The case rattled again, drawing a "Jesus!" out of Ethan as it shook off the top shelf and onto the floor.

Bob hovered over to the case and inspected it. "That hasn't happened before."

Ethan shivered and turned back to the desktop, muttering to himself, "Just ignore it."

"Well?" Bob asked, gesturing to the case.

"Well, what?" Ethan said, returning to his Google search.

"Well? I can't pick it up."

"Neither can I."

"Why not? Are your wittle pansy armsy-warmys too weak to wift it?"

"No. Buck said don't touch the cases."

"Oh, no. Bucky said don't touchy-wouchy the casey-waseys."

"Wow, you're annoying. Cut it out."

Bob put his hand to his mouth and said, "Did I hurt your feelings again? GET UP OUT OF THE CHAIR MAGGOT AND PICK UP THE GODDAMN CASE!"

"Fine!" Ethan yelled, standing up from his desk. He walked to the back of the room and stood right next to Bob, looking down at the case.

"Well? PICK IT UP!"

"Stop bossing me around."

Standing next to Ethan, Bob said, "Does it make you feel bad when I yell at you? Is that hard for you?"

"Shut up. Jeez, no wonder River takes off his badge so much," Ethan said, staring at the case.

"It's not going to bite you, bullet catcher. Just pick it up and PUT IT BACK ON THE GODDAMN SHELF! DAMNIT! DO IT! DO IT! DO IT NOW!"

"Fine! My God, you're annoying." Ethan yelled back. Bending down, he grabbed the leather case, reached up, pushed it back to the top shelf, and hustled back to his desk.

Bob hopped into River's chair and laughed hysterically. "Oh man. You're my favorite maggot. River never gets this worked up. You've got to toughen up if you plan on lasting."

"Fuck off," Ethan said as he dropped back into his chair and pulled up to his computer.

"Don't be that way. I'm just screwing with you. Look, the cases are fine now."

Keeping his eyes focused on his screen, Ethan said, "You know what? River's right. You are an asshole."

"Don't be sore. I was just playing with you, short round."

The briefcase vibrated again. With it, the entire shelf rattled, and the lights flickered on and off.

Bob crossed the room and inspected the briefcase. "Well, that's not good."

"Not falling for it this time, Sarge."

"No. Seriously. That wasn't right."

"Can you just leave me alone? I want to go home, get out of this damn suit, and go to bed sometime tonight."

Pressure built up in Ethan's ears as what felt like an earthquake crashed through the room, knocking mugs and pens off the desk and wrenching the shelf free from the wall, knocking down several briefcases as the lights flickered above.

"What the hell!" Ethan exclaimed.

"Well, now you've done it. Call Buck, now. Get them to come back." Bob backed away from the bookcase, his eyes locked on the pile.

"I don't know his phone number. Does he even have a cell phone? What's River's number?" Ethan said as he hustled across the room and began putting the fallen briefcases back on the wall.

"Why would I know the idiot's phone number? DO I LOOK LIKE I OWN A PHONE!"

"STOP YELLING AT ME!" Ethan grabbed the briefcase and immediately stumbled back.

His grip tightened around the briefcase as it vibrated violently in his hand. Sparks flew between his fingers, and the lights above him brightened before the bulbs completely burned out.

The rest of the lights followed suit and burned out.

Ethan stood in complete darkness until the small hallway emergency lights flickered on. Everything rattled and shook, and Ethan did everything in his might to keep hold of the briefcase.

"Uh oh," Bob said.

"Yeah, no shit. A little help here?" Ethan said, his eyes locked on the case.

"What class spirit is in that case?"

"How am I supposed to know?"

"Check the tag!"

Ethan tried moving his hand, but nothing happened. "I can't. You check it!"

"FINE!" Bob edged toward the case, but before he could reach it, the briefcase shook again. It flailed violently in Ethan's hand, flinging left and right. He was certain it was going to pull his arm out of his socket from the sheer force. Then it slammed down, and Ethan's legs gave out, crashing into the floor.

The case burst open. A rush of cold air blew from the case, condensing the warm air into a thick mist around it as yellow and pink lights flickered from inside. The scent of ozone filled the room, like the air during a thunderstorm. The light grew brighter and brighter until Ethan had to look away. Then a sound pierced his ears, a screech like an animal being burned alive.

"OH SHIT!" Bob yelled.

"WHAT DO WE DO NOW!" Ethan screamed, covering his ears.

Nine

Brief Encounter

E THAN SCRAMBLED AWAY FROM the screeching briefcase, lying open in the middle of the office floor, his hands covering his ears. His eyes darted around the dark office and found Bob, the pinkish light from the blowing briefcase lighting the space.

The army vet stood, positioned to pounce on the briefcase any minute now.

"GET READY!" he screamed over the screech.

"READY? FOR WHAT?" Ethan shouted in reply.

"COME ON SHORT ROUND, THINK! GET READY FOR THE ESCAPE!"

"ESCAPE? WHAT ESCAPE?"

The screeching stopped, but Ethan's ears were still ringing from the sound. He slipped his hands off his ears and eyed the glowing case.

He shot a glance at Bob, but Bob's eyes stayed locked on the case. After a long and awkward moment, Ethan whispered, "What's happening?"

Bob took a slow step forward, his fingers twitching. "Any second now, the enemy is going to make a break for it. You need to help me wrangle it back into the case."

Ethan eyed the briefcase, racing to get up to his feet and stand beside Bob. "What? How do I do that?"

Bob let out a slow growl. "Kid, this is why you should have read the manual."

Ethan looked over his shoulder at the desk, eying his manual. "Look, I've been a little busy if you haven't noticed," he hissed.

"Your badge."

"What?"

Bob turned and looked at Ethan for a split second, the vein in his incorporeal neck pulsing. "You can't touch the spirit, but your badge is like a hot poker. Use it."

Ethan pulled the badge from his belt, a trick Alexus had showed him when she clipped the badge backward so the metal touched her skin, and turned it over. Not sure what else to do with it, he held it out like it was a can of mace.

Bob nodded and locked his eyes back to the briefcase. "You didn't check the tag, and the wall had a few nasties on it. Treat it like it is a Class Four or higher."

"Cool, great. And how do I do that?"

"Don't let it touch you. Fives can possess. Before you know it, you'll be waking up somewhere in Northern Canada a week from now, buck naked, bare ass up in the sky."

"Speaking from experience?"

"FOCUS, MAGGOT!"

"Sorry. Sorry," Ethan said as he focused on the case.

Without warning, the light from the case flickered and then went out, leaving the only illumination in the room coming from the emergency light in the hallway.

Ethan's eyes adjusted, and he saw a young girl, no more than seven or eight years old, standing in the middle of the pile of fallen briefcases. She had loose blond curls draping over her shoulders and carried a small doll with the same hairstyle in her arms.

Ethan dropped his hand and looked over at Bob. "Oh. It's just a little kid."

"Don't think for a second that little kid won't eat your face off," Bob whispered.

Ethan shrugged off Bob's comment and took a step toward the little girl. She swayed back and forth, swishing the white dress she wore.

"Hey there," he said as he edged closer. "Uh, why don't you just go ahead and get back in your case? What do you say about that?"

The little girl looked up and smiled at Ethan. Her eyes were a bright shade of blue, and she looked no different from the kids his sister invited over to play.

Ethan looked back at Bob, who hadn't moved from his crouched over stance that made him look like he was ready to pounce any second. "I dunno what kid scorned you in the past, but you got me all worked up for nothing."

Bob shook his head, reaching a hand out toward Ethan. "Look, rookie. I was teasing you earlier, sure, but you better get your badge up right now. That's not a little girl anymore. She's the enemy, and she's going to make her move any second now."

The little girl ignored them, picking up her doll and pushing back her hair.

Ethan eyed the girl and shook his head. "Pretty cool doll you have there. My friend here thinks that you're the enemy, but I know better. You're just scared. If you want to talk, I'm here. They say I'm a good listener."

The little girl looked up from her doll, her eyes locking onto Ethan's. Cold air filled the room, and the little girl twisted her fingers tight around the doll's hair. The voice that came from her pierced through Ethan's ears, a raspy voice that shouldn't ever come from a child. "Momma doesn't like it when I talk to strangers."

"Oh, no." Bob said, taking a step closer to Ethan and passing a hand through his shoulder.

"Oh no, what?"

"That's gotta be Clara. She's—"

"Momma's gonna be here any minute. You're gonna make me get the paddle. It's all your fault. IT'S ALL YOUR FAULT."

Clara dropped her doll and clenched her fists at her sides. Her curly hair lifted from her shoulders, as if lightning were about to strike, and her blue eyes turned a deep glowing pink.

Before Ethan could react, the briefcase on the floor flew at him, landing perfectly in his gut and knocking him off his feet. He flew, a weightless sack of meat, before his head connected with the edge of the desk and his body slammed into the ground.

Bob's voice cracked through the newfound ringing in his ears. "WE'VE GOT A LEVEL FOUR!"

Lights danced around Ethan's eyes as he felt at the back of his head, seeing the red stains on his hand when he checked it.

Clara's voice permeated the air, a voice that drilled deep into the mind and forced you to hang on every word. "SHUT UP! SHUT UP! MOMMA WILL HEAR YOU!"

Objects flew at Bob, slipping through his incorporeal body and slamming into the desk behind him, knocking over Buck's mug.

The little girl's eyes glowed brighter, and she raced toward Bob, outstretching a hand that transformed and lengthened into a hand with long, pointed fingers. It wrapped around Bob's neck and lifted him off the ground.

He dangled in the air, clutching at the strange hand wrapped around him. He strained to speak, looking at Ethan, still on the ground. "GET UP . . . BULLET CATCHER! THOUGHT YOU . . . WEREN'T . . . WORRIED OVER A LITTLE GIRL?" Bob yelled.

Ethan propped himself on his elbows and took in a few breaths, clearing out the lights that blurred his vision. "What should I do?"

Clara shot a look at him, pink sparks lighting up her hair. "BE QUIET!"

Before he could even process, a briefcase flung itself off the wall, slamming directly into his nose.

He didn't know how long he lay on his back, staring up at the dancing lights on the ceiling. Papers and debris flew by, caught up in a ghostly windstorm. Occasionally, Bob would cross over his vision too. A part of him found it funny, a ghost somehow getting his ass handed to him by a little girl.

Ethan felt a cold chill run up his arm, and Bob's voice shouted in his ear. "YOU BETTER STOP BEING A WET RAG AND GET BACK ON YOUR FEET! WHY'D THEY EVEN HIRE YOU IN THE FIRST PLACE?"

That was enough to shock Ethan back into reality. He blinked a few times and felt his nose. Not broken. He scrambled backward when his vision finally came into focus and saw that Bob had bent down so his mouth was less than an inch from Ethan's nose.

"IF YOU DON'T HELP ME GET A HANDLE ON THIS LITTLE GIRL, THEN I'M GOING TO HITCH A RIDE ON YOU BEFORE SHE GETS A CHANCE. EVER RUN THROUGH ONE OF THOSE WALMARTS NEKKID?"

Ethan looked past Bob's face and saw that he had wrapped his other arm around Clara in a headlock.

"I CAN'T HOLD ON MUCH—"

She slipped through his arm and floated backward. Papers, keyboards, mugs, and Ethan's manual lifted off from the desks, revolving slowly around the spirit. "I SAID BE QUIET. Momma will hear you. She'll hurt me. NOT AGAIN!"

One by one, mugs and keyboards flew at him. Ethan shot up his hands at the last second, ceramic and hard plastic pelting his forearms.

"OW!" he yelped as the third mug cracked on his elbow. "Stop it! STOP!"

When he thought the coast was clear, he dropped his arms.

The girl still hovered in the air; an enormous grin spread across her face.

Ethan raised his hands. "Look, whatever happened to you. I'm sorry, but it's over. You're free."

She shook her head. "Never free."

She flinched, and the manual came hurtling at him.

It connected with the side of his face, and he fell to the floor once again. "DAMMIT! OUCH!" he screamed.

The door to the stairwell burst open, and Buck stepped in. "What in the hell is happening here?"

"Wait, isn't that the fucking little girl we cased last week? Shit, bro," River said as he charged forward with his badge extended in front of him.

River knocked back pens and mice as Clara hurled them toward him. Then she chucked a whole computer monitor, and he dodged behind his desk.

"I told this beatnik not to touch the cases, Honcho," Bob said.

Buck caught the second monitor and didn't even flinch, turning to place it gently on the desk next to him.

"What? Liar! You didn't tell me that!" Ethan yelled.

Buck crouched and squeezed the badge in his hand. He looked at River. "GO LEFT!"

River nodded and leaped out from behind the desk, dodging two more cases that Clara pulled from the wall.

Agile for his age and size, Buck raced forward, dodging and sliding under each briefcase she threw at him. He dove onto the ground, hand outstretched upward, and slid right beside her, ramming his badge into her leg.

The moment the badge touched her, Clara let out a loud howl. Smoke billowed from the badge, and the smell of ozone grew stronger. The office shook, an undulating vibration that nauseated Ethan as the lights above flickered on and off.

In an instant, the objects floating around her fell to the ground. River's badge pressed against her forehead, and she slowly descended closer to the ground.

"Briefcase. Ethan, now!" River yelled.

Snapping out of his daze, Ethan pushed himself off the ground and found the open briefcase inches away. He flung it forward, sliding it underneath the ghost.

A beam of pink light illuminated her, and Clara's eyes darted around the room. "NO! NO! NOT AGAIN!"

"Gotcha again, you evil bitch," River said.

Sparks of energy crackled up through the briefcase and closed in around the spirit before halting and reversing direction. She looked past Buck, reaching out her hand and trying to push past the beam, but the pillar of light stopped her.

Ethan followed her gaze and spotted the little doll, still sitting there, past Buck, out of Clara's reach.

Before he could say anything, Clara vanished inside the briefcase, and River snapped it shut. The doll vanished, an afterimage burned into Ethan's mind.

Buck brushed himself off and stood. "Dammit, rookie. I told you not to touch the cases."

"I gotta say, dude. This isn't cool. Seriously, you kinda suck," River said as he picked the briefcases up off the ground and stacked them back on the shelf.

"I told you this maggot wasn't ready. Hasn't even attempted to read the manual. He needs to go before he takes you all to the farm," Bob chimed in.

"Look, I'm sorry," Ethan said with a cough as he propped himself up on his elbows, wiping the blood off his face.

Extending his hand and helping Ethan stand, Buck said, "Go to the bathroom and clean yourself up."

"Thanks," Ethan said.

"Then get your ass back in here because you just tripled your paperwork," Buck said.

"So . . . I'm not fired?" Ethan asked.

River leaned against the shelf and laughed. "Did you forget the amount of paperwork Melissa would have to do for that? You're stuck here, dude. So, maybe stop trying to kill the rest of us."

Buck plugged the monitor back in and slapped the side, the light within coming back to life. "Looks like you're in it for the long haul. Hope you don't get too delirious from sleep deprivation."

Ten

Convention Full of NRDS

E THAN STEPPED OUT OF the van onto the red-brick sidewalk and marveled at the giant glass window and decorative steel awnings. Turning, he gazed up at the giant glass building across the street. He'd seen skyscrapers on his high school senior trip to Chicago, but they still seemed like something out of a Marvel movie.

"Welcome to America's Convention Center!" Trevor said as he pointed his phone at Ethan's face.

"Cool," Ethan said as he smiled and nodded.

"In downtown Saint Louis, Missouri, this amazing facility has over 80 meeting rooms, 502,000 square feet of prime exhibit space, and a 28,000 square-foot ballroom," Trevor said as he panned his camera around the entrance.

"Excellent parking job, as always, Doris. Glad to be dropped off right on the sidewalk," River said as he stepped out of the van and lit a joint. He nodded to the convention center and looked at the camera. "They've got all that space because there isn't shit else in Saint Louis."

Turning the camera back on Ethan, Trevor said, "The convention center sits next to the Dome at America's Center. The former home of XFL's BattleHawks and the NFL's Rams."

River blew a giant puff of smoke into the air before reaching into the van and slinging a backpack over his shoulder. He said, "Yeah. They were smart. Getting the hell out of here for LA."

Alexus stepped out of the van next, nearly tripping on the curb before asking, "Isn't this your home turf?"

River smiled. "Yep. And that's why I can talk all the shit I want to."

Melissa pushed open the passenger side door and stepped out, promptly tripping and falling into Ethan before standing to smooth her dress. "Has anyone seen Buck yet?"

Keeping his camera focused on Ethan, Trevor asked, "Did you know that this is the annual home to the Working Women's Survival Show?"

Ethan yawned and then asked, "What's that?"

"Women's survival show? Do they sell axes?" Alexus asked.

Trevor raised an eyebrow, "No . . . it's—"

"Ultimate girl's day out. The ladies get pampered all in one place. You can win spa treatments and junk. My mom loves it," River said.

"How does that have anything to do with survival? Do they fight to get prizes?" Alexus asked, cracking her knuckles.

"Is it 'Ignore Your Boss Day?'" Melissa said, waving her hands in the air. "Has anyone seen Buck?"

"He's too chicken to show until after the games," Alexus said with a scoff.

"Well, he better get over himself. I'm not parading in there without our whole team present. We're already late. Best to look somewhat put together," Melissa said.

"If I shave my head and act like a grouch, will anyone know the difference?" Alexus asked.

"If I answer, will I get punched in the arm?" River asked.

"Yes," Alexus said.

"I just wish that, for once, you two would be helpful," Melissa said, shaking her head.

Alexus shrugged. "Short of calling him, how else would we find out where he is?"

A gleam of bleached blond hair peeked out from the driver's side as Doris called out, "Am I just parking the van here or what?"

Melissa looked up and down the sidewalk. "I'm not paying for the tickets, Doris. There is a parking lot a block away. Do you think you can manage?"

"I can, but you wanted the whole team to walk in together?" Doris asked.

Melissa sighed and shook her head. "Just park the damn van, Doris."

Doris revved the engine before switching gears, the van jerking into motion as she drove up into the flowerbed before hopping over a curb to get back on the road.

Trevor panned the camera again around the driveway and asked no one in particular, "Did you know that yesterday the Missouri Bridal and Wedding Expo took place here? My wife almost dragged me down here early to look for dresses for her sister."

"That's kind of weird for the day before Halloween," Ethan said.

"Fucking Saint Louis. I bet there was no reference to the Bride of Frankenstein. Missed opportunity," River said.

"And next week is the Bands of America Super Regional competition?" Trevor asked.

Melissa eyed Trevor and put a hand on her hip. "Hey Trev. No one cares that you spent the last eleven hours reading up on St. Louis."

"I was just . . . trying to pass the time." Trevor said, slowly dropping his phone to his side.

"Aww, you made Trev sad. Don't worry man, you can interview me all you want about this place." River said.

Looking in her makeup compact to straighten her hair, Melissa said, "Jesus, people. Pull yourselves together and act somewhat normal. Upper management is going to be here, and we need to present a united front. Try not to look like you just spent the night in a van."

River took another big drag and then exhaled, running a finger through his unkempt hair. "We had plenty of opportunities to stop at a hotel."

"There's no budget for that," Melissa said.

River looked at the air next to him and rolled his eyes. "Yeah, but we all know Gerry and Buck booked a nice hotel up in Davenport. I could have crashed on the couch. Even Bob agrees the van sucked."

Ethan reached a hand in his pocket and pulled out his badge, having kept it off him to tune out Bob on the way there. Bob appeared next to River, shouting, "But we've got games to win, maggots!"

"Bob's right. Time to saddle up and kick some ass. That trophy is ours," Alexus said as she walked toward the giant glass doors of the convention center.

"Wait. No. Doris . . . and Buck. Well, I should go in first if you insist," Melissa yelled as she raced to keep up with Alexus.

Past the glass doors, Ethan gawked at the number of suits and ghosts all in one place. Agents were huddled in groups chatting, with ghosts in various civilian and military clothes huddled around them. "Wow. There are so many people here," he said.

River nodded. "Yep. And this is just the Midwest convention. You should see the Northeast one. It's in New York every year. There are like ten thousand agents at that one. Especially so close to headquarters."

"How many agents are here?" Ethan asked.

"I'd guess about a thousand, give or take," River said with a shrug.

"A thousand glorious soldiers all primed and ready to storm the beaches for the common good," Bob declared.

"Pretty sure that metaphor doesn't line up," Alexus said.

"Alright. We need a game plan. Someone put Buck on speaker so he can hear this," Melissa said.

Ethan reached for his phone, but then Alexus said, "Trev's recording, just make him watch the replay."

"Fine. Whatever," Melissa said.

"See? You need good old Trev," River said, shooting Alexus a wink.

"Don't you worry, I've got this all on tape." Trevor smiled.

"We know. God," Melissa said, shaking her head. Continuing, she pulled a map of the convention center from her purse and said, "So, as I was saying, upper management will be at all the keynotes. We need to split up so we can have a person in each one."

"No-fucking-way," River said, pretending to cough.

"Yeah. No. We're here for the games," Alexus said.

"We're going to kick some big city butts!" Bob declared.

"We don't have a big enough head count like the Chicago district. I know we have the office, but they have the head count. We need all of you at the presentations. We need to look like we're serious, ok?" Melissa said, holding her map out again for everyone to see.

River let out a loud giggle and darted his reddened eyes around.

Melissa shot him a glare, and he straightened up, fixing his tie. "Oh, yes. Sorry Captain. We need to . . . act like . . . adults," he said through fits of giggles.

A slim man in a sleek black suit joined their party and tapped Melissa on the shoulder. "Excuse me, ma'am. Are you Melissa Scott?"

Melissa straightened up and said, "Yes. Manager of the new New Richmond branch."

"Upper management is looking for you. Are you available to leave these . . . um, junior agents?" the slim man said, motioning to a small circle of older men standing seventy yards away.

"Hey, who are you calling junior agents?" River said.

"Shut up," Melissa said through gritted teeth. Then, turning to the slim man, she said, "Lead the way."

When Melissa was out of earshot, Alexus turned to the others. "Alright, we don't have enough numbers to compete in everything. We'll have to take on all the big pointers. River, you good to get through the house of horrors?"

Ethan held up a hand. "Wait, Melissa said—"

River grabbed his hand and pulled it down to his side, keeping a firm grasp on it. "What she doesn't know won't hurt her. Besides, she'll be happy when we take down Chicago's district."

"Well, then what's 'the house of horrors?'"

Bob stood in front of Ethan's face, waving his arms. "It's a haunted house so horrifying, so terrible, so disturbing that everyone taps out before they get to the end."

"Everyone but our boy here, four years running," Alexus said with a smile.

River lit up another joint and blew a huge cloud of smoke into the air. "Already prepping. It's in the bag."

"Nice. Okay, I've got the possession mummy wrap," Alexus said.

"And that is?" Ethan asked, more worried than before.

"That's where they lock you in a sealed box with a handful of Class Fives and you have to fight off possession," River said.

"They award points based on how long you last," Bob added with a smile. "Bug out too soon and you get nothing."

"You're going to do that?" Ethan asked, his mouth hanging open.

"I'm going to make those Class Fives my bitches," Alexus said with a wink.

"And you want me in the Bobs' Rotted Rumble, I'm assuming," Bob asked.

"What's that?" Ethan asked in a shaky voice.

"Hand to hand combat. The BOBs get to possess meat suits. Last one standing wins," Bob said with pride.

"To the death?" Ethan asked.

"I mean, till they can't keep wearing the meatsuits. They're already dead," Trevor said.

"And they named it after you, Bob? Why did they name it after you?" Ethan asked.

"My name's not Bob, it's—"

"Every branch has a BOB, bro," River cut Bob off. "And someone to carry around their bag of bones. You seriously have to read the fucking manual."

Alexus looked at Bob and said, "Hey. None of this old school honor shit. You fight dirty. I'm not losing to goddamn Chicago again. River, you'll drop him off on your way?"

"I'm on it," River said.

Turning to Trevor's camera, Alexus said, "Alright. You're our secret weapon. I put your name in for the pumpkin bowl."

"What's that?" Ethan asked, his voice raising an octave with his increased terror at the descriptions of the games.

"It's bowling. But with pumpkins," Alexus said.

"Oh. I mean, I'm honored. But I'm just here to record," Trevor said.

"Don't you think I didn't do my research. Bowling Champion, 2010 through 2014? You're part of the New Richmond branch, whether or not you like it. You better bring me that damn trophy or I'm going to jam that camera up your ass so far that Instagram's going to get a live stream of your next colonoscopy," Alexus said.

Trevor put the phone down and said, "Got it. Pumpkin bowling. I'm on it."

"And that leaves you, rookie," Alexus said.

"I don't . . . I mean . . . I'm not really up for being possessed or anything," Ethan said.

"As if." River laughed.

Shaking her head, Alexus said, "No. Former high school football star who ran the forty in four-six. You're playing Catch A BOB."

"You really did your research," Trevor said with a nod of respect. "What's—"

"If you say, 'what's that,' one more time, I'm going to get one of the BOB vets to possess your ass," Bob said.

River shook his head. "Man, just tell him. He doesn't know."

"It's a one-on-one against another branch, in a maze, trying to capture the BOB in a briefcase before they escape, then carry him across the finish line. It's a game of wit and cunning. A game of cat-and-mouse. And I've never been caught," Bob said.

"Look. There's nothing to worry about. All the BOBs are class ones or twos. You'll catch theirs in no time," River said.

Bob nodded. "You'll be fine, Rookie. Just as long as you don't go against Detroit's BOB. Crazy 'Nam vet. He's not right in the head."

"Got it. No to Detroit," Ethan said.

"Better stay away from Milwaukee's BOB as well. Native American shot in the French and Indian War. Still bitter about it. Not fun to tangle with," Bob said.

"Just stay away from all major metropolitan area BOBs," Alexus said. Looking over her shoulder at Melissa, who looked to be getting a stern lecture from upper management, and then looking back at the group, Alexus continued, "Look. I could tell you to do your best and it will be fine, but that's bullshit. I want to take that goddamn trophy from those Chicago fucks."

"Damn straight," River said.

"So, kick some ass. Let's put the New Richmond branch on the map," Alexus said.

"Yeah!" Bob yelled.

"Okay, meet in the food court when you're done. And if you lose, don't try to go hide, because I'll find your asses. And I'll hurt you," Alexus said. "Now, break."

Everyone scattered, leaving Ethan standing on his own. He looked around the room to see if there was some kind of map of the convention center, but there were only gobs and gobs of agents.

"Did everyone head out?" Melissa asked, making Ethan jump. He turned to see her playing with some kind of key fob.

"What's that?" he asked.

"Van keys," she said.

"I thought Doris had the van?" Ethan asked.

Melissa stuffed the odd-looking fob in her purse and said, "You know what, I'm your boss. You don't get to ask me questions. I ask you the questions. Got it? Now, where are we going?"

"Um. I'm competing in the Catch A BOB," Ethan said.

"Perfect, none of you listen. Fine, I'll test it there. Let's go," Melissa said, grabbing him by the hand and dragging him toward conference hall B.

Eleven

Run the Maze

"**S**TILL TRYING TO MEMORIZE it? It won't help." Melissa said from behind Ethan.

Ethan looked away from the map on the wall and over his shoulder, seeing the half-eaten chili cheese dog and enormous soda in Melissa's hands. "It's worth a shot. The maze isn't even that hard. Did you bring me anything?"

Melissa laughed. "Yeah right."

Turning back to the map, Ethan asked, "Did you ever compete in these?"

She took a long sip from her soda before rolling her eyes and saying, "Please. I'm management. We don't play kid games."

"But you had to be an agent at some point? Right?" he asked, tracing a finger along the various paths of the maze. They all intertwined, with only four dead ends. He figured if he could herd the BOB into one of those and get a case under him, he'd be set.

She shoved the final bit of her hotdog in her mouth and let out a loud belch. "That's not how the government works, kid. I started on a management track with USPS. Left there and took a supervisor's role at the FDA. Then I leveraged that experience to move to NRDS as a project manager for the upper management office in DC, but they shipped me out for my first post. I'll be back in their good graces by this time next year. Just gotta do my time."

Ethan paused and looked back at her. "Huh. So, you think I could, like, transfer to the FBI or something like that? I mean, not now. But in a few years?"

Melissa nearly dropped her soda as she doubled over laughing. "Oh, God. No. Jesus. That's funny though."

Ethan let out a sigh before turning back to the map.

Melissa patted his shoulder and took a long sip of her soda. "Look. Memorizing the map won't help. It's just a footrace to catch the BOB." Shifting her hand to his bicep and giving it an awkward squeeze, she continued, "A strong healthy boy like you shouldn't have anything to worry about. Nearly all the BOBs are ancient geezers or batshit crazy. I mean, look at them over there." She pointed at a group of BOBs standing in the corner, all waiting their turn at the games.

Ethan followed her gaze and spotted several BOBs with ghostly canes, and even one trailed a floating CPAP machine behind him. "I just don't want to let the team down," he said.

Putting her drink down, Melissa started rubbing his shoulders with both hands. "You've got this. BOBs get a thirty-second head start. Then you bring the briefcase and catch him before they open the door again. You can catch one of those old guys in five minutes, right?"

"Yeah. I guess."

"Of course you can. That's why I picked you," she said. Then, smacking him on the ass, she added, "Go team."

"I thought Alexus picked me," he said.

"I wear the big girl panties around here. Means I make all the decisions." She grabbed her soda and took another swig. "You know, I've got a little special something you could use, if you're that worried."

"Oh yeah? What's that?"

She dug into her purse, pulling out a simple white garage door opener. "This little baby here is going to make the BOB super easy to catch. Just point it at him, click the button, and viola. Easy-peasy."

Ethan took it and turned it over before asking, "Is this legal?"

"There's no rule against it," she said with a shrug.

Ethan pocketed the remote as the door to the maze unlocked. An athletic woman with a shaved head and dark skin burst through the doors, holding a case high over her head in victory.

A voice over the loudspeaker announced, "Agent Rodgers of Chicago, four minutes, fifteen seconds. Rodgers takes the lead. Way to go, Chicago!"

Cheers sounded from a group of agents on the far side of the room. They ran to surround Rodgers as she strutted from the maze.

"Wow. That's going to be hard to beat. Damn near the national record," Melissa said as she took another sip of her soda.

"Great," Ethan said, looking down.

"Oh. I didn't mean . . . don't worry. You can do this. Just, use the clicker when you have sights on the BOB."

"Agent Ethan Malik of New Richardson, please report to the maze door," the loudspeaker rang out.

"New Richmond! It's New Richmond, you assholes!" Melissa yelled at the ceiling. She huffed and looked at Ethan before smacking him on the butt again. "Get out there and win one for the team! Oh, and don't fuck it up."

"I'll try not to." He gulped.

He walked toward the door of the maze. A wave of relief washed over him as he saw the BOB waiting for him. The frail geriatric ghost with glasses far too large for his face leaned on a walker with tennis balls on its feet. The old ghost gave a toothless smile as Ethan approached, and Ethan whispered to himself, "Oh, thank God."

Arriving at the starting line, Ethan smiled and said, "Hello, sir. I'm Ethan Malik. I think I'll be racing you today."

The old man gave another toothless smile, looked Ethan up and down, and said, "Nice to meet you, sonny."

Ethan smiled, finally feeling light for the first time all day. "So, I guess we just wait here until they ring the bell?"

The old BOB took his glasses off and wiped them with a handkerchief. Putting them back on his nose, he looked at Ethan and said, "Sonny, I'm going to fuck you up so badly, you'll be running back to New Rockingham with your tail between your legs." Folding the handkerchief and placing it back in his pocket, he smiled and continued, "That is if you make it out of there alive."

Speechless, Ethan's mouth hung open.

Over the loudspeaker, a voice said, "Agent Ethan Malik. BOB from Detroit. On your marks!"

The old ghost folded his walker, attaching it to his back as if it were a sword, and then dropped into a runner's stance. Ethan, whose mouth was still hanging open, mumbled, "You're. Um. The BOB from Detroit?"

"Get set!" the voice in the loudspeaker yelled.

Looking up at Ethan, the old man said, "I'm going to fuck you Bad-Boys-Motor-City style and put your little bitch Ann-Arbor-wanna-be-pansy-ass in a jar to display on my mantel so I can always remember the day I made little Agent Ethan from New Where-ever-the-fuck shit his pants while weeping in a corner."

"Go!" the voice from the loudspeaker screamed as Detroit BOB took off like a gold-medal Olympic sprinter into the maze.

The digital clock above the door began counting down from thirty, and Ethan shook his head.

"Hey, kid," an agent said as he tossed a briefcase at Ethan.

Ethan caught it with both hands and looked at the clock. Fifteen seconds left. He rolled his shoulders and jumped up and down like he used to do before taking the football field. The clock hit zero, and he rushed through the door.

The nondescript plywood walls and sharp turns of the maze disoriented him quickly. Darting left, he spotted the old man.

"Here piggy-piggy-piggy-piggy!" Detroit BOB yelled with a cackle as he raced out of sight.

Planting his foot and pushing off the wall, Ethan cut around another turn. He could feel his football legs coming back to him. Pumping his knees, he raced down a straightaway and then took another sharp turn right. Detroit BOB was in his sights again. Without losing pace, he unclipped the clasps on the briefcase. Detroit BOB took a left down what Ethan remembered to be a dead end, and Ethan surged forward with excitement.

"Got you now, old timer!" Ethan yelled as he took the left turn and saw the old man trapped at the end of a hall.

"Come and get it, you little bitch," the old timer said with a smile.

"Suck it, old man," Ethan said with glee as he placed the case on the ground and prepared to claim victory in record time.

He cracked the case open, and Detroit BOB raced forward.

The old man phased through Ethan, a cold painful shock to Ethan's system. He tried to twist his body and turn the case, but he stumbled forward. Tripping over the briefcase, he rolled onto his back and slammed into a wall.

"Suck my taint!" Detroit BOB screamed, holding up his middle finger as he ran.

Ethan tried to shake off the pounding in his head. He reached into his pocket as he pushed himself up the wall. Gripping the garage door remote, he muttered, "You're going down, old man."

He picked up the briefcase, leaving it unlatched, and started the chase again.

"Come and get some, old timer!" Ethan yelled as he raced down another long hall.

"Olly Olly Oxen Free, you little bitch!" Detroit BOB screamed back.

Ethan whipped around a right turn, ran four paces, and then turned left. Catching sight of Detroit BOB at the end of a long straightaway, he pushed his legs to pick up speed. Crashing into the wall at the end of the hall and using it to propel him around the corner, he locked eyes with the old man.

The old timer stopped and turned to face him. Ethan skidded to a stop. "Come and get some," the old man said with a grin.

"Who's the bitch now?" Ethan asked, holding out the garage door opener. He clicked it with a massive grin on his face, expecting Detroit BOB to freeze or fizzle or fade. But the old ghost smiled, and lightning crackled in his eyes.

Pointing the remote at him again, in a panic, Ethan clicked it again and again. With each click, the old ghost seemed to grow in electric energy.

The plywood walls around them shook and trembled as a ghostly wind crashed into Ethan.

Blue lightning crackled through the old man's eyes. "Now we're playing with gasoline," the old man said, taking his walker off his back and holding it with one hand like a club.

"Oh, shit," Ethan shouted before the old ghost rushed toward him.

Before Ethan could even turn to run, Detroit BOB reared back with his walker and swung it forward like a softball pitcher hurling a strike toward the plate. The ghostly metal felt like a sledgehammer as it connected with Ethan's chin. His head rang as he felt his feet leave the ground. For a brief moment, he floated through the air, blood filling his mouth. His flight ended as his back crashed to the floor.

There was a rage-filled scream.

Ethan felt like he was about to throw up, the room spinning as he looked up, catching a blurred afterimage of Detroit BOB being sucked into the open briefcase Ethan had dropped when the old man had delivered the haymaker.

The voice from the loudspeaker rang out. "Agent Malik has done it! At three minutes and thirty-two seconds, Agent Malik of New—what was it again?"

"New Richmond, dammit," Melissa said through the loudspeaker.

"Agent Malik of New Richmond is our new leader!"

Ethan snapped the briefcase locks with a grin and wiped his bloody nose, "Suits you well, dick."

Ethan made his way to the food court after he reluctantly let Detroit BOB go. He found the others all together at a table in the middle of the room.

River was still puffing on a joint as Trevor laughed and stuffed cheese fries in his mouth. Even with her hair standing up on end, Alexus still looked ready to take anyone down in a chokehold if they said anything. Doris was zoned out, glued to her phone screen, scrolling through who knows what social media feed. Last, he spotted Buck and Gerry, shooting looks up at Alexus and whispering to each other.

Noticing the blood that had dried around his nostrils, Gerry asked, "What happened to you?"

"A BOB beat me with a walker."

"Next thing out of your mouth better be that you got that medal," Alexus said.

"I got mine," Trevor said with a huge smile.

"We both got ours too," Bob said as River held his and BOB's medals in the air.

Alexus pulled her medal out, "That makes four, rookie. Don't make me wait."

Reaching into his back pocket, Ethan pulled the medal and said with a grin, "Oh. I got it."

The table exploded in cheers, and Alexus pulled out a chair and called for Ethan to sit down between her and Doris.

"Who was your BOB?" Bob asked.

"Detroit," Ethan said.

Alexus whistled and clapped him on the back. "Shit, rookie. You've been holding back."

Gerry pulled up a duffel bag and dropped it on the table. "This is the perfect time to unveil my gift for this very special team."

He unzipped the bag and pulled out a stack of fresh black hats. In white lettering, they read: *NRDS.* Underneath, in smaller letters, were the words: *Special Agent.* "Penny embroidered them for me."

"This is awesome," Ethan said, taking his and putting it on.

"Pretty sure there are some copyright issues here," Alexus said.

"Oh shut up Alexus, who cares?" River said, squishing down his fluffy red hair with a hat.

"Great job today, team," Buck said. "I knew you could all do it."

"Maybe next time you won't bitch out." Alexus said.

Twelve

Protest Detest

E THAN STEPPED OUT OF his car, spotting Doris and Trevor at the edge of what looked like a mob surrounding the office.

"Hey there. What's all this about?" he asked, nodding toward the crowd of sixty-plus people blocking the doors of the office.

The mob of people may not have been as many as a New York City march, but for New Richmond standards, it was impressive. They waved signs proclaiming, "KEEP BIG GOV OUT OF NEW RICHMOND," and "1984 WASN'T MEANT TO BE AN INSTRUCTION MANUAL," and "DO YOU REALLY THINK IT'S GHOSTS? WAKE UP SHEEPLE!" and chanting, "FEDS GO HOME! FEDS GO HOME! FEDS GO HOME!"

Trevor panned his phone from the crowd blocking the door to the office over to Ethan and said, "Rookie Agent Ethan Malik, good morning. What are your thoughts on this little protest happening right outside the office?"

"Little protest? Uh . . ." Ethan started.

"Isn't it just awful?" Doris said.

"And . . . that's for us, right? They're protesting us?" Ethan asked.

Buck slid into the small huddle, coffee in hand, and said, "Yep."

Ethan looked at Buck, who smirked, and asked, "Why?"

JP RINDFLEISCH IX & JEFF ELKINS

"Because these two told 'em we're here," Buck replied, raising his cup of coffee to the phone as Trevor turned to him.

Doris paced back and forth, opening and closing her fists. "Oh no. Oh, no. She's going to kill me. This is awful. Never should have posted it."

"Wait. You think it's from that Instagram thing?" Ethan asked.

Trevor perked up, pointing the phone at him and said, "Oh, yeah. We got a hundred thousand views in three hours. Your intro went viral. We're at fifty thousand likes now."

"Is that a lot?" Ethan asked.

"Is that a lot? That's amazing. I was hoping for a few hundred. You're big news. Everyone wants to know about the ghost hunter renegade. Why don't you say something to all your fans?" Trevor said.

"This is all my fault," Doris muttered to herself.

A news crew pulled up in a van marked FOX 47 and raced to set up the camera and sound in the middle of the street. Within seconds, Kamila Gorski, whom Ethan had had a crush on since she first aired five years ago, was talking into a microphone with the rallying crowd as a backdrop.

Between the little dimple in her left cheek and the way her brown eyes twinkled in the light, Ethan couldn't take his eyes off her. "My grandma loves her."

Buck sighed and took a sip of his coffee.

Ethan could hear her voice projecting over the rally while she looked into the camera. "I'm here live in Downtown New Richmond where a rally has broken out after an Instagram video went viral. The video depicts agents from the government organization known as the National Recently Deceased Services discussing their investigations. Whether you believe in the afterlife, these government agents seem to, and the people are looking for answers about why DC has come to New Richmond."

Someone stepped in front of Trevor's phone, wearing an unusually colorful pink blouse that showed a surprising amount of cleavage. Melissa cleared her throat and looked at Doris. "This is all your fault. Once we get inside, you and I are going to have a little chat." She took a sip of her coffee, a cup three times larger than Buck's, before smiling into the camera. "Hello viewers. I'm the boss of this operation here. Name's Melissa Scott. Do I look like I care about what is going on inside your homes?"

"Jesus Christ," Buck mumbled.

The crowd suddenly changed from their chants to cheering and clapping. Melissa stopped and turned with the rest of them, Trevor holding his camera high to get a better angle.

Two middle-aged white men in suits climbed the stairs to elevate themselves above the mob. One of the two, the one whose eyes seemed to be red as if he'd been recently crying, Ethan recognized as Mayor Davies. Ethan had seen the other, who carried a bullhorn, before but he couldn't place him.

"Thank you! Thank you for coming to tell Big DC Government that we don't want them in our town!" the man with the bullhorn said.

The crowd cheered and waved their signs higher.

"Who's that?" Ethan asked.

Panning his phone over the crowd, Trevor explained, "The one on the left is Mayor Davies. The other one is Chax Tamish, his opponent."

"Oh yeah. I got a flyer in the mail about him," Ethan said.

Using the bullhorn to speak over the crowd, Chax continued. "DC is spending hundreds of thousands of your taxpayer dollars to do what? Chase ghosts? Well, we're here today to tell them WE DON'T WANT IT!"

The crowd roared again, and a chant of "WE DON'T WANT IT! WE DON'T WANT IT!" broke out.

Chax pulled up the bullhorn and shouted over the crowd. "That's right! We want better schools! Better roads! Safer streets! We don't want our hard-earned money going to this crap!"

"WE DON'T WANT IT! WE DON'T WANT IT! WE DON'T WANT IT!" the crowd screamed.

"We don't want it. That's right," Chax continued. "It's time for Big Government to go home. That's why we're both here. Two politicians, running against each other, coming together to face this together."

The chanting turned to cheers again as the crowd's anticipation grew.

"Now, my opponent and I have agreed to lay our differences aside to work together to put an end to this federal sham. Mr. Davies, you have the floor," Chax said, passing the bullhorn to the mayor.

His eyes still bloodshot, the mayor held the bullhorn to his mouth and said, "It's not right." His voice cracked, and he let the bullhorn fall to his side as fresh tears filled his eyes.

A hush came over the crowd as they leaned in to hear what the mayor would say.

Chax rubbed the mayor's back and encouraged him to try again. Raising the bullhorn back to his mouth, the mayor said, "It's not right that I had to bury my son. But. But then. For these outsiders. These Government Employees. For them to talk about him in videos like that. It's. It's not right."

"Do we want Big Government in our homes, scrutinizing every bit of our lives?" Chax shouted out to the crowd without the bullhorn.

"NO!" the crowd shouted.

"Leave the memory of my son to rest!" the mayor said before handing the bullhorn back to Chax.

"Do we believe them when they tell us they're chasing after ghosts?"

"NO!"

"Then why would we allow it here? They're using us. Making us vulnerable and giving us a 'second chance' to talk to those we lost, just so we spill the dirt on someone else. They're liars, and it's not right!"

Chax raised his hand in the air and started a new chant of "IT'S NOT RIGHT! IT'S NOT RIGHT! IT'S NOT RIGHT!" and the mob fell in with him.

"We should be debating city taxes or filling potholes. Instead, we've come together to fight a common enemy. Get NRDS out of New Richmond!"

Ethan looked away from the crowd, meeting Buck's eyes. "What is he talking about? His son?"

Buck shot a glare at Trevor's camera and raised his eyebrow at Ethan.

"What? Are you saying I did this?"

A voice spoke from behind Ethan, startling him. "Who else talked about a case while on camera? And a case about a kid?"

Alexus stood inches away from him, and he leaped back. "Jesus, how long have you been there?"

"Long enough," Alexus shrugged.

Ethan looked back at Mayor Davies. "So, he's Dylan's dad?"

Melissa chimed in. "Looks like we've got ourselves a high-profile case now, team."

"Wait, is that River?" Ethan asked as River slowly crept onto the top of the stairs next to the mayor and put his arm around the crying politician.

"Shit," Buck said.

Taking back the bullhorn, Chax spoke to the crowd again. "What we need you to do now—what we all must do—is call our representatives in DC and tell them to do their job! Get these . . . NERDS . . . out of our town."

River stepped forward, pumping his arm in the air while chanting, "CALL THOSE ASSHOLES! CALL THOSE ASSHOLES!"

With surprising speed, the crowd picked up on River's chant.

Chax glared at River before shouting into the bullhorn, "That's right! Call them! Let them know how you feel! They promised to put an end to Big Government overreaching. What do you think this is, but exactly that? We were doing just fine before, without them. Now they're creeping into our streets and making permanent residence. Not on my watch. Call them, and tell them what you think. Tell them about the votes they'll lose if they keep it up."

Again, stepping forward, River chanted, "FUCK THOSE ASSHOLES! FUCK THOSE ASSHOLES!"

Again, with shocking acceptance, although with some hesitancy, the mob followed suit and echoed, "FUCK THOSE ASSHOLES! FUCK THOSE ASSHOLES!"

Chax held up his hand to silence the mob. "Thank you! Thank you all for coming and showing your support! We've got another rally planned in two weeks. For now, call your representatives, night and day, and let them know what you want!" With a wave, Chax put his arm around the mayor and gave a big smile to the news camera.

Stepping in front of them, River again tried to change the chants. This time he screamed, "FUCK MY ASSHOLE! FUCK MY ASSHOLE! FUCK MY ASSHOLE!"

He gained a few members of the crowd before he devolved into a fit of laughter. The crowd quickly quieted, staring in confusion.

"This is what your money pays for. Remember that. Thank you, again, everyone," Chax said through the bullhorn as he ushered the mayor off the steps.

Kamila raced toward the politicians, the cameraman following behind her. "Mayor Davies, do you have a statement you want to make about the video?"

Ethan couldn't hear the rest of what he said over the crowd, but he knew it couldn't have been good. Mayor Davies lost his composure a few times before Chax wrapped his arm around him and guided him away from the camera.

"Well, that was something," Buck said.

"What do we do now?" Ethan asked.

Melissa grabbed Trevor's hand and pulled the camera toward herself. "I wasn't aware that NRDS employed a bunch of children for me to babysit. Clearly, I need to take action and talk to my supervisors. Perhaps they'll provide us with some backup to clean this mess up."

"It was a way to outreach the community. I'm so sorry. I . . . I didn't mean for this to happen," Doris said to no one in particular.

"You and I will talk more inside," Melissa said to Doris while still looking at the camera.

Kamila turned, holding her finger to her ear before looking right at Ethan. She waved her cameraman over and bounded across the street, microphone in hand. "Excuse me, are you Ethan? Ethan Malik?"

Melissa stepped in her path before Ethan could speak. "Hi, I'm Agent Scott of the NRDS, the head of the New Richmond branch."

Kamila's face brightened, and her entire composure changed. "Oh, then do you mind if we ask you a few questions?"

"How about you come with me inside? We've got nothing to hide, and perhaps an interview might help clarify a few things." Melissa started down the street without another word, leaving Kamila to chase behind her into the dispersing rally.

Bounding over to the gang with an enormous smile on his face, River said, "Did you guys see that? I even got a couple of them to say it!"

"Your mom would be so proud," Buck said.

"Hey, you don't know my mom. She would have been right up there with me," River said with a grin.

Trevor pointed the camera at River. "Tell everybody at home why you wanted the crowd to do that?"

As River droned on about his goals for the mob, Ethan looked at Buck and asked, "So, do we go inside now?"

With a sigh, Buck said, "Nope. Come on, kid. Let's go to work," and he turned to walk toward his car.

Following behind the older man, Ethan said, "Don't we need to get a case?"

"It's not all about cases and catching the mean ones. We need to get you back to basics, kid."

Thirteen

Back to Basics

A s HE PARKED THE car at the entrance to the Oakland Cemetery, Buck said, "Alright, kid. Let's have a chat."

Ethan shifted his weight in his seat and looked at the brick entrance gate and the dirt path that led through the pines and maple trees to the graveyard. He wanted to speak, but he didn't know what to say, so he just waited.

"You've had a big two weeks," Buck said.

Ethan looked over at the older man and then down at the floorboard and said, "I'm sorry I messed things up."

"You haven't. You still need to read the damn manual, but . . ."

"Yeah. I'm sorry about that."

"It's fine. That's not what I mean. Everything that's been thrown at you. Cases opening in the office, helping pull spirits out of a loop, and politicians rallying against you. That's not the job."

Ethan looked up at his partner and asked, "What do you mean?"

Pointing at the path in front of the car, Buck said, "This is the job, kid. The other stuff comes with it too, like it or not. But at its core, this is what we do. We show up and gather intel. Passing on what we learn. And we just try to help. That's the job."

Ethan nodded.

"So, let's put all that other stuff down and do the job."

"Yeah. Sounds good."

"Great. Get the clipboard," Buck said as he pushed open his car door.

Grabbing the case from the backseat and starting down the path, Buck said to Ethan, "You're in charge this time. Take the lead."

Staring at the clipboard and hurrying to keep up. Ethan stammered, "But. What should I do? I mean. What do I ask?"

Buck brushed past him, picking up the badge Ethan had left behind and handing it to him. "Just ask the questions on the form. Let the clipboard do the work."

"Got it," Ethan said, squeezing the badge and giving Buck a nod.

As they passed through the gates and started up the hill, Ethan spotted Mable wandering around the graves with her eyes closed and her arms out. He smirked as she called out, "Marco?"

"Polo!" the four giggling children called as they darted around behind graves and trees, laughing.

A warmth spread through Ethan, accompanied by a grin he couldn't get rid of, as he watched Mable lunge toward where she thought a child was. She passed through a tree, and all the children laughed as she grabbed at the air.

"Well," Buck said to Ethan.

"Oh, right," Ethan mumbled, stifling his smile. Looking at the clipboard and stepping forward, he called, "Um. Hey! Mable? We're back."

Opening her eyes and straightening up, Mable called, "Children. We have visitors. Everyone form a line, please."

Running over, the four children lined up in front of Ethan and Buck and gave the agents bright smiles. It shocked Ethan at first that they all looked the same, but then he remembered the dead didn't change clothes, or get dirty, or have their hair messed up. Eternally in their burial clothes.

"I see you brought backup," Mable quipped as she joined the children.

"I'm Buck. Nice to meet you," Buck said, tipping his hat.

"This one isn't going to smoke in my garden, is he?" Mable asked Ethan.

"Only morons smoke pot," one child said with a grin.

The other children and Buck laughed to themselves.

"No, ma'am. No one is going to smoke today. Buck is kind of like my boss. He's training me. I didn't really do things right last time. So, he came to make sure I don't mess it up again," Ethan said.

"Everyone makes mistakes now and then," Mable said.

"Thanks."

"Keep it moving," Buck muttered.

"Right. Can I get everyone's name?" Ethan said, looking at the first line of the document.

"I'm Mable Olsen. In order of how long they've been here, this is Harold Wagner, and Jean Peterson, and Angela Klein, and you've already met Dylan Davies."

Ethan looked up from his clipboard and confirmed, "Dylan. Your father is the mayor?"

"Uh-huh," Dylan said with a smile.

Scribbling the names into the first line on the form, Ethan continued. "Right. Um, how is everyone feeling today?"

All the children spoke at once, each saying they were doing well. Taking control of the chaos, Mable said, "We are all doing well. Thank you."

"Great," Ethan said, recording the response on his form. "Have there been any surges or fears of escalation in your, um, condition?"

"Angela wandered out of the graveyard last night," Harold chimed with a grin.

"Tattle-tale!" Angela whined, stomping her foot.

Looking down the line, Mable said, "Harold. We don't tattle."

"Sorry, Miss Mable," Harold said.

Turning back to Ethan, Mable explained. "She just wanted to see what the wildflowers over there looked like in the moonlight. No harm. No foul. Just a curious child."

"No one is, um, escalating though?" Ethan asked.

"We are all the same today as we were yesterday," Mable confirmed.

"Great," Ethan said, making a note. "Have any of you thought of anything that might keep you from transitioning?"

"Excuse me. Did you go see Tiger?" Dylan asked.

A surge of guilt ran through Ethan. "Oh. Um. I'm sorry. I haven't gotten to that yet."

Looking down at the ground, Dylan kicked at the dirt and said, "It's alright."

Letting the clipboard drop to his side, Ethan said, "But, hey. We'll do it today. Mister Buck and I will go as soon as we are done here and then come right back and let you know. Okay?"

Dylan looked up and smiled. "Thanks, Mister Ethan."

Ethan smiled and nodded. "Of course."

Buck cleared his throat.

Looking back at his clipboard, Ethan straightened up and said, "Right, so has anyone else thought about anything holding them back?"

"No. We're all just going about our day," Mable said.

"What about your murder? Have you thought anything about that?" Ethan asked.

"Stick to the script, kid." Buck grumbled.

"Now, I told you I wasn't interested in discussing that. I've got a job here to do. If I move on, who is going to care for all these children?" Mable asked.

"But don't you want to know who killed you?" Ethan asked, letting the clipboard fall to his side again.

"Table it," Buck said.

Ethan sighed and nodded. Picking back up his clipboard, he mumbled, "I just think you might want to know."

"I said drop it," Buck commanded.

"Sorry," Ethan said with another sigh. Running his eyes to the next question on the form, he asked, "So, um. Do any of you have any information for me about your surrounding community that might be helpful to our organization's mission?"

"As I told you the last time you were here, we are keeping to ourselves," Mable said.

"So, no information," Ethan said, making a note. "Okay, well. I guess that's it. We'll go check on Tiger and come back."

Mable smiled and said, "Thank you, gentlemen." Then, closing her eyes and raising her hands, she began to count, "Ten. Nine. Eight. Seven."

The children giggled and scrambled in different directions.

"Ready or not! Marco!" Mable called with a smile.

"Polo!" the kids all yelled back.

As they walked back to the car, Buck said, "First, don't make promises. Especially to kids."

"What do you mean? It's just checking in on a dog?" Ethan asked, again finding himself chasing after his partner, who seemed to speed walk everywhere.

Buck stopped at the car and looked over the top at Ethan. "It's not just a dog. It's an expectation. What if you can't find the dog today? Or the parents gave it away? What's your plan? Are you just going to walk up to a grieving mother and say, 'Excuse me. I'd like to know what you did with your dead son's dog?' How do you think that's going to go over?"

"Not great," Ethan said, looking down.

"That's right. Not great. Look, kid. Something as simple as finding a dog is never as simple as finding a dog. Don't make promises you can't keep," Buck said as he opened the back door and threw the briefcase into the backseat.

Once they were both in the car, Ethan asked, "Why didn't you want me asking about Mable's murder? I mean, I know it's bigger than finding a dog, but it seems like a pretty big deal. I don't get it."

Buck turned the keys and the old car engine roared to life. "Look, kid. She's right. Someone's gotta watch those kids."

"Why's that?"

As he pulled the car out of the parking lot, Buck explained, "Because. Children are unstable. They have a lot of pent-up emotion. It's rare to have so many in one place. Things there could escalate fast. Now, I don't think Mable knows that. But her instincts are good. We need to clear the rest of that field before we deal with her. Last thing we need is a bunch of children accelerating their condition to a Class Three or higher running around."

"I didn't think about that," Ethan said.

"I know. You'll get there. Now, pull out your phone and figure out where the mayor lives."

"Right. Tiger," Ethan said as he pulled his phone from his pocket. Searching on Google, he said, "Um. According to this article, they bought a new house a few years ago on West First Street. It's not too far. I can get us there."

"Great. Next time, ask the spirit for the address," Buck ordered.

"Right. Next time," Ethan said.

They drove in silence together besides Ethan's occasional interjection of "turn left here" and "turn right at the next light." At Ethan's instructions,

Buck brought the car to a stop in front of a beautiful two-story red-brick Colonial home with a hedge and iron gate surrounding the front lawn.

"Um. What do we do now?" Ethan asked.

"I don't know," Buck said.

Ethan gazed at the large home and swallowed. "But. Isn't there some kind of policy or form or something?"

"You want to fill out more forms?" Buck asked with a chuckle.

"No. I just. I mean. There has to be some kind of procedure. We have a procedure for everything, right?"

"This is a gray area, kid. This is where you have to get creative. You said you were going to check on his dog. So, go check on his dog."

"Do I just, like, knock on the door and say 'Hey. I was talking to your dead son. And he wanted to know if his dog is still okay.'"

"I wouldn't recommend that approach. That rarely goes well."

"But. What should I do?"

Leaning across Ethan, Buck pushed open the passenger side door and said, "Figure it out, kid."

"Figure it out. Great. Thanks," Ethan complained as he stepped out into the street.

Straightening his tie, he collected his small reserves of confidence and muttered to himself, "Hi. I'm from PETA. We'd like to know if you are taking care of your dog?" Shaking his head, he said to himself, "PETA. In New Richmond? So stupid." Ethan closed his eyes and took a deep breath. "Hi. I'm Ethan. I'm here to . . . um . . . to see if you are happy with your cable service? To see if you want to buy a new vacuum cleaner. No. To see if you are interested in joining the Church of Jesus Christ and His Latter-Day Saints?" The last one made him chuckle.

Ethan jumped when Buck leaned loudly on the car horn. Turning back to the car, Ethan said, "I'm going. I'm going."

Walking toward the house, he took more deep breaths, searching his mind for something that might make this go smoothly. So occupied by his thoughts, he was taken completely by surprise when he reached for the latch of the gate and ferocious barking ensued from inside the yard. The raging warning from the brown dog who had been peacefully sleeping in the yard gave Ethan such a shock that he fell backward, his ass colliding painfully with the sidewalk. Standing and brushing himself off, he said to the barking dog, "Hey, Tiger."

When Ethan opened the car door, he couldn't hold back his ear-to-ear grin. "Tiger's fine. Back at home, safe and sound," Ethan said.

"Great. Let's go tell the kid," Buck said, starting the car.

"Do you think it will help him move on?" Ethan asked.

"Doubt it," Buck said.

"I dunno, I've got a good feeling about this."

Fourteen

Don't Pout at Dinner

E THAN SAT IN THE passenger seat, staring out the window with his arms folded across his chest.

"You going to pout like that all through dinner?" Buck asked, his eyes focused on the road in front of them.

"No. I don't know. Maybe," Ethan said, refusing to take his eyes from the passing buildings.

"I can turn this car around. Maybe take you home instead?" Buck suggested.

"No, I'm fine. I'll stop." Ethan replied like a child who'd just been asked if he wanted to do chores.

"Good," Buck said as he turned the car left onto Knowles Avenue.

Ethan sighed and watched out the side window. The small one-story strip mall rolled by as the car passed through the beginnings of downtown.

Buck pulled the car off the road and into a parking spot in front of Maria's Pasta and Pizzas and killed the engine. Turning to Ethan, he said, "Well, get your act together. Else, I'm keen on making you sit at your own table."

Maria's, the only Italian food restaurant in town, was actually owned by the Martinez family, a Hispanic family who'd moved to New Richmond a decade ago. Maria, the owner, had spent a few years in Italy in culinary school before moving to the States with her husband Carlos. Together they ran the business, bringing authentic rustic Italian food that could compete with any five-star restaurant to a small town with a less-refined palette.

Ethan kept his arms folded across his chest as he followed Buck into the dining area. The small room was only big enough to hold five six-seater booths and six small four-seater tables. It wasn't much, but the Martinez family had done a marvelous job decorating. Each table had a white candle in the middle and was covered by a red and white checked tablecloth. There was also a massive mural on one wall, painted to look like the restaurant was overlooking a vineyard out in the mountains. The place was full for a weeknight. Almost all the tables were occupied.

Buck scanned the room and smiled when he found his partner sitting at a table in the back corner, sipping a glass of red wine and reading a novel. Seeing the old man smile made Ethan soften, but he quickly pushed the feeling away when Buck turned to him and said, "Best behavior. Got it?"

"You really know how to cheer me up."

Buck glared.

"Fine, yes. I will. Geez. I wouldn't dream of making an ass of myself in front of your husband because it might make you look bad," Ethan said, shoving his hands in his pockets.

Pointing his finger at Ethan, he threatened, "Damn right. Gerry worries that I'm too uptight as it is. Pull it together or I'll make you wait in the car."

Ethan straightened his back, gave a sarcastic salute, and said, "Sir, yes sir."

Buck sneered and shook his head.

"Bucky! Ethan! Back here!" Gerry called over the sound of the other customers eating and the dull hum of Sinatra playing through the restaurant's speakers.

Buck smiled again and lumbered to the back. Ethan followed behind him, refusing to let Gerry's comforting smile impact his mood.

Standing to greet them, Gerry kissed Buck before Buck took a seat. Sitting down in front of a copy of the Chicago Tribune Gerry had waiting for him, Buck took a pencil from the inside pocket of his coat and started skimming the front page.

Reaching out to Ethan, Gerry pulled him in for a hug. Ethan wasn't ready and somehow made things more awkward by wriggling his arms free and returning the gesture. Gerry was thinner than Ethan had expected, but his sweater was warm and soft, and even though there wasn't much meat on his bones, the hug still felt like home.

Pushing Ethan back but holding on to his shoulders, Gerry looked over his black-rimmed glasses into Ethan's eyes. "Well, someone looks grumpy."

Ethan looked down at the floor.

"He's pouting," Buck called.

Gerry bent down to find Ethan's eyeline and asked, "Pouting? How unfortunate. I don't think they serve pouters here. I guess we'll just have to sit down and talk. Tough day?"

Still looking down at his shoes, Ethan shrugged and said, "Yeah."

Hugging him again, Gerry said, "I've seen it plenty of times from this one over here. There's nothing a good meal, good friends, and good wine can't fix." Letting him go, Gerry said, "Now, sit, and be ready to turn that frown upside down."

Ethan pulled out a chair and sat down.

"Okay. So. Spill it. Better out than letting it bottle up," Gerry said as he poured a glass of wine for Buck and another for Ethan.

"He's not old enough for that," Buck protested.

"Pish Posh. Off by a year or two, who cares? Old enough to risk his life, but not for a good glass of wine? Nonsense." Topping off Ethan's glass,

Gerry explained, "Now this is a Cabernet Sauvignon. It's the 2017 Opus One. Buck and I got it in Napa a few years ago."

"You brought your own wine?" Ethan asked.

Gerry nodded. "I brought a few over, for Maria to try. I told her I'd get her a new supplier if she liked them."

Buck sipped his wine, opened the newspaper on the table to the crossword section, and said, "If he gets arrested, it's on you."

"Take two more sips before you speak again, please," Gerry said, rolling his eyes and shaking his head at Ethan.

Ethan laughed and picked up the glass of wine. "You know they have wine here. I don't think you need to bring your own bottle."

"They do, but I've spent decades collecting only the finest. Why let them sit on our shelves back at home when Buck insists we have dinner out on the town?"

"You shouldn't be cook—"

Gerry held up a finger, "Ah-ah, how many sips was that?"

Buck paused, then reached for his glass and took another sip.

Gerry turned to Ethan. "Okay. Take a sniff. Sip. Hold it in your mouth. Experience it. And then, swallow," Gerry explained with a demonstration.

Ethan followed the instructions. The creamy yet crisp warmth in his mouth sent a wave of relaxation through his chest, followed by the flavor of blackberry pie with a hint of licorice. He swallowed, put the glass on the table, and said, "I really like that."

Reaching over and taking Buck's free hand, Gerry said, "Stick with us, kid. We'll take care of you."

Ethan didn't fully understand why, but a knot caught in his throat. Unsure if his face was reddening too, he looked down at the tablecloth and shrugged.

"Ethan. I hope you like Italian. Maria Martinez, you know her, right? Well, I've shared my recipe for spinach and ricotta cannelloni, and she's already in the back with the chefs making it," Gerry said.

"You couldn't just order from the menu," Buck complained.

"Hmm, you're still being sour, I see. Two more sips. You're still not ready for civil conversation, dear," Gerry said, using his free hand to pat Buck's arm. Obediently, Buck put down the pencil and took another sip from his glass.

Ethan smirked but wiped it off his face when Buck shot him a glare.

Gerry sipped his wine and then asked, "Alright. So. All this pouting and grouching has got me thoroughly invested. Either of you going to tell me what happened? I suppose I could call Rosemary and bring her over here. I'm sure she'd have plenty of stories about Ethan here to entertain me."

"Wait, how do you know—"

"Ran into her at the grocery store. You two look a lot alike. She offered me a seat in her bridge club. Seems like Annie might get the boot soon for all her no shows."

Looking across the table at Ethan, Buck said, "Don't get him started. I'm sure he knows way more about you and this town than you'd want him to." Buck looked at Gerry. "The kid thought he was going to fix one. Didn't pan out."

"Oh no, I see," Gerry said.

"It should have worked," Ethan complained.

"It's always tough when they can't figure out what they need," Gerry said with a nod.

"It's a kid," Buck said, picking up the pencil and going back to his crossword.

Gerry took a deep sigh. "Oh. That makes it so much harder."

Still looking down, Ethan said, "I just really thought that the dog was going to do it. We went to the house. We saw the dog was okay. And then we went back. And he was just like, 'Great. Thanks. He's a good dog.' And then he ran off like nothing had happened."

"Blond author. Fifteen letters," Buck said.

"Joyce Carol Oates. So, he didn't go into the light?" Gerry asked.

"No. He just acted like he didn't even care," Ethan said.

"Did he give you any hint as to something else it might be?"

Ethan crossed his arms again and said, "No."

"Poems of praise. Four letters," Buck said.

"Odes, dear. You know. Sometimes it takes time. When he was first starting, Buck worked on one child every week for seven years before they figured it out."

Looking up with wide eyes, Ethan's mouth fell open as he said, "Seven years?"

A small Hispanic man arrived at the table carrying a tray with three plates on it. "Here we go. Three cannelloni," he said as he placed one in front of each of them.

"Thank you, Carlos. This looks simply amazing," Gerry said.

"Well, thank you. My wife wants to put it on the menu next week," Carlos said with a smile.

"Excellent news. Tell her I picked it up from the oldest man in Sicily when I was backpacking in my twenties. Lots of history that I'd be happy to sit down and tell her." Then, leaning closer, Gerry asked, "And how's everyone enjoying that bourbon?"

"It's wonderful. I had to limit the staff to one pour, or nothing would ever get finished tonight," Carlos whispered back.

Looking up with a grimace, Buck asked, "Which bottle?"

Gerry rubbed his arm and said, "Bucky. Carlos is our new neighbor. I had to bring gifts on our first visit. It was a new one you picked up. Sweetens Cove, I think?"

Buck groaned, took another sip of his wine while shooting a playful glare at Gerry, and went back to his crossword.

As Carlos headed back to the kitchen, Gerry turned back to Ethan and said, "I'm sure Buck has told you this already, but sometimes it helps to hear this more than once, so here it is. If you are going to survive in this job, you can't worry about the wins and losses."

"Yep," Buck said without looking up from his crossword.

"When Buck first started, I can't tell you how many times he came home with that exact same expression on his face. If you let it, this job will drag you down into some dark places."

Ethan nodded.

Taking Ethan's hands in his own, Gerry smiled and said, "Death isn't easy for anyone. People take time to process, on both sides. Some longer than others. Take it one day at a time. Be there for them and do the best you can. And then come home to people you love. Have a good meal. A great bottle of wine. And do something that helps you relax."

Ethan smiled and nodded.

Putting the crossword aside and looking up at Ethan, Buck said, "It always hurts, kid. But you can't let it wreck you."

Ethan nodded, took a deep breath, and said, "Yeah. Thank you. I think I'm starting to get it."

Going back to his crossword and picking up his fork with the other hand Buck said, "You'll be fine. One day at a time."

Also picking up his fork, Gerry said, "Wonderful. Now, let's eat. And after, maybe you can help me take my medicine in the parking lot. I find it works better with company."

Ethan took another sip of wine and asked, "Medicine?"

Grinning, Gerry reached under the table and pulled out a sandwich bag with five joints in it.

Not sure what else to say, Ethan asked, "Did you get those from River?"

Laughing, Gerry said, "No. Please. I got it from my doctor. It's medicinal."

"For what? Glaucoma?" Ethan laughed, his mouth hanging open again.

Gerry took a bite of his cannelloni, savored it in his mouth, swallowed, and then took a sip of wine. Whispering across the table to Ethan, he said, "Don't tell, Bucky. But I've got the cancer."

"That's not funny," Buck said, not looking up from his crossword.

"Bucky doesn't think cancer is funny," Gerry said with a mischievous grin.

"Wait. So, you really have cancer?" Ethan asked, his cheeks turning red from his previous joke.

"I do. But it won't take me today, so no use pouting over it," Gerry said with a smile.

Buck sighed, put the crossword down, looked at his partner, and said, "I love you."

"Love you too, Bucky Bear," Gerry said as he leaned in for a kiss.

Ethan nodded again and took his first bite of the pasta. Without a doubt, it was one of the best things he'd ever tasted. "Wow. This is amazing," he said after he swallowed.

"Maria doesn't play around," Gerry said with a smile. Topping off Ethan's wine glass, he said, "Now. Eat. Drink. And tell me all about you. I want to hear everything."

Fifteen

Nursing Home Shenanigans

E THAN STUMBLED OUT OF the backseat of Buck's car and into the street, barely keeping his legs underneath him.

Through the open passenger side window, Gerry said, "Now you just go inside and get a good night's sleep."

"Will do," Ethan said with a wave as he stumbled toward his house. He wasn't sure if it was the rich food, the wine, the weed, or all of it together, but he felt like he was floating in a half-asleep and half-awake dream.

"Tomorrow will be a new day, my boy. Wait and see," Gerry called.

Ethan turned to face the car, smiled, and said, "Thanks. I like . . . I had a great time."

"Go sleep it off before you get arrested," Buck called from the driver's seat.

"Sleep well, young Ethan. Don't hesitate to come by if you need any more . . . medicine," Gerry said with a grin.

Buck nudged Gerry and gave him a glare.

"Pep talks. I mean pep talks, my boy." Gerry gave Ethan a wink.

"And don't be late tomorrow," Buck added.

"Oh, stop it. You'll stress the poor kid out," Gerry said, pushing on Buck as the car pulled away.

Ethan watched the car's taillights stream away like ribbons and thought about how much he'd enjoyed the night. Maybe a few more dinners like this and the job would be worth it, even when things didn't go according to plan. Regardless, it was way better than working retail.

With a deep breath and a half-closed stare forward, he turned to head up the walk toward the house but jumped in panic when a voice behind him said, "Hey. Rookie."

"What the fuck!" he exclaimed as he spun around to see Alexus standing in the middle of the street, her hands tucked into the pockets of her black leather jacket.

"Get in the car," she said, nodding toward the black Mustang across the street.

Ethan put his hand to his chest, trying to slow his racing heart. He looked at the car, then back at Alexus. "But? I mean. Like. You know, where?"

"Where did I come from? Over there," she said, nodding at the car again.

Ethan bent down and leaned his hands on his knees, hoping to steady himself. Partially from the wine and weed, and partially from the scare, his head was spinning. "But. I mean. What? Like? What are you . . . like?"

"Oh, my God, it's like talking to a three-year-old. Come with me, in the car."

Ethan stood back up straight and took another deep breath. He eyed the dark mustang, then looked back up to his house. "But. I mean. Like. Why?"

"Questions in the car. Don't make me use force," she said, turning and walking toward the mustang.

Ethan stood still, watching her go. An acidic burp erupted from his gut and escaped his mouth.

From the car, she called, "Gerry got you drunk and gave you some of his weed?"

Ethan gave her a half smile.

"Great. So, you're over your typical self-wallowing bullshit?" she asked with an eyebrow raised.

"Yeah, I think so," he laughed.

"Good, then it's time to work. Come on. Car. Now," she said, pointing at him.

Burping again, he moved as quickly as he could to the passenger side door.

He sat down and felt his leg brush up against something sharp. He grabbed the handle of whatever it was and pulled it up to get a better look. "Is . . . Is this a machete?"

Alexus pulled on her seat belt and started the engine. "Every woman should have a machete."

She drove faster than his stomach was prepared to handle, and she took turns like a getaway driver after a bank heist. With each one, he let loose a small burp.

"If you puke in my car, you better know how to run fast," she said, patting the handle of the machete before she shifted into a higher gear and punched the gas.

"Sorry," he gulped, gripping his seat belt, and eyeing her.

He looked out the window and tried to get his bearings, but his head was still spinning, and she was taking turns too quickly for him to track where they were. "Uh, you gonna tell me where we're going?" he finally asked.

"I need you for a job," she said.

He burped again. "Like? Are we going to rob someone?"

"Yep. I'm going to break into the town bank and bag some cash and thought, 'you know who would be a good lookout? The drunk, stoned rookie.'"

"I'm not, um." He burped again. "Really at my best right now." Rolling down the window, he stuck his head out and let the wind cool his face.

"Look. Don't worry about what we're doing. You're just the bait."

"The bait. Uh-huh, great." he said, his eyelids suddenly feeling painfully heavy.

He may have drifted off or no time may have passed. It was impossible to determine and didn't matter. What did matter was that when Alexus screeched to a stop, he screamed "Ouch!" as his head slammed into the corner of the window jam.

"We're here. Let's go," she demanded as she exited the vehicle.

Ethan obediently followed behind. His feet were heavy, and his head was now pounding from the sudden stop. It took a moment for his eyes to adjust to the darkness, but as he looked around, he realized where they were. "Hey. This is Cedar Villa."

"Yep," Alexus said as she marched across the street to the front door of the elderly home.

"I thought they closed this place," Ethan said as he chased after her.

"They reopened after Northwoods burned down. Took in some of their tenants." She reached back, grabbed him by the arm, and pulled him away from the front door and toward a patch of bushes near a window that looked into the lobby. Pushing him against the wall next to the window, she grabbed him by the shoulder and pulled him down until he fell on his ass. Hidden completely by the hedge, she pointed into the lobby. "See that guy there?"

Ethan squinted in the direction she was pointing at a heavyset man in scrubs sitting behind a desk. "Oh, hey. That's my cousin," he said with a smile.

"Yeah. I know."

"He's such a good guy," Ethan said dreamily.

Alexus slapped him on the back of the head, and he yelled, "Ouch!"

"Focus. I need you in the game."

Rubbing his head, tears built in his eyes, and he said, "You didn't have to hit me."

"Don't be such a big blubbering baby. NRDS Agents don't whine. Shake it off."

Ethan closed his eyes and said, "I had, like . . . a hard day. And Gerry . . . He said I should go to sleep."

"You'll get sleep when I'm done with you. For now, you get action. Like distracting your cousin while I slip past him."

"Slip past him? But like . . . why?"

Looking through the window, Alexus said, "Here's the deal. I need to get to room twelve B."

"Twelve B," Ethan parroted.

"But your eager beaver cousin won't let me through."

"Did you, like . . . Um . . . Did you, like, um . . . Did you like, show him your badge? Because we're official and stuff."

"No. Jeez, you know what? I didn't think of that."

"Really? It's the first thing I try. I'm like, badge. Badge. Badge," he said as he pretended to show his badge to people.

She rammed her fist into his chest and knocked out the air in his lungs. "Of course I thought of that. Tried a couple nights ago. What do you think I am, some kind of idiot? Jesus."

"Jesus. Where?" he asked, clutching his chest and looking around.

Grabbing him by the arm, she yanked him down again and exclaimed, "Goddamn it, Gerry."

"Gerry's here too?" he asked with amazement. Whispering, he asked her, "Does he have more weed?"

"No. Jesus."

"Does Jesus have the weed?" he whispered.

"No. Focus," she said, grabbing his chin and forcing him to look at her.

"Ouch," he said.

"I need you to go in there and distract your cousin so I can get to twelve B. Got it? My next plan involves the machete, and you don't want to guess what happens then."

"Got it. Twelve B," he said with a gulp.

"Shit. I should just move on to the next plan."

"No, wait. No. Why are we here, like now? Like. Why not in the day or something?"

"Less nursing staff to hear the shouts from the guy in twelve B who doesn't want to see me."

". . . Oh. Ok, got it," he said as he stood up. He puffed up his chest and looked into the building. "Distract my cousin. Twelve B," he said as he pushed through the hedge.

"Dammit. Sure, now works," she said, creeping behind him.

Forcing his feet to move, Ethan made it to the sliding glass doors. Leaning up against them, he felt his stomach turn. He took a deep breath, willing the contents of the evening to stay where he'd put them. After another deep breath, he knocked on the glass and called, "Hey! Andy! Open up!"

His cousin stood up from his desk and peered toward the window. "Ethan? Is that you? What are you doing here?"

Ethan burped. The rancid taste lingered in his mouth longer than he was comfortable with. Taking his badge from his coat pocket, he banged it against the window and yelled, "Open up. Official business. See, look? I have a badge!"

Walking to the door and shaking his head, Andy said, "Do you know what time it is?"

"No," Ethan said, raising an eyebrow in disgust at the question. With a surge of frustration, yelled, "Badge! Respect the badge!"

"Dude, it's too late for visitors. What agency are you with?" He stepped closer and looked at the batch.

"The NRDS. This is my badge! And I have an important miss . . . mission," Ethan said.

"Nerds? Like that one gal who tried coming in here a few days ago after the day shift kicked her out?"

"I just need to ask you a few questions. In and out, I promise."

"Look cuz, I'm just supposed to sit here and call the ambulance from time to time. That's it. But if Granny Mae hears I let you go in whatever state you're in right now, she'd tell my mom and I'd be dead. Are you gonna do anything weird if I let you in and sit down?" Andy asked as he reached for his ring of keys.

Ethan shook his head and said to himself, "Badge works. Every time."

"Good, just sit down next to me. You can ask all the questions you want as you sober up." He grabbed the key that went to the front door, unlocking it.

The automatic doors slid open, and Ethan crashed into the lobby. Andy bent down to help him stand, but Ethan pushed him off and said, "No. Bro. No. Respect the badge." Taking a step back, he put his hands on his knees again and looked up at Andy. He realized he did not know what to say. His head pounded and his stomach rumbled again.

"You don't look so good. I can call my sister. She can drive you home. Does Granny Rosemary know you're out this late?"

Ethan tried to explain that he was a grown man who didn't need his grandmother's permission to do his job, but instead of words, an explosion of half-digested Spinach and Ricotta Cannelloni, Tiramisu, wine, and stomach acid burst from his mouth, covering Andy's blue scrubs and the carpet of the lobby in vomit.

"Oh. God. Dude, no! Gross," Andy exclaimed, holding his arms out and examining his vomit-covered shirt and pants.

"Sorry," Ethan said with a burp.

"Come on, Ethan. Why, man?" Andy complained.

"I'm sorry. I. Um. Look at the badge," Ethan said, bending over again, afraid round two might escape at any second.

"God. This is so disgusting. Okay. Just. Just sit down over here. Don't move. Okay," Andy said as he backed away.

"Okay," Ethan said, taking deep breaths.

"I'm going to clean up. You stay right there, or else. I'll be right back," Andy called as he disappeared down the hall.

Laughing, Alexus stepped over the puddle of puke and said, "Not exactly what I'd do, but . . . nice job, rookie." After looking in the direction Andy had gone, she ran down the opposite hallway.

"No. Wait. We're supposed to stay right here," Ethan said as he chased after her, holding his stomach.

He followed her, passing closed door after closed door, down a second hallway and a small cafeteria, until finally she stopped in front of a brown door with the number 12B next to it. "Alright, you son of a bitch," she said as she turned the door handle.

Stepping into the room behind her, it took Ethan's eyes a few minutes to adjust to the darkness. There wasn't much to the space. A small TV on a stand stood against one wall. A worn armchair faced it. Seemed like a lonely nightmare of a place to grow old.

Alexus stood behind the armchair, looking down on a bed where an elderly man in light blue pajamas was sleeping. He looked withered and small in the bed. Reaching to her back waistband and under her leather jacket, Alexus drew a six shooter and pointed it at the sleeping geriatric.

"What the fuck?" Ethan exclaimed.

Coughing and sputtering, the old man stirred.

"Get up, you old bastard," Alexus said as she poked him with the nose of the gun.

The old man opened his eyes and smiled. Alexus, keeping the gun trained on him, took a step back. Stretching and grinning, the old man sat up and put his feet off the side of his bed. "So, the bitch is back," he said with a laugh.

"It's time, old man. I'm sick of this game," Alexus said.

Ethan looked at the old man's determined grin and then at the look of hate in Alexus's eye. Certain he was about to witness his first murder, he said, "Oh shit."

Sixteen

Dearly Departed

A LEXUS POINTED THE SIX-SHOOTER at the elderly man. "You know why I'm here."

Ethan slouched against the entrance to the old man's room, the mixture of weed and booze still in his system. "No, please don't kill the sad old man. He looks so lonely."

"And, who's this fucker?" the old man said, nodding toward Ethan as he scratched his rather rotund belly, covered by a white tank top, and reached for a lit cigar at his bedside.

"Oh, no. He's so angry," Ethan muttered to himself.

The man took a drag off his cigar, and Ethan said, "Hey, you can't smoke in here."

"Like I give a shit?" the old man said, savoring the strong oak-scented cloud.

Alexus stepped further into the room; her gun still pointed at the man. "He's my partner tonight."

"The agency is really scraping the bottom of the barrel, huh?" The old man snorted.

Ethan frowned and pushed himself off the wall. "I changed my mind. You can shoot him."

Alexus scoffed. "Gladly, after I get what I came for."

"I could report you to upper management for this," the old man said, taking another drag off his cigar.

"Last I heard, they weren't taking your calls. Something about too much crying on your end," Alexus replied.

"Wait, is he an agent?" Ethan asked, his mouth hanging open.

The old man laughed. "This greenhorn's really killing it."

"Enough. Give me what I came for, and you can stay in this hellhole. They don't have to know," Alexus said.

"Hellhole? They have shuffleboard and all the pudding you could want." Alexus took a step closer.

Ethan looked at Alexus, then the old man. "Look, man, I'd do what she says. You know she keeps a machete in her car?"

Looking at the barrel of the gun, the old man asked, "And you're sure that's it? Doesn't look old enough."

Alexus shrugged and spun the gun on her finger, catching the barrel with her palm and pointing the butt at the old man. "Museum said it was from Dodge City. 1879."

Taking the gun, the old man turned it over. "How do I know you're not full of shit? Could be a fake?"

Alexus shrugged. "Could be. I'm sure there are tons of shops selling six shooters up here. But I keep my word. Do you?"

"I've got the case, alright. Had to convince a few old friends to get it pulled from storage."

"Wait. He's an agent too?" Ethan asked again.

Alexus shot a glare at Ethan. "Greenhorn's a good name for you. Agent Malik, meet ex-Agent Stephenson. The only asshole who got kicked out of the agency for some shady business. Agent Asshole, meet Agent Malik. Greenhorn? Yes. But also a bit drunk and stoned at the moment."

"Nice to meet you," Ethan said with a smile and a wave.

"Okay. Deals a deal. Where's the case?" Alexus demanded.

"Such a needy little bitch," Stephenson said. He stood and threw the gun on his bed, exposing a little too much through his boxers before reaching for a robe. Then he walked to the closet, pulling open the door. Inside were a few shirts, a few pairs of slacks, and some worn coats Ethan imagined he had worn on the job.

There was a square black safe on the floor of the closet. Spinning the dials, Stephenson mumbled the numbers. There was a click, and then Stephenson turned the handle. From the steel box, he drew a weathered briefcase, passed it to Alexus, and said, "Here you go. Fair trade."

Inspecting the case, Alexus said, "This better be the right one, or I'm going to come back and kick your ass."

Sitting back on his bed, letting his robe expose his upper thigh, he said, "It's the right one."

"I'm so confused," Ethan said.

Stephenson held the gun in the air and examined it. "Simple exchange, greenhorn. I want revenge and money. She wants some old case. This baby is going to take care of some old grudges."

Alexus grabbed the briefcase in one hand and Ethan's arm in the other. "Let's go. The old man will talk your ear off if you let him."

"Nice doing business with you," Stephenson called behind her.

Flicking him the middle finger through Ethan's arm as she left the room, she called, "Hope you rot in here alone."

"Already am."

"It was nice to meet you," Ethan said, fighting against Alexus to look at him.

"Hey, greenhorn. Buck part of your office?" Stephenson asked as he examined the gun.

"Yep. Best agent there if you ask me," Ethan said.

"Give him a message for me. Tell him Stephenson said, 'I hope you fucking die,'" the old man said with a grin.

Ethan stammered, then shook his head, letting Alexus pull him along. "No. I'm not going to do that."

They both raced past Andy at the front desk, ignoring his shouts, and headed straight for the car. As Ethan climbed in, Alexus said, "Nice work, rookie."

"Thanks," Ethan replied. He rolled down the window again to feel the breeze on his face as she drove. "So, does that mean you're done calling me greenhorn?"

Revving the engine and pulling out of the parking lot, she said, "Depends. How are you feeling?"

"Better," he said with a yawn. "What's in the case?"

"Wanna tag along and find out?"

His eyelids felt heavy. "Sure," he said with another yawn. "So, what's the deal with that guy, anyway?"

"Big shot asshole in Chicago. Buck caught him doing some shady shit and got him kicked. Way before my time, but I suspect he and Buck both know it didn't end with Stephenson."

Ethan could feel his eyes closing against his will. After a third yawn, he said, "He could be the guy. The reason behind all the ghosts here. The reason you and Buck are here."

"Maybe, if he weren't a complete idiot," Alexus said just before Ethan's world went black.

Ethan jolted up when he felt a sharp stab at his side. "Ouch!" he said.

Withdrawing the pen she'd poked him with, Alexus said, "You drooled on my seat. We're here."

Ethan squinted out the open window. His head was pounding, and everything felt too bright. The sky was a dark pink as the sun peeked over the horizon. "Where are we?" he yelled to Alexus, who had already exited the vehicle.

"Saint Joseph's in Baraboo," she yelled back.

"Baraboo. That's like three hours away."

"Move your ass, greenhorn," she yelled.

With a sigh, Ethan dragged himself from the car to find she'd parked it in the grass on the side of a two-lane road next to a huge plowed field. "Gross," he said as his sneakers squished into the mud. Running across the street and through the stone gateway that led into the cemetery, he called, "Why are we in Baraboo?"

"Because I thought I'd start the weekend off with some camping, maybe check out Devil's Lake."

"Really?" he called, running to catch her.

"No," she said as he finally caught up to her.

"Slow down. Wait," he said, gasping for air. "My head is killing me."

"You wanted to come along. I need to get this done," she said.

"Can you at least walk a little slower?"

"NRDS Agents don't whine. Greenhorns do," she said as she picked up her pace.

They moved through the graves to the north side of the cemetery. Here the headstones were small and well-worn from the elements. Ethan reached inside his pocket, wrapping his hand around the badge, noting the few spirits on the way. Alexus didn't slow to do more than nod to them as she strode by. She didn't slow until they reached a woman wearing a white dress with lace fringe.

The woman perked up as she saw them approach. "Is that? Is that him?"

"I think so," Alexus said, placing the briefcase she'd taken from Stephenson on a gravestone.

"I can't believe you found him. I thought he was long gone," the woman said, clutching her hands together at her chest.

"Hey, I'm Ethan," Ethan said with a wave.

The woman shot a quick glance at Ethan, raising an eyebrow before locking her eyes back on the case. Biting her bottom lip, she asked, "Nothing, um, happened to him in there. Did it? Like he'll remember me? And our life?"

"He was a Class 4 when they caught him. There's no knowing what's left of him. Only way to find out is to open it. But first, our deal?" Alexus asked.

The woman smiled and nodded. "Marietta Estevez. Died three years ago. Chicago. I remember."

Alexus swallowed. "And. You'll tell her?"

The woman took a step toward her. "I'll tell her. You love her. You miss her. And you're sorry. But if she waits for you, you'll make it up to her."

"Thanks," Alexus said.

"Of course. Now the case," the woman said.

Ethan shoved his hands in his pockets and looked at the ground. He had a thousand questions, but he held his tongue.

Alexus dropped the case to the ground and rested her hand on the locks. "Let's get you two to the other side."

The woman wiped down the front of her dress, removing wrinkles that weren't there, and then patted at her hair.

Alexus flipped the clasps on the case and stepped back.

Blue light spilled from the seams before the lid flipped open. A beam of light shot into the sky.

Long fingers reached out from the inside of the case and grasped the edges as an unnaturally tall man clamored out from inside. His eyes were white, and his hair whipped wildly in the windless air.

He let out a long howl, and his eyes settled on Ethan.

Before Ethan could think, he stepped forward. His body moved without his will. The floating man reached out a hand and let out a raspy laugh.

Ethan turned to Alexus, his eyes wide. "Help! Um. I."

The ghostly woman stepped in front of Ethan, facing the angry spirit. "Todd! It's me. Todd. I'm here. We're here. Please."

The angry spirit paused, white eyes on the woman. His mouth worked up and down before a crackling voice sounded. "Dar . . . Darlene?"

She nodded, and the whites of the man's eyes filled with color. The blue tint faded away, and his height shortened. A man in his late forties, dressed in a simple tuxedo, looked at Darlene.

The pull on Ethan vanished as the two spirits ran to each other and embraced. Todd squeezed Darlene as if he would never let her go and said, "I missed you so much."

"I love you," she whispered as a white light formed around them.

White light beamed off them, shining into Ethan's eyes. He covered his eyes with his arm and looked at the ground.

As quickly as it had begun, it vanished, and Ethan looked up to find he was alone with Alexus at the gravestone.

"NRDS Agents don't look away. Not at that," she said, blinking her eyes with a nod.

"You brought them back together? And they crossed over?" he asked.

"Look at you. Paying attention. Rookie's finally catching on," she said as she collected the case and started toward the car.

Racing to catch her, questions flooded from him. "But how did you know that's what she needed? And why did Stephenson have that guy in a case? Was that guy, like, locked away somewhere for being bad? Did the case make him worse? Or did Stephenson, like, catch him when he wasn't supposed to? And how did you know Stephenson wanted the gun? And I totally thought you were going to shoot him. And why are we in Baraboo? And how long had Darlene been waiting?"

Making a hard stop and turning to face him, Alexus held up a finger and said, "You get one question."

"That's not fair," Ethan complained.

"NRDS Agents—"

Cutting her off, he said, "I know. I know. NRDS Agents don't whine. Fine."

Alexus started walking again, and he followed her.

"Alright," he said as they arrived at the car. "Who's Marietta Estevez?"

Alexus took a deep breath and got in the car.

Ethan sat down in the passenger seat and waited.

Alexus started the engine. Looking out at the road, she said, "Marietta is—was—the love of my life. I was reckless. And stupid. And I got her killed."

"I'm . . . I'm sorry," Ethan said.

"That was your question. No more." Alexus reached down and flicked on the stereo, and the hardcore screams of the Old Wound's Son of No One blasted through the speakers, filling the car.

"Thanks for bringing me," Ethan yelled over the blaring lyrics of Judas Priest.

"Glad you came, rookie," Alexus said as she put on a pair of black sunglasses. She slammed on the gas, spinning the wheels in the grass before the car roared onto the road.

Seventeen

Office Announcement

"**H**EY ROOKIE, THE HELL are you doing here?" Buck asked as he stepped into the office.

Ethan blinked a few times and looked away from the computer monitor. He leaned back in his chair and noticed the sunlight streaming in from the windows. "What? What time is it?"

Buck took off his tattered trench coat and hung it on the coat rack by the door. "Before nine. How long have you been here?"

Ethan rubbed his eyes and yawned. "I wanted to get an early start on the day."

"Huh." The old agent paused, looked Ethan over, then nodded. Walking over and sitting in the chair next to Ethan, he asked, "What are we looking at?"

"Oh. Well, um. I thought I might take a stab at Harold."

"The Oakland kids."

"Yep. He's been there the longest, looks like."

"Ambitious."

"Really?"

"Old spirits are hard to dig back up. Most records are sparse."

Ethan looked down at the keyboard and sighed. "Oh. I just . . . needed a break from the Dylan case. Since I couldn't help him and all. Figured I could switch gears."

"That's smart. You've got to be able to handle all your cases, and you've got four kids to tend to."

Ethan smiled.

"So, what have you found?" Buck asked, leaning into the computer screen.

Ethan started to answer but was interrupted by the office door swinging open.

River strode in, giving them a halfhearted two-finger salute from the edge of his St Louis Cardinals stocking cap. "Gentlemen," he said as he took his blue winter coat off, threw it on the floor, and crashed into his chair. Looking over the top of his sunglasses, he said, "You both look chipper this morning. Someone put a little upper in your coffees?"

"No," Buck said, keeping his eyes on the computer screen.

"Where's Bob?" Ethan asked, looking back at the door.

"Pouting in the hall," River said as he smiled and leaned back in his chair.

"That's not like him. Did something happen?" Ethan asked.

River waved his hands up in front of him defensively. "Woah woah, no need to throw around accusations."

"River," Buck said, shooting him a glance.

"Okay, fine. I might have forced him along to my D&D group last night."

"That doesn't sound so bad," Ethan said.

"Right? I thought it was awesome. It was a ten-hour campaign. We got down into this labyrinth in the basement of this one castle and found these dragon-born maidens. I mean. Let's just say my d20s were lit with crits. Things got hot, if you know what I mean?"

"I don't," Buck said.

"Sounds fun?" Ethan offered.

"Hell yeah it was. I practically maxed my character on persuasion. I had those maidens—"

"Wow. Already a party," Trevor announced as he stepped into the office. "I thought I'd be the first in this morning."

"Morning," Ethan offered.

"What are you doing here early?" Buck asked.

"I wanted to get set up and start recording before the protests kicked up again," Trevor said with a shrug as he took his coat and scarf off and hung them up on the coat rack.

"You think they'll be back again this week?"

"Absolutely. It's all over the web. Angry parents, campaign ads . . ." Trevor said with another shrug as he pulled out his camera and started setting up, pointing it out the window.

"Who broke Bob?" asked Alexus, who had walked in and stood right next to Ethan before he realized she was there.

"Jesus! Where did you come from?" Ethan jumped.

"Wait, you can break a BOB?" Trevor asked, looking up from his phone.

River laughed and raised his hand. "Apparently. Had a D&D one shot last night."

"An X-rated D&D one shot," Buck added.

"Like you or I know what that is," Alexus said.

Taking off his sunglasses and rubbing his red eyes, River nodded confidently and said, "Let me set the scene."

"Please do," Alexus said as she plopped down in her chair and wheeled over to River.

Swiveling in his chair, River continued, "So, we're at my boy Squiggy's place."

"Squiggy," Buck grunted.

"Yeah, super great DM. That's a Dungeon Master. Like, top tier. Super hard to book time with."

"I'm already sorry I asked," Alexus said, rolling back to her desk.

River grabbed the back of her chair and rolled her back to him. "Squiggy kicks off with this Dungeon crawl from the Book of Vile Darkness. I mean, it wasn't a full game. He'd just put together a short campaign for the night because his sister Queef was in town."

"Queef?" Buck asked.

Trevor yanked his phone off the makeshift stand and turned it on River. "That can't be her real name."

Spinning to face Trevor, River explained, "Her real name is Vanessa. That's just what we call her on account of the time that we were all at the state fair and I got this giant corn dog—"

"No. Absolutely not," Alexus interrupted. Waving her finger in the air, she said, "The next words out of your mouth better be about this D&D thing or I swear . . ."

Spinning his chair back to face her, River continued. "So, Squiggy kicks it off. And we're in this crazy castle, right? And Queef and I and Todd, we're just throwing these perfect rolls. I mean, I critted like five times in a row. All my spells laid waste to my foes. Like it was crazy stuff. Spells I never get to use. Like, he let me mix two of them to summon the ghost of my enemy's mom and—"

"Wait. Actual spells, or this D&D stuff?" Trevor, who turned his phone camera on River, asked.

"Oh, yeah. Like I'd be working here if I could cast spells in real life," River said with a mocking laugh.

"I mean, we talk to ghosts for a living," Ethan offered.

"Yeah, with special badges. We don't do spells. I'm sure that's a different department, like the Department of Unique Magical Badges and Superstitious Shit or something," River said.

"This is great and all," Alexus said. "But how does this lead to why Bob is sitting in the stairway?"

"Uh, I kinda forgot I had his bag in my pack when I went over," River explained. "I mean, I got the sense that he was around, but I just ignored it. And then, once things got steamy down in the dungeons and my character was deep in a harem of maidens he saved, the table shook. Slipped my hand in my pocket, grabbed my badge, and there he was, bitching up a storm."

"Harem of maidens?" Alexus rolled her eyes.

"Wait, but if he was bitching. How did you break him?" Ethan asked.

River leaned back. "Well, he demanded we leave. I may have tossed the badge in my pack. And we may have kept on playing for six more hours. Then . . . when Squiggy left. Well, let's just say things got steamy between Queef and I."

Buck blinked and looked up from the screen. "Go apologize."

"What? No way, man," River said, throwing up his arms. "I'm not apologizing because he can't handle me having a good time."

"You shouldn't have brought him out like that," Buck said.

"The guy bitches nonstop about getting out. I'm not putting my life on hold to go to some old war museum every weekend," River said.

"You could have left him in the car. Or the office," Buck said.

River grinned and asked, "Where's the fun in that?"

"Yeah. You just wanted an audience when you and this Queef girl were banging," Alexus said.

"Maybe, I did. And maybe Bob shouldn't have been an asshole last time I hooked up with someone in front of him," River said with a grin as he leaned back in his chair.

"Good morning, everyone. I have coffees," Doris said as she stepped into the office carrying two four-cup carriers filled with coffees.

Everyone converged on her desk, swiping up the beverages. River inspected his cup and raised an eyebrow. "They're all black?"

Doris reached into her purse and pulled out handfuls of creamer. "I didn't know how everyone took it, so I filled the bag with creamer and sugar."

Trevor searched through the pile of packets and grabbed the artificial sweetener. River dumped creamer after creamer into his until the light brown liquid reached the top of the cup.

Wheeling her chair away from River before he continued recounting his sexual escapades, Alexus nodded at Buck, and asked, "What's this you've got?"

"Research on one of the kids in Oakland," Ethan said.

"How long ago?" Alexus asked.

"Twenties," Buck said.

"You won't find anything there," Alexus said as she sipped her coffee.

"Wait? What?" Ethan asked.

"They don't keep digital records like that in the great Midwest. Not for a spirit that old," River said as he poured a ninth sugar packet into his coffee.

Ethan slumped in his chair and folded his arms. "Really? What then?"

"Nothing *digital*. Keyword," Alexus said.

Standing, Buck moved to the coat rack. "They're right, kid. Let's go."

"Go? Go where?" Ethan asked as he stood.

"Library trip," River sang.

"Library trip?" Ethan asked.

"Public records, newspapers, microfiche. Better hope you're not allergic to dust," Buck said.

"Awesome," Ethan said as he put his coat on.

"Can I come with you too?" Trevor asked.

Bursting into the office like a drunken toddler, Melissa declared, "No one is going anywhere!" Pointing at Buck, she said, "Sit." Pointing at Trevor, she demanded, "And turn that off or stand outside with Bob. Mandatory team meeting, now."

"Oh, team meeting! Do you need me to take minutes?" Doris asked.

"What? It's an official meeting. Someone better be taking minutes," Melissa said. Then, moving her hands in a rushed circle, she said, "Well? Come on. Get writing."

Doris rushed to get a pen and paper from her desk.

Pointing at Buck and Ethan again, Melissa said, "Official meeting. Sit down."

Raising his hands in surrender, Buck moved back to his chair, and Ethan followed suit.

Straightening her skirt and fixing her hair, Melissa continued, "Okay. Well, upper management is not pleased with the handling of our public relations as of late." Pausing, she turned to Trevor and said, "Ok, turn it on. Now. Start the thing."

"Yes, ma'am," Trevor said as he started filming again.

Shooting him a quick glare before the red light turned on, Melissa continued. "New Richmond is a beautiful, exciting place. And as GOOD and UPSTANDING community members, we are going to take part in the town's Winter Wonderland Festival."

Alexus snorted a laugh.

"Yeah. I'm gonna be super busy that day," River said.

"What day is it?" Doris asked.

"Doesn't matter," River said.

"Usually the last Thursday before Christmas," Ethan offered.

"Knew it. Totally have plans," River said.

"Nope. Clear your schedules. There's only Winter Wonderland, and attendance is mandatory," Melissa demanded. She outstretched her hands to the entire office, she said, "And all my little lovely agents are going. Okay? Great. Doris, you'll print off a sign-up form. Each of you will volunteer at a booth or with setting the street up with decorations. You understand?"

"What do you want on the form?" Doris asked.

"Why don't you just figure it out, Doris!" Melissa barked through gritted teeth.

"Will do," Doris said, scribbling notes on her page.

Melissa shot a look at Trevor, "Off. Now. I presume you'll edit that to make us look good, after our . . . talk?"

The red light on Trevor's camera shut off, and he nodded.

"And no one leaves today until their names are on the sheet. Got it? Because we're going to be the happiest and most helpful goddamn volunteers this town has ever fucking seen. Do you hear me?" Melissa asked, looking over the office. When no one responded, she smiled and turned, "Bring me the list when it's done."

Punching River in the arm, Alexus said, "This is your fault because you broke Bob."

"Ouch," River said as he rubbed the new bruise.

Holding a pen in the air, Doris asked. "Well. Does anyone know what happens at Winter Wonderland?"

Ethan took a deep breath and said, "I can help you put it together."

"Aww, thank you Ethan," Doris said, and she clapped her hands together. "Just come over here and . . . oh, just sit at my computer and I'll watch what you do."

Ethan pushed off his chair and crossed the room. "No worries. Faster it's done, the faster we can get to the library."

Eighteen

Flying off the Shelves

"**H**EY, UM EXCUSE ME, Ms. Peterson?" Ethan asked as he approached the circulation desk of the New Richmond Library.

An old librarian with a hooked nose that sported a pair of glasses resting right on the tip held up a long bony finger. Her eyes were locked on the contents of an old red hardcover book with gold lettering titled *Sense and Sensibility* as she let out a slow hum and said, "Just one second, Willoughby has gotten himself in a real mess."

After turning the page and closing the book with a slight sigh, she trained her eyes on Ethan. "How may I help you?"

"Well, um, Ms. Peterson—"

She pulled her glasses off and let them dangle off a thin gold chain around her neck. "How many times do I have to tell you to call me Joan, Ethan? I play bridge with Rosemary for Pete's sake."

"Ok. Joan. Sorry, Ms. Pe—Joan."

"Is this about the papers? I see your red-eyed friend and that dapper man you were with already left. No leads?"

Ethan shook his head. "It's all regional stuff. Doesn't New Richmond have their own paper?"

"Papers dated from the twenties? You're lucky we even had regional coverage back then."

Ethan sighed. Buck, River, and he had been reading through newspapers for four hours and hadn't found a single word about Harold and his family. Not an obituary. Not an explanation about a child's death. The regional paper was silent on all of it. Looking at the librarian, Ethan shrugged and said, "Well, I guess that's another dead end then."

"What is it you're looking for, if I may ask?"

"An obituary or an article on someone's death back in the twenties. He was a kid, so I can't imagine the obituary would be anything long," Ethan said.

"When my sister died, there was barely a mention of her in the paper. From what I know of the area back in the twenties, some families just kept the news to their congregations, or neighborhood," Joan said.

"Well, shit," Ethan muttered.

Joan pursed her lips and raised an eyebrow.

"Uh, Sorry Ms. Peterson."

"You're with the National Recently Deceased Services, correct?" Joan asked.

Ethan felt the blood rush from his face. Friend or foe, he wouldn't know until he asked. "How d'you know that?"

"I'm a librarian. We know everything," she said, her face serious and stern.

"Oh. Um," Ethan started.

Joan smiled. "And I may be old, but I have Instagram. Seems like you've all caused quite the stir."

"Yeah, who knew being recorded talking about the mayor's recently passed son would cause an uproar."

Joan let out a laugh. "Perhaps not the best thing to have done, especially with that goat of an opponent looking for votes. It'll all blow over. It always does."

"Tell that to the protestors camped out in front of the office."

"NRDS has been in this part of the woods for decades. Never had an office, but similar uproars sprout up every couple of years."

"Wait, I've been here all my life, and this is the first time I've even heard of NRDS."

"You were young last time, and nobody likes to talk about things close to death. But I remember it like yesterday, when someone just like you was asking for obituaries."

Ethan's eyes widened. "Really? That's—I didn't know."

Joan pulled open a drawer and pulled a set of keys. "Luckily, for you and him, newspapers aren't the only thing to dig through around here."

"Yeah, but I don't think books are going to—"

"This library has had an ongoing project of retaining the history of the town through journals and book collections. I assume that might pique your interest?"

"You have all that? Here? Journals, I mean. Even from the twenties?" Ethan asked.

Joan nodded. "I'm sure there is something that will help down in the basement. But I have to warn you, the boxes have gotten out of hand."

"Sounds more promising than the newspapers," Ethan said with a grin.

"I'll make a deal with you. I haven't been able to make it down there in ages. Bad hip and all. Help me rearrange some boxes and make it easier for an old lady like me to move around and catalogue, and you can take whatever you need as long as you bring it back."

"Deal!" Ethan said, a grin stretching across his face.

Joan pushed herself off her seat and led Ethan to the back of the library. She stopped at a door with the word "Basement" hanging above it. "Well, I'll hold you to it. Just be warned, there are a lot of boxes."

With a click, she unlocked the door. "Light switch at the top of the stairs is broken. You'll have to flip the one at the bottom on the pole. The entire room is on motion sensors, so just keep walking and they'll pop on."

Ethan looked down at the shadowy pit and gulped. As he started down the steps, stale air and dust tracking up from his footsteps assaulted his senses. He called up to Joan, "You weren't kidding about nobody coming down here."

"When you get your bearing, there may be something you'll want to look for. An old NRDS agent's belongings by the name of Stephenson. Never know if they were on to something," Joan yelled from upstairs.

"Hey. I think I met him," Ethan yelled back.

"That's . . . nice, dear." Joan called in a tone that communicated apathy so perfectly, Ethan could feel it.

Feeling his way along the stair railing as he descended into the windowless darkness, he choked as a cobweb filled his mouth. His foot reached the bottom stair, and he began groping for the light switch. Ramming his leg into a heavy table, he grunted in pain. "You said there's a pole?" he yelled.

"To the right," Joan yelled back.

Moving to the right, he felt what seemed to be metal shelving. He ran his fingers down it and failed to discover a switch. "Are you sure it's to the right?" he yelled.

Then he felt it. Three taps at his left shoulder. His spine straightened, and a chill surged through his body. Spinning with eyes wide, he flung his hands left and right, trying to find what had reached out to him, but he only grasped at empty air. "Joan? Are you down here?" here he called.

"Maybe it's left? It's to the left," Joan called from upstairs.

"Uh. Yeah. Okay, thanks." Ethan muttered; his hands still outstretched in front of him. He was certain every one of his hairs was standing on end. Reaching to his left, his hands found a round metal pole. He ran his fingers down it until he came upon the switch.

The bulbs above him bloomed in an incandescent light, revealing stacks of boxes and piles of books on dusty tables and shelves. He tried peering deeper into the darkness, but he could only guess that the space went on for eternity, with the same narrow passages blocked by boxes and shelves.

A cold sweat formed on his brow as he imagined a stack of boxes crushing him, and he wondered if anyone could even get to him in time.

He sidestepped his way down the left aisle, lights flickering on to guide his path as he glanced at the scribbles and names scrawled on each of the cardboard boxes. It seemed like every book ever owned by someone in New Richmond would find its way to this tomb.

Spotting a box that looked like it had an "St" on it, Ethan turned down one of the aisles. Flipping open the top, he pulled out the first book. It was a paperback copy of "The Haunted Mask" by R.L. Stine. Ethan flipped through the pages affectionately, remembering when he'd read the book as a child. Pulling the box down and setting it on the ground in front of him, he looked in it and found other books by Stine. "Not Stephenson," he muttered to himself as he put the books back.

Icy fingers brushed along his back, and a tingling jolt of electricity shot up his back. He shoved his hand in his pocket and wrapped his palm around the cool metal of the badge. As he spun around, he pulled the badge out and held it in front of him. His eyes darted left, then right, and the sound of footsteps echoed off into the black distance. "Hello?" he called. "Who's down here?"

The lights that trailed his way flickered and died out one by one until he stood under the only source of light.

Gripping his badge tight, he shifted to the next stack of boxes and started scanning names. Several other boxes started with "St", and he was thankful that, even in this mess, someone had the sensibility to organize the boxes somewhat.

Flipping open a few of the boxes, he found piles of hardcover Grishams, a complete Clancy collection, and a stack of Nora Roberts novels.

Footsteps raced behind him, sending his heart pounding. He shot a glance up and down the aisle and through the boxes. "Hello? I know you're down here. I can hear you."

He waited, seconds passing by like hours, but there was no response.

Slowly, he backed down the row again, monitoring the aisle behind him. "Why can't I just go somewhere and experience some normal shit?" he whispered.

Looking at the boxes again, his eyes fell upon a small briefcase stuffed into the side of the shelf. One of the hinges was broken, and the name "Stephenson" had been scrawled on a metal plate across the top.

Ethan dropped to his knee and carefully pulled the briefcase free from the shelf, the leather flaking off under his grip. With one hinge already broken, it took little to bypass the locks and pop open the top. Inside, he found stacks of small brown leather journals.

Pulling one off the top, he flipped to the middle and read the precise handwriting. "Herschel and I discussed his wife and children. He begged me to give his wife my badge so he could talk to her one more time. I, of course, had to refuse. He'd lost touch with his son. Possible name change?"

Ethan wondered if this could be the same Herschel he'd met on hist first day when footsteps sounded again, bounding toward him, echoing louder and louder in his ears. Lights flickered on as boxes fell off shelves, and Ethan shoved the journal back in the briefcase and shut the lid. At that moment, a wind blew past him, sending his teeth chattering from the shock of cold.

"What the fuck. Just show yourself." He hopped to his feet, stumbling forward and releasing his grip on his badge from a sudden loss of balance.

A voice screeched right in his ear. "NO TALKING IN THE LIBRARY!"

Ethan turned around, his back slamming into the metal shelf. Inches from his face stood the outline of a ghostly woman in an ankle-length dress and ruffled collar.

The only thing clear to him were bright blue eyes and huge circular glasses. She let out a loud howl and lunged back. As she did, books flew off the shelves, pelting him over and over.

He dropped to his knees, covering his face with one arm while the other searched frantically for his badge.

His arm slammed into a shelf, knocking a large box off balance and topping more books on top of him.

The ghost screeched again, followed by, "NO! NO MESSES IN THE LIBRARY!"

His hand felt the metal of his badge, and he whipped his arm up into the air between him and the screaming ghost.

Immediately, the screaming stopped. He lowered his arm and looked down the empty aisle before tucking the old briefcase under one arm and holding out the badge with the other.

He made a run for the stairs, flipping the lights off as he passed and taking the steps two at a time.

He slammed the basement door behind him and rested his back against it, huffing air.

Joan's head peeked out from behind the circulation desk and asked, "Find what you were looking for?"

"Well. I found something." Ethan said, holding up the tattered briefcase.

"Excellent," Joan said, walking toward him with a key in hand. "I hope it wasn't too much of a mess down there. I'm pretty sure I hear the occasional box toppling over now and then. Breaks my heart."

"Well, I definitely think it is something I can help you with," Ethan said, trying to slow his breathing. "I think I can even convince the others at the office to come and help too. I'm sure they'd love the . . . resources down there."

Joan gave him a smile as Ethan clutched the briefcase and headed toward the exit.

Nineteen

Winter Wonderland

"**B**oss Granny, this is Crowd Surfer, do you copy?" Ethan asked into the walkie-talkie.

He eyed the street, lined with booths and vendors all the way down and around Main Street. Standing on his tiptoes, he looked over the sea of heads, searching for the lefse food cart.

Rarely did New Richmond get this busy, except Winter Wonderland, when all the residents and visitors from neighboring towns piled into this one street for food, music, and Santa.

He darted his eyes to his sister, working both the frier, griddle, and cotton candy machine simultaneously. "Hey, Ellie. Did the lefse cart come by to pick up their last load?"

The walkie talkie crackled to life. "This is Boss Granny. Use your code name dear, over."

Ellie spun a paper tube into the cotton candy machine, and a blue cloud materialized. She stuck it in a holder with several others before looking at the metal pan filled with lefse. "Nope. I'm running out of space too. They better get here soon, or people are gonna start crowding here and demanding food like last year."

Ethan sighed and looked up to the third-floor window of the YMCA where Granny had set up her command center. He could vaguely make out her binoculars peering through the middle window at the crowd below. Clicking the button, he said, "Boss Granny. This is Crowd Surfer. Over."

"Go for Boss Granny, Crowd Surfer. Over."

Ethan rolled his eyes. "I can't see the lefse cart. Ellie, I mean Fuel Station, is going to bust at the seams."

"Crowd Surfer, please say 'over' when you've stopped yapping, so I know you're done. Over."

Ethan leaned against the table. "Boss Granny. I can't see the lefse cart. Over. Better?"

"Almost, Crowd Surfer. Got intel from Sweet Cakes that the funnel cakes are all sold out. Does Fuel Station have enough batter to restock? Over," his grandmother rattled back.

Ethan turned around and found the shelf where the plastic containers of pre-made batter were being stored. "Four full containers left. Over."

"Crowd Surfer, acknowledge who that comm was for. Over." Granny crackled back.

He squeezed the walkie talkie, considering how far he could chuck the thing. "This damn thing only links to you," Ethan said to himself before clicking the button and saying, "Boss Granny. There are four full containers left. Over."

"Also, tell her I'm starting on the sweet potato fries now," Ellie said as she put another cloud of cotton candy on the stand.

"Boss Granny. Child Labor in Fuel Station is moving on to sweet potato fries as we speak. Over." Ethan said with a smirk.

"Hey! My Home Ec teacher counts this toward extra credit." Ellie complained.

"Crowd Surfer. Tell Chef Cupcake her time management skills are wonderful. Then I need you to carry two batter containers to the Funnel Cake Tent. Over."

"What about the lefse?" Ethan said.

"Crowd Surfer. You're breaking up. Please repeat with proper designations. Over."

"Boss Granny. What do we do with the stacks of lefse Tiny Demon Child has made? Over."

"If I wasn't doing all the work in here, I'd take that away from you," Ellie said as she took a batch of fries from the frier, dumped them on a tray, and seasoned them.

"Crowd Surfer. Who did you put on the lefse duty? Over."

Ethan thought for a second and said, "Boss Granny. Alexus from my office. Over."

"Crowd Surfer. Perhaps you should hoof it to the funnel cake tent and find the lefse cart on the way. Over and out."

"Ha ha, finally some peace and quiet." Ellie mocked as she put another cloud of cotton candy on the tray.

Their grandma had put them on Winter Wonderland duty since they could walk, which meant they both knew the safety of the tent compared to shoulder-to-shoulder streets. But this year, Ethan had to step it up, per Melissa, and play the role of ringleader.

Ethan clicked the walkie-talkie again and prepared a snarky come back. Then he paused, let go of the button, and stacked the two trays of lefse before wedging them between his elbow and ribs. Ellie was all too giddy to stack the batter on top and mouthed the words "good luck."

He stepped out of the tent, and the walkie clipped to his jeans came to life once more. "Crowd Surfer, this is Boss Granny. Great work Cupcake Chef. Over and out."

Ethan turned around and stuck his tongue out at Ellie before braving the streets. He walked slowly, carefully weaving between groups and steering clear of anyone who had a beer in their hand.

The booths were all nearly the same as they were every year: Mildred's homemade jams, Roy's paintings of squirrels, Kent's wood carvings, and Susie's leather work. Then the kids craft tent, the library's book sale, and the face painting tent.

The band, aptly named Five Fat Germans, settled near the middle of Main Street. Their polka style was way more entertaining than the polka they had in previous years, and it paid off. The crowd was heavy around them, dancing to the music and laughing when one of the band mates would intentionally sabotage the music and get chased around by the big guy with the tuba, all while still playing music.

More booths surrounded the street past the band, the new entrepreneurs who either wanted to try their hand at managing a booth or were fighting for a permanent spot next year. He passed by Kathy and John, who'd tried their hands at honey making this year. Old Angela Barnett had a haphazard tent selling crystal stones and jewelry, and the Bradly sisters were giving tarot readings.

All in all, this year Granny had organized seventy-six booths and ten rolling food carts.

Ethan slipped past the massive line in front of the funnel cake tent and stepped inside. "Hey, man. How's it going?"

River turned back, his hair tied back in a bun and sweat beading up on his brow. His face was also covered in so much powdered sugar that he looked like an eighties Wall Street tycoon who'd dropped his nose into a mound of cocaine. "How do you think it's going? I'm not made for this kind of pressure."

He looked back at the massive vat of oil, prodded at three funnel cakes bubbling, then pointed at the table next to him. "Just drop the goods off there."

A walkie-talkie next to River crackled, and Granny's voice rang out in the tent. "Powder. This is Boss Granny. Reports coming in, you're cooking those cakes too long. Over."

Shaking his fist at the sky, River let out a "Goddamn it!" and then pulled out the funnel cakes and dropped them into paper baskets.

"She's right. They are a little brown," Ethan said, eyeing the three cakes.

"Fuck you very much," River replied, shaking a heap of powdered sugar on each.

"At least you're still here. I think Alexus bowed out."

"Is that an option? Pretty sure you owe me big time for putting me in here. I said something easy."

"It was this or the kids' tent. Would you have wanted unknown sticky hands? I can make that happen," Ethan said, reaching for his walkie.

"I hate you and your whole family," River said as he poured more batter into the oil.

"So, any chance you saw Alexus?" Ethan asked.

"Through this crowd? You're kidding, right?" River asked as he passed the plate to a customer.

Ethan's walkie crackled again. "Crowd Surfer. This is Boss Granny. There's a holdup at the Wrapping Station. Investigate please. Over."

Picking up the walkie, Ethan replied, "Boss Granny. Crowd Surfer is on it. Over." He let go of the button and patted River on the back before picking up the lefse trays. "Good luck, dude. You got this."

Deftly crossing the street and moving four tents to the right, he made his way to the gift-wrapping tent. Without having to balance the batter on top of the trays, he could navigate the long line of angry citizens waiting for their turn to wrap their last-minute gifts.

He spotted Trevor behind the booth, slowly and precisely measuring paper to match packages with Doris working the tape. What he didn't see was the problem; no one was covering the ribbon-tying station.

"Uh, looks like you're down a person." Ethan asked.

"Really? Hadn't noticed from the long line of bitching customers," Doris spat back.

"Next year, I want face painting duty. Got it?" Trevor said.

Doris slid the package she was working on across the table and jumped around a wall of ribbon, deftly pulling an absurdly long strand and haphazardly twisting it around before tying it off.

"Where is your third?" Ethan asked.

"Oh. You mean Melissa? She up and left us." Doris said as she raked scissors across the tied ribbon to curl it and then passed it to the waiting customer.

"I'm sorry, but I wanted a green ribbon," the customer said.

Doris smiled, a wild look in her eye, and through gritted teeth said, "Well, Santa said silver this year. Happy Holidays!"

She shoved the package into the customer's hands, and the line shuffled before they protested. "Did you see where she went?"

"Said she had a last-minute meeting. Something about upper management coming for an inspection if she didn't get on the phone with them," Trevor said as he wrapped paper around an enormous stack of books.

"Is there anyone we can get to help us? I'm afraid I'm going to lose my grip if I keep up at this pace," Doris said as she crumpled wrapping paper around a stack of books.

Picking up his walkie, Ethan said, "Crowd Surfer to Boss Granny. We've got another AWOL at the Wrapping Station. Over."

"Crowd Surfer. This is Boss Granny. Reinforcements on the way. Over and out."

"There, you should get someone soon," Ethan said. Then, looking around, he asked, "Has anyone seen Alexus and the lefse cart?"

"You mean the cart right behind you?" Trevor asked, pointing across the street with scissors.

"That's the one," Ethan called after he spun around. He raced to it and immediately noticed that the person standing at the cart was absolutely not Alexus.

Their back was to him, but he knew she would never be caught dead in the red and green striped elf suit. Grabbing the elf's shoulder and spinning them around, Ethan said, "Hey. Who—"

Cutting him off, Gerry turned around and gave Ethan a huge smile before giving him a side hug, "Hello!" The bells on Gerry's shoes, belt, and hat jingled as he moved. "Isn't this all just fantastic? I mean, who knew this sleepy burg could throw such a wondrous event?"

Gerry looked down at the trays and clapped his hands. "Oh, excellent. I had to turn people away." He took the two trays and stored them in the warmer. "Have you been listening to that Bach Trumpet? He's really been carrying the rest of the band."

Clicking on his walkie-talkie, Ethan said, "Boss Granny, this is Crowd Surfer. Located Potato Frisbee. Gremlin is AWOL and has been replaced by Gerry. Over."

"Is that Rosemary?" Gerry said, taking the walkie-talkie away from Ethan. "Rose dear, is that you?"

"No. Wait," Ethan protested, unsure what the punishment would be for giving up his walkie-talkie.

Holding Ethan back with his arm, Gerry continued, "You've really done an outstanding job. Why don't you come down here and enjoy it?"

"Connoisseur, what are you doing? You're supposed to be at the North Pole." Rosemary replied.

"Connoisseur? Why do you get a cool name?" Ethan stammered.

Gerry waved Ethan off and continued in the walkie-talkie, "Rose, come down here and have some lefse with me."

"I would if I could, but someone's gotta keep an eye on all this. Mind telling me what happened at the North Pole?" Rosemary asked.

"Santa never showed, so I had to improvise." Gerry said, giving Ethan a wink.

There was a pause on the walkie before it came back to life. "Crowd Surfer, Investigate. Now. Over."

"Mind repeating that? I didn't hear who it was from. Over," Ethan said with a smirk.

"Ethan, dear. Speak with Gerry and go to the North Pole. Find out what happened, or I might let it slip to Gerry and the others that time in sixth grade when I found something behind your box of dinosaur toys."

Heat flushed Ethan's face, and he darted his eyes to Gerry. "Crowd Surfer to Boss Granny. Understood. Over and out."

"What did she find?" Gerry asked, a smirk on his face.

"Nothing. So, Santa is missing? That doesn't answer why Alexus isn't here."

"Ok, so, Bucky was on security, which he loved, by the way. I told him that Santa went missing from the North Pole. He started looking, couldn't find him, and the kids were getting restless. I was ready to take the role. Having been Macbeth a few times in my past, a little Santa wasn't about to scare me. However, my knees have been aching and I can't sit that long, so Bucky had to step up."

Ethan's eyes widened, "Wait. You're telling me Buck is Santa?"

Gerry nodded. "Yep. And Alexus, poor dear, was overwhelmed by the adults trying to talk to her. I gave her my job. Just stand there, usher kids in and out, and don't have to say a word. I had an extra costume, so she was ready in no time."

Ethan's mouth hung open. "You put Buck and Alexus on North Pole duty?"

"Probably the best decision I've made all day." Gerry said with a smile.

Ethan shot a glance down the road, toward the candy cane poles and the nexus of garland. "Oh no."

Twenty

Santa!

"WHY, GERRY? WHY?" ETHAN mumbled to himself as he shouldered through the crowd toward the massive line of parents, candy cane poles, and nexus of garland.

He pressed on, even though the crowd kept trying to carry him away from Santa and toward the food tents. It was like Ethan was a salmon trying to swim upstream.

What was Gerry thinking, assigning the role of jolly Santa to Buck? And with Alexus as his helpful elf? He strained his ears, assuming the loud crowd was just suppressing the inevitable children crying.

His pulse pounded as he worried about what carnage he might see and the wrath of his grandmother after she heard about this.

Finally, he found a break in the crowd between the people passing up and down the street and the line of bundled-up, anxious kids, mostly looking like a mascot for the Michelin tire company. Some clung to their parents in fear; others moved back and forth with the excitement of telling Santa all their hearts' desires for Christmas morning.

He still couldn't see Alexus and Buck, but a light haze in the corner of his eye pulled his attention to Bob. He hadn't seen him when he was in the funnel cake tent, too preoccupied trying not to laugh at all the powdered sugar on River, but Bob was there now, a few feet from the tent.

Bob danced wildly as the Five Fat Germans played a song called Hoop Dee Doo. He seemed almost enchanted by the music as he hopped up on stage, moved through the guitar, accordion, drums, trumpet, and bass, flinging his arms and legs almost in rhythm to the music.

Yelling over the crowd, Ethan screamed, "Yeah, you go, Bob!"

Bob looked over and gave him a firm salute as he continued to spin and whirl to the music.

"Would not have guessed he liked polka." Ethan laughed to himself.

He shook his thoughts away and refocused on the mission at hand when his walkie-talkie came to life. "Crowd Surfer. This is Boss Granny. Over."

Holding the device to his face and looking up to the third floor of the YMCA where his grandmother's makeshift command center was, Ethan replied, "This is Crowd Surfer. What's up Boss Granny? Over."

"Crowd Surfer. AWOL Ribbon Curler spotted leaving the tarot tent. Please engage with haste. Boss Granny, over and out."

Ethan gave a big thumbs up to the YMCA building, knowing his grandmother was watching with binoculars. Diving back into the sea of people, he pushed off a child that bumped into him, too focused on weaving through the sea to look back.

The crowd cleared when he reached the side of the tarot tent. Avoiding the lines, he slipped into the small alley between the tarot tent and the palm reader. As he moved to the back of the tent, two voices whispered at the edge of his hearing. He paused, out of sight, and strained to listen.

"Upper management is expecting a full report," a pointed voice said.

"I don't know what more you want me to do. You should have enough evidence from the conference." Melissa said.

"That wasn't enough."

"I shouldn't have to listen to you. They should come up here and tell me directly, not send over some little intern."

"Well, this little intern is telling you to figure it out."

"How should I be doing that when you all put a bunch of veterans on my team? River, I get, but Buck and Alexus? Come on."

"Get it done, or upper management will find someone else looking for that promotion."

"Don't threaten me. You all have no one else gutsy enough."

"You have your orders. I'll be back in two weeks to confirm your progress."

At that point, Ethan backed up, then walked full speed into the alley. "Hey! Melissa! Boss Granny sent me. Doris and Trevor are swamped at the gift-wrapping station without you." He looked over at the man, recognizing him from the Halloween conference. "Hey. Do I know you?"

"No, and I'd like to keep it that way," the man said as he turned and started down the alley.

"Oh great, it wasn't like we were talking or anything." Melissa called after him. She turned to Ethan. "Were you spying on me?"

Ethan raised his hands defensively. "What? No. Boss Granny said you were in this tent. I wasn't expecting you to be in some secret meeting."

"NRDS business. Upper management is just demanding more work on the hauntings."

"And he's upper management?" Ethan feigned surprise, nodding toward where he last saw the man.

Melissa let out a laugh. "No. He's the peon they sent so they didn't have to leave DC. Best to forget what you saw."

"And they want us to speed up the haunting investigations?"

Melissa looked at her watch. "Oh, wow, look at the time. I bet those two knuckleheads are at wits' end without me. Well, break's over. Best for both of us to get back to work."

"That's what I came to tell you."

She pushed him back down the alley between the two tents. "Seriously, Ethan. Stop screwing around. We're supposed to be making a good impression at this thing."

"I know. And. That's what—"

Shoving him into the crowd again, she said, "You need to stop distracting me. I've got ribbons to tie. Go on, do whatever it is you are supposed to be doing." With that, she disappeared into the crowd.

Clicking on his walking talkie, Ethan said, "Boss Granny. This is Crowd Surfer. AWOL Ribbon Cutter is heading back to her post. Over and out."

"This is Boss Granny. Good job, Crowd Surfer. Over and out."

Then Ethan turned back to the crowd and candy canes. Nodding with determination, he said to himself, "Alright Crowd Surfer. Let's get back through this tide and do this."

Wading into the crowd without regard for the visitors, he pushed through families and friends who were chatting. He separated a woman holding hands with a young girl. He pushed a child with a balloon to the side and listened to the cries as the balloon floated into the sky.

Finally, Ethan broke free from the crowd only to come back to a line to see Santa that was twice the size he'd left it. He took in a deep breath and marched forward, pushing past family after family.

The crowed greeted his manhandling with, "No cuts!" and "Hey, Mister! Wait in line like the rest of us!" and "Hey asshole! This is for kids!" and "Mommy, why does he get to be naughty?"

Ethan ignored all of them, pressing forward in his goal to make Granny's Winter Wonderland what it was supposed to be.

He found Alexus dressed in an elf hat, elf ears, and a leather jacket at the front of the line. He pushed past a final little girl who said, "Hey! Elf Lady! He's cutting!"

Pursing her lips, Alexus asked, "Why are you pissing off my line?"

"You can't say 'pissing off' in front of the children. You're supposed to be a Christmas elf," Ethan lectured.

"Can I say dick? As in, man, this guy ruining the vibe of my line is being a total dick?" Alexus said with a sneer.

"He is being a dick," the little girl said.

"That's right. And what do we do with dicks?" Alexus said to the child.

"Castrate them!" the little girl said with a smile on her face.

Ethan's mouth dropped open, and Alexus let out a loud laugh before patting the girl on the head. "What a smart girl you are. I'll put in a good word to Santa."

"Hold up, this is Santa's tent. You can't say dick and castrate," Ethan said.

"That's what happens to our cows. My dad said when the bulls start being dicks, we castrate them," the little girl said.

"I knew this was a terrible fit. You've got the kids cussing? I'm getting you reassigned," Ethan said.

"She already knew the words. I didn't teach her anything. And before you showed up, I was a happy little elf. Right little evil girl?" Alexus asked.

The little girl nodded. "Then the bulls stop being dicks. Some of them disappear anyway, then we have steak for weeks. Dad doesn't think I know. But I know." She grinned ear to ear and looked up to Ethan.

"So, moral of the story. Line cutters are also dicks. Want to help me hold him down?" Alexus said to the little girl.

"I get to help?" she replied. Her eyes beaming.

"What? No," Ethan said.

"Absolutely," Alexus said.

"Stop. No. No one is getting castrated. This is serious," Ethan said to Alexus. Looking at the little girl, he asked, "Where are your parents?"

"Away. Helping my brother. What's it to you, line cutter?"

"I'm watching her," Alexus said.

Ethan sighed. "Fine, whatever. Just let me through so I can make sure Buck's doing it right."

"No," Alexus said.

"What? You can't say no. Let me through," Ethan said.

"No," Alexus said again.

"But. Boss Granny said I should. I need to get in there," Ethan said.

"Not until you promise to me that you won't change my post," Alexus demanded.

"Wait. You like it here?" Ethan asked.

"Um, yeah. I boss people around. I don't have to move. Every once in a while, a runner brings me food, and I get to hang with cool, partially deranged kids," she said, giving the little girl a high five.

"Oh. Um. Yeah. Sure. As long as the parents don't complain," Ethan said.

"Then you may pass, but remember, Santa is just through those doors. Have you thought about which list you'll be on this year, buddy? You wouldn't want Santa stuffing your pockets full of coal, would you?" Alexus said, stepping aside and opening the curtain.

Ethan stepped into the tent and found Buck in a full Santa costume, beard and all, sitting on a throne with a young boy on his knee. He spoke in a low voice, but with a smile on his face that Ethan hadn't seen before. "Now, I don't know if Santa can get you all those things. Maybe let me know what the most important thing is."

The mother, standing near Ethan, mouthed, "Thank you."

The little boy thought for a minute and then said, "Maybe just the basketball then."

Glancing at the mother and seeing a thumbs up, Buck said, "A new basketball. We can do that."

Ethan looked down and asked, "Um. Do you need anything?"

"Nope. All good," Buck said as he helped the child off his lap. The kid ran to his mother, smiling with glee about the possibilities of things to come, and Buck asked Ethan, "You alright, kid? You look a little pale."

"I'm fine. I mean. I don't know. I really thought you and Alexus would mess this whole thing up," he confessed.

"What? Really? We don't exude holiday cheer?" Buck said with a grin.

"And I ran into Melissa. She was meeting this guy; pretty sure he was with upper management. Same guy I saw in Saint Louis."

"Huh," Buck grunted.

"Something about upping our haunting investigations. It was weird. Maybe it was nothing."

"Maybe."

Ethan's radio crackled. "This is Boss Granny for Crowd Surfer. Crowd Surfer. Status Report. Over."

Ethan held up a finger to Buck and pulled up his walkie talkie. "Boss Granny. This is Crowd Surfer. Everything is great at the North Pole. Over."

"Crowd Surfer. I need you back at Tourist Fuel. Princess Cupcake Chef needs help with unclogging the Cloud Maker. Over and out."

Buck let out a deep chuckle.

Ethan shook his head and said, "She has me running all over the place. Doris is losing it with gift wrapping. River looks like more sugar has gone up his nose than on the funnel cakes. Oh, and Bob is a huge fan of polka music, apparently. You should see him dancing."

"You watched Bob dance?"

Ethan felt suddenly flushed. "Yeah. I mean. You couldn't help it. He was going crazy."

"Where's your badge?"

Ethan felt his face grow hot. He patted his pants, then shook his head. "I mean. I. I left it at home. I didn't think I needed it for this."

"If you don't have a badge, how can you see Bob?"

Ethan looked down, confused and nervous. "I. Um. I don't know."

"Nothing is ever dull with you around, kid. And things just keep getting weirder around here."

Twenty-One

Audits and Donuts

T HE FIRST THING ETHAN saw as he entered the office was a lanky man in a dark blue suit clicking through files on Buck's computer. "Uh, hi. Can I help you?" Ethan asked as he hung up his coat and hat.

"I suppose that remains to be seen, Agent Malik," the man said as he turned the chair to face Ethan. He was younger than what Ethan remembered, but he knew it was the same blond-haired, blue-eyed man from the convention in Saint Louis and the same man he'd caught talking to Melissa at the Winter Festival.

"Well, that's Buck's computer. Probably best you're not sitting there when he comes in," Ethan said, wishing he hadn't been the first one in the office.

"Ah, but this seat seemed to be the most comfortable," the man replied.

"It's alright, kid," Buck said, entering the office and pulling off his long coat and scarf.

"You sure it's alright? He's going through your files," Ethan said as Buck walked past him for the coffee machine.

"Agent Hampton. Pleasure to see you again," the man said.

"Pleasure's all yours," Buck said with a grunt.

"Oh, fuck no," River said as he walked into the office. "No fucking way." He tossed the bag marked BOB under the coat rack as he turned and walked out.

"River," Buck shouted toward the door. "Get your ass in here, or you are going to get the Waste Management case."

"I'd rather take a fucking sick day," River called from the hall as he pretended to cough.

"Excellent," Bob declared, walking through the door.

"Wait. What's going on?" Ethan asked.

"Inspection Day!" Bob said, elated.

"We're being audited," Buck said, leaning against Doris's desk.

"Partial audit. Think of it more like a friendly check-in on our newest branch," the auditor said, pulling out a clipboard from his briefcase.

"Well, sir, this branch is in tip-top shape. Ready for a call at a moment's notice," Bob announced with pride.

"Yeah, not going to listen to a kiss ass all day," Alexus said, tossing her badge on her desk as she sat down in her chair.

Ethan jumped and did a double take from the door, where a puffy black jacket now hung, to Alexus's desk. "When did you get here?"

"Honestly, get your eyes checked," she replied with a menacing grin.

"Hey, gang. Check out these great shots I got of the protest," Trevor said, his eyes on his phone as he stepped into the office and nearly tumbled over the bag marked BOB.

The auditor stood and scribbled on his clipboard. "Ah, the Social Media Intern has arrived. Trevor, is it?"

Trevor raised an eyebrow, tapped his screen, and held up his camera to the auditor. "That's right. And who are you?"

"He's a peon from upper management," Buck said, slipping past the auditor, cup of coffee in hand, and reclaiming his seat.

"Name's Agent Fillmore, thank you. And you're the one who posted the video that caused the protests, are you not?" the auditor asked as he made notes on his clipboard.

"I mean. Who's to say what caused the protests to happen?" Trevor said, lowering his camera and darting his eyes around the room.

Agent Fillmore flipped through the sheets on the clipboard, "October 6th. Looks like the contents of that video were the initial catalyst for the protests. Unless my information is wrong?"

"You're in for it now," Bob said with glee.

"There hasn't been a protest for a while now. The town's moving on," Buck said.

"Five days since your last protest is hardly 'moving on,'" Fillmore said.

"Last protest was a stupid soccer mom I chewed out at the grocery store, a bank manager who wouldn't give me a loan, and some old lady who kept telling me I looked like a whore. I don't think they even really count as protestors," Alexus said.

"Oh, I'll come back to you. Looks like those anger management classes have really made an impact," Fillmore said.

"I'd say so. It isn't like I hurt any of them. Well . . . None of them had to go to the hospital." Alexus smirked.

"Back in my day, if you had an anger problem, you went out back with the captain. A swift knock to the head seemed to set them right," Bob said with a smile.

"No one's gonna punch Alexus," Ethan said.

"Oh, is that what Bob's saying? I'd like to see him try," Alexus said, cracking her knuckles as she looked at Bob.

"This banter is all very interesting, but—"

"That old lady who called you a whore is Mildred. Used to teach at the school. Mildred Banger. She calls everyone a whore," Trevor said.

"Shut up, ingrate," Bob said. Looking at the auditor, he nodded. "Please, go on."

"He can't hear you, suck up." Ethan said.

Agent Fillmore pulled back his blazer and flashed a shiny badge. "I see your BOB just fine."

"Hold up. Banger?" Alexus laughed. "Please tell me little prepubescent Trevor and friends would make 'bang her' jokes?"

Trevor smiled and nodded.

"This is how you all work most days? I can see why there are so many delays," Fillmore said as he scribbled.

Melissa burst through the office door, waving her arm wildly as she regained her balance. "Never fear, everyone. I'm here and I've brought donuts!" Looking behind her, she yelled down the hall, "Doris! I said I brought donuts!"

"Oh, dammit. Oh, I'm so sorry," Doris said as she rushed into the room and placed a box of donuts on her desk.

"Time for a little office check-in," Melissa said, tearing open the donut box and grabbing an overly filled Bavarian creme.

"Excuse me. Do you have any gluten-free options?" Agent Fillmore asked.

"Oh. You're here. No. I don't." Melissa said.

"More for me," Alexus said as she jumped out of her seat and plucked two jellies from the box.

"That is quite unfortunate," Fillmore mumbled as he scribbled on his clipboard.

"Be sure to let upper management know that we run a tight ship here," Melissa said.

Picking up two glazed donuts, Doris mashed them together and said, "As tight as two people squished together."

"Uh, was that a sex joke, Doris?" Alexus said.

"What? No. I just meant it because I was smashed in Melissa's car this morning. That thing is not meant for two people," Doris said.

"So, you and Melissa are smashing in her car?" Trevor asked with a childish grin.

"It was a tight squeeze, but I kept the box intact," she said, holding up her donut monstrosity.

"I bet that box did just fine," Alexus said with a grin.

"Well, that's enough of that." Melissa scolded, tossing her coat haphazardly onto the coat rack.

Ethan watched as a small gray clicker fell from her pocket onto the floor beneath her coat.

Melissa started again, waving her donut in the air. "Our dear *intern* here has come at the behest of upper management to audit and ensure that you are not behaving like animals." Looking at the auditor, she said, "Do you see what I have to deal with?"

Ethan brushed past Melissa and eyed the donut box, putting himself between the clicker and everyone else.

"You mean dealing with hot and heavy car rides with Doris?" Alexus said with a giggle. Trevor, Bob, and Ethan all laughed.

"You are all children." Melissa said.

Ethan stepped back and crouched down, fiddling with his shoelaces while swiping the clicker from the ground and pocketing it.

"If you all are going to act like children, then donut Thursdays are off."

"Donut Thursdays? Since when have you brought in donuts on Thursday?" Trevor asked.

"I was thinking about it. Either way, just get back to work." Melissa said before grabbing the box of donuts and stomping off to her office.

Agent Fillmore turned and surveyed the room before clearing his throat. "Would someone please explain to me the wall of filled briefcases?"

"We have about five requests pending for pickup," Buck said.

Agent Fillmore walked over to the wall. "Regulations clearly state in section 35b of the Spirit Disposal Procedure in Subsection D that there should never be over twenty filled cases in this office at any given time. I count thirty-five. Who is to blame for this oversight?"

"The manual also says the regional office will pick up briefcases every Sunday, but we haven't had a pickup for four weeks," Ethan said.

"Oh shit," Alexus exclaimed with pride.

"Rookie? Did that come out of you?" Bob asked.

"Oh, Ethan, look at you," Doris said with a warm smile.

"What am I missing?" Trevor asked.

"Our little boy's all grown up," Alexus said.

"You read the manual," Buck said.

Ethan smiled, "I read the manual."

"Was reading the manual considered optional in this branch?" the auditor asked.

"No," Buck said.

"I should hope not," the auditor said.

Standing, Buck began putting his coat back on and asked, "You're here to observe the office, right?"

"That's correct," the auditor said.

"Great. Alexus will give you a tour of our ongoing cases," Buck said.

"Fuck I will. I got my own shit to do. Make the rookie do it," Alexus said.

"Ethan and I have work at the library, and River is sick," Buck said.

"What business might you have at the library?" the auditor asked.

Ethan said, "There's a—"

But before he could finish, Buck interrupted. "Research. Nothing too exciting. The librarian has some old journals and notepads we've been cataloging. You are free to join us if you want."

"No. No. That sounds terrible. This doesn't get you out of the interview, Agent Hampton," the auditor said.

"Yeah, yeah, I know. You won't miss us," Buck said as he pushed Ethan out the door. Looking back at Alexus, Buck added, "I owe you one."

"You do, you old bastard!" she yelled as Buck pushed Ethan to the elevator.

Once the doors closed, Ethan asked, "Why'd you rush me out of there?"

"You told me the other day you could see Bob without the badge. You really want to work a case with an auditor around? I don't. Not until I know what's going on with you. Unless you'd rather them cut you open to find out," Buck said.

"Oh. No. I don't want that," Ethan said.

"Good, then let's get a move on," Buck said.

Twenty-Two

Late Fees

E THAN STEPPED OUT OF Buck's car and slammed the door before saying, "Okay, so, like I was saying, the only thing I really got from it was that it can throw books."

"Be careful with her," Buck cautioned.

"With the ghost?"

"No. With my car," he replied as he opened the back door and pulled a briefcase from the backseat.

"Oh, yeah. Right. Sorry," Ethan said, nodding. "But, um, back to the ghost. How do you think we go about taking her down? At least I think the ghost is a woman. I couldn't tell. Do we need to talk to her first?"

"No," Buck said as he walked up the steps to the library entrance.

Ethan chased after him. "But, like, what if she knows something? Bet she knows something about the children. Should we at least try to get something out of her?"

"No," Buck said again.

"But she nearly took my head off. I was lucky I even got Stephenson's briefcase out of there alive. She attacked when I found it. That has to mean she knows something about it. Right?"

Turning around to face him, Buck said, "Or she came out of it and doesn't want to go back in. Either way, doesn't matter. Old ghost, no record of hauntings, and signs of Class Three or above activity. Case first. Ask questions later."

"Oh, yeah. I just. She could know something."

Buck grabbed on to the door of the library, paused, and looked back at Ethan. "Look, we're not action heroes. We don't fight monsters and get medals pinned to our chests. We're social workers. We solve problems where we can, we document everything, and we do a shit-ton of paperwork. So, stop thinking that you are some kind of comic book figure. If you go about asking hostile ghosts questions, you're going to end up dead, or worse. Got it?"

Ethan nodded. "Be happy doing paperwork. Stop asking questions. Boring. Not action heroes. Got it."

Buck rolled his eyes and pulled the door open and stepped inside.

Following suit, Ethan stood beside him and scanned the room, which appeared to be empty besides Jean standing behind a desk on their right.

With a boney finger, she turned a page of the book she was reading, *The House on the Cerulean Sea*. Ethan chuckled when he noticed the book was upside down. Calling to her, he said, "Hey, Ms. Peterson. I'd like to take another look in the basement if you don't mind."

Not looking up from the book, she said, "Oh, of course, deary."

"Doing some brain exercises?" Ethan asked, laughing as he pointed out the book.

"A sharp mind finds joy in all kinds of reading," she replied, her eyes still trained on the book.

Buck handed Ethan the briefcase and said, "Why don't you go ahead, kid. I've got a couple of questions for Ms. Peterson. Why don't you at least get the lights on?"

"Everything alright?" Ethan asked.

"Yep. All fine. You go on ahead. I'll be down in a minute," Buck replied, his eyes locked on the librarian.

Taking the case, Ethan shrugged and said, "Alright. I'll, um, go turn on the lights I guess." He grabbed the set of keys off the desk and headed to the back. He eased down the rickety wooden steps, muttering to himself, "Here ghosty, ghosty, ghosty. I'm back for round two. Come out, come out, wherever you are."

He flipped the switch at the bottom of the stairs, and the lights flickered to life. It was in far worse condition than when he'd left it. Several of the large metal shelving units were knocked over, boxes were tossed all about, and books were everywhere.

"You've been a busy little ghost, haven't you?" Ethan called as he stepped over a box and waded into the mess. He gripped the briefcase tightly in one hand and his badge in the other.

He waited for what seemed like forever, motion sensors killing the lights in the basement except for the ones above him.

Ethan eyed the top of the stairs, whispering to himself, "Well, Buck, are you too scared to come down? Guess I'll just do it myself then."

He chewed on his lip, then thought of a grand idea. "Oh no, ghosty, I bet you don't want another mess down here." He pushed a box off the shelf, spilling books all over the little space left on the floor.

He waited and listened.

Nothing.

Picking up a dusty copy of "*A Wocket in Your Pocket*," he opened it to the middle and said, "Uh-oh. You better come and stop me. I'm messing with books." He slowly ripped a page from the middle, held it up, and waved it around. "Look. I'm wrecking stuff. Oh no. You should come and make me stop."

He waited and listened.

Nothing again.

Crumpling the page, he said, "Oh, no. Now it's destroyed. What will I do next? Someone should really stop me." Without thinking, he put the page in his mouth and started chewing and mumbled, "M-oh mo. Mew hould mome smop me."

His mouth full of dust and paper, he waited.

But there was nothing.

He spat out the page onto the floor, brushing his tongue off with his hand while trying not to gag. He looked to the stairs and yelled, "Buck! Something's wrong. It's not down here."

He sighed and backed away from the mess he'd made. The lights flickered on behind him and when he turned, something on the floor caught his eye.

"Hey, Buck. You there?" he called as he reached down and picked up a broken pair of glasses. He held them up to take a better look at them.

"Uh . . . Buck!" he called, straining his voice as he realized he'd been holding the pair of glasses Joan had been wearing the day she let him down here.

Ethan's heart pounded as he skipped steps while racing up the stairs. "Buck! Buck!" he said, bursting through the door; but Buck replied with a calm smile that brought Ethan to a halt.

"Hey, kid," Buck said. He was standing in front of the door, his badge in his hand.

Ethan looked at Joan. She gripped her upside-down book with both hands and stared intently at its pages. "So, there isn't a spirit down there. Not anymore," Ethan said, keeping his eyes locked on the librarian.

Buck smiled, but his eyes told a different story. "Well, good thing you read the manual, because you know that this happens sometimes."

Ethan gripped tight onto the briefcase, darting his eyes back and forth between Joan and Buck. "Yeah. Those pesky Class Four spirits are great at hiding."

"Well, I suppose you know what we've got to do next, right?" Buck asked, his eyes shifting to the librarian.

Ethan swallowed. "You want to get the door?"

"Already on it," Buck said.

"You think they've gone out the back?"

"Checked there too, but it was blocked off, so I think we're good," Buck said.

Ethan took a deep breath, stepping out from the basement door, and then smiled at Joan. "Okay, well, Ms. Peterson. We're, um. We're going to go."

The librarian looked up from her book for the first time.

In one swift motion, Ethan placed the briefcase and unlatched both locks, setting it between himself and Buck. As he stood, he reached into his pocket. "You know, while I'm here, I've been having trouble with my, um, library card. Do you think, maybe, you could look?"

The librarian's eyes looked at the briefcase and glowed a strange green. She let out a low hissing noise that sent a chill down Ethan's spine before throwing the book right at Ethan's head.

He dodged it, holding up his badge seconds before her bony fingers grabbed him. She froze, her eyes transfixed on his badge.

"Careful, kid," Buck said. He edged closer to the case, ensuring his body stayed between the librarian and the door.

"Now, Ms. Peterson. I don't really like how you're looking at me," Ethan said, taking another step closer.

She took a step back, hands swaying side to side. In a deep and raspy voice that sounded nothing like Joan, the librarian said, "Ms. Peterson's not here right now."

Even though he knew the sound of the otherworldly voice, Ethan's breath caught in his chest.

"Easy, kid," Buck said.

Ethan kept his eyes on the possessed librarian. "I'm going to need you to vacate that body."

"I'm going to need you to go fuck yourself, you tiny-dicked pissant," the librarian said in the deep voice. She backed up into a cart, halting any chance she had of running away.

Ethan frowned and said, "Now, that's just rude."

"Poor little baby Ethan. What are you going to do, wet yourself again like you did in the third grade?" the librarian rasped.

"Wait, how did you—" Ethan started.

Then the librarian wrapped her hand around the cart and whipped it forward, slamming it into Ethan's hip and knocking him off his feet. With an ear-piercing scream, she blasted a foul-smelling gust of wind at Ethan before inhumanly leaping over the counter.

Ethan stumbled to his feet and held out his badge, leaping forward, hoping to catch her gaze again.

Instead, as he fumbled around the desk, a fist met his jaw and stars blurred his vision.

He looked back at Buck only to see a swarm of flying books thwarting any help from him.

She stood over him, holding another hardcover book high above her head. She swung the book down onto his face, and his nose exploded with blood.

"No," Ethan coughed, blood filling his mouth.

Holding the book high again, blood staining the cover now, she grinned and brought it down on Ethan's face a second time. Moments before it connected, Buck smacked her in the jaw with his badge.

A howl echoed in the entire library as she stumbled away, followed by Buck.

"Kid! Case!" Buck yelled.

Ethan watched in amazement as Joan fell to the right and the spirit fell to the left.

Holding his badge out, ready for the spirit to attack, Buck screamed again, "Kid! Get the case!"

Ethan scrambled to his knees and crawled to the case.

Again, foul-smelling air rushed over Ethan and Buck as the spirit screamed, "Noooooo!" Soaring above Buck, the ghost raced for the door.

"Now, kid!" Buck screamed.

"On it!" Ethan yelled as he opened the case and slid it toward the door, hoping it would intercept the spirit's path.

There was a scratch as the ghost, inches from the door, was caught by the pull of the briefcase. It clawed at the door as it tried to escape the pull of the prison.

"Not again!" it screamed, but the case was too strong. Green light dimmed to nothingness as the ghost vanished inside and the case slammed shut.

Ethan raced over to the briefcase, one hand holding his nose while the other pushed the latches closed. He held it up and looked back at Buck with a huge grin on his bloodied face. "Got it!"

Buck leaned over Joan and reached down to take her pulse. "She's alive, but she's going to be in some serious pain when she wakes up."

Ethan collapsed against the door and slid to the floor, briefcase wrapped in one arm. "Wow. That was. Something."

Buck shook his head and let out a chuckle, walking over to him and holding out a hand. "She had a hell of a right hook. Good thing you read the manual, kid."

Ethan took a deep breath and let it out. His ears were still ringing from the blows he'd taken. Looking up at his mentor, he asked, "So, what do we do now?"

"What we do every day. Paperwork," Buck said, offering a hand to Ethan.

Twenty-Three
Walking Retired

E THAN STARED AT THE Cedar Villa Retirement Home sign as Buck pulled into the parking lot. "Are you sure you want to do this? I mean, I don't remember a lot from that night, but I remember Alexus holding him at gunpoint."

Buck killed the engine, straightened his red tie, and grabbed the door handle. "Stephenson's a bully. He only responds to authority or violence. If we don't, then we're doing a disservice to Herschel and everyone else in his journal."

As they walked through the sliding glass doors, Ethan spotted his cousin Andy sitting behind the front desk in his security uniform. "Hey, cuz. Looks like I'm, um, back again."

"Oh, hell no!" Andy said, jumping up from his desk and rushing to block Ethan's path.

Ethan held up his hands. "Hold up. Wait. I know what you are going to say, but last time I was in a bad way."

"You puked all over me. And all over the carpet!" Andy yelled.

"I know. I know," Ethan said.

"I had to smell that for three days before they ended up trashing the carpet and getting a new one. Three days, Ethan!"

Ethan looked down, noticing the change in the carpet. "I'm really sorry about that. It looks way better, though. Less like a horror movie from the eighties."

Andy shook his head and put a hand on Ethan, pushing him back. "You and your friend can just turn around and take your sorry asses back to your damn car."

Buck pulled his badge from his blazer and said, "We're here to talk to Stephenson in 12B."

Andy eyed the badge and cleared his throat. "Well, Mr. Stephenson gave specific orders. Unless they have a warrant, no agents are welcome here."

"Hold up. Mr. Stephenson gave orders? The old guy?" Ethan asked.

"He bought the building before retiring," Buck said.

Andy nodded. "That's right. And what he says goes. So, no agents. Especially no NRDS agents."

"Wait. Hold on. He owns the building? Why is he in 12B? That room wasn't anything special." Ethan said.

Andy shrugged. "It's a corner room. But other than that. No clue."

Buck put his badge back in his pocket and straightened his suit jacket. "Look, kid. I'm coming in to see him one way or another. Best you pick up your phone and tell him Buck Hampton is here to see him before I pick option two."

Andy shifted his gaze between Buck and Ethan. "Option two?"

Buck sighed and cocked his neck from side to side, cracking it. "Trust me, kid. Ten bucks an hour isn't worth the pain. Stop fucking around and get him on the phone."

"It's twelve, but yeah. No," Andy said.

"Twelve dollars? For security? Well, fuck this guy," Ethan said.

Andy picked up his radio and pointed at them. "You two stay right here until I get back."

After Andy scurried past the doors to the main hallway, Ethan whispered to Buck, "That was awesome!"

Buck chuckled.

"You're, like, a certified badass," Ethan said.

Buck shook his head.

In a grumbly voice meant to sound like Buck, Ethan said, "Ten bucks an hour isn't worth the pain I'm going to cause you."

"Enough," Buck said.

Ethan cleared his throat and grinned. "Sorry."

Andy popped his head back into the lobby and said, "You two come this way. He's eating lunch right now."

As they stepped through the doors and into the hallway lined with doors as if it were some type of hotel, Ethan asked, "Wait, your residents eat lunch at two-thirty in the afternoon? Seems a little late."

Andy shook his head. "Mr. Stephenson prefers to eat alone. On his terms."

Buck elbowed Ethan's ribs. "An entitled asshole, remember? Stand strong."

They entered a large dining hall looking out into a snow-covered courtyard. Tables that seated between four and eight people lay empty all around the room, chairs resting upside down on the tables. All but one table next to the windows, where the old man Ethan had surprised with Alexus sat in blue pajamas.

In front of him was a bloody, half-eaten porterhouse, a loaded baked potato, and two empty beer bottles. An attendant dressed in a white nurse's outfit, white skirt and all as if it were pulled from the 1950s, stood behind him to the left, waiting on his every need.

Buck and Ethan crossed the room in silence. As they neared his table, Stephenson stopped cutting the bleeding meat, looked up, and said,

"Hampton. Fuck you," before jamming a bleeding piece of steak into his mouth.

"Stephenson. Same bitter piece of shit as always," Buck said, taking off his hat and pulling out a chair.

Pointing his knife at Buck, Stephenson said, "Did I say you could fucking sit?"

"Did I suggest that I fucking cared?" Buck sat down and looked at Ethan. Hurriedly, Ethan followed suit.

Stephenson grunted and shifted his beady eyes over to Ethan before pointing his knife at him. "I see you brought the blitzed greenhorn too. Where's the broad? I'd rather the apology come from her."

"He's not here to apologize."

Stephenson leaned back in his chair and started using the tip of the knife as a toothpick. "You know, Bucky ol' pal, I really should have you both killed. Right here."

Leaning over to Buck, Ethan whispered, "Wait. Can he do that?"

Buck shot Ethan a withering look and said, "He can't take a piss without help."

Stephenson laughed. Snapping his fingers to the attendant behind him, he said, "Sweetie. Why don't you go get my friends here a beer."

"Yes, sir, Mister Stephenson," the attendant said as she walked away.

Putting his fork and knife down, Stephenson sat back in his chair and asked, "So, why are a couple of NRDS agents ruining my lunch? I gave the broad what she wanted. What else could you possibly want from little old me?"

Ethan leaned forward and pointed a finger at him. Either it was the arrogance of Mr. Stephenson, or the pep talk from Buck, but either way, Ethan couldn't hold himself back. "You listen here, motherfucker. You're going to tell us what we want to know or I'm going to fuck you up. I mean, come on. You pay twelve dollars to my cousin for security? He's worth more than that. So why don't you get your ass off that high horse of yours and answer our questions."

Stephenson crossed his arms and looked at Buck.

Buck rested a hand on Ethan's shoulder and squeezed. "You came on a little strong, kid."

Ethan let out a deep breath and nodded. "Okay. Yeah. That sort of just . . . came out."

Stephenson rolled his eyes. "Look, my lunch is getting cold. Maybe now, after that little tantrum, the adults can talk. Just know, I don't do shit for free. You want something done. It's going to cost you."

"Oh, I haven't forgotten," Buck said.

The attendant returned and placed two beers in front of Ethan and Buck, and a third in front of Stephenson. Stephenson took a swig of his, but Ethan looked at Buck. When Buck didn't move to drink his, Ethan waited too.

Buck pulled the old brown journal from his coat and placed it on the table. Tapping it with his finger, he said, "We need some answers."

"Look at that. I haven't seen that thing in decades," Stephenson said with a grin. "Guess that old bitch I left in the basement didn't keep it as safe as I thought she would."

"Wait, you left—" Ethan started, but Buck turned and shot him a glare.

Picking the journal back up and tucking it into his jacket pocket, Buck said, "Herschel's kid. We need the name."

Stephenson took another swig, swishing the beer in his mouth before swallowing. "Which one is Herschel?"

"Died in '42. He's over at St. Patrick's?" Ethan offered.

"He fucking knows that already," Buck said.

Stephenson chuckled. "Ah, yeah. That's right. That's right. Herschel. Angry old guy? He's still there with his buddy. The soldier. Charlie? Surprised you didn't make him a BOB yet. Left him there for you."

Buck clenched his jaw before saying, "Kid's name. What is it?"

"His kid? Huh. I'm sorry. My memory just isn't what it used to be. You sure it wasn't there in the journal?" Stephenson said with a wide-toothed grin on his face.

Ethan leaned forward in his seat and spoke before Buck could cut him off. "You know damn well it isn't. You suspected Herschel's kid changed his name. You know that's what's holding Herschel here, and I bet you figured it all out, but didn't write his name. Funny too, all the records that could have helped us are missing too. So, just give us the name, and we'll take care of it."

"Right, the kid's name . . . but, you know. I tried to help Herschel. I really did. But he had nothing of value to offer. I told him I'd tell him what happened to his son when he could pay for it. Doesn't seem like he has anything new to offer yet," Stephenson said with a shrug.

"Wait? What? That's not how this is supposed to work," Ethan stammered.

"He's not too quick, is he?" Stephenson asked Buck.

"Just give me what I want and let me close it out. Or would you rather I dig up a couple skeletons in your closet?" Buck growled.

Stephenson laughed. "Please, if you had anything on me, you'd have already exposed it. You're too good to have leverage. You know how this works. What did you bring me? And if someone tries to threaten me with management again, then this meeting is over."

Ethan cracked his knuckles. "Pain. We're going to offer you pain."

Stephenson took another swig of beer. "Child. The adults are talking now."

"Northwoods," Buck said.

"Northwoods?" Ethan asked.

Stephenson cocked his head to the left.

"I have evidence that he burned it down before re-opening this one. He didn't want the competition." Buck said.

"No way. People got hurt by that. Like bad. You're like the devil," Ethan said.

Stephenson shook his head and laughed. "You've got nothing."

"Did you know that one resident was a retired librarian? She was a real mean one back in the day. I could keep going, if you want. But know that this won't stop with NRDS. You'll be talking with other law enforcement pretty quick," Buck said.

"You're bluffing. I go down, and I'm gonna take you with me," Stephenson fired back.

Leaning forward, Buck sneered. "There's nothing on me. So, you're going to give me what I want every fucking time I come here, or you can kiss your steak and beer goodbye. Unless you want to call that meat they serve in prison 'steak.'"

Ethan clapped his hands together and chimed in. "That's right. You're our bitch now."

"You don't have shit. You'd have turned it in," Stephenson said, his eyes locked on Buck.

Buck leaned back and smiled. "Fuck around and find out."

Ethan smacked the table and stood up. "Oh shit. Fuck around and find out. Oh. You. Are. Fucked."

"Reel it in," Buck said.

Ethan cleared his throat and sat back down. "Yeah. Uh. My bad. You're still our bitch, though."

Stephenson sneered and picked up his knife and fork, jamming another piece of steak into his mouth. He chewed with his mouth open, the blood seeping through his teeth. "After his mother died, Herschel's son moved to Chicago and changed his name to get away from his father's debts. He opened a butcher shop under the name Franklin Murdock. His kid still runs it. Out on North Halsted."

Buck stood and picked up the beer, taking a long drink from it before setting it down. "Pleasure doing business with you."

He turned and headed for the door without another word.

Following Buck's lead, Ethan chugged his beer. Through a loud belch, he said, "Yeah. Nice working with you, bitch."

Stephenson pointed his knife at Ethan. "Watch your fucking mouth, kid. Talk like that to me again and we'll see who kicks the bucket first."

Ethan stared at Stephenson, wide-eyed. "Uh, yeah. Um, sorry." He gave an awkward bow and quickly chased after Buck.

Twenty-Four

Cold Case

E THAN'S LEG BOUNCED UP and down in the passenger seat of the Oldsmobile Cutlass as Buck cruised down South Knowles Street. Shops flew past the window in a blur as Ethan picked at his nails. "Any chance you can go faster?" He asked after they passed by the one and only cop on duty.

"Stop moving your leg." Buck said.

Ethan stopped for a second, then the bouncing started all over again. "I can't."

"What's gotten into you?" Buck asked, his eyes on the road.

"I mean, how often have I been a part of delivering actual good news? It's always been, 'this is a routine check-in.' It feels like we've got the missing piece to a puzzle. I dunno, it just feels like we're actually doing something. It's exciting."

"Don't get your hopes too high, kid. Remember Tiger? Just because Stephenson's journal says it's going to work means nothing."

Ethan slumped in his seat, threw his head back, and complained, "Don't remind me about Tiger, ugh. Sometimes, you're the worst."

"Fix your suit and sit up. We're almost there."

Ethan buttoned his shirt and straightened his tie, checking himself in the mirror. Still not a perfect fit, but he'd been glad his gran had taken him to a get a real suit after weeks of wearing baggy, oversized ones.

Buck took a left turn and pulled up in front of an old red-brick church. The sign out front read "St. Patrick's Episcopal Church."

Ethan had been back here nearly every week since he started working for NRDS, but the memories still came flooding back. "You remember my first day?"

"Yep."

"You showed me the ropes. I didn't even know ghosts were real until then."

"I remember."

Ethan looked over at Buck and smiled. "Well, thanks."

"Of course, kid," Buck replied, pulling into a parking spot near the iron gate entrance to the cemetery.

Ethan squinted, looking past the few hundred graves and focusing his eyes on the other side. Two blobs of light formed in his vision, floating along the southern fence, heading toward them. "I think I see them, headed this way."

Buck killed the engine and looked at Ethan's hands. "You're getting good at that. Even with the badge, that'd be out of range."

Before Buck could rope him into another conversation about his sight, Ethan unbuckled and hopped out of the car, wrapping his hands around his badge and watching the blobs of light take shape. He jogged up the path to the gate and pulled open the iron gate. "Morning, guys. Hope you two are doing alright."

"Well, he's awfully chipper," Herschel said. His tan suit was wrinkled in the same places it always was.

"Ethan!" Charlie called with a smile. "Man, you will not believe what's been going on with Anthony and Martha. So much has happened. I've been making mental notes."

"Gentlemen," Buck said as he stepped beside Ethan.

"I know. I know. I have to wait until you get to the right place in the form. It's just, there has been a lot going on," Charlie said with a grin.

"No forms today," Buck said.

Herschel raised his eyebrow. "Why's that, Buck? What happened?"

Ethan bit his bottom lip and rocked on his feet. "Can I do it? Come on. I found it."

"Sure, kid," Buck said with a nod.

Ethan clapped his hands together and smiled. "Ok. Yes. Herschel, you may want to sit down."

"I'm dead. What do you think I'm gonna faint or something?" Herschel shot back.

"Good point. Okay, fine. Buck and I have been doing a ton of digging in records and journals this week, and we've got something to show you," Ethan said.

Herschel leaned against the fence and waited.

Taking out his phone, Ethan held it up for Herschel to see as he talked. "So, there is this butcher shop in Chicago, see? From what we found, it's doing really well. It has a ton of Yelp reviews. Evidently, it's like the best place to get meat in Chicago." Scrolling, Ethan said, "And there's a deli and they serve coffee. It's like a real cool spot people like to hang out at."

"I saw a place like that when I was in Europe. Little cafe in London. It was great," Charlie said.

Herschel took a step closer to Ethan and looked down at his phone. "Why are you showing me this? It's not like I can make it out to Chicago soon."

Looking back at the phone so he could find the "About" page of the website, Ethan said, "No. Sorry. I guess that would be confusing. Let me back up. So, you had a son."

"Yes," Herschel said.

Holding out the phone again, Ethan explained, "And Buck and I learned recently that after your wife died, you lost track of him, right? You were worried because he assumed all your debts, then one day he just disappeared."

Tears formed in the old spirit's eyes, and he looked away, sniffling and wiping his nose.

Ethan zoomed in on the photo, holding out an image of a young man standing in front of his new butcher shop.

"We're pretty sure that he didn't die at the hands of the debt collectors. We think he ran. He changed his name so they couldn't find him. Franklin Murdock showed up in Chicago shortly after your son disappeared, working a few different jobs before taking one with a butcher. Ended up marrying the man's daughter and, after a while, opened his own shop."

Herschel's mouth hung open as a tear rolled down his cheek.

"The kid looks a lot like you. 'Cept he somehow turned your ugly mug into something much more handsome," Charlie said.

"Murdock was my wife's name," Herschel whispered.

Ethan scrolled to the next picture and held it out again, continuing, "His shop was a huge hit. Movie stars, athletes, tons of celebrities swear by it. Jordan even used to get his meat there. In fact, it's still family-owned. Franklin's son runs it now. That's a picture of him, your grandson, Herschel Murdock."

The old man took a step back, tears freely running down his cheeks.

Buck cleared his throat. "We wanted to be certain this was him before sharing this with you. At this point, we are certain that your son lived a long and happy life."

Herschel wiped the tears from his eyes. "I didn't know what happened to him. I was worried I'd . . ."

"Your debts didn't bury him," Buck said.

"He got out of this town and created a beautiful life for himself," Ethan offered.

Herschel took a deep breath. Looking down at the ground, he said, "Thank you."

"Our pleasure," Buck said.

Charlie nudged at Herschel's ribs. "Now maybe you can stop moping about."

Herschel smiled as a faint glow hazed around him. He looked over at his grave and gasped. "Charlie. I—I can't," the old man started.

Charlie rested a hand on Herschel's shoulder. "Oh no you don't. This is your time, and you better not be thinking of sticking around for me. Get out of here, you old goat."

"You're the worst," Herschel said, a grin wide across his face, and he walked up to his grave.

Buck stepped forward. "We'll take care of Charlie, don't worry. Go find your wife and son."

"Thank you," Herschel said again as he stepped onto his grave. Light grew bright around him, blinding Ethan into closing his eyes. In his last moments, Herschel said to Charlie, "Stay out of trouble, dummy."

"See you on the other side, old timer," Charlie shouted back as his friend of fifty years vanished with the glowing light.

"We did it," Ethan said, his smile so big it threatened to cut his ears.

"Great work, rookie," Buck said.

Charlie looked around the empty cemetery and out into the fields of corn before kicking at the grass. "So, um. I guess it's just me left here to keep watch."

"Not exactly. We have good news for you too," Ethan said.

Charlie looked back at his grave. "Seriously? Don't play with me."

Buck shook his head. "It isn't anything to do with crossing over. Not yet. But we put in the paperwork for you to join the BOB program. They accepted you this morning."

Charlie jumped and thrust his fist into the air in celebration. "No way! That has to be good, right? Saving souls, hunting ghosts. Surely that helps get through the pearly gates."

Buck nodded. "Many BOBs find the light from their service. Especially the ones who weren't able to find closure in their lives."

"And besides, I know you're going to make a great BOB," Ethan said.

"Oh, man. You guys will not be sorry. I'm going to make you so proud. I get to be a NRDS agent and be out in the field. See some action again. This is going to be amazing!"

"We still have additional paperwork to fill out," Buck said.

"Of course you do. Guess I better get used to that too." Charlie laughed.

"An extraction team from management will be here to exhume your remains in a few days. They'll take you through basic training," Buck said.

"I'm going to bust so many ghosts. You'll see. I'm going to be the best BOB in history. Do I get to work with you guys?"

Buck shook his head. "We only get one BOB out here, and that position is currently filled. They'll put you somewhere else. I will put in a good word."

"I'd love somewhere with a nice fall. Like Maine? Or Connecticut? These fields really cramp the fall vibes sometimes. But I guess it doesn't matter. I'm just pumped about getting out of here."

"You'll do great, I know it," Ethan said.

Clapping his hands, Charlie said, "Oh crap. I almost forgot about the news I've been sitting on. So, this dude showed up, big guy. He looked pissed. Anyway, he showed up and he and Anthony got into a big fight. Chipped Anthony's tooth too. It was bad."

"What do you think it was? A lover's quarrel?" Ethan said with a grin.

"No. The big guy kept talking about money. Sounded like a real estate thing. The guy was here to yell at Martha, but Anthony stepped in. He threatened her. Said she needed to stop telling the parishioners not to sell," Charlie said.

"Did the man say anything else? Like why they are trying to buy?" Buck asked.

"No, sorry. He didn't," Charlie said.

"Did you get the guy's name?" Buck asked.

"No, but he said he worked for a Chaz something?"

"The guy running for mayor? Chax Tamish?" Ethan asked.

"Yeah. That's right. He even said she better get her head on straight before Chax becomes mayor, or she'd be sorry," Charlie said with a grin.

"Nice work, Charlie." Buck said with a nod.

"You got it, boss. Heh, really boss, now that we're on the same team," Charlie replied.

"We'd best be off. Thanks for the good work, Charlie. I'll find out where they end up posting you. Maybe we'll come by for old times' sake." Buck said.

Ethan and Buck walked to the car and got in. As Ethan fastened his seat belt, he said, "Man, I love this job."

"It has its moments," Buck replied.

"You want to call Gerry? We should go celebrate."

Fastening his own seat belt, Buck said, "I don't know if you can handle another Gerry dinner."

"What? Please. I can handle another night with Gerry. I did great last time. I just. Just make sure Alexus doesn't kidnap me again."

"Alright, rookie. Call him and ask him where he wants to meet up," Buck said, tossing Ethan his phone.

Twenty-Five

Fresh Case

R IVER KICKED IN THE office door and jumped into the office, arms outstretched and a grin on his face. "Good morning, guys and ghouls. You are not going to believe what we just saw."

Bob phased in through the door behind him and glared at River. "Don't take joy in other people's misery, chickenshit."

"I'm not 'taking joy', you happiness-munching asshole. I'm just sharing news," River shot back as he threw his coat on his desk.

"You're late," Buck said, keeping his eyes on his computer.

Alexus spun in her chair and threw a pen up into the ceiling panel. "So, are you calling him a jerk that chews on joy, or—"

Ethan jumped in, spinning in his chair and launching himself across the room to side up against Alexus. "Or is he, like, a sphincter that literally consumes happiness?"

"Clearly the second," Trevor added as he picked up his phone from Doris's desk and panned the room.

River plopped down in his chair and sneered at Buck. "I got here exactly when I intended to get here. But thanks for keeping tabs, Dad."

"Try calling me that again. See what happens," Buck said in reply.

River looked around. "Wait, where's the boss?"

Ethan shrugged and looked at her empty office. "Said she needed to fly out to DC for a meeting. She'll be back next week, I guess."

Bob grunted and shook his head. "'You're so full of shit. Exactly when you intended? Sure. After you slept through three alarms. Undisciplined dullard."

"Wow, Bob. Tossing out them big words," Ethan clipped.

"Wait, what'd he say?" Trevor asked.

Doris smiled and patted his leg. "It's frustrating, isn't it?"

"Undisciplined dullard," Buck said.

Turning the phone to Buck, Trevor asked, "Wait, is that what Bob said or are you calling someone that?"

Bob leaned against the wall leading to the break room and crossed his arms. "You're awfully chipper today, Rookie. Find yourself a moose to bang?"

"A moose?" Ethan asked.

"You know, a girlfriend. Finally found someone to take pity on you or just give yourself the old one-hand salute?" Bob said.

"He sent one over yesterday," Buck said.

Alexus stuck out her hand and high-fived Ethan so hard the pop echoed in the room. "Nice. Finally popped that cherry."

Ethan rubbed his hand as it turned a bright red. "Thanks. It was pretty awesome."

River rolled into Trevor's view and waved his arms at the camera. "Just for everyone's information, I didn't sleep through three alarms. I strategically set those alarms so I can get up by the third one. Not all of us are morning people."

Bob pushed off the wall and walked behind Doris, eyeing her computer. "Maybe if you didn't hotbox yourself in every night and read a book or two instead, you'd only need one alarm. We didn't get no second or third alarm. When the horn went off, if you didn't hit the deck, your ass was beat."

"Like you ever read when you were alive. Don't you fucking lie," River snapped back.

"Wait? Is Bob lying? Come on, can somebody translate," Trevor begged, moving his camera around the room.

"What does reading a book have to do with waking up? That doesn't make any fucking sense," Alexus said.

Stomping his foot, causing Doris's monitor to flicker on and off, Bob yelled, "I'm so flabbergasted by all you disorderly crybabies not comprehending the words coming out of my mouth!"

"Seriously? What's with the vocabulary upgrade?" Ethan asked.

River turned to Ethan and laughed. "I got super high last night and passed out to some British history documentary," River said.

"Come on, guys. Is anybody going to tell me what's going on? Please?" Trevor pleaded.

Still yelling, Bob declared, "This is how I always talk, you unruly clowndicks!"

"He called them unruly clowndicks," Buck said, still not looking away from his computer screen.

"That's not a vocabulary upgrade," Trevor mumbled in confusion.

"It most certainly is not," Doris agreed.

"Yeah, pretty sure I rolled over on the remote at some point and switched it to Comedy Central," River said.

Bob sat down in an empty chair near the entrance and crossed his arms. With a pout, he said, "You dimwits would turn old Catholic nuns into Buddhists from the shit you talk about, 'cause there is no way in hell anyone could get this dumb in one fucking lifetime."

River held his stomach as he let out a loud laugh. "Now, that one was pretty good."

"Three points to Bob. Who's keeping score?" Ethan said.

Trevor sighed and tossed his camera onto the desk. "Goddamn it."

"Hey! Listen here, you motherfucker. Don't you take the Good Lord's name in vain," Bob shouted.

River wadded up a piece of paper and threw it through Bob. "Hey, dipshit. He can't hear you."

Doris took a sip of her coffee, pushed up her glasses, then asked, "I'm sorry, but didn't you say you saw something?"

Smacking the table, River said, "Oh shit! Bob, you asshole. You almost made me forget."

"Go drink a warm cup of shut-the-fuck-up, you dumb peon," Bob griped.

"Eh, that didn't stick the landing like the last one," Alexus commented.

Ethan smirked. "Should we take points off the board for that?"

Bob glared and stood up from his seat, pointing at River, and shouted in his best drill sergeant voice, "Fine, you want an insult? You should have been a blowjob, you dumb shit! If I wasn't a ghost, I'd 300-Spartan kick your ass into the next dark pit I see to save everyone else from the fucking waste of breath you make, bitch!"

River, Alexus, and Ethan all gave Bob a slow clap of respect as Buck continued to type.

"Ugh, when will you get me a badge, boss?" Trevor said, turning the phone to Doris.

"Ha! I don't get one, so you certainly won't. So, River . . . what did you see?" Doris asked River again.

Standing up for dramatic effect, River held up his hands and said, "Okay. Okay. Okay. Look. There must be some major shit going down. I mean, like eat-a-four-pound-burrito-and-now-you-regret-it-shit happening. I mean, like, crack the porcelain throne big. Big. Major something's-going-down-in-tiny-town news."

Bob let out a huff and interrupted, "We passed a house covered in caution tape with five police cars out front."

River slowly turned and met Bob's eyes; mouth wide open. "What? Come on, man. Why do you have to be so mean to me?"

Bob smiled.

Ethan raised an eyebrow. "Huh, I think New Richmond only owns two squads? That means they pulled in some state-level stuff."

"Jesus. Please. For the love of everything that is holy, someone fill me in," Trevor begged.

"House, caution tape, five police cars," Buck said as he typed.

"Oh, you mean the triple homicide?" Trevor asked.

Alexus sat up in her chair, eyes glistening like a puppy and trained on Trevor. "Wait. A murder?! Go on."

He picked up his phone again and scrolled, pausing on the screen before saying, "News broke out like an hour ago. Looks like it's made it national. Trending on Twitter too. They're calling it the #brotherlylovemurder. That's pretty dark. Anyway, some dude offed his three brothers and then shot himself."

"Wait, are you talking about the Meyers?" Ethan asked.

Trevor nodded.

"Holy shit. There was a rumor that they were going to kill each other, all living in the same house, but shit. I mean, they all hated each other," Ethan said.

Alexus and River both jumped up from their chairs at the same time and shouted, "Dibs!"

Alexus shoved River and said, "Nope. I called it first."

River stomped his feet and looked at Buck for support. "Come on. I don't want to be stuck in the office today. It's a triple homicide-suicide. Guaranteed that nothing like this is going to happen here again."

Still typing, Buck interjected. "Both of you go. And take Ethan too. With a potential of four angry spirits, you're going to need the extra hands."

Alexus practically skipped across the room and pulled down two empty briefcases from the wall. She threw them at Ethan and said, "Malik's the chauffeur." Taking two more, she thrust them at River and said, "And I've got shotgun."

River looked at Bob and glowered. "Well, now I don't know if I want to go."

"You're going, so suck it up," Buck said.

Trevor hopped up and blocked the exit. "Wait, can I come too? Pretty please? Maybe I can stream the action."

"If it gets you out of here, fine. But you stay behind the police tape. Got it?" Buck said.

"Aww, no fun. Can I at least get a badge?" Trevor asked.

"No," Buck and Doris said at the same time.

Alexus pulled on her black leather jacket and pushed Trevor out of the way. "It's a party then. Let's go, dum-dums."

Trevor, River, and Bob all squeezed into the back of Ethan's car. River physically pressed himself up against the side of the car while Bob took the center seat. Not knowing any better, Trevor hopped into the car, sitting partially through Bob. He shivered and rubbed his arm, looking at Ethan. "Geez, man, it's freezing out. Why do you have the air blasting cold?"

Ethan held up the keys, "Dude, you're half inside Bob. Car's not even on."

Trevor's eyes widened, and he looked to the center of the seat, moving himself against the glass while slowly slipping his hand in and out of the center. "That's so fucking cool."

"Ha-ha, Trevor's inside you."

Bob looked at River. "Tell him to cut it out or all your coffee is going to be cold here on out."

River grimaced and reached through Bob and grabbed Trevor's hand. "Stop, or Bob's gonna possess you."

"Really? Oh geez. I'm sorry, uh, Bob. I didn't mean—"

"You two cut it out. We need our game faces on if we're gonna get past the cops," Alexus said.

"Wait? The cops know about us, right?" Ethan asked.

"Yeah, but doesn't mean they like us. Just walk up with your badge out and say you're with the Feds. Works every time," Alexus said.

"Not every time," River said.

"Maybe not for you." Alexus added.

"Yeah, and she doesn't look like a little bitch who calls his mommy before bedtime," Bob said with a grin.

Pointing at Bob, River yelled, "Hey! She just had knee surgery, asshole!"

Trevor flipped through his phone and sighed. "We need to set some ground rules about you guys telling me what the ghost says."

In a high-pitched whine, Bob mocked Trevor. "We need to set some ground rules."

"Bob, what the fuck? What's got you all hyped up today?" Alexus said.

River laughed. "He's still mad at me."

"For what?" Ethan asked.

"I told him we'd watch Braveheart last night. Poor guy's never seen it. Anyway, I let him watch the first two hours. And then, right in the middle of a battle, I flipped it to an antique roadshow."

"Motherfucker," Bob complained under his breath.

Turning in her seat, Alexus reached back and pounded River on the knee.

"Ow!" River screamed, gripping his knee with both hands.

Alexus pointed a long finger at him and said, "You're supposed to take care of him, asshole."

Still holding his knee, River looked out the window and said, "I didn't ask for this shit."

"Nope. You slept with your supervisor's daughter, then broke her heart by sleeping with her brother. Dumbass," Bob said with a laugh.

"Wait? What?" Ethan asked.

"Lucky you didn't get fired for that and were just assigned a BOB instead," Alexus said.

Trevor tapped on Ethan's shoulder and pointed to a two-story building up the street. "That's the house up there."

Police swarmed around the property like ants, weaving through the caution tape. Not only were the five cop cars still there, but now two ambulances were parked out front, along with a growing crowd of people.

"You think someone survived?" Ethan asked.

"Nope. They're carrying in body bags. Pull up over there," Alexus said, pointing to an empty curb a half-block from the house.

Alexus hopped out of the car first, before Ethan killed the engine. The others had to run to catch up with her, reaching her before she approached the nearest cop, held up her badge, and said, "I'm with the Feds. Where are the bodies?"

Twenty-Six

The Clicker

E THAN HELD ON TO the two briefcases, racing to keep in step with Alexus as she reached the police line and held out her badge. "I'm with the Feds. Where are the bodies?"

The chubby cop eyed her over his clipboard and grimaced. "The Feds aren't here yet."

Bob slipped past them, sticking out his hand and passing it through the cop, laughing as the man crossed his eyes and let out a shiver. "I'll get a closer look."

River pushed past Ethan, holding the other two briefcases in his hands and Bob's bag under his arm. "Who's the detective in charge?"

Lowering his clipboard and rolling his eyes, the officer said, "I am."

"Bullshit you are," River said, looking him up and down.

"Yet I'm on this side of the line, and you're not. Want to be over here? Be on my list," the cop shot back.

Holding up the camera on his phone, Trevor said, "Hi, officer. I'm streaming this. Would you care to explain why you're holding up a federal investigation?"

The officer sneered at the camera. "Why don't you get back in your clown car and drive back under whatever rock you crawled out of? I don't care what kind of fake badges you flash at me; I'm not letting you by."

From thirty yards ahead, Bob yelled, "Will you guys hurry? I can't get a good vantage point from here."

Putting her finger in the cop's face, Alexus said, "Listen here, tubby. If you don't let us by—"

Before she could finish her threat, a deep voice from up the hill called, "Let 'em through, Terry" Ethan looked past the heavyset officer to see a short man in a rumpled suit and tie.

Officer Terry pointed to his eyes and then to Alexus and River and said, "I'm watching you."

Alexus shoved past the officer and knocked down his clipboard. "Don't poke your eyes out, Doorstop."

Following behind her, River laughed and said, "Yeah, yeah, Doorstop. Always watching."

Bob ran forward, pressing up against his invisible barrier. "Yo! Pothead! Just throw the damn bag!"

"You're not getting in there before me, asshole!" River yelled as he raced up the hill after Alexus.

"He's talking to Bob again?" Trevor asked.

"Aren't you supposed to stay behind the tape?" Ethan replied.

"Aren't you supposed to mind your own damn business?"

As they approached the house, they passed four mud-covered pickups and a rusted swing set in the front yard. The wrap-around porch and two stories were covered in peeling blue paint, and the small, round attic window was busted out. Atop that, broken shutters and weed-infested flower beds showed the state of care that had been missing from this house for a long time.

Arriving at the second officer, Alexus flashed her badge again. "I need to get into the house."

Bob slipped in through the door and shouted, "Hallway, clear!"

Giving them a halfhearted smile, the detective said, "Yeah, yeah. I've worked with you vultures before. My guys are almost done."

"Vultures?" Trevor asked.

The detective laughed. "Because you clean up the dead?"

Alexus stood inches from the detective's face and said, "Cool, insults. Listen up, donut wrangler. If you don't want one of your men to get himself possessed and wake up a week later with his bare ass up in the air on some sandy beach with no recollection of how he got there, then I suggest you let us through."

The detective raised his eyebrow. "Well, that seems highly specific. Look, my guys are almost done. Nothing's even happened yet."

Ethan shifted his weight and heard something fall onto the porch.

Trevor moved in behind him, picking it up. "Oh, is this one of those fancy ghost things? Do I press it?"

Ethan turned and looked at the clicker he'd stolen from Melissa. "No! Don't press—"

Trevor pressed the button.

River looked at Trevor, then Ethan. "And what the fuck is that?"

Dropping his briefcases and grabbing at his hair, Ethan yelled, "Oh, Jesus! Why would you do that?"

Alexus snapped her fingers at him. "Hey! Focus! What the fuck is it?"

Ethan snatched the clicker out of Trevor's hands and shoved it back into his pocket. "I swiped it from Melissa. She made me use it back at the conference to ramp up Detroit BOB so I'd catch him off guard."

River set down his cases and lit up a joint. "Well, shit's about to get interesting."

Screams echoed from inside the house, followed by a cacophony of loud crashes. Bob came shooting out the second-floor window and slammed into the ground. "Holy motherfucking shit! Confirmed Class Fours, maybe a Five."

"Bob, you okay?" River shouted.

"Like I'm about to fucking explode. I think they did something."

Officers ran out of the house, knocking the detective back and clearing a path inside.

"What about the bodies?" the detective yelled at them.

"Fuck that. Shit's flying everywhere," one cop clapped back.

A silver toaster came flying through the door, nearly colliding with the detective's head before it passed through Bob as he stood. "Bastard hillbilly assholes!"

"Can we go in now?" Alexus asked the detective.

He waved her off. "Fine. Take care of it. We need to get those bodies out of there and to the morgue before they start causing a stink."

He turned and gestured for the officers to follow him back to the police line.

Trevor held up his camera to the open door and said, "So, what now?"

Alexus picked up a briefcase and turned it over. "There's no talking them down now. Thanks to Ethan."

"Hey, why me? Trevor pressed the—"

Alexus jabbed a finger in his chest. "You brought the stupid clicker. So shut up and grab a briefcase. Bob! Intel, now!"

"They got strong. Quick. They're all fighting with each other. Three of them have gone to Class Four, one of them is at Class Five. There are guns all over the place too, so if one of them gets their hands on one . . ."

Ethan turned to Trevor. "Bob says they have guns."

"Wait. Like ghost guns or real guns? How are they . . ." Trevor trailed off.

Alexus looked at River. "Remember Midville Factory?"

River took a long drag on his joint and nodded. "How could I not? All twenty-two ghosts, peaking at Class Five, all cased in one fell swoop. Man, primo work."

"How many exits?" Alexus asked Bob.

"Just two. Front door and back door. Go in the front, past the living room, into the kitchen, hang a left, and you're going out the garage door. But the house is a mess. There's crap everywhere."

"Okay. River, I need you setting up the cases in the garage. The rest of us are going to prepare for Midville and chase them out." Alexus said.

"Hold up. You want us to run into a house full of guns and ghosts?" Ethan said.

"Yeah, I'm out." Trevor said and turned away from the house.

Alexus grabbed his shirt collar and pulled him back. "We have to stall so River can set up too."

"I'm not supposed to be back here. Buck said I should stay behind the police line," Trevor said with a nervous laugh.

River dropped a stack of briefcases in Trevor's arms. "And yet here you are. You're coming with me for that sweet shot for the social, mkay?"

"Alright. You got two minutes. Got it?" Alexus yelled.

River gave her a thumbs up as he kept walking. "I'll ping your phone when I'm ready."

Alexus looked at her watch. "On four, we run for it."

Bob looked at Ethan and said, "If they go for a gun, duck."

"Wait, what do I do?" Ethan asked, looking at the entrance and back at Alexus.

"Run in like an idiot and keep their attention. Ready? One."

"Fuck. Fuck. Fuck," Ethan muttered.

"Four!" Alexus screamed as she charged up the front porch stairs.

"Ahhhh!" Ethan and Buck both screamed as they ran behind her.

Alexus raced through the open door and stopped in the foyer. Ethan crashed right into her, and Bob passed right through them. The house was terrifyingly silent. Straight ahead of them were stairs and a hallway that led to the kitchen. To the left was a living room filled with torn-up furniture, beer cans, and pizza boxes. To the right was another room that was void of furniture but was still littered with beer cans and other trash.

"Well, isn't this lovely? Bob, where are they?" Alexus said.

"Oh, they're here," Bob replied.

"Are you sure? It's so quiet," Ethan said.

"Look out!" Bob screamed, pointing up.

Ethan and Alexus glanced up just in time to see a forty-five-pound dumbbell flying toward them from the ceiling.

"Move!" Alexus screamed as they jumped out of the way, and the weight slammed on the ground with a giant crash.

"Incoming!" Bob screamed again as more weights came flying from the second floor.

"Run!" Alexus yelled as she darted into the empty room.

Ethan charged the other direction as another weight crashed into the floor behind him.

"Don't worry. I got this one!" Bob yelled as weights continued to rain down around him.

Ethan only got a foot into the living room before he had to react. He threw himself into a backbend, narrowly avoiding a baseball bat that swung inches from his face.

As he regained composure, his foot clanked through beer cans and stumbled on the wooden floor. A transparent Meyer brother, dressed in denim overalls, smiled right at him.

Popping up, Ethan held out his hands and said, "Hold up. Luke, right? Let's just take a breath."

A different Meyer, this one in jeans and a bloodied T-shirt, appeared at the door to the kitchen. Gripping a cast-iron skillet in his right hand and a waffle maker in his left, he screamed, "Get out!"

Luke laughed and charged at his brother. His bat collided with the frying pan, sending a loud clang through the house. The T-shirted brother countered with his waffle maker, but it flew through Luke's head and burst through the drywall instead.

"What the hell, guys?" Ethan shouted.

Both brothers turned to face him and screamed together, "Get out!"

Dirty T-shirt Meyer screamed "Grah!" as he threw his waffle maker as hard as he could at Ethan while Luke charged again with his bat at the ready.

Ethan ducked the waffle maker but was smacked in the head by the cord. "Dammit! Gary, fucking stop," he yelled in pain as he reached into his pocket to grab his badge.

Passing through the couch in the middle of the room, Luke took his shot and swung at Ethan again with all his might. Dropping to one knee and rolling to the left, Ethan moved out of the way just in time. Rolling a second time, he avoided the bat's downward arch as it crashed into the floor next to him. "No!" he yelled as he scrambled backwards, nearly dodging the frying pan coming for his head.

Sitting on his butt, trapped in the corner of the room, Ethan held out his badge. His heart raced as he said, "Now just wait! Shit!"

The two Meyers approached, laughing to themselves.

"I'm a federal agent! I'm here to help!" Ethan yelled, holding out his badge.

Gary leaned in and looked at the badge. "Don't give a shit," he said with a grin. Raising the frying pan above his head, he was about to strike when suddenly there was an explosion of activity from the foyer.

Forty-five- and twenty-five-pound dumbbells flew into the living room like frisbees as Bob raced through the doorway. "Got the Five on my six!" Bob screamed as he pivoted to dart through the kitchen.

In the doorway, a raging Meyer appeared. His eyes burned red with fury. He held a weight in each hand. Seeing his brothers, he screamed, "Why won't you bastards die!" as he hurled a weight at Luke and Gary. The weight spun through the room, passed through Gary's chest, and lodged itself into the drywall an inch above Ethan's head.

Ethan's heart raced as he looked up at the weight that would have taken his head off had its aim been a few inches lower.

The brothers in the living room turned and sneered. Charging through the couch with their weapons at the ready, they advanced on their brother. With a laugh, the red-eyed brother dropped the weight he was holding and reached to his right for a shotgun that was leaning against the wall. "You two aren't gonna gang up on me ever again."

"Take cover!" Bob screamed at Ethan.

Ethan curled into a fetal position, covering his head with both arms, as a shotgun blast rang through the living room. Dust from shattered ceiling drywall sprinkled around him. Glancing up, he saw all three brothers swinging their weapons wildly at each other, none of them making contact, until the red-eyed Meyer dropped his gun and opted to use his fists. With a powerful right hook, he clocked Luke, causing the bat-wielding brother to fall backward and crash to the ground.

Gary took a step back, and before the red-eyed Meyer could advance, Alexus raced through the kitchen screaming, "Now! Now! Now!" A lumbering, heavyset Meyer plodded after her.

Jumping to his feet, Ethan yelled, "Hey! Dipshits! You remember me?"

All four brothers paused their fight to look at him. The red-eyed one cocked his head as if he were searching for a memory.

Smiling, Ethan said, "Playoffs. Fourth and twenty-four. You were up by three. Then I ran past all three of your stupid asses for the touchdown."

Recognition flashed on the Meyers' faces.

"And then," Ethan continued with increasing gusto, "I banged your cousin Elli under the bleachers to celebrate!"

The four Meyers raised their weapons. "Kill the twerp!"

"Run!" Bob screamed.

Ethan's eyes grew wide, and he scrambled for the opening to the kitchen, ducking as the frying pan flew across the room and smashed into the wall above him. Taking a sharp turn, Ethan saw the door to the garage open in front of him.

"Incoming!" Bob screamed.

Refusing to look back at the crashing behind him, Ethan raced for the glowing blue of open cases that filled the garage door. At the threshold, he dove headfirst, soaring over four open briefcases. The heat from the cases burned his skin as he passed above them. Landing on the concrete floor of the garage, he heard the cases snap closed behind him.

"Yes!" Trevor yelled.

"Nice job, rookie!" Bob yelled, walking into the garage.

Leaning down to help him up, Alexus said, "I totally thought they'd shot you."

Coming to his feet, Ethan looked at the four closed and smoking cases on the ground. His heart still pounding in his chest, he said, "I thought they were going to kill me."

Offering him a lit joint, River said, "You really bang their cousin?"

Ethan took a drag and let the smoke rest in his lungs. Blowing out, he said, "I wish. She's crazy hot."

"Alright, dummies. Grab the cases. Beer is on me," Alexus said.

Twenty-Seven

Sex Ghosts

A LEXUS PULLED INTO THE parking lot and flipped open her center console. "Alright douche nozzles. Badges, in here."

"Wait. What? I thought this was a mission?" Ethan said from the passenger seat. He had on a new navy suit that didn't quite fit, restricting him from turning fully.

Alexus whipped around and looked in the backseat. "What the fuck, River? You were supposed to tell him."

River, wearing a flowing knit cardigan and multicolored hippie pants, tossed his badge into the console and plopped Bob's bag on the seat next to him. "Dude, trying to convince this idiot that the three of us were going to some speed dating event together was worse than talking to Buck about . . . well, anything."

"So, it is a mission?"

Alexus rolled her eyes and pulled lipstick out from a small purse. Two things Ethan had never seen her handle. "Yeah. We're here to see why the hell the auditor is here," she said as she checked her lips in the rearview mirror.

Ethan pulled his badge from his pocket. "And we don't need these?"

Alexus shook her head. "We are about to go into an old-ass hotel in the middle of a gay district, in a conference room full of horny people using a dating mixer as a cover to get laid. Do I really need to put two and two together on what kind of ghosts you might see in there?"

"Wait. What?" Bob shouted, his eyes focusing on the building in front of them.

Ethan was the only one that looked at him, badge still in hand.

River patted the bag on the seat next to him. "And you get to stay in the car."

Bob swung at him, and River shivered. "If you sons-of-bitches don't take me in there, I'm going to . . ." The overhead light in the car started to flicker.

Alexus looked up. "Bob, if you fuck with my car, I'm going to burn your bones."

The lights stopped flickering.

Ethan tossed his badge into the center console with the other two. "Maybe you should take him? Like, what if we get attacked by horny ghosts?"

"It's a good thing you're pretty," River said.

A silhouette of Bob nodded, more like an after image now that Ethan wasn't holding his badge. He gulped and blinked, but Bob just became more and more clear. "On second thought, maybe he should stay in the car. And I could stay here and keep him company?" Ethan said.

The lights flickered again as Bob began thrashing in his seat like an angry toddler.

River picked up the bag and popped open the door. "Okay. Okay. I don't need Alexus punching me for you being a dickwad. You can play with the horny ghosts."

Minutes later, they stepped into the hotel. Ethan was sweating in anticipation of what he might see. As they walked through the lobby, he had to do his best to ignore a heavyset naked man ghost going to town with a significantly older spirit while a family sat next to them, completely unaware of the acts happening inches from their faces.

"You feeling alright? You're, like, dripping in sweat?" River remarked.

Ethan laughed uncomfortably. "Yep. Um. Nothing to see here. Nothing at all."

"Weirdo," Alexus said.

Ethan hoped that was going to be it. A little fornication in the lobby—two happy spirits having a good time with each other—but stepping into the conference room, all his hopes were dashed.

In the first second in the room, he saw more ghost dicks, ghost boobs, and ghost assholes than he could have possibly imagined. They filled every corner of his view, coming at him in all shapes and sizes. Large, thin, young, impossibly old—you name it. They filled every empty space with their gyrating hips and ghostly moans.

Bob stood right next to Ethan, his eyes averted upward and constantly clearing his throat as a large-breasted female spirit passed him by, rubbing his crotch with her hand. "Sorry. On duty," he mumbled.

Alexus snapped her fingers in Ethan's face. "Yo. Earth to Ethan."

"Wha-what?" he stammered.

"You gonna sign in or what?"

He shook his head, trying to keep the images burning his eyes from sticking to his brain. "Uh, yeah. Sign in. Um, you didn't really say why there'd be horny ghosts. Am I just to, uh, assume I'm surrounded by, like, an orgy?" He tried to fake a laugh.

River elbowed him in the ribs. "Orgy, ha! No, nothing like this attracts that much attention. You know that thing people say they can feel? That . . . sexual tension. Well, it's real, and it's like cocaine to ghosts. I bet there's ten in here, tops, just doing their thing."

Ethan quickly scanned the room and stopped counting at thirty.

River patted him on the back. "Now go sign in like a good little boy and mingle. Signal if you get eyes on the auditor."

Before Ethan could say anything else, River dove into the crowd of people.

Bob turned to follow River, then froze as a burly naked man stared at him with his hands on his hips. He shouted into the crowd. "I . . . I think I'll stay here and guard the perimeter." Of course, River couldn't hear him, but nonetheless, he stood at attention, hands behind his back, his eyes gazing at the ceiling.

Ethan shook his head and looked at the sign-in table. He'd expected to see a sign-up sheet or nametags. Instead, there were three ghosts, fucking. Two men and a woman sprawled out on the table, interlocked and balanced in ways Ethan wouldn't have imagined possible.

"Hi there. Are you looking to sign in?" A voice called behind the undulating spectacle.

"Uh, yes, where do I . . ." Ethan said as his eyes locked on a bubbly brown woman sitting at the other side of the table.

"Fill this out, and we'll get you signed in. Feel free to skip any questions you aren't comfortable answering. This is a safe space."

Ethan took the clipboard and looked over the questions. A myriad of preferences and pronouns filled the sheet. Minutes later, he felt like the most vanilla person in the room as he handed the clipboard back.

She handed him his nametag with two colored stickers and a little notecard. "These stickers indicate your preferences. Here is a cheat sheet so you know how to decode everyone else. Go ahead and mingle, and we will send you a text with possible matches for you to find. Good luck!"

He turned and looked at the crowd. Every living person looked normal. Most of them were well dressed and holding cocktails. But in between them, it was a clusterfuck of gyrating nudity as parts were thrust into other parts and bodies shifted back and forth.

Deciding not to walk into that, he retreated to a clear space against the wall with a glass of wine as his barrier between him and whatever hell Alexus and River had dragged him to.

Ethan jumped as a nasally voice next to him said, "Not one for large crowds?"

Ethan turned and saw the auditor leaning against the wall next to his right. Shocked by his presence, Ethan said, "Shit, uh, Mr. Fillmore. I'm sorry. I, um, didn't see you there."

"You can call me Bryce." He waved his phone screen at Ethan. "Looks like we might be a match."

Ethan pulled out his phone and saw one new missed text message that read, "Bryce Fillmore."

"We could sit here in silence for a little bit. Make that matchmaker feel like she did her job, or we could fill dead air? I'll leave it up to you."

Ethan shifted against the wall and gulped. "I . . . I guess we could talk. What do you want to talk about?"

Bryce smiled. "I'll take it easy on you. Let's start with something easy. How about you tell me about something exciting you've done?"

Sweat covered Ethan's palms, and he almost dropped his wine glass. "Oh, well. Um . . . I don't really get out much. Not anymore. I guess there was this one time. A few buddies from high school went whitewater rafting out in Colorado. That was pretty exciting. I got this scar on my thigh from it." Ethan's face flushed at the mention of his thigh.

Bryce smiled. "An adventurer with the wounds to prove it. Very nice."

"What about you?"

"I can't say I've done anything as daring as whitewater rafting, but I was once pulled onstage at a drag show in New York and forced to sing Cher against three other guys."

"Did you win?"

"Absolutely not."

They both laughed, and the animosity Ethan had been holding against him started to fade. At that moment, Bryce just seemed like a normal guy. An uptight, rule following, potentially nefariously intentioned guy, but normal—with a life outside of the office, friends, and maybe even a family—who was just looking for love like everybody else.

Bryce reached his hand into his pocket and nodded off to the crowd. "I saw the other two in that mess of people. It's a little strange for three agents to be close enough to go out on a speed date together. Wouldn't you agree?"

"I mean, I don't know how weird it is. Seems pretty normal. Just some co-workers at a ghost orgy."

"I mean, that pothead agent of yours is carrying a Bob around, if I'm not mistaken."

"Not much else to do around here, I guess."

Bryce nodded. "Or maybe you aren't here for the ghost orgy. Maybe you came to spy on me. Did you come to spy on me, Agent Malik?"

Ethan laughed nervously. "What? Spy? Come on. That's ridiculous. How would we even know you were going to be here?"

"It's on my inter-office calendar."

"What? I didn't even know that was a thing."

He pulled out a keychain with a small handheld device that looked like a smaller version of the clicker Ethan stole. "Want to see what I'm up to, Agent Malik?"

"Wait? What's that?"

Bryce clicked the button. Suddenly, the crowd of ghosts all gave out a loud and haunting moan as the lights above flickered off and on for a few seconds. The crowd of people gave a collective gasp, and once all the lights came back on, they let out a resounding chuckle. "It seems that every time I press this button, the crowd gets more and more interested in each other. Odd that a mixer event like this has become so much more intimate than any other one I've been to. It's practically an orgy of conversation, don't you think?"

A naked old man came running through the wall and through Ethan, leaving him nauseated as he watched the ghostly man's ass run head-first into the orgy mosh pit.

"Wait, are you causing the ghosts to—"

River and Alexus flanked them right at that second.

"Hello creepy auditor man," River said. "Fancy meeting you here."

"You three as well." Bryce said.

"This is a mixer for locals. Why are you here?" Alexus said.

"That's none of your business." Bryce straightened his suit jacket and looked at Ethan. "Well, our conversation was rather pleasant. Perhaps we can continue this chat in the future?"

"I . . . Um. Yeah. Maybe."

Bryce nodded and turned on his heels, leaving the conference room.

Alexus snapped her fingers at Ethan. "Yo, lover boy. You see anything?"

"Yeah. He had another clicker."

River shivered as a very curvy naked woman and a tall bearded naked man sporting a beer gut passed through him. He shut his eyes. "I don't want to know."

Alexus tapped her chin and looked at the crowd. "Could be ramping up the sexual tension in the room?"

Ethan's eyes stayed on the ghostly woman longer than he'd intended, and Bob shouted, "Avert your eyes, Private Pervy."

Ethan darted his eyes to the ground and muttered, "I'm not a pervert."

Alexus tilted her head. "Uh, who are you talking to there, buddy?"

Ethan's eyes flushed red. Had he just spoken to Bob without his badge? In front of Alexus and River? "Shit. Shit. Shit."

River looked at Alexus and smirked. "He just talked to Bob."

Alexus stared at Ethan.

"What? No."

Alexus stared at Ethan longer.

"Alright! Alright! Yes. I see him. I see all this. I see those ghosts over there in a sixty-nine, and I see that old granny gesticulating in ways her hips should not allow her to, and that couple over there—Jesus! I don't even know what the fuck they're doing. And when he hit the clicker, it got worse. And you're wrong, River. It's a big-ass, pun literally intended, orgy in here. Like hundreds of giant asses and old asses and all the asses that you never want to see! Dammit! So many fucking asses fucking each other! FUCK!"

River let out a roaring laugh and held out his hand to Alexus. "Pay up."

She fumbled through her purse and threw a wad of cash at him. "I'm never letting you trick me into another bet again."

"You knew?" Ethan asked.

River flipped through the wad of cash and neatly placed it in his pocket. "I suspected. You're super easy to read."

"You're not going to tell anyone, right?"

Alexis shook her head. "Fuck no. They'll ship you off to HQ if they find out you're psychic. NRDS doesn't get its hands on many these days."

"Psychic? I'm not a psychic."

River wrapped his arm around Ethan's shoulders. "Medium, psychic. Basically, the same thing. Regardless, you see without the badge, and that makes you a little more interesting in this Podunk town."

Ethan let out a sigh and let go of the questions he had bubbling to the surface. Instead, he looked at the crowd, seeing several living people breaking the awkward tension and making out right in the middle of the room. "What do we do about them?"

Alexus shrugged. "Pretty sure the intake girl has a stash of condoms. Seems like she's hosted more than one of these before. With Captain Clicker gone, I think it'll die down."

River loosened his tie. "Oh, I don't think so. Pretty sure it's just getting started."

Alexus held out her hand. "So, you want me to take Bob and you can get yourself an Uber in the morning?"

River shook his head and smiled. "Nah, Bob can stay. I'm sure he needs to relax too."

Bob's eyes widened, and he gulped, his eyes dropping down to the ghosts and back up to the ceiling.

Ethan rubbed his face with his palms, "I . . . I think I need to bleach my eyes."

Twenty-Eight

Beer Can Graveyard

E THAN GRABBED HIS CLIPBOARD from the passenger seat and stepped out of his car. He looked at the brick entrance to Oakland Cemetery, straightened his tie, and smiled. He'd finally gotten into the groove, and with cases piling up back at the office, he was free to handle his cases alone.

He stepped through the entrance and looked around the empty graveyard. "Hey, Mable? It's me Ethan."

"Over here," the elderly spirit with the gray streak in her hair called from the corner of the cemetery.

Scanning the graves, Ethan cocked his head and asked, "What'd you do with the kids? Are they in a time out?"

Mable rolled her eyes and said, "No, we're playing hide-and-seek."

Ethan held his hands up. "Well, I don't want to interrupt."

"Do you want to play?" she asked.

"Yes! Please Mister Ethan?" Hairs on the back of his neck rose as a ghostly child's voice yelled from behind him.

Ethan spun, looking to see where the voice came from, but he saw nothing. Looking back at Mable, he grinned. "How does it work?"

Mable tilted her head and looked at Ethan like he was an idiot. "It's hide-and-seek. You don't know how to play hide-and-seek?"

"No. What? Of course I know how to play hide-n-seek. I'm like a hide-n-seek master."

Haunting giggles echoed from all over the graveyard. Ethan spun to look in different directions but couldn't find anything.

"Oh, you're a master, are you?" Mable said with a suspicious tone in her voice.

Laying his clipboard on the ground, Ethan began stretching. "Oh yeah. Might be a bit rusty, but back in my prime, no one could hide from the Hawk."

"They named you 'the Hawk?'"

Ethan shrugged. "I might have named myself. You know, like Ethan Hawke. And the Hawkeyes."

Mable continued to stare at him.

"Come on. It's a good name!" he said.

The children all laughed again.

Bouncing on his toes and shaking his arms like he was getting ready for a football game, he said, "Are there any special rules I need to know about? Is this forty forty or Brazil style?"

Mable shook her head and laughed to herself. "Just regular hide-and-seek. If you find someone, you just need to call their name and then they are out."

Ethan scoffed. "I just have to call their name. Shoot. I thought I was going to have to tag them. This is going to be easy."

"Alright then, Master Seeker. Have at it," Mable said.

"I don't have to close my eyes and count or anything?"

Waving her arm over the cemetery, she said, "They're already hiding."

"Ready or not, here I come!" Ethan yelled as he began running around, weaving in and out of the graves. He jumped around one of the larger headstones and yelled, "Got you!" But no child was there.

JP RINDFLEISCH IX & JEFF ELKINS

The children all giggled, and the sound swirled around him, lingering longer than it humanly should.

Straightening his suit jacket, he looked up and down the graveyard, scouting for other potential hiding places.

He feigned a step to his left, then raced to his right down a line of headstones. Peeking around a black marble headstone, he shouted, "Got you!"

For a second time, he came up short; and with it, giggles echoed again from every corner of the graveyard.

"Mister Ethan. You're kinda bad at this," Dylan's voice echoed.

"Oh, but he's a master, children. I'm sure this is all part of his schtick," Mable said as she examined her fingernails.

"I'm just warming up," Ethan shot back as he spun quickly, trying to look in all directions at once. He felt a chill in the small of his back, spinning on his heel as fast as he could. He yelled, "Dylan!"

Again, giggles came from all around him and there was no child to be seen.

One of them started a chant, and the others joined in quickly after. "Master Ethan has no cred. He can't catch us, though we're dead."

"I'll show you cred."

The chill returned, but this time was at the back of Ethan's calf. Kicking out, he yelled, "Harold!?!"

"Nope," a small voice whispered in his right ear. The voice was so close to his head he stumbled backward, twisting left and right in search of the child.

Giggles rang out from around the graveyard again.

"Over here," the voice whispered in his left ear, sending another cold spike down his back. Spinning toward it, he yelled, "Jean! It's Jean!"

The children giggled.

Ethan lurched forward to look behind the headstone in front of him but found nothing. Standing up straight again, he took a few steps back, looking left and then right, trying to anticipate how the child would sneak up on him again.

"They're just children," Mable said.

"Sneaky little bastards," Ethan said, creeping backward another step.

"Language!" Mable shouted.

"Oh, shit . . . sorry. Ah, sorry again."

"I thought you said you were a master," Mable said.

Ethan rubbed his hands together. "Oh, I've got th—AHHHHHHH!"

His last word turned to a blood-curdling scream as one of the children popped up from the ground and swatted at his feet.

Stumbling backward, Ethan tripped over the grave behind him. "Annngeeellllaaa!" he screamed as his head and shoulders flew toward the ground and his legs shot into the air.

"Awww," Angela said, rising from the earth and stomping her foot.

Lying on his back, his feet hanging on the gravestone, Ethan cheered with joy, "Angela! Got you! Angela, Angela, you are toast. Caught you, even though you're a—"

"What the fuck are you doing!" a deep voice shouted from across the cemetery.

"What? Who?" Ethan sat up and looked around.

"Oh no," Angela said.

"Game's over, children. Everyone out of hiding. West side of the graveyard. Right now," Mable command.

Harold, Jean, and Dylan all phased out from different headstones around Ethan, leaving behind a blue mist.

"What the fuck did you say?" the man on the path demanded again.

Ethan finally spotted him. He wore the signature blue denim overalls the electricians in New Richmond wore, and in his right hand he carried a six-pack of beers with three missing. "You! Asshole! What did you say?" he screamed.

Ethan looked at Mable.

Mable stomped her foot and demanded again. "Children! Corner! Now!"

Dylan and Harold stepped forward first, both taking one of Angela's hands. Dylan said, "Come on. Let's go see the wildflowers."

"Yeah," Harold said, pulling at her. "I bet there are some new ones coming up."

Angela stood frozen, staring at the man.

Ethan looked at the man, who stumbled into a headstone. "Who the hell put that there?"

The man looked up at Ethan, and his eyes looked strikingly familiar. He looked back at Angela and immediately saw the resemblance.

Mable grabbed Angela's shoulder and gently pulled. "Go see the flowers with your friends, dear. You don't need to see this. I'll come get you when he's gone."

Motioning for her friends to follow, Jean said, "Come on, Ang. We can practice poking the bees."

"Hey, you! Fuckwad! Get off of that!" the man said again.

As the children walked away, Ethan pushed off the headstone and scrambled to his feet. "Oh, hey. Sorry. Um. Hi. This might look a little weird."

The man staggered up to him, only an arm's length away, and Ethan could smell the alcohol all over him. "What the fuck are you doing? You some kind of weirdo who enjoys laughing at others' misery?"

Ethan waved his hands and took a step back. "No. No. You've got me all wrong. I'm. Um—"

The man stepped forward and poked him in the chest. "I'm um. I'm um," the man mocked him. "You're some fucking asshole. Respect the dead. What the fuck is wrong with you?"

The man chugged his beer, crunched the can in his hands, and tossed it over his shoulder.

Mable let out a sigh and eyed the can resting in a flowerpot.

Ethan stepped up to the man and looked him in the eye and said, "You pick that up."

"Ethan. Calm down," Mable said.

The man sneered and stared into Ethan's eyes. "Listen here, you entitled bag of shit. You going to tell me why the fuck my daughter's name was coming out of your mouth?"

Ethan took a step back and fumbled for his badge. He held it in the man's face and said, "Sir, I'm a federal agent, here on official business. Please keep your distance."

"Official business?" The man laughed. "You're one of those ghost fuckers stirring up shit in our town. Fuck you. And fuck your badge."

Ethan tucked the badge back in his jacket pocket and tried his best to smile at the man. "I get it, I do. I'm a local too. But I am just doing my job, sir, I swear."

"You were just screaming her name. Did you know I was coming? Know I'd hear you, so you can question me?"

Mable stepped between them and looked at Ethan. "Take it easy on him. He hasn't taken her passing well."

Ethan nodded and looked past Mable. "Listen, man. It seems like you might have had a rough day. What's your daughter's name?"

Ripping off another beer off the six-pack, he cracked it open with one hand and took a drink. "Angela. Her name's Angela."

A part of Ethan knew the man was going to say that, even so, when the words left his lips, a weight settled in his stomach. "I see. And where is she buried?"

The man took another drink and pointed behind and to the left of Ethan. "Over there."

Ethan put his hands in his pockets. "You, uh, want to go see her?"

Mable looked back at the man, nodded, and started toward the children. "Thank you."

The man wiped his nose with the back of his sleeve and looked at the ground. "I've been coming here almost every week, trying to build up the courage."

Ethan nodded. "You mind if I walk with you?"

The man shrugged and held out the two beers left on the six-pack. Ethan pulled one off and cracked it open. "Here's to Angela," he said, tipping his beer to the man before he took a sip.

The man took a drink and said, "Let's do this," as he trudged over toward his daughter's grave.

Ethan followed him in silence. They arrived at a headstone that read, "Angela Klein. Beloved Daughter. Gone too soon. 1996 to 2015." Standing together, they sipped their beers and looked at the grave.

The man finished his first, crushed it against his leg, and shoved it into his pocket. He then dropped, taking a seat in the grass.

Ethan followed suit and sat down next to him.

The man cracked open his last beer and took a drink.

Ethan took another sip. "Do you mind if I ask how she died?"

"Car accident," the man said.

Ethan nodded. "I'm sorry."

"Her mom and I were fighting. I don't even know what about anymore," he said, taking another swig of his beer.

Ethan nodded and took a drink too.

"She was in the backseat. I'd told her to buckle up, but . . ." The man's voice caught in his throat. He stopped and took another drink and then took a deep breath before continuing. "But. She'd dropped her crayons. And. And I wasn't watching because I was yelling. And. And I ran a red light. And." He took another drink.

Ethan put his arm around the man. "I'm so sorry."

The man sighed and shook his head. Closing his eyes, he said, "If I could, I'd go back and just do shit different. You know."

Ethan squeezed his shoulder, then let go, picking at the grass near his feet.

The man chugged the rest of his beer, crushed the can, and slipped it into his pocket next to the other one. "Wife couldn't take it anymore. She left me too. Divorced me 'cause I just couldn't let go."

Movement in the corner of Ethan's eye caught his attention, and he saw Mable and the children approaching.

The man sighed. "I wish I was your age again. I could do it all differently. God, I was such an asshole." His gaze lumbered over to Ethan, and he said, "Don't be an asshole. Okay?"

"I'll try not to be."

The children stood around Angela's grave. Quietly staring at Ethan and the man.

Angela looked at her dad, then rushed over to his side, her arms slipping through him.

The man shivered and rubbed his arms. "It still feels like she's here, you know?" He shook his head. "It's stupid."

"It's not stupid to miss your kid," Ethan said.

Ethan looked at Angela and smiled.

Leaning toward her dad, tears fell down her cheeks, and she said, "I love you, Daddy."

The man leaned into Ethan, and a tear trickled down his cheek. They sat in silence, the children looking on, staring at Angela's grave.

After a few minutes, Ethan patted the man's shoulder and stood up. "It's going to be dark soon. My gran's making fish fry. Why don't you come over?"

The man wiped his nose on the back of his sleeve and struggled to stand without Ethan's help. "I. I think I'd like that. Name's Jeremy, by the way. Jeremy Klein."

"Hi Jeremy, I'm Ethan."

Looking past the man, Ethan winked at Angela.

"Thank you, Mister Ethan," she said.

Twenty-Nine

High-Speed Chase

E THAN STEPPED OUT OF the office and turned around, waving his hands at Buck as he relayed the events to his partner. "So, a week later, I took the guy out again, right? To that same Italian place you and Gerry took me."

"Don't do that," Buck said, interrupting.

Looking both ways and then stepping into the street, Ethan said, "Wait? What? Why? But I already did it."

"I mean, don't do it again." As they arrived at his car, Buck waved to the three remaining protestors who were still hanging out on the curb. Calling to a thin man in a red, white, and blue trucker hat holding a sign that read, "We Don't Need More Nerds!" Buck yelled, "There's no E. It's an acronym."

The man looked at his sign, then back at Buck, his face glowing red. "Fuck you!" Turning to the other two protestors, muttered something to them, and they all started chanting, "No more nerds! No more nerds! No more nerds!"

Buck sighed and looked back at Ethan. "You can't allow yourself to get emotionally attached. We invest our time with the spirits because they'll move on. This guy is going to keep coming back, even after she's gone."

"But it was an excellent dinner. I learned a ton about Angela and her mom that I wouldn't have learned otherwise," Ethan protested over the top of the car.

"And you spent your own money, didn't you?" Buck asked.

Ethan's eyebrows perked up. "Oh, wait. Can I, like, turn in receipts and get reimbursed or something?"

Buck smirked and shook his head. "Yeah right. They won't budget for a new coffee maker after Alexus threw the old one out the window, but they'll reimburse dinner."

"Really?"

Buck grimaced at his naïve partner. "No." Climbing into his car, he mumbled to himself, "Stupid rookie."

Ethan opened the door and plopped into the passenger seat. "But listen. You weren't there. You didn't see Angela's face. I'm pretty sure she's hanging around because her dad is so lonely."

"Uh-huh," Buck said as he adjusted his mirror.

"I'm thinking that if I can just get him on tinder or something . . . you know, get him a date or get him laid? Then he'll stop showing up drunk at her grave and then Angela will be able to move on."

"Oh, you fucking bag of shit!" Buck declared as he stared into the rearview mirror.

Ethan dropped his gaze to his feet. "I didn't think it was a bad idea. But, okay. Maybe getting him laid isn't the answer."

"No. Not you. Back there!" Buck said, turning in his seat and pointing to the rear window of the car.

Ethan turned and spotted the spirit standing out in the middle of the road, stretching. She wore a purple eighties-era tracksuit with neon yellow lightning bolts on the sides and the sheer volume of her hair sprayed, back-combed blond hair could rival drag queens.

She pulled on one arm, then the other, then hopped in place. There were two black lines under her eyes, as if she were a football player and she appeared to be sucking on a lollipop.

"Can ghosts eat?" Ethan asked, confused.

"Tell me you put a briefcase in the trunk," Buck said, starting the car.

"Yeah. Yesterday. Why?" Ethan said, staring at the ghost, who was still leering at them.

"Go through the backseat and get me that case!" Buck demanded as he revved the engine.

Ethan unbuckled and turned, pushing himself halfway through to the backseat. When he looked back at the ghost in the tracksuit, she winked at him and then jumped into the air, vanishing inside the engine of the old red pickup truck that was parked right behind them.

"Whoa!" he said as the truck roared to life.

Movement in the corner of Ethan's eye drew his attention, and he watched the protester in the trucker hat drop his sign and stare wide-eyed at the keys in his hands. "Hey! That's . . . That's my truck."

The headlights behind them flashed, and the truck's engine revved a few times.

Buck revved in response and squeezed the steering wheel. "Fine, we're doing this again? You're going down, wannabe Christine."

"What's going on?" Ethan asked, his heart racing with panic. He cautiously started climbing into the backseat, trying his best to wiggle back there while keeping his ass and junk out of Buck's face.

The pickup truck's wheels squealing against asphalt, kicking up smoke as the horn sounded behind them.

"No! Wait!" the protestor screamed, running to his vehicle with his hand outstretched.

"Hurry up! I need that case!" Buck yelled.

"Alright! I'm going!" Ethan said as semi-stood in the backseat, reaching for the pull that released the backseat to the trunk.

The truck threw itself into drive and nearly clipped them as it spun out from the parking spot behind him. It fishtailed into Main Street and sped away, doing at least sixty in a thirty-five.

"Hang on!" Buck shouted as he slammed on the gas.

The car lurched forward, launching Ethan headfirst into the rear window. After he peeled his face off the glass, he saw the protestor standing in the middle of the road shouting, "Nooo!"

"Get that case!" Buck screamed.

Ethan blinked a few times to get the stars out of his vision and felt for the latch. "What's going on? Who is that?" he yelled back at Buck.

"Hang on!" Buck yelled again as he took a hard left, chasing the car down a side road.

"Jesus!" Ethan screamed as he fell off the seat and wedged into the floorboard.

The car tires squealed as Buck took a hard right, throwing Ethan onto the other floorboard. "Where's that case?" Buck yelled again.

"I'm trying goddammit!" Ethan yelled, pushing himself up off the floorboard as Buck floored it through a red light after the pickup truck. "Tell me what's going on!" Ethan demanded.

"She fucking found me! Been waiting for this day. Probably thinks she is so fucking clever. But she's going to be sorry because I'm casing her this time!" Buck said as he spun the wheel to the right, taking another hard turn after the pickup truck.

This time, braced for the turn, Ethan was able to maintain his position in the car. Reaching up, he found the release for the backseat and opened it. "So, you know her?" he said as he reached into the trunk.

"Fuck. We're not gonna make it." Buck shouted as he pressed the pedal all the way to the floor.

"Not going to make what—oh shit!" Ethan turned and looked out the windshield. Red lights indicated the railroad crossing blinked back at him, and he traced the tracks back to a train racing to cut them off.

Slamming on his horn, Buck screamed, "Brace yourself!"

Ethan held a hand on the roof of the car as Buck hit the railroad tracks with such force, the car took flight for a full two seconds. Ethan was certain they were about to die, the train lights streaming into the car.

The car landed, and sparks flew around them as it crashed back to the ground.

Ethan watched the Welcome to New Richmond sign race by, and the roads opened up to corn fields. He waited until the road looked straight enough before scampering into the trunk and grabbing the case. He pulled himself out as Buck took another turn and clutched the briefcase to his chest. "Got it!" he said.

The pickup waited until the last minute and turned left, skipping tires on the road before racing down the road.

"Not this time!" Buck yelled.

Ethan stretched his arms out to brace himself, and Buck wrenched the wheel, drifting the car before catching a grip and racing down the road.

"Who is this girl?" Ethan demanded, praying the car didn't flip.

Buck sped up right behind the haunted truck. "I don't know her name, but I've been chasing her for twenty years. It's some kind of sick game she likes to play."

The truck behind them swerved, and Buck nearly lost control.

"You've done this before?" Ethan said, deciding not to try and climb back into the front seat, but rather look for a buckle in the back.

"Doesn't matter where I transfer, she always finds me. But this time, she's going down!" Buck said, pressing harder on the gas, causing the engine to roar louder.

The pickup approached another crossroads and slowed, swerving lanes and feigning a turn before hopping back onto the country road. Buck stayed the course, keeping control of his car.

"Ha! Not falling for that!" Buck yelled with glee.

Ethan looked into the rearview mirror, spotting a crazed look in Buck's eyes that he hadn't seen before.

Buck grinned. "Alright! Here's the plan! I'm going to get in front of her. You need to open the back door and throw the open case out so she drives over it! Got it?"

"What? No!" Ethan said.

"Figure it out then!" Buck yelled as he punched the pedal all the way to the floor and swerved out beside the truck.

Ethan buckled his seat belt and cracked the locks on the case. "Are you sure about this?" he asked as blue light poured from the briefcase's seams.

"Almost!" Buck said as the driver's sides matched up along the empty pickup.

"Son of a—shit—fuck!" Ethan screamed as the truck rammed into their car.

Sparks flew, but Buck didn't slow. Pushing ahead, he yelled, "Almost there! Almost there!"

Ethan cracked open the door to the car.

Buck raced ahead. As the trunk of their car passed the hood of the pickup, he screamed, "Now! Now! Now!"

Ethan threw open the back door and leaned out. The pavement raced by below him. Opening the briefcase, the blue light blinding him, he tossed the case on the ground toward the pickup's path.

The truck swerved, smacking the briefcase off course while losing control and spinning completely around.

Staring into the rearview mirror, Buck yelled, "Fuck!" as he pulled on his wheel and spun his car around.

The lights on the pickup all flashed bright and then died at once, and the tracksuit-wearing ghost leaped out of the car and rolled on the road in front of them while the truck raced off into the cornfield.

"Aaah!" Ethan yelped as Buck passed the ghost and slammed on his brakes.

Ethan turned to look out the back window.

Putting the car in reverse and slamming on the gas again, Buck screamed, "I'm gunning for you, asshat!"

"Oh, shit!" Ethan yelled as the car raced at the ghost at top speed.

The ghost hopped to her feet, popping a lollipop in her mouth and smiling. She didn't move as Buck raced right through her, but to Ethan's shock, she completely vanished the moment she touched the car.

Buck slammed on the brakes, lurching Ethan forward and into the back of the front seats.

The car came to a stop, and Buck said, "Wait! Where'd she go?"

Ethan looked all around. "I don't see her!" he said.

"How close were we to the case?" Buck asked.

Ethan spotted the blue light coming out of the case near the side of the road. "It's still open."

His eyes wide, Buck said, "Oh no."

The car roared to life as the wheels spun on the asphalt and the radio came to life at full volume. "It's Britney, bitch."

Music blared from the speakers, and the doors automatically locked.

Buck screamed, barely audible above the music. "Abandon ship, kid!"

Watching Buck jump from the car, Ethan unbuckled his seat belt and unlocked the door. He dove out of the back door just before the car sped away. He watched as Buck's beloved car raced into the horizon.

Running after the car, waving his fist in the air, Buck screamed, "I'll get you next time, you motherfucker! You better fucking watch out!"

Thirty

NRDS Behind Bars

E THAN SHOOK THE BARS to the jail cell and called down the hall, "Hey! You can't keep us here without a phone call!"

River paced back and forth behind him, mumbling to himself. "I knew I shouldn't have answered the damn phone."

"Hey! Lawyer! I want a lawyer!" Ethan yelled again.

"'We're stranded, come pick us up,' you said. 'We're having car trouble,' you said. Why did I listen? Why didn't I question why you were out in the boonies in the first place? Stupid River. I should have sent Trevor," River whined as he continued to pace.

Buck lay on the bench against the wall, his eyes closed. "Will you two just calm down and have a seat?"

"Have a seat? But this is against our constitutional rights! They can't hold us here," Ethan yelled down the hall again.

Buck snickered. "Yeah? Which one?"

Kicking at the bars, Ethan said, "I don't know. That one about people having a right to an attorney."

River stopped his march and spun on his heels, pointing a finger at Buck. "You know I hate prison, old man. It fucking sucks. With what they've already got on me, I'm not getting out of this."

"Relax. Lie down. Walking back and forth won't get you out of here any sooner," Buck said with a laugh.

"I don't want a fucking nap! I want my car back, and I want to go home," River said as he started pacing again.

Ethan turned and leaned against the bars. "Why didn't they just take our statement and go? It's not like we stole that dude's truck."

"Oh, really, genius!" River snapped as he walked. "So, they see you two yahoos getting into my car full of weed. No other car in sight. Oh, and the stolen truck in a ditch. Who else stole it? Huh? Who?"

"It was that ghost. The one with the tracksuit." Ethan said with a shrug. Buck snorted a laugh.

Not breaking his stride, River pursed his lips and straightened his back, putting on a sophisticated voice. "Ah, well, let me see if I understand you correctly, mister Malik. You want this court to believe that a ghost—the spectral remains of a deceased person—stole good Mr. Protestor's truck? Is that what you would have the court believe?"

Ethan shrugged again. "That's what happened. I mean, we're a whole government agency who works with the deceased. Why wouldn't they believe us?"

Buck let out a laugh. "Nice try, kid. But no one wants to believe that ghosts are actually real. And we can't prove it to them without putting a badge in their hands, which goes against protocol."

River nodded at Buck and came to a stop in front of Ethan's face. "Mister Malik, are you trying to say this court is fucking stupid? Ghosts? And are we going to forget that when the police searched that rather attractive young man's car, we found a holy fuck ton of weed in his car? Do you think we're stupid, Mister Malik? Is that it?"

"Um. No, you're not stupid, but why does that matter?"

"You'd like for this court to accept your fucking Casper-Did-It defense? With no evidence of the matter. And at the scene of the incident, you just so happen to have someone with both marijuana and human remains in their car. How fucking stupid do you fucking think we are?" River screamed.

"Objection," Buck said, still without opening his eyes. "There were far too many fucks given in that accusation, Mister Prosecutor."

River started his pacing again and pointed a finger at Buck. "Don't fucking start with me, old man. This is your fucking fault."

"So, what, when the truck took off, we were supposed to just let her take it out for a joy ride?" Ethan asked.

"Yes! We are NRDS Agents! We barely have jurisdiction over haunted houses, let alone chasing down some Christine wannabe!" River yelled, throwing his hands in the air.

Ethan rolled his eyes. "Look, we didn't know the cops were going to get there that fast. How would we have known that?"

River paused, his mouth hanging open in mock surprise. "Oh. I don't know? Maybe. Let's see. Could it maybe have been the car theft that tipped you off? It's a fucking small town. Cops from three towns over would be on that like flies."

Buck sat up and rubbed his eyes. "We almost had her."

Ethan nodded. "We were really close. You should have seen it. We can't let her run around taking cars as she pleases."

River looked at the floor, shook his head, and started pacing again. "And now you're out a car and they impounded mine. Oh, and we're in fucking jail, unless you forgot," he said in a mocking tone.

"This isn't jail. Calm down. Jail would be way more fun than this," Buck said with a grin.

Ethan laughed. "At least I'd get my call in jail."

River waved his arms in the air in frustration as he paced. "Great, they both have jokes now! Do you know how hard it is to get a felony off your record?"

"Okay, killjoy. Will you just take a seat?" Buck said.

Still pacing, River asked, "This is the crazy chick you've been chasing for decades, right? How many times have you almost had her? Did you even tell him that?"

Ethan looked from River to Buck and then back at River.

"I've heard the numbers are in the twenties, at least. And you won't even report it like you're supposed to," River said.

Buck lay back down, folding his hands behind his head, and said, "It's been forty-three."

"Forty-three? Including today?" Ethan asked, his mouth hanging open.

Keeping his eyes closed, Buck said, "Nope. Today was forty-four."

"Jesus. Fucking forty-four times?" River laughed. "When are you going to learn, old timer? You're never going to catch her."

"Forty-four times," Ethan said, his mouth still hanging open.

"And now you've pulled me into it. Dammit. I'm not going to jail, Buck! You're getting me out of this shit!" River yelled.

"No one's going to jail," Buck said.

"Wait. What?" Ethan asked.

"They found enough weed in my car to light up the whole town, Buck! You were in it. And you don't even know what I've got in the trunk. It could be a dead body? You don't know!" River screamed.

"Shit, wait. How am I involved with what was in your car? I won't jail for that, right? Right Buck?" Ethan asked.

"You were in the car, dumbass. All three of us are guilty until proven innocent." River said.

"We're federal agents. I guarantee Melissa is calling the higher ups and talking with the mayor to pull us out. This is just the locals flexing their muscles," Buck said.

"Until they open my trunk. Then we're all fucked!" River yelled.

"Wait. Do you have a dead body in the trunk?" Ethan asked.

"What? You fucking think I'm some kind of serial killer? Is that what you think of me?" River complained.

"That's not a no," Buck said with a smile.

Ethan turned to look down the hall again as he heard a door open. A woman with a microphone entered the hallway along with a man who had a news camera on his shoulder. Mayor Davies followed behind them, wearing a beige suit with a blue and yellow striped tie. "Heads up. Media," Ethan said to River and Buck.

"Fuck them!" River said.

The woman with the microphone stopped at the edge of the hall and said, "Mister Mayor, why don't you stand in front of the bars so we can see you in front of the prisoners?"

The mayor nodded and positioned himself near the bars, but out of reach from Ethan. "How's this?" he asked.

"Perfect," the reporter said as she came to stand next to him with her microphone.

"This should be good," Buck said.

It wasn't until Ethan took a seat next to Buck's feet on the end of the bench that he saw him. "Oh shit," he said as he caught a glimmer of young Dylan standing next to the cameraman, watching his father.

"You good, Andy?" the reporter asked the cameraman.

"Rolling," the cameraman said.

"No, no, you're fucking not! We haven't consented to being filmed," River said as he raced to the other end of the cell and pressed himself against the wall.

"What's going on?" Buck whispered to Ethan.

The reporter looked past the mayor and at River. "Actually, your boss consented for you. It was part of the terms the mayor has been negotiating."

Ethan's eyes locked on Dylan, who was coming more into focus the longer he looked at him. Ethan leaned in toward Buck and explained, "Dylan's here. He's out of the graveyard."

River covered his face with his hands and muttered, "If those fucking fucks see this, we're all fucked. You know that, right?"

"Dammit," Buck said.

"Hey, Mary? Um. We need him in the shot," the cameraman asked, pointing at River.

"Fuck you and your camera! Point it at me and you'll be sorry!" River screamed, his body still shoved as tightly to the wall as he could manage.

Mary looked behind her to stare at River who pressed his face as hard as he could against the wall. She laughed and looked back at her cameraman. "More work between the mayor and their boss, I guess. Let's just get this done."

Ethan lowered his voice and looked at Buck. "What do you think it means? Him being here?"

"It means that Mable's losing control," Buck said. "Things are escalating."

The cameraman pointed at the reporter, which cued the reporter to say, "This is Mary Crenshaw of Channel Five News, here today with New Richmond's Mayor Davies. A major car chase rocked this small downtown this afternoon after a car was stolen. After a chase through the streets, several thousand dollars' worth of damages, and a major drug bust, the criminals were apprehended. Mister Mayor, would you be willing to comment on today's events?"

Looking into the camera, the mayor said, "The citizens of New Richmond are good people. Hard-working people. And you should feel safe to walk the streets of your own town."

"Ugh, he's good," Buck whispered.

"Yeah, he really knows how to capture an audience," Ethan said with a grin as he waved to Dylan.

Dylan's eyes grew wide, and he slid behind the cameraman's leg.

"But ever since these interlopers—these transplants, these so-called federal agents—showed up in our town, we've seen nothing but chaos. I am here today, fellow citizens of New Richmond, to show you we have apprehended the miscreants behind the events today."

Ethan giggled and nudged Buck's foot. "He called you a miscreant."

"I heard," Buck said.

Continuing, the Mayor said, "And I will make it my duty to ensure that if you re-elect me as Mayor, these so-called fake federal agents will not get a moment's rest until they leave our town."

Smiling at the camera, Mary the reporter said, "You heard it here first, folks. Sounds like these federal agents are in some hot water today. Back to you Tucker."

"Annnnnd, we're clear," the cameraman said as he took the rig off his shoulder.

Dylan scampered over to stand by his father's leg, shifting his eyes to Ethan. "Um. Hi Mister Ethan."

"That was great, Mister Mayor. Thank you for the exclusive," Mary said as she wrapped up her microphone cord.

While the Mayor was distracted, Ethan stared bug-eyed at Dylan and mouthed, "Go back to the graveyard."

"Any time," the mayor said. "Now, if you don't mind. I'd like a word with these gentlemen."

"Of course," Mary the reporter said as she and the cameraman began to leave.

"Is it fucking over?" River yelled from the wall.

"Not yet. Stay there," Buck said with a smile.

"It's over," Ethan said. Approaching the mayor, he smiled and said, "Sir. How are you?"

"Here's how I am, son. I heard you were up at my son's grave again early this week." He pointed a finger at Ethan and prodded his chest. "Now, I'm only going to say this once. My son is gone. And I don't need some freak like you picking at old scars. Understand me?"

Ethan nodded.

Dylan leaned in closer to his dad and yawned. "Dad. Can we go back home? I want to see Tiger."

The mayor shuddered from a phantom chill and pointed a finger at Ethan. "Now, I know some people in town still see you as the football state champion, but I see you as a pimple that I need to pop. So, don't push me, boy, or I'll dig my fingers in so hard your head comes clear off."

River pulled himself from the corner and walked toward the mayor. "Hey! You can't talk to us like that, asshole! We're federal agents!"

"Back down, Cujo." Buck said.

Mayor Davies smirked and straightened his tie. "You're the kind of federal agents that no one cares about. You're the forgotten child of an ancient era of fear and paranoia. You have about as much power in my city as the garbage man, except I actually want them here."

He turned and started down the hall, Dylan at his side, before pausing at the door. "I seemed to have misplaced your papers for release in my emails. I'm sure it will all be straightened out in the morning. Goodnight, gentlemen."

"Fuck you very much!" River screamed down the hall after him.

Dylan waited at the door, looking at Ethan for a moment longer before taking a step through the door.

"No! Dylan!" Ethan hissed. "You need to go back to the graveyard."

Dylan phased back through the wall and pouted. "But I want to—"

"No, Dylan. Go back. Right now," Ethan said.

Dylan stomped his foot. "Fine!" Then he marched away, through the door and out of sight.

The three of them stood in silence for a while longer before River plopped down on the bench. "So, what now?"

Buck settled on the bench and yawned. "Now you shut up and wake me when the sun comes up."

Ethan rested his back against the cell bars and slid down. "Fuck."

Thirty-One

Insubordinate FUCS

"**A**ND DO YOU KNOW how goddamn early it is?" Melissa shouted as she burst into the front doors of the NRDS office.

Ethan rubbed the back of his neck while he, River, Buck, and Bob filed in after Melissa. "And we thanked you for the hundredth time."

Buck started toward his desk, but Melissa growled. "My office. All of you. Upper management wants a meeting. Now!"

River pointed and mouthed "Ha. Ha." while Buck spun on his heels and followed Melissa to her office.

She tried jamming her key into the door while shaking it furiously. "I don't want to be up this goddamn early. Do you think directors have to deal with this bullshit?"

"Do you want me to do that for you?" Buck asked.

Melissa shuddered and turned, her eyes like portals into the deepest pit of hell. "I will ask for help if I need it. Agent Hampton."

With a smirk, River elbowed Ethan in the ribs and said, "It's tricky. You kind of have to jiggle it a little."

Melissa's demon eyes locked on him, and he paled. "Now you? Don't even start. Do you know what I had to promise to get you out? What in the ever-living fuck were you doing with that shit in your trunk?"

"Wait. What's in his trunk?" Ethan asked.

Melissa turned back to her jigsaw puzzle of a door as Bob jumped in front of Ethan. "So, this moron thought it was a good idea to—"

"No! Nothing! None of your fucking business!" River screamed, holding his badge as he swung his arms through the ghost's face.

Bob coughed and backed away, holding his hands up in surrender.

"Enough. Just let me help," Buck said, pushing past Melissa and opening the door. He stepped back and motioned for her to go in.

"I had it. I fucking had it," Melissa said as she flipped on the lights and stomped into the office. Buck and Ethan followed her in, and River stood in the doorway.

"Coffee? You want coffee?" River asked before turning and walking into the break room.

Ethan heard several metallic clangs before River said, "Does anyone know how to work this thing?"

Melissa pinched the bridge of her nose. "I work with idiots."

Bob phased through the wall and shook his head. "Dumbass finally found the filters. I think you're all safe."

"When is the meeting with Internal?" Buck asked.

"Any minute now." Melissa held up her badge. "I need a briefing. Bob, report. Now."

Bob stood at attention. "I followed protocol while these three duds were held up."

"Hey, who are you calling a dud?" Ethan asked.

"And? Did you find anything useful?" Melissa asked, leaning back in her chair and resting the palms of her hands on her eyes.

"Yes ma'am. Stacks of unsolved murder files. More than they've been reporting. Way more than a town this size should have," Bob said.

"Murders like Mable," Ethan nodded.

Buck crossed his arms and leaned back in his chair. "We knew they were hiding that, though."

River clapped his hands from the break room, followed by. "Aha! Coffee is brewing, bitches!"

Melissa sighed. "Anything else? Anything useful we can use as leverage next time I have to talk to them?"

Someone cleared their throat behind Ethan, and he jumped in his seat. He turned and saw the mousy Agent Bryce Fillmore standing in the entrance to Melissa's office.

"Oh. What the fuck are you doing here?" Melissa said.

He stepped into her office and pulled off his beige trench coat, wrapping it over his arm as he stood beside her desk. "Quite the story on the news last night."

"Wait, they sent a temp to discuss internal affairs?" Melissa laughed.

Agent Fillmore rolled his eyes and grinned. "Actually, Agent Scott, I'm not a temp anymore, and the directors have personally hired me as liaison between you and upper management. So please, continue."

Melissa stammered. "Oh, that was . . . well, see. I needed to negotiate with the locals. And they said to release our agents they needed to—"

"Upper management has expressed concern over the attention this office is bringing in. I see you still have protests nearly every day. Now this?" Fillmore said.

"I'll file the report right after this meeting. It was my error," Buck said.

"While I appreciate the tenacity, the routine failure of this office to maintain public decorum is the issue."

River slipped into the office with several mugs in his hand, spilling coffee on Melissa's desk as he set them down. He then produced several packets of sugar and creamer from his pockets before standing opposite Agent Fillmore and taking a sip of coffee. He gagged, swallowed hard, and poured in several more packets of sugar. "I don't know what you're talking about. We're the epitome of fucking decorum."

"Discipline and honor. That's us," Bob added with a smile.

"The spirit from yesterday wasn't from our area," Buck clarified as he reached for a mug of coffee and cautiously sipped it.

Choking down his coffee again, River added, "Yeah. It hitchhiked all the way here to pick on poor Buck."

Melissa clapped her hands and grabbed a mug of coffee, taking a swig and instantly spitting it back into the cup. She cleared her throat. "Well, that's fucking disgusting. Clearly, the spirit came from Chicago. That office should be under investigation for negligence."

"We're already on it but thank you for the input. This meeting is to discuss the second spirit you encountered." Agent Fillmore's eyes fell on Ethan.

Ethan laughed nervously. "Second spirit?"

Buck downed the rest of the coffee and set it on Melissa's desk. "Only one spirit stole the car."

Melissa opened her mouth. "That spirit has a history of—"

"Agent Malik," Fillmore said, cutting Melissa off again. "Exactly who were you waving to during the news report?"

Bob let out a laugh and put his hands on his hips. "Oh, you're in the shitter now."

Ethan tried his best to ignore Bob and bit his lip. "I was, um. Waving at the camera?"

Melissa darted her eyes between Fillmore and Ethan and cut in. "He's a greenhorn. I'm sure he was just nervous. Never had to be on TV before."

"That's why I stayed in the corner. I don't need IA up my ass about waving at the fucking camera." River said, taking a swig of his coffee and choking it down.

Agent Fillmore sighed, removed his glasses, and cleaned them with a handkerchief. "I find that hard to believe. Had you looked into Agent Malik's past, you'd see he was somewhat of a celebrity in high school. Been on the news several times."

"Ha-ha, he's got your number, rookie." Bob laughed.

"Second, our investigators noted that Agent Malik clearly waved at someone approximately two feet below the camera line. Odd, since there was no record of anyone that height in the room."

"It was a kid," Buck said.

"Living or dead?" Fillmore shot back.

"Living. Obviously." Melissa said, shaking her head.

Agent Fillmore kept his eyes locked on Ethan and raised his eyebrow. "Obviously. However, Upper management has no video of a child coming in or out of the police station while these three were incarcerated."

Buck cleared his throat. "It was the mayor's son. He's deceased. First time we've seen him break loose."

Fillmore put his glasses back on and nodded. "With or without a badge?"

River dropped his mug. "Uh—"

"With. They confiscated mine and River's but failed to get Ethan's," Buck interjected.

"I'm sure I will confirm that in the report when I visit the station. Now, about this child," Fillmore said.

Melissa threw her hands up in the air. "Our office can't be held responsible for the natural progression of things. With the spikes we've been seeing—"

"The issue is not the single spirit. The directors are curious about the lack of reporting with these escalations," Fillmore said.

Melissa looked stunned. She stammered, searching for an answer. "But. I. We've just been. You know?"

"What do you think I know, Agent Scott?" Fillmore asked, looking down his nose at her. The word "agent" jabbed from his mouth like a dagger piercing the flesh of her pride.

Buck stood from his chair and pointed a finger at Agent Fillmore. "Can it. We all know about the clicker."

Fillmore furrowed his brows. "The what?"

Ethan slowly stood and looked at Agent Fillmore. "The clicker. The thing you two have been using to escalate ghosts."

Bob rubbed his hands together and smiled. "Now the shit's hitting the fan."

Melissa looked at everyone standing in her office and pushed herself up out of her chair to join them. "I said nothing to them."

"Ethan took it from you," River said with a grin.

"Traitor!" Bob roared.

River pointed at his chest and said, "I'm not going down for this shit! This is on all of you!"

"You used one at the speed dating thing," Ethan said.

Agent Fillmore's mouth hung open. "We were having a moment. That was supposed to be between us."

"Now who's breaking protocol?" Melissa said with a grin.

"I didn't break protocol. The experiment was authorized and signed off on." Fillmore said.

"Oh, I bet every rule was followed at the giant ghost sex orgy," River said with a sarcastic nod.

"I can tell you that there were no protocols being followed by anyone at that abomination," Bob said.

"I have a hard time believing that was an authorized experiment. Are there ghost STIs? I mean, did you vet all the ghosts?" Ethan said.

"When was there a ghost orgy? I didn't see a report on that," Melissa complained.

"We were off the clock," River said.

"If you see spirit activity, you are duty bound to report it," Melissa said.

Pointing at her, River declared, "I didn't 'see' anything. Besides, you don't want to know what I do in my free time! Or do I have to explain the thing in my trunk to you?"

"I can affirm that. You don't want to know," Bob said.

Agent Fillmore took a step forward. "Enough. They sent me here to warn you. If there are any more unwanted disruptions from this office, the fucks will come."

"Fuck!" River yelled.

"Don't blame me for the fucks!" Bob chimed in.

"There has to be something you can do. We can't allow the fucks to penetrate our operation," Melissa said.

"Hold up. I'm really confused. Fucks?" Ethan said.

"Not fucks, FUCS, F-U-C-S. Those FUCS are coming," Buck said.

"I know how to spell fuck. That doesn't help," Ethan said.

"Wait. You know fuck has a K, right?" River asked with a grin.

Ethan rolled his eyes. "Yeah. I know it has a K."

River stood up straight and spouted, "Well, these FUCS are the Foreign Unworldly Census and Seizure. Bunch of racist assholes."

Fillmore frowned. "You know it's Federal, not Foreign, right?"

River ignored him. "These assholes go around rounding up all the ghosts of immigrants and sending them to the shredder. You can't tell me that wasn't some racist shit that went down in Cleveland."

"The Italian Mob incident?" Bob asked.

"The fucking Italian Mob incident. Never saw so many spirits of Italian immigrants rounded up and taken by those FUCS. Did they care to take anyone else? No. Cause they're racist assholes."

Buck tilted his head. "Wasn't that the case where ten spirits created a murder house and sat on a hoard of prohibition-era cash? They killed like two hundred people before the FUCS came in."

"My entire team is a bunch of morons," Melissa complained.

Ethan looked at Agent Fillmore. "Federal Unworldly Census and Seizure?"

Fillmore nodded. "If we're the FBI, they're like Homeland Security."

"So, they're another federal agency? And they do what we do? Seems redundant." Ethan said.

"No," Buck said. "We help spirits cross over or catch and release. They shred them."

Bob shuddered, and Ethan stared blankly at Buck.

"He means they destroy spirits. As in, no more afterlife for you," River said. "Especially the foreign ones."

"That would mean no more Mable? And the kids too?" Ethan said.

"That's right, kid," Buck said.

"Fuck," Ethan replied, looking down.

"That's why I was told to bring you here. If you all end up on the news again, or you keep fucking up, then those FUCS are coming, and the directors can't help you."

Melissa clapped. "Okay! Time to tighten this ship up. No more messing around." She pointed at River. "You need to pull yourself together. And get that shit out of your trunk before you get pulled over again."

"Fine," River said with a pout.

"And you," she said, looking at Ethan. "No more clicker." Before Ethan could defend himself, she pointed at Buck. "And you. I don't care if that ghost steals a tractor trailer. You let it fucking go."

"We'll see." Buck said.

"The fuck we won't." Melissa said.

Fillmore pulled on his coat. "Well, I have some reports to confiscate from the police station. Agent Scott, I'll leave it to you to get this in order."

"Don't worry, boss. I'm all over it," Melissa declared.

Fillmore looked at Ethan and cleared his throat. "And you. Dinner? Tonight?"

Ethan's face flushed. "Uh. Sure."

Fillmore smiled and said, "Excellent." before walking out of the office.

Thirty-Two

Please, No Creepy Dolls

E THAN SHIFTED HIS WEIGHT from one foot to the other as he looked at the front door of The Christmas Haus. "I don't know. This one seems super creepy," he said as he watched all the fake Christmas trees in the store blink on and off in random patterns.

Trevor nodded. Pointing his phone at the storefront, he said, "I mean, it's going to be like, what? Nine months before they make another sale? So, maybe we just leave whatever is in there, in there, and it will take care of itself."

"You two better not bitch out on me now," Alexus said as she sipped her coffee. Tipping her coffee to the front door, she added, "But I see now that the owner's a Chax-head, so on second thought, maybe we let it burn."

"Chax-head?" Ethan asked.

"Forty-something dude. Slicked back hair. Nice suit," Trevor said.

"Running for mayor. Started the protest in front of the office," Alexus added.

"Guys, I know who Chax is. I mean, how do you know the owner's a Chax-head?" Ethan asked.

Alexus rolled her eyes and shook her head in disbelief. "I don't know, maybe because there's a Chax for Mayor sticker on the front door?"

Ethan looked over and spotted the huge sticker plastered on the center of the door. "Oh, right. But my gramma loves this store. She comes in all the time."

"Even when it's not Christmas?" Trevor asked.

"She said she likes how it smells."

"And how does it smell? Like old sweaty Santa suits and children's tears?" Alexus asked.

"Uh, no? Like cinnamon and pine trees," Ethan said.

"Oh, that sounds nice," Trevor offered as he turned his phone camera on Ethan.

"Yeah, I'd go with her, but there are also all these terrifying, like, dolls," Ethan said as he shivered.

Alexus laughed. "Aww, is the big man afraid of dolls?"

"Ok, but you would be too if you saw them. I think the owner collects them or something. They're all around the store on the top shelves, just staring with those dead eyes," Ethan explained.

"Like the porcelain ones in the big white dresses?" Trevor asked.

Ethan nodded and pointed at the store. "Yeah, and there's like a thousand of them in there."

Trevor shivered. "Yeah, I hate those things."

Alexus laughed again. "Wow, didn't know I was working with a bunch of wimps."

A woman shouted behind them, and the three turned, "No! No! Absolutely not!" Fighting to come toward them was a middle-aged woman sporting a classic Karen haircut and dressed in a green and red dress, while an overweight cop halfheartedly stepped in her way. "I don't want them anywhere near my store!"

"Mrs. Klein. Please. Stop. It's not safe," the cop said as he attempted to block her.

She pushed past him and marched straight up to the agents. Pointing her finger at them, she threatened, "If any of you take one step near my store, I'll sue. I'll sue all of you."

Alexus sighed and muttered to Ethan, "Great, and she acts like a total Karen too."

"Mrs. Klein. You need to calm down," the officer said.

Stomping her foot, the woman barked, "Stop calling me Klein, Carl! You know we're divorced."

"I'm sorry, Kitty. It's just a force of habit," the officer said.

Pointing at the NRDS again, she demanded, "And tell them they have to leave! They're destroying the town, and I don't want them in my shop!"

"Wait. Klein? You're Jeremy's ex-wife?" Ethan asked.

Spinning to face him, the woman said, "And who the fuck are you?"

Ethan held out his hand and said, "Oh. Um. Sorry. I'm Ethan Malik. Agent Ethan Malik."

Kitty looked at his outstretched hand and crossed her arms, laughing to herself. "Well, thank you, Agent, for coming by. Now, please, get the fuck out of here. The police have this handled."

The officer held up his hand to get Kitty's attention. "Um, actually Kitty. We're not going in there."

She spun around and yelled at the officer, "What do you mean you aren't going in there? I think I need to speak to your supervisor."

A laugh echoed out of the store at that second, followed by flickering Christmas trees. The cop shook his head. "Yeah. No. We're not getting involved."

Kitty's mouth hung open. "But. It's your job. You're the police."

"And if there'd been a crime committed—like, say, you'd been robbed or something, then we'd go in. But this doesn't look like that, and these fine agents feel they need to investigate," the officer said.

"I called you, the police, to come check on my store and make sure there wasn't an intruder," Kitty said.

"And there wasn't, but you failed to mention that shit was literally flying off the shelves. What do you want me to do, Kitty? Arrest a snow globe?"

"You're fucking worthless, Carl," Kitty said to the cop.

Ethan interjected. "Listen, I know you don't like us and all, and I know Chax Tamish has said some pretty weird stuff about us, but this is kind of what we do." He held up a briefcase for her to see.

Kitty looked at her shop and then down at the ground. "Alright. Fuck. Fine. Go. But don't break anything."

Ethan smiled. "We'll do our best."

Alexus stepped forward, tossing her coffee in the trash and pulling a notepad out from her back pocket. "We've got a few questions for you before we go in. First, did anyone die here recently?"

Kitty took a step back. "No. Why would you ask that?"

Alexus scribbled some notes. "Part of the job. Do you know who it could be?"

"Who what could be? Are you seriously going on with this whole ghost facade? Carl, can you get on the phone with an electrician? It has to be just wiring or something."

"How about antiques? Get any antiques recently?" Ethan asked.

Alexus looked up from her notepad and smiled. "Nice."

Ethan crossed his arms and grinned. "Reread the manual last night. Page seventy-eight."

Alexus smiled and dropped her voice low, impersonating Vince Vaughn, "Our little baby's all growns up."

"I had a clock come in. A big grandfather clock. Handcrafted. It came all the way from Germany," Kitty offered.

"That's gotta be it. Let's go get this old geezer," Ethan said with a nod.

"I'm going to wait out here," Trevor said. "I'll stream from the window. So, don't die."

Alexus laughed and picked up her briefcase. She strode to the front door of the store with Ethan chasing behind her. Grabbing the door handle, she looked at him and said, "You don't have that damn clicker, do you?"

"No. Melissa took it back," he said.

"Good," she said as she yanked the door open and rushed inside.

Ethan stepped in behind her and took in the store. The tight aisles, kitschy keepsakes, and the row of dolls staring down at them were eerily illuminated by the unceasingly flashing Christmas trees at the front of the store.

"Ugh. You're right. This place is from my nightmares," Alexus said.

"I know, right?" Ethan asked, as he looked at the dolls all staring back down at him.

A voice echoed past them in a low whisper, "*Sterben.*"

Alexus let out a sigh. "Great. Here we go."

One of the dolls at the end of the aisle fell from the top shelf and landed in the middle of the dimly lit floor.

"Oh, fuck." Ethan said.

The doll spun its head around and sat up, staring at them.

Without skipping a beat, Alexus grabbed a large wooden candy cane with one hand and held it like a bat. "Creepy ghost. Check."

Ethan held on to his badge, noting the strands of wispy fog emanating off the doll. "Alright, you old German bastard. *Sprichst du Englisch?*"

A low voice screeched from the doll as a small porcelain arm pointed toward them, "*Du wirst hier verrecken!*"

"Uh. What the fuck?" Alexus said.

At once, all the dolls on the top shelf leaned forward and looked down at Ethan and Alexus. Ethan gripped his badge tighter and shook his head. "Uh. It said something about us dying."

The dolls fell, one by one, from the top shelves as a shout echoed through the store. "*Strib! Strib! Strib!*"

"Oh hell no," Alexus said, dropping her briefcase and holding on to the candy cane with both hands before swinging it at the nearest dive bombing doll.

It shattered in one hit and flew into several others before she swung again and again, smashing every creepy porcelain doll that dared near her.

The ones that landed near Ethan rose like spiders on their little porcelain arms and legs and skittered across the floor as their heads spun in circles.

Ethan punted one across the store before three leaped onto him and started crawling up his leg. "Fuck, Ahh! Alexus, a little help!"

Alexus swung the bat, lodging a shattered doll head into the candy cane, and kicked off the other two. Once they were cleared, she straightened her jacket and pointed the bat at the first doll, still sitting in place. "That all you got, you creepy-ass fucker?"

Ethan peered at the doll and followed the wisps of smoke to the silhouette of an old man with small round glasses hiding behind the row of snow globes. "I think I see him."

Alexus kicked the briefcase to him. "Great, then case the fucker."

Then the music from every snow globe went off at once, creating a strange melody of discordant noise.

The silhouetted man became clearer to Ethan, and he saw a smile grow on his face.

"Fuck. get ready," Ethan said.

One by one, snow globes flew into the aisle at Ethan and Alexus.

"Take cover!" Ethan yelled, as the globe shattered against his briefcase.

Alexus swung her candy cane bat at one, shattering it to pieces, and took another to the shoulder before turning quickly to look at Ethan. "Go around and case the dick! I'll keep him distracted."

Ethan nodded and scampered behind a rack of greeting cards as a fourth globe crashed into the metal shelves, sending shards of glass, water, and glitter in all directions.

He crouched down low and raced into the next aisle over, keeping close to the garlands and tinsel.

Another crashed from the next aisle over and Alexus yelled, "Ethan, hurry the fuck up!"

He unclasped the briefcase as he neared his target, the old man's focus drawn solely on Alexus and his dwindling collection of snow globes.

He flung the case forward, and it flapped open, shrouding the man in blue light.

The ghost turned and looked at Ethan, the snow globe in his hand falling to the ground. "*Nein! Nein!*"

When the briefcase snapped closed, Ethan raced to pick it up and collapsed on the floor, hyperventilating.

Alexus walked over to him, swinging her bat haphazardly while her shoes crunched on shards of porcelain and glass. "Well, that was easy."

Ethan glared up at her and laughed. "The fuck it was. Is it always this insane? What happened to the whole going to the graveyard with a clipboard thing?"

Alexus held out a hand and pulled Ethan up, wiping the glitter off his shoulder. "Little more insane than usual, but this is the job, rookie. You don't get to pick your ghosts. You just deal with them as they come."

Bursting through the door, Kitty screamed, "Oh, my God! What did you do to my shop?"

Alexus patted the briefcase that Ethan was still clutching, "No worries, ma'am, we've got your culprit right here."

Trevor stepped through the door, panning his camera around the shot. "Holy hell, looks like it was a feisty one."

"I'm going to sue! I'm going to sue all of you! I knew I shouldn't have let you in here! You ruined my shop!" Kitty wailed as she marched around, taking in the damage.

Alexus waved her glass-covered candy cane bat at the woman. "I'm keeping this. Might come in handy later."

The woman's face turned red, and her eyes looked as if they were about to bulge out of her head.

Ethan carefully stepped over the remnants of the broken snow globes. "I uh. I think we should just go."

Kitty didn't say another word as they escaped from the shop.

Alexus patted Ethan's back and looked into Trevor's camera, mimicking Vince Vaughn once more. "Our little baby's all growns up."

Trevor laughed and finished the quote, "Because you're growns up and you're growns up and you're growns up."

Thirty-Three

Clowning Around

"WAIT, WHO DIED?" ETHAN asked Buck as they stood on the grassy hill overlooking a funeral procession as pallbearers carried the casket to the designated plot.

"Some twenty-year-old kid. Worked for Tamish," Buck said.

A man, dressed in a long black robe, stood next to the casket while nearly sixty others surrounded him. Ethan scanned the crowd and spotted Chax Tamish, the mayoral candidate, dressed in a crisp black suit.

"And what are we waiting for?"

"Just wait, you'll see."

Ethan focused on the faces of every person, recognizing most as the people who stood outside their office on more than one occasion. Everyone was in black. Everyone but the clown, wearing a giant red wig and orange and yellow suit that stuck out like a sore thumb.

"Is. Is that a clown?"

Buck adjusted his glasses, grabbed on to his badge, and nodded. "That is correct. But not what I meant."

"Well, that's pretty out of place."

"The kid should be here."

Ethan kept his eyes locked on the clown as he moved uncomfortably close to the casket. "How do we know he's going to be a spirit?"

"We don't. But if we can, it's better to catch them when they're fresh. Plus, it was this or paperwork," Buck said.

"This is better than hearing Melissa calling me jailbait again," Ethan said, shaking his head.

"You're telling me. If I hear another joke about being framed, I might consider crimes that will keep me in a cell."

Ethan cocked his head and shifted his focus completely to the clown, who started blowing up balloons and twisting them into animals. First a giraffe, then a dog, and then a sword. Once he finished one animal, the clown drew an oversized needle from his sleeve, popped it, and then did a little dance. All the while, the minister continued as if nothing was happening.

"My god, this clown is desperate for a laugh," Ethan said.

"Good for us, though. If this kid's still around, I don't think he'd appreciate a deranged clown dancing on his grave."

"Did you find out how he died?" Ethan asked.

"Nope," Buck said.

"I mean, it would have made the papers if it was something big, like a car wreck."

"Yep."

"Jeez, what is wrong with this guy?" Ethan asked as the clown hopped off the grave and next to the minister. He stood cheek-to-cheek with the older man and pulled out a small horn, sounding it with perfect precision.

"May HONK be upon all who HONK, and HONK all the bereaved among us. HONK us into eternity."

The clown made faces at the man of shock and disgust, and Ethan snorted in a suppressed giggle.

"What the fuck? Do we just let him do that?" Ethan asked.

"Give it another minute."

The minister started singing Amazing Grace, followed by the others surrounding the casket. As if on cue, the clown hopped onto the casket and began dancing in a combination of the macarena and chicken dance to the slow and melancholic beat.

Finally, someone in the crowd clapped. A man in a sleek blue suit came forward from the back, passing through the crowd and clapping at the clown. He shouted. "I fucking get it. Thank you, you dick."

As the song ended, the minister looked at the casket and said, "We commit this body to the ground, earth to earth, ashes to ashes, dust to—fuck!"

At that second, the clown cartwheeled off the casket and through the minister, and the unsuspecting pious man nearly fell to the ground as he shivered.

The minister stood up straight and cleared. "Dust." He then rested a hand on the casket and signaled for the crowd to disperse.

One man broke from the crowd, his eyes looking up the hill, right at Ethan and Buck.

"Here we go," Buck mumbled as mayoral candidate Chax Tamish approached. His black trench coat swished as he walked, and Ethan realized how cool Chax looked, like an action hero in a movie. Ethan half-imagined Chax pulling an automatic weapon from the coat and lighting them both up like in a Tarantino flick.

"Gentlemen," Chax said once he was close enough to be heard without yelling. "Stalking me at a funeral, I see? Is there anywhere you poor excuses for government officials won't go?"

"Well, that's rude. I think we have better things to do than stalk you." Ethan laughed.

"We're doing our jobs," Buck replied.

"Which includes intimidating civil servants and the public by looking over them at a funeral? Is that your job, agent?" Chax fired back.

"We're not here for you, dude. We didn't even know you were going to be here," Ethan quipped.

Chax grinned. "Right. Okay. So, my assistant dies, and you didn't think I was going to show up? You just thought I, what? Wouldn't come to his funeral? That's the story you're going with?"

"You're giving us too much credit," Buck said.

Ethan rolled his eyes. "Put it together, man. Government agents that talk to ghosts are at a funeral. What do you think we're doing here?"

"Government agents who think they talk to ghosts come to a funeral to intimidate the people trying to defund them. That is the story here. Do you really think Lester is one of your ghosts? Come on!" Chax said with an exaggerated laugh.

"If we wanted to intimidate you, we'd let a ghost or two loose in your bedroom," Ethan said.

Buck snickered at the thought. "Maybe the little girl in the pink dress who sings lullabies in that creepy whisper."

"Oh. I was thinking of the German doll man we just caught, but that's way more terrifying," Ethan said.

"Great, and you two think you're funny?" He reached into his coat pocket and pulled out his phone. "I need to document this. You two stay right there."

Ethan sighed. "Great, a male Karen."

"Smile for the camera," Buck said.

Holding up his phone, Chax took multiple pictures of the two agents. "Oh, my campaign is going to eat this up. Worthless government agents have nothing better to do than try to intimidate me."

"Yep, that's exactly it. Wasting your government dollars," Buck said as he waved to the camera.

Chax nodded and put his phone down. "Gentlemen, I hope never to see either of you again." Turning and walking back down the hill, he called, "Vote for Tamish."

"I hate that fucking guy," Ethan said.

Buck shrugged. "We're probably going to get shit for those pictures."

"So much for staying out of Melissa's way."

Nudging Ethan with his elbow, Buck said, "We just can't win, kid."

Looking at Buck, he smiled and held up his clipboard. "You got that right. Ready to do some work?"

They walked down the hill together and approached the man in the blue suit and the clown, who stood shoulder to shoulder facing the grave.

Buck cleared his throat and said, "Gentlemen. I'm Agent Hampton. This is Agent Malik. We're with the National Recently Deceased Services."

The two men turned around. Beneath his thick-rimmed glasses, the one in the sleek blue suit had eyes that were red and puffy. The clown extended his hand. The smile on his face was almost as big as the makeup around it. "Ah, the NRDS have arrived. Love what you guys have been doing with the place. Name's Bingo Bango."

Ethan reached out to accept the handshake, and as he expected, his hand passed straight through Bingo's as if it were moving through cold air. However, what he didn't expect was the numbing sensation that left his hand tingling.

Ethan stared at his hands while Bingo waved his arms in the air in celebration. "Aha! Gotcha! I'm a ghost, you sad excuse for a meat suit! BOO!"

Ethan smiled. "Yep, you got me."

Bingo put his arms down and said, "Wow. A smile?! I haven't got one of those in years. Maybe you aren't such a sad excuse after all."

"And you're Lester, I presume?" Buck asked.

The man in the blue suit took his glasses off and cleaned them with a handkerchief from his breast pocket. "That's correct." Putting his glasses back on, he took a deep breath and said, "Lester Buchalter. So, this is all real, right?"

Ethan nodded and began taking notes on his clipboard. "Afraid so. Buchalter. Could you spell that for me?"

Bingo jumped in front of Lester and did a dance while singing out his name, "B-I-N-G-O B-A-N-G-O!"

Ethan let out a short laugh.

"Now a laugh? Sweet Jesus. For a while there, I thought the living were all dead inside," the clown said.

"B-U-C-H-A-L-T-E-R," Lester said.

"Well, we'll get you in our system, then our job is to care for you until you figure out how to cross over to the other side," Buck said. "Today, we just want to do a preliminary assessment on both of you to get some basic information. And Bingo, we haven't forgotten you too."

"Sounds good," Lester said.

Pulling a fake flower from his sleeve and giving a bow, Bingo said, "Hope is a lot like a flower. Looks pretty, but in the end—" When he dropped the flower, it evaporated before hitting the ground.

"That's a little dark," Ethan said.

The clown let out a laugh and fell backward, landing flat on his back and looking up at the sky.

Ethan looked at the clown, then at Lester. "I guess we'll start with you. Can you tell us a little bit about how you died?"

"Oh. Um. Sure. I was murdered."

"Wowzers!" Bingo shot up from the ground, and a deck of cards flew from his sleeves, filling the air. "Bury the lede like they bury the dead, why don't ya?"

Ethan giggled as the cards evaporated around them.

The clown looked at Ethan and smiled, his voice raspier. "Seriously, kid. I'm here all night. People are dying to get in, but I think I can save you a headstone at my next show," the clown said.

"What do you remember?" Buck asked.

"It's foggy. I remember I was in the campaign office, and I was arguing with . . . With someone. And. I think I was shot. Maybe. I remember there was blood and . . . and I was lying on the floor." Lester held his head as he spoke, like he was having a massive migraine. "I don't know. It's fuzzy."

"You experienced a traumatic event. It'll probably come back to you slowly. Don't rush it," Buck said.

"Yeah. Okay," Lester said.

"You don't have a joke for that one?" Buck asked Bingo.

"Hey. Murder's no laughing matter," Bingo said. Pulling a rubber knife from his sleeve, he added, "Unless we're talking about the time my therapist told me time heals all wounds, so I stabbed him fifty times and watched to see what would happen."

Ethan let out a loud laugh. "What the fuck? You're not serious, are you?"

The clown froze in place, his smile stretching farther across his face than normal, and a strange hunger filled his eyes. "I don't know, kid, am I?"

There was a long pause, and Ethan looked to Buck, then back at the clown. Then, on the flip of a dime, the clown honked his horn and started cartwheeling around, flinging his rubber knife at Ethan.

Buck took Ethan's clipboard and looked at the clown over his glasses. "Alright, funny man. What's your real name?"

"Bingo Bango. I, A, double B, double N-G-O."

"Seriously?"

"Rarely," Bingo said.

"We want to help. What's your non-clown name?" Ethan asked.

"Tell that to the last guy that tried helping me. Like I told him, no idea what the name is, so I go by Bingo Bango."

"How about when you died? Do you recall the date?" Buck asked.

"I think she was tall, blond, red dress."

"The day!" Ethan laughed. "What about where your headstone is? Remember that?"

"Nope."

"Well, what do you remember?" Buck asked.

"I remember the grouchy agent."

"Agent Stephenson," Buck said.

"Yep, that's him. Grumpy Gus. Not like this chucklehead," Bingo said, motioning to Ethan.

"How often did Stephenson come by?" Buck asked.

"Just the once. He introduced himself, asked my name. When I told him I didn't know it, he said, 'I don't have time for this clown shit.' Then he marched away. I've been welcoming the new residents to this eternal abode ever since."

"If it makes you feel any better, we all think Stephenson is an asshole. We'll work your case and see if we can help get you out of here," Buck said.

"It's alright. The funerals aren't too bad to play. The audience is a little stiff, if you know what I mean."

Ethan laughed again.

"I like him," Bingo said to Buck.

Buck wrote on the paper. "Noted. So, here is how this will work. Someone from our office will come by once a week to check in on you. If you remember anything about who you were or how you died, let us know. It might be a clue to getting you to the other side."

"What are we supposed to do in the meantime?" Lester asked.

"Don't worry, dirt buddy. All the others are just dying to meet you," Bingo said, putting his arm around Lester. "We've got an a cappella group who sings on Thursdays in the back corner. When all of us are going, the old lady comes running out of her house and speaks tongues at us."

Buck scribbled another note. "Yeah, you should probably stop that."

The clown frowned and squeezed Lester's shoulder. "Aw, no fun. Too bad you can't stop us." He steered Lester away and kept talking. "On Sundays, we like to scare the groundskeeper. We've gone through three this year."

Thirty-Four

Who Invited Gerry?

E THAN TOOK A SIP of his beer and looked around the bar. For a small spot outside of town, it wasn't half bad. The tables were clean, at least.

A group of men, who seemed to be regulars, sat at the bar laughing and watching the game together. A few couples were spread out around the room, but it was too poorly lit to see their faces.

Ethan smiled at his date and then looked down. They'd only been sitting at the table for a few minutes and already it felt awkward.

"How's your beer?" Bryce Fillmore, the liaison for upper management, asked.

"It's a beer. I never know what to pick with the craft stuff, so it's just the same old stuff for me," Ethan said with a shrug. He couldn't believe he'd said yes to this. Taking a breath, he nodded toward Bryce and asked, "How's your, um, your drink?"

"It's a Gibson. And it's nice."

Ethan laughed. "I don't really know what that is."

"It's gin and vermouth," Bryce said with a smile.

Ethan scrunched up his nose and pursed his lips. "I don't know what that is either."

Bryce chuckled, his eyes full of happiness as he looked at Ethan. "I started drinking them in college. Back then, it felt sophisticated to order something with gin in it. Usually it comes with pickled onions, but they didn't have any."

"Pickled onions?"

"It tastes different than it sounds."

Ethan nodded and took another drink of his beer.

He looked around the room again. There'd been a time not too long ago when everyone in a room like this would have known who he was and, depending on which high school they'd graduated from, would have adored him or despised him; but those days were gone. Now he was just a guy in a T-shirt and jeans who seemed vaguely familiar to strangers, but not familiar enough for them to care about, with another guy sharply dressed in suit pants and a button-up.

He looked back at Bryce. "So, um. Where did you go to college?"

"Columbia," Bryce said.

Ethan felt a surge of excitement. "Like in South America? What was it like? Do you know Spanish?" he asked, leaning forward.

"In Manhattan," Bryce said with another sweet laugh.

"Oh. Like, New York?"

"That's the one."

"Well, that's cool too," Ethan said. He thought about being surrounded by tall skyscrapers and racing through crowds of people to get from one place to another. He couldn't think of a question to ask, and the seconds dragged on.

He took another sip of his beer and made quick eye contact with Bryce. It occurred to him he'd never dated anyone with glasses before. He was out with a nerd, and he didn't mind. "Did you like it?" he finally asked.

Bryce leaned on the table and looked up at the ceiling. "I don't know. It's not really something you like or dislike. It's more something you survive."

Ethan leaned back in his chair and asked, "What's that mean?"

"It's a lot of pressure. And it requires a lot of focus. And then it is over far too quickly. There were things I liked about it. I like that I could jump on the subway and be anywhere in the city in minutes. I'd go to jazz clubs in Harlem or have dinner in Central Park, or take a Saturday and tour the Met, or walk the Brooklyn Bridge. I do miss the city. There was this little bagel shop near my apartment. I lived in a one-bedroom hole in the wall on the tenth floor of a building that felt like it might collapse at any minute. Anyway, there was a bagel shop on the corner that had beautifully baked fresh bagels and dark coffee. I miss things like that. The sights. The smells. Just being in the middle of everything with life churning all around you. It was magical."

Ethan found himself leaning on the edge of his seat when Bryce stopped speaking. He could have listened to the wistfulness of his voice for the rest of the night. "That sounds amazing."

"Have you ever been to New York?" Bryce asked.

Ethan took a drink from his beer and laughed. "Me? No. I've never been farther east than Pittsburgh. I want to go sometime, though. That'd be cool."

"You should. I'd love to show you around."

Ethan's face flushed red, and he looked down. "I, um. Yeah. Maybe."

Bryce leaned in. "I'm sorry. I didn't mean that to sound awkward. I. Well. I mean." He took in a breath and looked away. "I don't date much, if you can imagine."

"Me neither," Ethan said with a smile. Desperate to change the subject, he asked, "Uh, how'd you get from New York to the middle of nowhere?"

"Well, after school, I went through the intern program. They had me try field work for a few weeks out in Chicago, but that was just a formality so I could get in with management," Bryce said, returning his glasses to his face. Ethan liked how they gave his features depth.

"That seems like a quick ladder to the top."

"My family is part of the agency's legacy. My great-great-grandfather was one of the first agents when President Pierce founded the agency."

"So, this is like a family business for you?"

"It's in the blood. My father is the Chief of the Northeast Region and my older brother runs the office in Baltimore. I was sent out here to learn the ropes before I get pulled back to the East Coast."

Ethan shrugged. "That's got to be nice. To have people putting it together like that for you. Before I got hired, I thought I'd be stuck working at Walmart for the rest of my life."

Bryce smiled. "And yet, here you are. Doing something you hopefully love."

Ethan stared into Bryce's eyes and smiled. Bryce stretched out his hand and rested it next to Ethan's, his pinky brushing up against Ethan's hand.

Ethan's stomach fluttered, and he reached for his beer and glanced around the room. "Do you come here a lot?" he asked, immediately regretting the question.

"Never. This is my first time," Bryce said, pulling back his hand.

"Oh. Yeah. Me too."

"I Googled it right before I texted you. It had a four-star Yelp review. It has that going for it, I guess."

Ethan laughed. "Well, a four-star yelp review around here is like. I don't know. A restaurant that's a huge deal in New York?"

"Well then, I'm honored to share this high-quality Midwest experience with you."

Ethan smirked. "I bet."

Bryce sipped his Gibson and said, "I was a little surprised you agreed to meet me. I wasn't sure I was your type."

"Yeah. This is the first time I've dated someone who went to Columbia," Ethan said, tipping his beer to Bryce.

"I'll try to do the alma mater proud," Bryce said with a grin.

"I was surprised, though. I didn't know if there were rules or something against dating people in management. So, I didn't tell anyone in the office. I hope that's okay?"

"It's not encouraged, but I'm not your direct supervisor, so there are no rules against it," Bryce said.

"I figured you'd know," Ethan said, moving his chair forward and brushing his knee against Bryce's. They held each other's gaze and smiled.

Before he could ask Bryce something else about his time in New York, he heard the bells jingle, indicating someone was entering the bar.

As if his aura was preceded by some form of magical energy, a hush fell over the bar, and everyone turned to see who was blessing the establishment with his presence. Striding through the door, Gerry looked around the restaurant and said, "Looks like Dana didn't listen to me about the decor. She's going to regret it. Now, where is my little Ethan? Would someone please point me toward where he is being kept?"

Ethan turned to Bryce in a panic. "Okay. I might have told Gerry."

"Your partner's husband?"

"I didn't know what to wear, and I needed advice."

"But you're in a T-shirt and jeans? I mean, don't get me wrong. It's working for you."

"Gerry said the same thing." Ethan's face flushed. "He said jeans did wonders for my ass."

Bryce let out a laugh as Buck stepped in behind Gerry and pointed to where Ethan was sitting.

"Ethan! Never fear! We're coming!" Gerry called as he crossed the bar.

"Oh, God," Ethan said as he slunk into his seat, wishing he could disappear from the moment.

"This should be entertaining," Bryce quipped, leaning back and crossing his arms.

"I'm so sorry," Ethan said.

Stepping up to the table, Gerry extended his hand to Bryce and said, "Why you must be the young lad in upper management Buck has told me so much about? Agent Fillmore, is it?"

"I'm off the clock. You can call me Bryce. And you are Gerry, I presume?" Bryce asked with his back straight and a smile that could swoon a road-raged trucker off his feet.

Gerry tilted his chin down and took Bryce in. "Initial presentation is acceptable. Firm jaw. Intelligent eyes. And damn you for that smile. Ethan, this one gets my initial approval."

Buck sat down in the chair next to Ethan and glared at Bryce. "Hey, kid," he said to Ethan.

Ethan put his forehead on the table and said, "Hey, Buck."

Picking up Ethan's beer, Gerry held it up to the light, sniffed it, took a sip, and grimaced. "Oh, Jesus, Mary, and the great goddess Betty White, may she rest in peace. No. No. No. No." He placed the beer at an empty table behind them and then picked up Bryce's glass and sniffed it. "A Gibson. God. Really? What is this, a Mad Men reunion? Excuse me while I get us some proper drinks," he said, walking behind the bar with Bryce's drink. He dumped it in the sink and pulled bottles off the top shelves.

Ethan picked his head up off the table, looked at Buck, and asked, "Why are you here?"

Still glaring at Bryce, Buck said, "Chaperoning."

"How very Victorian of you," Bryce said.

"I'm a grown man. I don't need a chaperone," Ethan complained.

Buck grunted toward Bryce.

"We were having a nice time," Ethan said.

"I bet." Buck sneered.

Ethan watched Gerry pull several bills from his wallet and hand them to the bartender before returning with a tray filled with three martini glasses and a tumbler of dark amber liquid. "Double bourbon for my dearest," he said, placing the dark liquid in front of Buck. "And French martinis for the rest of us," he said, placing the three martini glasses in front of himself, Ethan, and Bryce.

Ethan took a sip and said, "Fruity."

"Yes, yes. Freshens the breath up in case you two decide to do the tonsil tango later," Gerry said.

While Ethan's face turned beet red, Gerry turned to Bryce and asked, "Now, mister upper management. What are exactly your intentions with our young Ethan? Because Buck and I will not tolerate any shenanigans."

"Shenanigans?" Ethan asked in disbelief.

"I am a no shenanigans type of guy," Bryce said, raising his hands defensively.

"We'll see," Buck said, still glaring.

"I can't believe I told you where we were meeting," Ethan mumbled.

"And you," Gerry said, turning his attention to Ethan. "What exactly is this outfit?"

Bryce laughed to himself.

"You said the jeans made my ass look good," Ethan said, looking down at his white T-shirt.

"They do, but what kind of slob wears a plain white T-shirt on a first date? You're not a San Fran daddy, so don't even try. I know you have a tie because I've bought you a few," Gerry complained.

Picking up his martini glass and motioning toward Ethan, Bryce said before he took a sip, "I think you look cute."

Ethan shot a smile at Bryce while a server appeared with a plate of onion rings, fried cheese curds, and a container of beer cheese. "This is perfect, Hans. Thank you."

The server nodded. "We made the call last week to the butcher you recommended, and the steaks are being prepared just like you asked."

Slipping the server a palm full of cash, Gerry said, "That's for you and the boys in the back. Tell them thank you for humoring an old fool."

"You ordered for us?" Ethan asked.

"And you're welcome for saving you from the chicken strips and French fries you were no doubt going to order," Gerry said, looking at Bryce and then Ethan.

Ethan shrugged. "I like chicken strips."

Buck laughed.

Gerry grabbed Ethan's hand and squeezed as he said, "Oh, girl, I know."

"I still haven't heard what your intentions are with my partner." Buck sneered at Bryce.

But before Bryce could answer, another person stumbled through the front door. They all turned to see a heavyset man in blue denim overalls, so drunk he could barely walk. "Oh shit. That's Jeremy!" Ethan said.

"I only got four steaks," Gerry complained.

"It's a work thing," Buck said.

"This is Mr. Klein? The one from your report. His daughter Angela is the spirit," Bryce said, suddenly attentive.

"Ger. Give this guy a point for reading my report," Buck said.

"Your reports are impeccable," Bryce said.

"Give him two points," Buck said.

"It's Jeremy!" someone from the bar called as Jeremy shuffled toward him.

"How you doing, man? How'd that job at the laundromat go?" another guy called.

"I need more beers, please," Jeremy said, holding up a finger.

"You got it, man," one guy said as he ordered a beer and passed it to Jeremy. Jeremy held it with both hands close to his mouth like a kid would hold hot chocolate.

"Something's off," Ethan said, squinting his eyes at Jeremy. There was an odd halo around him that Ethan couldn't quite make out.

"Thank you, Mr. Kaper," Jeremy said.

The man from the bar laughed and put his hand on Jeremy's shoulder. He shivered and yanked his hand off him in an instant. "Jeez Jeremy. You're freezing. You alright?"

Jeremy shook his head and looked down. "No. It's bad. I just want my mom and dad to get back together. I messed up. Now they hate each other even more. I just wish I'd never been born," Jeremy said as he choked back tears.

"Oh, shit!" Ethan exclaimed.

"Yep," Buck said, pushing back his chair and slowly standing.

"Can we just have one evening without this nonsense?" Gerry said as he sipped his martini.

"What's wrong?" Bryce asked.

Ethan gave Bryce a look and said, "You and Gerry get out of here. That man isn't Jeremy. I mean, it is. But he's not himself. That's Angela. His daughter! She's possessed him!"

Thirty-Five

Bar Fight

E THAN STARED ACROSS THE bar from his table as Jeremy took another beer from the man next to him and shotgunned it. The man beside him grabbed the bottle from Jeremy and glared, "Woah man, take it easy. Buy your own."

Jeremy winced and stuck out his tongue, "Blech, I don't know why daddy drinks this. It tastes like pee."

Tracing the aura around Jeremy, Ethan knew in his mind that Angela had possessed her father. He shook his head and cleared his throat. "We've got to do something before this goes sideways."

"And what exactly is that supposed to mean?" Gerry said as he swirled his martini.

Buck finished his whiskey and pointed his empty glass at Jeremy. "See that big guy there? His little girl possessed him."

"Wait, the little girl from Oakland? She was low risk." Bryce said as he took his glasses off again and cleaned them.

Ethan looked at Buck. "Well, she's a five now. And I don't have a case. What are we going to do?"

"We're going to do what we do," Buck said, standing.

Bryce sipped on the martini Gerry had ordered for him before standing and grabbing his coat. "Say, Gerry, how would you like to retire with me to the parking lot while these two gents take care of this mess?"

Gerry swirled his martini again and held up a finger to Bryce. "I'm not going anywhere. I never get to see my man in action, and now I have a front-row seat. He's always telling me, 'Gerry! Wait in the car!' or 'Gerry! This one's too big! Close your eyes and stand in the corner.'"

"I've said none of those things," Buck said.

Gerry reached up and squeezed Buck's shoulder. "Dear, don't ruin this moment for me."

"But I never said those things. This isn't like your wrestling shows. You could get hurt."

"Dear, I'm not leaving. So, you can either continue arguing with me, or you can get that fine ass over there and let me see my man in action."

Pushing his glasses up and sitting back down, Bryce said, "Fine. We'll stay, but you're going to be back here with me, out of the way, while they go to work."

Gerry smiled and grabbed Ethan's half-finished martini and set it next to his own. "I can agree with those terms."

Buck looked down at Ethan, who was still seated, and said, "This is your case, kid. How do you want to play it?"

Ethan looked across the room and watched Jeremy take another beer from one of his friends and start chugging. This man was more attentive and shoved Jeremy, knocking him back into a wall.

Jeremy dropped the beer on the floor and held his shoulder. Tears fell down his face, and he pouted at the men. "Hey! That was really mean."

Ethan stood, his eyes locked on the glowing aura around Jeremy, which seemed to glow brighter and brighter as he frowned at his friends. "We should get him outside, I guess?"

"Lead the way," Buck said, motioning for Ethan to step forward.

Ethan sized up the men as he approached. He gulped, realizing that each of them was at least twice his size, and he couldn't help but wonder how he was about to get out of this without a bloodied nose. Jeremy alone could squish him like a bug if Angela really went for it.

Jeremy pushed off the wall and stumbled into the bar, leaning heavily on it while he whimpered. "It's just so bad, Mr. Kaper. I tried. I wanted them to get back together, but she just wouldn't listen." Burping, he added, "I think I might be sick."

Kaper took a swig from his own beer and patted Jeremy's back. "Hey, it's going to be okay, man."

The men from the bar all surrounded Jeremy and patted his back, echoing the sentiment with supportive "yeah-mans" and "that-sucks-bros."

"She won't even talk to me. And it's all my fault," Jeremy wailed, tears flowing down his cheeks.

Kaper continued rubbing his back and said, "Jeremy, man, you can't keep beating yourself up. She left you years ago. Maybe it's time to move on?"

"Move on? I can't move on, knowing my ma and dad aren't going to get back together."

"But I thought your mom died like ten years ago, man?" a man at the bar said.

"Yeah. Yeah. Didn't she have cancer?" another man asked.

"We had like a jar up and everything," a third man noted.

"No!" Jeremy screamed as he slammed his fist on the bar, and a wave of cold energy radiated off of him, causing everyone to shiver. "That was grandma. I'm talking about my mom. My mom hates my dad."

Kaper raised his eyebrow and slowly lowered his hand back onto his friend. "Listen, man. Maybe you just need to sleep it off. I think you've had too many tonight."

"I can't. I can't sleep," Jeremy wailed. "I never sleep." Looking at the man next to him, he grabbed the beer out of his hand, sloshing some on the floor before drinking it with both hands.

Angry, the man growled at Jeremy and said, "Hey! That's my—"

Ethan stepped forward, pulling his badge from his pocket and flashing it at the men. "Excuse me, gentlemen. I need to have a word with Mr. Klein here."

"Oh, no. Mister Ethan," Jeremy said, his eyes wide. "I'm sorry. I know I'm not supposed to be here. The other kids told me not to."

"We need to get you back," Ethan said.

"I know. Please don't be mad. I just needed to try," Jeremy pleaded. He let loose another foul burp that made the men at the bar all move back from him.

Kaper stepped in front of Jeremy and loomed over Ethan. "Look, man, I don't know who you are, but we've got this. Jeremy's our friend. He's just having an off night."

Ethan stepped back from the massive man, eyeing up his arms—thick from decades of manual labor—that could easily crush him.

"Yeah. Cut him some slack; he lost his daughter," a man from the bar called.

Buck held up his hands defensively. "We're not cops. We're with the National Recently Deceased Services. We just need to have a word with your friend."

Jeremy looked at his friends and shook his head. "They want to make me go with them. They want to take me back to the cemetery."

One man pushed Jeremy behind him and pointed a finger at Buck. "Wait. I know you! You were on the news."

Kaper squinted at Buck, then nodded. "Yeah. You got arrested for ripping up downtown."

Ethan looked past them at Jeremy. "Hey, look at me. We need to get you out of here. It's not safe."

"Please don't make me go back there," Jeremy wailed.

"She's going to find out. You're not where you're supposed to be, Angela," Ethan pleaded.

The aura around Jeremy quivered, and fine tendrils lashed out, latching on to Kaper and the other men around Jeremy.

The men all blinked a few times, then Kaper took another step forward and several of the men from the bar fell in behind him. "Look. I don't know what kind of game you're playing, but I said we'd handle it."

From across the room, Gerry waved his empty martini glass and yelled, "Don't let him push you around, sweetie! You've got this!"

Buck looked down at the floor and shook his head.

"And Ethan, I was right. Those jeans are doing wonders," Gerry added.

Ethan strained to see past Kaper and said, "Angela, let them go. This is getting out of hand."

Kaper took another step forward, his chest bumping into Ethan's. Ethan looked up and saw the faint glow in his eyes as he let out an onion-ring-and-stale-beer-filled breath. "Maybe you should think twice before using a name like that."

Another man stepped up beside Kaper and nodded, "Yeah, bro. Using a name like that could get you a black eye."

All their eyes glowed even brighter, and a second man stood next to Kaper, cracking his knuckles. "Seems like someone needs to teach you some manners."

A third man stood and joined the party. "Yeah. I'm gonna teach your face some manners with my fist."

The second man's eyes flickered to normal, and he frowned, turning back to the man and saying, "Come on, man. Be serious. We're about to fight."

The third man's eyes flickered, and he replied, "Well, I thought it was clever. You know. Because I'm going to punch him in the face."

"Why do you always have to ruin everything, Donnie? God," the first man behind Kaper complained.

"Sorry, guys. I was just going to help pound these guys, you know?" Donnie said, holding up his fists.

"Just more punching and less talking, alright?" the second man said.

Jeremy stomped his foot, and all the men stood at attention, their eyes glowing once more.

"Guys! Focus!" Kaper demanded.

Behind them, Jeremy grabbed a half-finished beer and drank as he said, "I get why daddy does this. It takes away the sad."

"Drink as much as you need, buddy. We've got these losers!" Kaper called.

From behind Ethan, Buck whispered, "When it starts, grab Jeremy and get him out of here. Distance should break up whatever he's doing to his friends."

"When what starts?" Ethan whispered back.

Buck grabbed Ethan's shoulder and pulled him back, stepping face to face with Kaper. He adjusted his suit and loosened his tie. "Enough talking. You boys want to rumble? Then stop picking on the kid."

Kaper laughed. "Why don't you go take a seat with your boyfriend back there, old man, before you break a hip?"

Buck smirked. "Here's what's going to happen. We're gonna take Jeremy with us. Now, you boys have a choice. You can finish your night over there drinking yourself to sleep or in the emergency room while they put you all back together."

"And I said, leave Jeremy alone," Kaper said as he jabbed two fingers into Buck's chest.

Buck didn't move back. Instead, he looked into Kaper's glowing eyes and said, "Touch me again and see what happens."

Gerry clapped from across the room. "Keep fucking around and you're going to find out!" he called. Pushing on Fillmore, he added, "Buck hasn't been in a bar fight in at least a decade. This is so exciting."

"Come on guys," Ethan said, smiling and trying to make eye contact with Kaper. "You don't have to do this."

"But they do," Jeremy whined. "I don't want to go."

Kaper grinned, and his eyes glowed brightly.

Buck sneered.

"Look, old man," Kaper said again, pushing his two fingers toward Buck's chest a second time.

Buck grabbed the man's meaty fingers before they touched him and twisted them up. There was a loud popping sound, and Kaper screamed in pain.

"Now, kid!" Buck yelled right before his fist demolished Kaper's nose, spraying blood across the floor.

Ethan raced around the mob, surging toward Jeremy. Kaper staggered backward, cradling his broken hand and letting loose a stream of obscenities. In the confusion, Buck threw a powerful right hook into the next man's belly, causing the man to double over.

"Yeah! Give him the chair!" Gerry cheered, standing and clapping on the other side of the room.

Ethan ducked a punch from a man who'd jumped up from the bar. He then grabbed the man by the back and tossed him forward while Ethan pressed on. Glancing back at his partner, Ethan saw Buck take a shot to the jaw. Buck didn't flinch. Instead, he returned the jab, hitting the taller brute right in the throat and then turning on the next man and punching him across the jaw with a left cross.

Ethan gaped at the display of skill and deftness his partner showed as he laid out three younger men three times his size and was now moving onto a fourth.

He shook his head free and turned, grabbing Jeremy by the arm. "Sober up. It's time to go!"

Yanking his arm back, Jeremy took another chug of a beer. The threads of energy coming off him glowed brightly, and the men who were sprawled out on the floor jumped up and raced toward Buck.

"Now, Angela!" Ethan demanded.

He looked back toward Buck, seeing him stagger backward after taking a strong shot to the jaw.

Ethan knocked the beer out of Jeremy's hands and pointed to the men attacking Buck. "Do you see what you're making them do? Do you want your dad's friends to end up in the hospital?"

Jeremy looked at his friends and whined, "I'm sorry. I didn't want to start a fight. I'm sorry."

Ethan grabbed Jeremy's arm again, feeling the chill that stung his hand on contact. He pulled him off his barstool and toward the door. "Outside! Right now!"

"Fine. Okay. Fine. You don't have to be so mean about it," Jeremy said.

Ethan pushed Jeremy out into the chilly air, and all the threads of energy snapped back into the aura surrounding him.

Ethan took in a breath of cold air and shivered before glaring at Jeremy. "What were you thinking? I can't believe you'd do this!"

"I'm sorry. Please don't tell Ms. Mable. She's going to be so mad at me," Jeremy said, dragging his feet.

"I'm sure she's noticed you're gone," Ethan said.

"Oh, no," Jeremy said as he came to a hard stop.

Ethan pointed to his car and said, "Yeah, I can't imagine she's going to be happy. So, let's get back now before you're in any more—"

"No," Jeremy cut him off, pointing ahead of them. "It's not that. Look."

Kitty Klein stood several yards in front of them, sporting a green and red reindeer sweater with small Christmas ornaments hanging off it and clutching her purse to her chest. Her cheeks were tear stained, and her mouth was hanging open.

"Son of a bitch," Ethan muttered.

"Hi, again. Mom." Jeremy waved, looking down.

"Fuck me," Ethan mumbled.

Thirty-Six

Snow Cones and Snickerdoodles

J EREMY, WHO WAS STILL possessed by Angela and very intoxicated, stood outside the bar waving at Kitty as she approached.

Kitty Klein stopped several yards in front of them, sporting a green and red reindeer sweater with small Christmas ornaments hanging off it and clutching her purse to her chest. Green eyeliner streamed down her cheeks, only adding to the crazed Christmas woman look.

"Fuck. Fuck. Fuck," Ethan muttered.

"Jeremy! We weren't done! Don't make me get the lawyer for this!" she shouted, ornaments swinging left and right under her arms as she yelled. She rushed forward like some holiday-themed harpy ready to strike.

Ethan jumped between her and Jeremy and held his hands up. "Ms. Klein. Please. I'm sure this night has been difficult, but this isn't a good—"

A powerful smack to the face cut him short as it rattled his teeth.

"I've been meaning to do that for weeks," she said.

Grabbing his throbbing jaw with both hands, Ethan looked up at Kitty, ready to ask her why, but she reeled back her jingling arm and smacked him again.

"Mom! No, stop!" Jeremy yelled as he stumbled back and leaned against a car to keep himself from falling over.

Ethan blocked the strike with his forearm and instinctively pushed her back with both hands, realizing too late that both his hands had fully cupped Ms. Klein's breasts. "I. Uh. I'm—"

"How dare you! Pervert!" Kitty yelled, stepping back and covering her chest with both hands.

"Hey! Mr. Ethan! Don't touch my mom like that!" Jeremy yelled, taking a swing at empty air and falling to his knees. His face turned green, and his wide eyes looked up at Ethan. "Uh oh."

A flood of vomit came shooting out of him like the end of a firehose. Ethan lowered himself and jumped forward, wrapping his arm around Ms. Klein's waist and picking her up, racing away from the torrent of vomit.

"Let! Me! Down!" Kitty shouted, ramming her fists into his back.

"I'm sorry! I'm sorry!" Ethan said, setting her down carefully as they reached a safe distance.

Kitty brushed herself off and glared at Ethan, raising her hand to prepare for another smack.

Between breaths, Ethan lifted a finger and said, "If you smack me again, so help me God."

Ethan looked back at the ground, his body not quite in shape enough to have carried a grown woman across a parking lot. Something hard smacked the top of his head and bounced off. He watched a bright green ornament fall onto the pea gravel and shatter.

"I've got plenty more where that came from, perv," Kitty yelled.

"Now, wait a damn minute. You started it. And I just saved you from taking a trip to the splash zone of your husband's vomitorium."

Kitty looked up and down the parking lot before throwing another ornament at Ethan. "Where's your little friend with his phone? He didn't have any problems recording you destroying my store, but when you assault me in a parking lot, he's suddenly nowhere to be found!"

The sounds of vomiting turned to dry heaving, and Jeremy whimpered. "I don't feel so good."

"Hold up. You assaulted me! I was defending myself. And I didn't destroy your store," Ethan declared.

"You and your friends didn't? Then who caused the disaster in there? Who threw all my snow globes?" The remaining ornaments on her sweater leaped to the rhythm of her arms as she waved her hands to explain what she'd seen. "Racks were flipped over. The cards were scattered everywhere! And my poor beautiful babies. You destroy my dolls, you monster!"

"Ok, those dolls were creepy. But, no, we didn't. That was the ghost."

"Ghost? Really? You're still on about that? Admit it, it was just an excuse to come into a Christmas store and destroy everything. Who does that? Why do you hate Christmas?" she asked as tears fell from her cheeks.

"No. What? I don't hate Christmas," Ethan said.

Jeremy stumbled past Ethan. "Mom. I want to go home. Can we go home, please?"

Kitty stepped back from him. Through sobs, she said to Ethan, "And now you've got my ex talking like this? You people are monsters."

"Mom? Please. I just want to go home," Jeremy said.

"Please. Just stop," she said. Her eyes shifted, and her eyebrows furrowed. She pushed Jeremy away from her and screamed, "Stop it! Stop calling me that!"

"Mommy. I don't understand," Jeremy said as he leaned against a car and slid down to the ground

Kitty shook her head, massive tears flinging off her face. "Why Jeremy? Why did you have to do this tonight? Tonight, of all nights!"

Looking down into his lap, Jeremy picked at his fingers and said, "I just missed you. And I love you, mommy."

"Wait? What's so special about tonight?" Ethan asked.

Jeremy let in a haggard breath and looked up at Ethan. "Tonight's the night."

Kitty turned her back on the both of them and held her face in her hands.

Ethan looked at Jeremy. "I can't help if you don't tell me what's going on. Please."

Kitty looked up at the night sky and let out an exasperated breath. "Tonight's the anniversary of . . ." She stopped and closed her eyes, pinching the bridge of her nose and facing Ethan. "Tonight is the night my sweet girl left us."

"It's my unbirthday," Jeremy said with a burp.

"How dare you speak as if you are her. We are both hurting, you know. Ugh, I hate you. I hate you so much," Kitty shouted.

Jeremy cried. "Please, Mom. Don't say that."

"Stop calling me that!" Kitty yelled again as she took a step forward.

"No! Wait!" Ethan yelled. "That's not Jeremy!"

Kitty laughed at him. "You really want me to believe that my daughter is here? You agents will have us believe anything just to get whatever crap it is that you want."

"Think about it," Ethan said.

"Do you remember the snow cones?" Jeremy said.

Kitty frowned; her eyes locked on Jeremy.

"The night before it happened. You and I got snow cones. Said it was our secret."

Kitty shook her head. "No. It can't. I don't. I don't understand."

"Mommy, it's me. Angela," Jeremy bit his lip and smiled awkwardly at Kitty.

"But how?" Kitty asked. "How did this happen?"

"Sometimes spirits get restless and can't move on. And those that really can't move on sometimes take matters into their own hands," Ethan explained.

Kitty pointed to her ex-husband, who was slumped over on the ground. He let loose a loud burp right before she spoke. "So, that's my daughter. In my husband's body?"

"Yes. Exactly," Ethan said.

"Can I go and . . . I don't know . . . Can I talk to her?" Kitty asked.

Ethan relaxed and looked back at Jeremy, whose eyes filled with tears. "I think she'd probably really like that."

Kitty walked past him and knelt next to Jeremy. "Hey? Um? Is that really you?"

Jeremy rubbed his eyes and nose with his forearm and sniffled. "Mom, I'm scared."

Kitty sat down next to Jeremy and wrapped her arm around him, her ornaments jingling as she did. "You don't need to be scared, baby. I'm here."

Jeremy nodded and picked at the tinsel weaved into Kitty's sweater. "I really like your sweater, Mommy."

"I've missed you. I miss you so much." Kitty looked up to the sky, fresh tears rolling down her cheeks, and she bit her lip.

"I missed you too. Why don't you visit me anymore?"

"I. I couldn't." Kitty looked back at Ethan and asked, "How is this even possible?"

Ethan rubbed a hand against his jaw, wincing where Kitty had slapped him. "We don't know. It just is."

Kitty pressed her cheek against Jeremy's and flinched. "Baby, you're so cold."

"It's the possession. She can't stay much longer or Jeremy's going to need a hospital," Ethan said.

Kitty looked at him again and said, "I . . . I don't know what to do?"

"Just be there. Be her mom."

"I don't know if I can . . . It's—" she swallowed again. "It's been a long time."

"She needs help moving on," Ethan said. "She needs to know everything is going to be okay when she leaves."

Kitty pet the top of Jeremy's head, and he looked up at her with an innocent, drunken smile. "Baby. I'm sorry I didn't visit. I love you. You know that, right?"

"I love you too, Mommy."

"The agent over there said you need help. Do you need help, baby?" Kitty asked.

Jeremy started crying again and looked down. "It wasn't daddy's fault. I was . . . I was mad. Daddy didn't see Mr. Bigby go under the gas pedal when I threw him. He didn't. It wasn't. I'm sorry."

Kitty's face paled, and her grip tightened on Jeremy. "Oh baby. It wasn't your fault. You couldn't have known." She paused for a long second, then ran her fingertips along Jeremy's head. "Neither of you could have known."

"It's my fault you don't love Daddy anymore." Jeremy sniffled. "I just want you two to be happy again."

"Aw, sweety," Kitty said, leaning her chin on Jeremy's head. "Did you think that was why we weren't together?"

"It's not?" Jeremy asked.

"No. Honey. No. Sometimes mommies and daddies move on. We had a happy time together, but we were just ready for something else."

"But if I hadn't died, you'd still love each other?"

Kitty squeezed Jeremy's hands and said, "Baby, your daddy and I decided it months before the accident. It wasn't your fault. It was never your fault. You were perfect. My perfect little girl. And I love you. And your daddy loves you too. Have you been able to tell him that?"

Jeremy nodded. "He's listening now."

Kitty lifted Jeremy's head and looked into his eyes. A smile passed between them, and she said, "I think we both needed to hear that, sweetie. Thank you. Now, why don't you give your daddy his body back?"

"But I don't want to go. What about—"

"I think we're both going to be okay now. And you need to go to heaven, baby. I know a certain granny who'd love to see you again," Kitty said.

Jeremy's eyes lit up. "Will she have snickerdoodles?"

"I think she'll definitely have those waiting."

The aura around Jeremy glowed a brilliant white, emanating from his heart and extending in all directions.

Both Ethan and Kitty shielded their eyes as a young girl materialized in front of her seated parents, wearing pigtails of shimmering fluorescent pink.

"Oh, baby. You're so beautiful," Kitty said.

Jeremy reached out toward Angela. "I. I'm sorry. I'm sorry for all the times I drank at your grave."

Angela reached out a hand and caressed her father's. "It's okay, Daddy. You'll be better now. I know it."

A second bright light appeared behind her. So bright, it consumed her light and forced Ethan to look away.

"You were right, Mommy. I can smell the cinnamon. I love you both," Angela called one last time as her light was absorbed into the brighter light; and then, as quickly as they had appeared, they vanished.

Kitty held on to Jeremy as they sat, leaned up against the car in the parking lot. Ethan took a step forward, about to say something, but backed away, leaving them alone to mourn.

He grinned and was headed back toward the bar when the door swung open.

From it emerged Gerry, Bryce, an extremely bruised Buck, and all the men from the bar. They had their arms around each other and were laughing as if they had all spent the evening drinking together.

Gerry looked past Ethan and smiled. "Looks like everything's been taken care of," he called. "You've missed all the fun. These men are absolutely delightful."

"I take it they didn't care that they were being beaten up?" Ethan asked, confused.

Bryce shrugged. "Buck and Gerry have a way."

Ethan met Bryce's stare and grinned, his heart fluttering in his chest.

The beaten men all slapped Buck's back and waved him off, heading over to Jeremy and Kitty to help them to their feet.

"Make sure you put a steak on that eye when you get home, boy!" Buck called after the one named Kaper.

"Will do, you old bastard! See you next weekend?" Kaper yelled back, his arm around Jeremy.

"Absolutely."

"I'm so confused," Ethan said.

Gerry stepped between Bryce and Ethan, stretched his arms overhead, and rested his hands on their shoulders. "Well boys, the night is young. I know this place about an hour away. Anyone have a hankering for midnight cheesecake?"

Buck spit a mouthful of blood onto the ground and said, "I'll go where you want me to."

"I don't know that we can beat the first place, but I can't say no to dessert," Bryce said, looking at Ethan.

Ethan smiled and nodded. "Yeah, this double date's just getting started."

Thirty-Seven

Resurrection Day

E THAN LOOKED OUT THE passenger side window and up at the giant inflatable Jesus that looked down on him. "Man, Granny is going to be pissed that I'm missing the service."

Buck killed the engine and looked out to the cemetery. "Work never stops."

"Yeah, but why today?" Ethan said, shifting the bag of bones in his lap.

Bob scoffed in the backseat and said, "It's Resurrection Day. Busiest day of the year."

Buck looked in the rearview mirror. "He doesn't know what Resurrection Day is, Bob."

"Probably because of all the pot," Bob said.

"I know what Resurrection Day is. And what are you talking about? I don't smoke pot," Ethan said.

"Except when you're with Gerry," Buck snickered.

Ethan stared slack-jawed at Buck. "Okay, that was one time."

"Sure, rookie. That one time at the Italian place. And that one time you ran into him at the grocery store. And that other time, you two went bowling. And then last week at the bar after you sent back Angela," Buck said with a laugh.

"Ok, partner, thanks for throwing me under the bus. Those were all just one-offs," Ethan protested.

"And I bet you still have that flamingo lighter he gave you in your pocket," Buck said.

Ethan felt the lighter in his pocket. "What? No. If I did, it was because it was a gift, thank you very much."

"You and River, reprobates of the office," Bob said.

"Hey, we offered to take you with us when River called in sick. Why do you have to be so mean?" Ethan said, turning in the backseat.

"You're wasting your life away. How many one-offs is it going to take before you see you're an addict?" Bob ranted.

Ethan stared forward in his seat and crossed his arms. "I think you have me confused with someone else."

"He's just projecting," Buck grunted. "He's mad that River didn't take him home for Easter, and now he called in sick for Resurrection Day."

"Hold up," Ethan said, "Aren't those the same thing?"

"No," Buck said, opening the car door and stepping out.

"You're dumber than a box of rocks." Bob laughed, phasing through the backseat door.

Ethan got out of the car and held out the bag of bones, hovering it over the car seat. "If you keep being a dick, I'm going to leave your bag here."

Bob flitted his eyes between the bag and Ethan. "Fine, look, rookie. Resurrection Day is a ghost holiday. Just so happens to be on Easter this year, but something with the magnetic pull of the earth or location of Saturn or something. No one knows. The point is, on one day a year, ghosts have superpower possession. Any ghost, not just the special ones, can jump into anything or anybody."

"Oh great, I can only imagine this ending well." Ethan said.

Buck laughed. "That's where we step in. All the NRDS in the country are on double time today, registering and confirming that no ghost is going to fucking think about it or we'll case them."

"Huh," Ethan said as they started toward the cemetery. "So that's why Mable kept reassuring me there'd be no shenanigans in her cemetery? I figured she was just being weird. I mean, those kids are always up to something."

Bob laughed and looked at Ethan. "Yeah, if you don't report a cemetery as 'clear' on Resurrection Day three years in a row, then you can bet a clean-up crew is going to show up."

Ethan frowned. "What? Clean-up crew? What do they—"

Bob stopped dead in his tracks, and Ethan accidentally stepped right through him. Ethan shivered and glared at Bob. "What the fuck, Bob?"

Bob pointed, his finger passing through Ethan. "What in the eternal fuck of all fuckery is that?"

Ethan turned around and spotted the clown, Bingo Bango, waving at the fence of the cemetery.

"Bob, meet Bingo." Buck said.

Bob turned around and marched back toward the car. "Oh, absofuckinglutely not."

Ethan tugged on the bag of bones, and Bob fell backward. "What? Are you afraid of clowns?"

Bob stood up and leaned against the invisible barrier, glaring at Ethan. "No. I am not."

Buck leaned toward Ethan. "He is."

Bingo phased through the fence and cartwheeled in front of Ethan. "Wahoo, the clowns in suits have arrived. And who do we have here?" Bingo peered past Ethan, right at Bob. "Vietnam? Paging Vietnam? You hear?"

Bob shook his head. "No! Get away from me until you take that costume off!"

"Well, that's rude," Ethan said. "You know he can't take it off. He's dead."

Bob glared at Ethan, and his clothes shimmered and changed to match Ethan's suit before shimmering back into his army uniform. "You were saying?"

"Aww, is the poor army man afraid of a little clown? I'm not so scary, I promise. Here, have a little gift."

"No," Bob said.

"Check your pocket," Bingo said.

"No."

"Come on, Bob, check your pocket," Ethan said.

Bob slowly unlatched his left breast pocket and stuffed his hand inside. He pulled out a wallet-sized picture of Bingo with an autograph scrawled across it. Bob threw the card like it was on fire, and it instantly vanished.

"Ta-da!" Bingo declared, taking a bow. When he came up, he was holding a white rabbit by the ears. "Oh, whoops! Sorry about that," he said, holding the rabbit out to Ethan. "Would you mind holding this for me?"

Instinctively, Ethan reached out to take it, but as he touched it, it disappeared.

"Ta-da-ta-da!" Bingo declared again.

Ethan clapped. "You got me."

"That's enough," Bob yelled, huffing and stomping toward Bingo. "Put on some goddamn normal clothes like the rest of us."

"Sir, yes, sir," Bingo said with a smile. Spinning on one leg, he became a momentary blur. When the spinning stopped, Bingo was wearing the same uniform as Bob, but still with his white face and big red nose. He saluted four times, stood at attention, and then let out a loud honk on his nose. "Is this more acceptable, Sir Officer Sir?"

"Good form," Buck muttered with a nod.

Bob jammed his finger into Bingo's chest. "You take that off right now!"

"Oh my, getting fresh already and we haven't even been on our first date," Bingo said, honking his nose. Bingo leaned in toward Ethan and whispered in a Jerry Seinfeld voice, "What's the deal with that drill sergeant? He wake up on the wrong side of the morgue?"

"I'm serious, maggot! Take it off right now!" Bob demanded.

Snapping his fingers and replacing his clothes with a lab coat, Bingo held up a clipboard and said in a heavy German accent, "The patient's fear of clowns is superseded by damage to the ego. Perhaps he wasn't loved as a child?"

"Okay Bingo, enough," Buck said.

Snapping back into the clown suit, Bingo slumped his arms and kicked his oversized shoes at the grass. "Fine, you guys are no fun."

"Sorry Bingo, we've got some slack to pick up, and it's Resurrection Day too. Are you, Lester, or anyone else here planning anything?"

Bingo hit the side of his head, and glitter came shooting out of the other ear. "Nothing in there, sir. Not even ideas."

"I'm serious, Bingo. I take it you've heard of the cleaners?" Buck asked.

"Yes, sir. I promise I am up to only good on this fine day," Bingo said.

Ethan looked over at the cemetery and frowned. "Where's Lester?"

"Lester-Pester the Grave Digger Molester," Bingo sang. He shrugged and added in a somber tone, "I've got no idea who you're talking about."

Bob rolled his eyes and pushed on Bingo's shoulder. "Look, maggot. These fuckers will happily case you if you keep acting up. You want that? You want to be trapped in a case for decades, making friends with cobwebs while they forget about you?"

Bingo sighed and looked at Ethan, "Why'd you have to bring Captain Buzzkill?" Pointing back to the entrance, he said, "He went to the church hoping to grab someone as they came out. Told me to distract anyone that comes."

"Goddamn it, let's move!" Buck said, turning and running to the car.

"Hey! What did I say about taking the fucking Lord's name in vain?" Bob yelled.

Ethan saluted to Bingo. "Well, see you next week."

Buck revved the engine, and the car's wheels spun before the car raced from the cemetery. Flying through the cemetery gate, Buck raced past the giant inflatable Jesus toward the front door of the church.

"What are you doing?" Ethan screamed as he used both arms to brace himself.

"If we don't find him before the church service lets out, he'll possess someone, and we'll have our asses handed to us!" Buck yelled.

He brought the car to a screeching halt in front of the church and popped the trunk. Ethan hopped out and grabbed a case, joining Buck at the steps leading up to the church.

"Lester? Come out!" They both called.

Hymns sounded from inside, and based on the time, the service was nearing to a close.

Buck pulled the case from Ethan's hands and tossed it on the ground. "Lester! You better come out right now or I'll open this case. And if I open it, you damn better expect I will case you. Do you want that?"

Ethan looked at Buck's wide eyes and stammered. "Uh, Lester. You better come out. I think Buck's snapped. I've never seen him like this. He'll do it."

"That's it, Lester! Last fucking chance!" Buck yelled as he bent down and cracked the case. Blue light poured from the seams.

"Oh, God! Lester! Don't make him do it!" Ethan screamed.

"You better get out here before it's too late!" Bob yelled.

Buck cracked the case open a little more and yelled, "Lester! I will find you. I will hunt you down."

Finally, from behind a large hedge, Lester came out with his hands up. "Fine, fine!" he said. "I don't know how to possess someone, anyway. Close the damn case."

Buck smirked and latched the case shut. "You little shit. Get your ass back in the cemetery before I have to report you as a Class Three."

With his head hung in shame, Lester started toward the cemetery. "It's not my fault. Bingo and Denise told me I had to try it."

Buck stood straight up, his face paling. "Did you say Denise?"

Lester turned on his heel. "Yeah, said she knew you, Buck. You two were old friends or something."

Buck looked left, then right, then froze, his eyes back in the cemetery parking lot. "Son of a bitch!" he yelled.

Buck's nemesis, the woman in the purple eighties-era tracksuit with the neon yellow lining and lightning bolts on the slides, stood mere feet away from the giant inflatable Jesus. She winked at Buck.

"Buck," Ethan said, carefully stepping closer to him, "Don't do anything crazy."

"Step the fuck away from Jesus!!" Buck screamed, pointing at the ghost.

She took the lollipop out of her mouth and ran it across her throat in a slicing motion and then pointed it at Buck.

"Quick, kid. Toss me Gerry's lighter," he whispered to Ethan.

"What? No. I told you. I don't have it with me," Ethan said.

"You want my help?" Bob asked.

"No, stick with Lester! She can up your class," Buck demanded.

The ghost, or Denise as Ethan now knew her as, smiled and took a step back, slipping into the towering Jesus.

The flailing arms went rigid in an instant, and the massive five-foot-tall head peered down at them.

"Hand me the fucking lighter, kid!" Buck demanded.

Mega Jesus took a step forward, the electric fan scraping along the asphalt.

"Look. Take it easy. You can't burn Jesus on Easter," Ethan said.

Mega Jesus took another step forward, and the ropes holding him to the ground all snapped.

"Ethan! Now!" Buck demanded, holding his hand out.

Ethan pulled the flamingo lighter from his pocket and tossed it to Buck.

Mega Jesus took another step closer, reaching with its long arms and wrapping underneath an old pickup truck.

Ethan took a step back. "Wait, you don't think it can—"

The truck screeched, then flipped over with enough force to come tumbling toward them.

Buck and Ethan dodged on either side while it passed through Bob and Lester.

"Get the case, rookie, and follow my lead," Buck shouted.

Ethan picked up the case and nodded.

Mega Jesus tipped over a minivan, causing its alarm to ring out through the parking lot.

"Now!" Buck yelled as he ran forward, gripping the flamingo lighter in his hand.

Just as they raced forward, the doors of the church cracked open, and congregants began pouring out of the worship service.

A little girl pointed at the marauding Mega Jesus and screamed for her mother.

An older man screamed and raced back into the church, "He has risen! Take cover!"

A small child tugged on his father's coat and shouted, "Daddy! Jesus flipped the minivan!"

Ethan stepped in front of the crowd and waved his badge. "Federal Agent. Everything's under control. Please, go back into the church."

"Out of my way!" mayoral candidate Chax Tamish yelled as he elbowed through the crowd. He took one look at Ethan and shouted. "Now you're pulling this at church? Is nothing sacred? This is harassment!" he said as he took out his phone and hit record. "You guys won't get away with this."

"Ethan, where are you?" Buck shouted.

Ethan turned on his heel and saw Buck, already standing next to Mega Jesus. "No! Buck! Don't!"

Buck flipped the lighter right at Mega Jesus's ankles. Flames raced up Mega Jesus's plastic body in an instant, and he transformed into a massive burning man.

"That man killed Jesus again, mommy!" a child cried.

Other kids started crying, shouting, "He's dead!" over and over again.

"I'm suing you! I'm suing all of you!" Chax Tamish shouted.

Mega Jesus fell to the ground in a heap of flaming plastic, and Ethan took in the surrounding wreckage. "I fucking love Resurrection Day," Ethan said, just before he broke into a fit of laughter.

Thirty-Eight

The Cleveland Cleaver

A SEA OF PEOPLE and picket signs blocked the entrance to the NRDS office, shouting "No MORE NRDS! NO MORE NRDS! NO MORE NRDS!" as Ethan stepped out of his car. He counted at least thirty signs in a crowd of over a hundred, which was impressive for a Wednesday morning in New Richmond.

He rested up against the brick building across the street, Richmond Roasting Company, and eyed the signs as he considered calling in to watch this dumpster fire unfold. Most of the signs were basic and shallow, constructed by someone lacking the art skills of a four-year-old, scribbled with "NRDS GO HOME", "NO MORE FEDS", and many more which just read "NOT IN MY TOWN." Based on the official posters and banners hanging from the makeshift podium outside the offices, "not in my town" seemed to be the slogan Chax had adopted for his mayoral campaign.

The best picket sign by far was a picture of Chax's face, altered into a Pac Man chasing four ghosts with the letters N, R, D, and S on them. Written in exploratory text on the sign was, "NRDS PLEASE GHOST US."

"This shit again?" a voice said beside Ethan.

He jumped and turned, noting Alexus inches from his face. "Jesus Christ Alexus! Stop doing that."

Alexus smiled, adjusted her signature leather jacket, and brandished a rather large ax. "Never."

"What the hell is that for?"

"Can't a girl carry around an ax?" Alexus asked.

"I mean. I don't know. I guess? But why?"

She smiled and ran a finger along the edge of the ax. "Never know if there's a tree or two you need to take down."

Ethan sidestepped. "Okay then. Just as long as I'm not that tree."

"Aw, do you feel threatened by a strong woman with an ax, rookie?"

"Yes. Yes, I do," Ethan confessed.

Alexus smiled. "Good."

The door beside them chimed, and Doris stepped out of Richmond Roasting Company, carrying a basket of muffins. "Oh, great. This again."

"Yep. I vote we sit back and watch this shitshow," Ethan said.

Doris held up the basket. "Well, want a muffin?"

Alexus reached in and grabbed a perfectly shaped muffin dotted with chocolate chips. "I thought you told us you baked these yourself."

Doris laughed, "You think I bake? I just said they were freshly baked. You all assumed."

"I like your style," Alexus said before chomping down on the top of the muffin without even unwrapping it.

Ethan watched in horror. "Who eats like that?"

Through mouthfuls and between cramming the muffin in her face, Alexus said, "What? I'm hungry."

Fillmore rounded the block, having waited the agreed ten minutes after Ethan left his apartment, and stood next to Doris. "Well, isn't this just what everyone wanted to see on a Monday morning," he said as he adjusted his glasses.

"Why are you still here?" Alexus said, eyeing Fillmore as she licked the wrapper clean.

Ethan felt his face flush red when Fillmore shot him a glance. They'd kept their relationship quiet from almost everyone but Buck this whole time, knowing that River wouldn't let it go the moment he caught wind of it.

Fillmore smiled and said, "Upper management hired me on as a liaison between headquarters and this region. Since an office is here, it only makes sense to use it as my home office."

"Ugh, whatever." Alexus said.

"Muffin?" Doris offered.

"Why, thank you, Miss Doris. How's Mr. Westminster Tabby doing?" Fillmore said, selecting a blueberry muffin from the basket. After gently removing the wrapper, he took a delicate bite from the side.

"Well, thank you Bryce. At least someone around here cares. He's fine. Turns out it was crystals, so special cat food for my special boy."

Ethan eyed the basket, and his stomach growled. "Hey, can I get one of those?"

Doris shoved the box at Ethan. "Yeah, sure, whatever."

He copied Bryce and grabbed a blueberry muffin, carefully peeling the wrapper off, and picking off a tiny bite.

Alexus snickered and punched his shoulder. "Who are you trying to impress?"

Ethan locked eyes with his muffin, sweat forming on his brow.

"Aww man! How long has this been going?" Trevor said, racing up to them on the sidewalk. He pulled his phone from his pocket and held it up to the crowd. "Did I miss the speech?"

Bryce frowned. "There's going to be a speech?"

Trevor turned the camera at his face and waved before turning it back to the crowd. "Yeah, my boy Chax is definitely going to give a speech if he hasn't already. The dude is practically running on kicking us out."

"Just keep streaming. No speeches yet," Alexus smiled, leaning on the handle of her ax.

Ethan stared at the crowd, listening to the chants coming from them, and suddenly realized that he hadn't seen the people of New Richmond so united around a single cause before. He scratched his head. "Hey, Doris. You've been here a while."

"I beg your pardon. What do you mean by a while?" she asked.

"Oh. I just mean. Well. Do you remember New Richmonders ever getting this mad about something?"

"There was that tech billionaire who tried to claim a bunch of houses with eminent domain. I'd say people were pretty mad then," Trevor said.

"Yeah, but did anyone protest? I only remember people complaining about it at the grocery store," Ethan replied.

"Well, there was that one time that Farmer Elmore tried to start a nudist colony on his property. People protested that," Doris replied.

"Oh, Right! I remember that," Trevor said.

Bryce laughed, "A nudist colony? Doesn't it get a little cold here?"

"When was that?" Ethan asked.

"At least a decade ago," Doris mused.

"Twelve years. Met my wife that year. I remember because I tried to convince her to join," Trevor said.

"Really? I didn't peg you as a nudist," Ethan said.

"Well, I don't want you pegging me at all. But hey, back then, I'd join a nudist colony in a heartbeat," Trevor said.

"So, the nudist colony," Bryce said, looking at Ethan, "Is it still around?"

Doris shook her head. "Oh, no. Elmore never actually got anyone to join. It was really just him baring it all to the world while he picked weeds out of his garden. The town protested and said some pretty nasty things. Then the Chief of Police finally went out and offered to build Elmore a privacy fence so the church ladies would leave him alone."

Alexus snickered. "Now, that is pretty badass."

The mob's chanting turned to cheering as a news van pulled up, followed by a black SUV. A camera crew funneled out of the news van, pointing it to the SUV behind them.

"Ah man," Trevor said. "I was hoping for an exclusive this time."

Ethan looked at the others and frowned. "Hey, has anyone seen River or Buck? Or Melissa? Or Bob?"

"I bet Buck and Melissa are inside already," Bryce said. "It's Buck's performance evaluation this morning."

Alexus sighed. "Aw, dammit. I would love to see the two of them at it."

"Maybe we'll get a rundown from River if he made it in before this," Ethan said.

"Well, we might," Alexus offered. "River and I got wasted last night, and he slept it off in the office. If Melissa didn't find him sleeping under his desk, then I bet he caught an earful."

The crowd's rumbling turned to a focused chant of "Chax! Chax! Chax! Chax!" as the mayoral candidate stepped out of the SUV and headed to the makeshift podium.

A scrawny man in an oversized suit jumped up to the microphone and announced, "Good people of New Richmond and the surrounding counties, your mayoral candidate Chax Tamish!"

The crowd cheered and clapped as Chax smiled, showing off his insanely white teeth. He waved, his biceps pressing up against a form fitting suit, and Ethan nearly found the urge to join in and clap.

Alexus bumped into Ethan, knocking him out of his trance. When he looked over, he saw her pulling a small makeup compact from her back pocket. She applied some heavy bone-white makeup on her face.

"Um, doing alright over there?" he asked.

"What now, rookie? Strong women in war paint scare you too?" she snapped back.

Ethan shrugged and said, "When it's that kind of war paint. Yeah. A little."

Chax's voice boomed over the crowd. "We've all gathered here this morning to give the federal government a simple message! We don't want you here! We don't need you here! Pack up your fake, worthless, psychic losers! And get them out of our town!"

The crowd went wild. A chant of "Get them out! Get them out! Get them out!" rose from the mob.

"Get them out! Get them out! Get them out!" Doris muttered, shaking her fist.

"Doris, what the hell?" Ethan asked.

She immediately stopped and smiled. "He just speaks with so much authority. Sorry."

Chax continued, "And you know, good citizens of New Richmond. These people aren't just full of baloney, but these so-called federal agents are destroying our town!"

"So-called? He just called us federal agents like twenty seconds ago," Trevor said.

"Us? You're not an agent, cameraman," Alexus said, coating her face completely in white makeup.

Trevor lowered his phone and pouted. "But I'm a part of the team, though. That's. That's all I meant."

Doris patted his back. "Of course you did, dear."

"They've taken over a historic building in town! They've caused untold amounts of damage to some of our most important streets! They destroyed Christmas Town! And just last Sunday, they desecrated the Easter celebration at the First Christian Church of New Richmond!"

"More like we saved their asses," Ethan said.

Bryce pushed up his glasses. "I heard there were several vehicles damaged. Let alone the emotional damage those kids were put through. I mean . . . who thought it was a good idea to burn Jesus?"

"Hey, it wasn't my idea!" Ethan shot back.

Alexus snapped the makeup compact closed. "Okay, shut up, you lovebirds."

"Dammit," Ethan said under his breath. "You know?"

She smiled, "I do now."

"Don't tell River."

"Fine. How do I look?" Alexus said.

Ethan stared at her white face and did his best to hold back a laugh. "Like you just came out of the morgue. Or maybe after your first day at clown school."

"Perfect," she said, picking up her ax.

Chax's voice continued, "And that is why, if you elect me mayor, I will demand that the federal government remove these charlatans from our town! They must go!"

The crowd joined Chax in chanting, "They must go! They must go! They must go!"

Something moved in Ethan's peripheral vision, up on top of the NRDS office. When he looked, he spotted River with his shirt off, spinning it in the air, a megaphone in the other hand.

He held down a loud siren and waited for the crowd to fall into silence as Chax looked up.

"Citizens of New Richmond," River yelled. "I am a federal agent with the National Recently Deceased Services! What we do is important!"

The crowd laughed and booed, and Chax turned to his microphone. "Government dollars at work, I see. Why don't you do something useful in this town for once?"

Bending down, River retrieved a briefcase from the roof and held it high so the entire mob could see it. He stumbled for a moment, then caught himself before saying, "We protect you! In this briefcase, I have the most vile! The most horrible! The most murderous ghost ever caught in the Midwest! The Cleveland Cleaver of '59!"

"Oh God, River, what are you doing?" Ethan said.

"There's no such ghost," Bryce said with a nod.

"I should hope not," Doris added.

"Do you want these ghosts on your streets? They are the ones who ruin your homes, tear up your streets, and possess your balloon Jesus. Not us. Do you want that?" River screamed.

"Your scare tactics don't work on us. We know the truth. We know what you're really doing. All the intel and questions. You will not own us!" Chax screamed back.

River stumbled again and shouted, "You don't get it! You'll never get it!" Then he stumbled backward, and the briefcase left his hands.

It flew up in the air and descended right into the middle of the street.

The second it landed, blue light and mist exploded out from inside the briefcase, and every single face in the mob turned white.

"That's my cue," Alexus said, as she lifted the ax over her head and sprinted through the blue fog toward the crowd.

She let loose a blood-curdling scream as she swung her ax wildly in all directions.

"It's the Cleveland Cleaver! Run!" someone from inside the mob yelled.

Then, panic.

The crowd dispersed in an instant, a multi directional stampede filled with screams. Even Chax raced to his SUV to seek shelter.

When Alexus reached the door, she gave one more bone chilling scream, then looked back at the team on the sidewalk and said, "Alright, Let's go to work."

Ethan stared, bug-eyed and slack-jawed. "What the hell was that?"

"Effective," Fillmore said as he started toward the office.

Thirty-Nine

Stash Thief

"O H, MY. WHAT HAPPENED here?" Doris asked as she shoved open the office door.

Ethan peeked over her shoulder, noticing the large amount of debris strewn across the floor of the office. As he stepped into the office, he saw that the reception desk was completely flipped over, and all of Doris's office supplies were thrown onto the floor. Even the basket she kept muffins and donuts in was completely smashed.

Alexus ran over to the remains of the basket, dropped her ax, and fell to her knees. She let out a scream, and with the white face paint still caked onto her face from her performance as the Cleveland Cleaver, she looked like some kind of horrific ghoul. "Not the muffin basket! What kind of monster would kill the muffin basket? Seriously!" She picked up the pieces and cradled them, murmuring, "I loved you, little basket. And all your sweet, delicious goods."

The muffin basket wasn't the only thing destroyed. As Ethan surveyed the room, he found most of the drawers in the agents' desks had been pulled and smashed to bits. Computer towers were torn apart, and screens were cracked nearly in half. The filing cabinets were tipped over and all the files had been thrown haphazardly across the floor. Even the coat rack had been broken in half. "Wow, this place is trashed."

"No shit, Sherlock," Buck said, peering up from an overturned desk. He lifted a stack of files and set them on a chair while Bob hovered next to him.

"I take it the performance review didn't go well?" Fillmore said, a grin stretched across his face as he entered the office.

"It was like this when Melissa and I came in. Now, can one of you maybe say something intelligent or get your ass over here and help, please?" Buck complained.

Bob phased through the desks and glared at the office crew. "The enemy has infiltrated our lines, men. We have a traitor in our midst."

"We don't know that Bob," Buck shouted.

"Oh, but we do." His eyes widened and his head cocked. "How else would someone be able to do this? One of us had to let them in!"

"Aw, man! They took my desk weed!" River tossed a drawer on top of a pile of other drawers and threw his hands in the air. He then ran over to a filing cabinet and started fishing around inside of it.

Arriving last, Trevor looked at the remains of his desk and said, "Anyone seen my stool?"

Bob raced over to the doors, blocking the exit. "Well. Well. Well. The gang's all here, which means the mole is in the room right now!"

Ethan rolled his eyes and looked at Bryce. Bryce laughed and nodded toward Buck. In tandem, they joined Buck on the floor and helped him pick up the files. "Have you implemented a system yet?"

Buck sighed. "Off the record, yes. I submitted the request for a tracking system four months ago but got back crickets. The files are categorized by case number and date on the header and a page number in the bottom right corner. Once this mess is picked up, we should see what's missing."

Marching over to Trevor and shoving a finger in his face, Bob said, "I'm onto you, maggot. Newest leech in here, always recording everyone too.

Where were you this morning? Did you do it? Did you let the mob in to destroy our office?"

Trevor shivered and rubbed his cheek. "Did anyone else feel that? It was like my jaw got a jolt or something."

Ethan sighed, keeping his eyes on the piles of paper. "Hey, Bob? Trevor doesn't have a badge. He can't hear you."

"Wait, that was Bob?" Trevor said as he stared at Doris.

Bob leaned in closer, so his face was inches from Trevor's. "I bet he can hear me. Traitors have all kinds of secrets. Isn't that right, maggot?"

"Bob, come on," Ethan said. "He was with us outside this morning. Besides, they probably broke in last night."

"I'm still watching you," Bob said to Trevor.

Trevor shivered and picked up Doris's chair, dusting it off before setting it beside her. "Well, at least you have your seat."

Doris sat, purse in lap, and looked at the heap on her desk. "Well, thank you, dear."

"Fuck! Not the coat rack!" Alexus screamed, picking up the broken pieces and holding them in the air for all to see. "Now where am I going to hang up Darlene?"

"Darlene?" Doris asked.

Alexus flexed her leather jacket. "You know, trusty Darlene here."

"Fucking hell," River shouted, waving his arms up in the air. "They got my filing cabinet weed too! These bastards!" He ran over to Buck's desk and lay down on the floor, searching beneath it.

"I think I have a full file here," Bryce said, passing a full manila folder to Buck.

Buck thumbed through it and said, "Perfect." Then he placed it on a stack of five other finished files.

Alexus picked up her ax and walked over to the remains of her desk and ran a hand across a gash in the drywall. "Motherfuckers scratched my damn wall!"

Bob turned his gaze toward her and stomped over. "You seem awfully dramatic this morning. Maybe too dramatic? Was it you? Huh? Did you destroy our office? Confess! Confess and we'll let you live!"

Rubbing her finger along the hole in the wall, she gave Bob the side-eye. "If you don't step the fuck back, I will find a way to put you in a body and then torture that body until you die a second time."

Bob stepped back and announced, "Everyone! I have cleared Alexus! It was not her!"

River jumped up from Buck's desk and screamed. "What in the ever-loving shit? They took my Buck's desk weed! Argh! Is nothing sacred to these bastards!" He frowned and raced into Melissa's office, closing the door behind him.

Ethan, Buck, and Fillmore continued organizing and adding cases to the pile while Bob paced around the mess, deep in thought. After a few moments of silence, he pointed his finger to the ceiling and announced, "Melissa! That traitorous bitch. She's not here. It has to be her. She sold us out and then left us here to clean up her mess!"

Bryce frowned. "Us?"

Ethan smiled.

Buck shook his head. "She and I got here at the same time, before the protests. She went to the police station to give a statement after we called them."

Bob nodded. "Fine. That checks out." Then he mumbled to himself. "She's still a traitorous bitch."

Alexus left the wall and stepped over the heap of paperwork, ignoring the mutterings from Ethan, and to the untouched shelves filled with briefcases.

She ran her fingers up one briefcase before snatching it from the wall and saying, "At least they didn't get my favorite."

"You have a favorite briefcase? Who's in it?" Ethan asked, looking up from the file he was putting together.

Alexus looked up from the case and glared. "I don't fucking know."

Ethan frowned. "Wait, if you don't know who's in it, then why is it your favorite?"

Running her hand over the edges of it, Alexus said, "The stitching is perfect. It's a really well-made case."

Bryce handed Buck another stack of papers and looked at Alexus. He nodded and said, "It is a nice case. What is that, Italian leather?"

"Has to be," Alexus said, her voice cracking slightly.

River burst from Melissa's office. "Well! They also found the three bags I stored in Melissa's office! These weed-thieving motherfuckers were thorough." He paused, jumped, then raced to the back corner of the room, picking at the edge of the carpet.

Alexus set the case back on the shelf and surveyed the destroyed office. "It's just so sad. I can't believe they destroyed so much stuff," she said.

"You know," Bryce said, looking up from the file he was working on. "Upper management will replace everything that was damaged."

Alexus perked up and said, "Everything?"

"Of course," Bryce said with a nod.

Alexus crossed over the pile of papers again, nearly stepping on Ethan's hand, before picking up her ax. With a wild look in her eye, she hefted the ax above her head and swung it down onto her desk. She did it again, and again, and everyone else in the office stopped what they were doing to watch as she cackled.

Once the desk had been thoroughly murdered into splinters, Alexus breathed heavily as she looked at everyone staring back at her. "I really hated that desk."

"Noted," Ethan said.

"Send me what you want, and I'll see to it," Bryce said with a laugh.

"No! No! No! No!" River screamed from the corner where he'd pulled up a section of the carpet to reveal a hole in the floorboard next to the doorjamb. "They even got my spare stash."

"I was wrong. Drug dealers clearly robbed us with drug-sniffing dogs!" Bob declared. He leaned in close to the carpet and stomped around. "Does anyone see any dog hair? We could match it and find the stinking culprits."

"I don't think it works like that," Ethan said, adding his last file to the stack.

"It absolutely does not," Bryce said, adding his last file to the stack.

Buck put the final loose file on the stack and said, "Hey, Grass Man. No one took your weed."

"What are you talking about? It's all gone! Of course they took it!"

"No. They didn't," Buck said.

"Then where did it go? Where's my desk stash?"

Alexus laughed. "You smoked that last week."

"Oh! Shit! Well, what about my filing cabinet stash?"

Ethan shrugged. "I saw you take that out like, two weeks ago? You said you'd forgotten about it."

"Fuck! Okay. Okay," River replied, becoming increasingly frantic. "What about my three stashes in Melissa's office? Huh? What about that?"

"I mean," Trevor said, "if you hid weed in my office, I'd smoke it."

"That sneaky, no good—God! Fine! But! But! My stash in Buck's desk was missing, too! We all know he's not going to smoke it. So, ha!"

"I told you if you put that shit in my desk, I was going to throw it away," Buck said.

"You threw my stash away? You heartless old bastard! How could you?"

"Keep your shit out of my desk," Buck said as he flipped through the completed files.

"Well? But? What about my super-secret corner stash? Huh? What about that? Someone stole that. No question!"

"Well, dear. I'm so sorry," Doris said.

Ethan's mouth fell open. "Doris?"

"Oh, my God! Yes!" Alexus exclaimed with a laugh.

"I was going to replace it," Doris said with a frown. "But I don't know where to buy more."

"Doris. Sweet Doris," River said, tears forming in his eyes. "You smoked my corner weed? How could you?"

"Oh sweat heavens, no. I didn't smoke it," Doris said with a smile. "You told me I had to make you pot brownies for your Dungeons and Dragons party. I saw you hide some there, so . . ."

"It's not a party, Doris. God. It's a serious game. Okay?" River complained.

"This is my favorite part of the day," Alexus said with a smile.

Bryce stood and started putting the files Buck had finished back in the filing cabinet. "Did you figure out what's missing yet?"

Buck stood and started putting the files back too. "Only two files. Mable and that new kid Lester," he said.

"The murder victims?" Ethan asked.

Buck nodded.

"But they had to know we had everything backed up online?" Alexus commented. "What kind of morons break into an office, destroy the perfect muffin basket and coat rack, only to steal stuff we can just print off again?"

"I suspect they are more interested in knowing what you know," Bryce said.

"And they were hoping the protest would slow us down. That bastard Chax! We should let ghosts go into his house!" Bob declared.

"Let's not jump to conclusions. It might have been a coincidence," Buck said.

"So, what do we do?" Ethan asked.

"Get back to work. We don't catch murderers. We help the murdered. Do our job and everything will come to light," Buck said.

Forty

Blue Clicker

E THAN'S BRAND-NEW LEATHER DRESS shoes squelched through mud as he followed Melissa deeper into the woods. "Get out," was the only thing she'd said when they pulled off the side of the byway by mile marker ninety.

A branch snapped back into Ethan's face, and he grunted. "Wait. Where are you going? Why are we doing this?"

"Performance evaluation, Agent Malik," Melissa replied. She hadn't said a thing about tromping through mud. Even her wardrobe, a blazer and skirt with flats, didn't suggest they'd be hiking until she'd rounded to the trunk when they pulled over and slipped on thigh-high rubber boots.

Ethan smacked a bug on his neck. "But shouldn't Fillmore be here?"

Mocking him, Melissa imitated the voice of a whiny child. "But shouldn't Fillmore be here?"

"I don't sound like that."

"I don't sound like that," Melissa said, still mocking him with the whining voice.

"Seriously? What, is this part of the evaluation or something?"

Melissa slapped at a bug on her arm, then pulled bug spray from her purse and started violently spraying herself. Between coughing fits, she said, "No. You're just annoying."

Ethan walked into the cloud of bug repellent and nearly choked. He stopped walking and put his hands on his hips. "Can't you just tell me what we're doing here? I'm about to report you for trying to kill me with this spray."

Melissa sprayed once more in front of her and said, "Oh no. You're going to report me? To who? Buck? I'm the boss, not him." She turned around and started walking deeper into the woods. "God. I'd just like a little respect from all of you."

Ethan followed behind. "I just don't understand why Buck got to do his evaluation in the office and we're in the middle of nowhere."

Melissa spun back around to face him. "You weren't at Buck's evaluation. So how would you know if it was different?" She pulled out her phone and glanced at the map on the screen. "Jesus. How far is this place? God. I hate the woods."

She veered right, her eyes glued to the screen.

"Well, I know Fillmore was supposed to be at Buck's."

"What, you want Fillmore here to watch your evaluation? If you love him so much, why don't you just marry him?"

Heat flushed in Ethan's face. "What? No. I don't love Fillmore."

Melissa's eyes grew wide, and she laughed. "Oh, my God. That was a shot in the dark. You do, don't you? You actually love Fillmore."

"What? No. That's crazy," Ethan said, brushing a fly away from his face.

"It all makes sense now. His reassignment. How the two of you keep giving each other weird looks in the office. You're in love with that dork. Oh. This is amazing."

Ethan pushed another branch back so it wouldn't hit his face and sped up to catch her. "No. Don't change the subject. My evaluation. I just didn't know why this is just you and me."

"Oh. This trek into the woods already paid off. God. You and Fillmore? Wow." She stopped again and checked her map. She took another sharp right. "You know he's only upper management because of his daddy, right?"

Ethan puffed up his chest. "There is nothing between me and Fillmore."

Melissa laughed. "Yeah. Right. Okay."

"I'm serious," he pleaded.

"Fillmoreloversayswhat."

"What?"

"Ha! Got you, bitch. You love him!" Melissa checked her phone again, laughing hysterically. "Oh, finally. Almost there."

Ethan looked down at his shoes, noting the mud that not only coated them but had seeped up his suit pants and into his socks. "We've had like three dates. Okay?"

"And you like him," Melissa said in a sing-song voice. "You want to marry him? You want his babies."

Ethan snorted a laugh. "That's not how babies work."

She spun around and pointed a finger at him. "Ha! But you didn't deny that you wanted to marry him."

"I . . . fine, whatever, yes. I like him. I just get nervous talking about it."

"Well, you should," she said, starting her walk again. "You just told your boss in the middle of your performance evaluation that you are having an inter-office romance."

Ethan bit his lip. He hadn't thought about that. "Oh no. Um . . . but . . . well, Bryce said it would be okay because he's not my supervisor."

"Is that what he said? Was that before or after he stuck his tongue down your throat?"

"What? Geez. No. It's not like that."

"Don't hold out on me now. You're now my ace with upper management."

"Um, excuse me?"

Melissa shrugged. "I'm just saying. If they try anything funny with our branch, I've got you to report that he was sexually harassing you."

"Wait? What? What is wrong with you? No. I would never."

"You say that now."

"No. That's not . . . I mean it."

"Sure kid, keep that determination. If the time comes to report him, you'll need it."

"No one is making an accusation. That's not happening."

"Uh-huh. Just know, people like him aren't looking for anything long term with people like you."

Ethan clenched his jaw, holding back every vile thing that came to his mind.

"Oh good, we're here," Melissa said, pointing ahead.

They broke free from the woods and stepped into a small, overgrown graveyard with seven weather-worn headstones. Melissa stood in front of a short, crumbling stone wall with an iron gate encircling the small family plot.

Ethan stepped up beside her, peering at the closest headstone, trying to make out a name. "So, what's the evaluation, then?"

"Performance evaluation. Go stand over there, in the middle of the graveyard," she said, waving her hand toward the graves.

Ethan frowned. "Just, like, over there?"

She dug around in her purse and waved at him. "Yep. Tell me when you spot a ghost or something."

Ethan stepped over the stone wall and ran a hand against the smooth stone gravestones. He felt a slight chill from the touch, but the minute graveyard was empty. The second gravestone had a small, legible name poorly carved into it. *Applejack*. Which Ethan figured was a last name. "I don't see any spirits here," he called. "Did we get a report on this place or something?"

Melissa pulled a contraption that looked like a small TV remote from her purse and waved it in the air. "Found it!"

"What's that?" Ethan asked.

She held it out to him, a small light bulb aimed at him, and said, "Say cheese."

"Say what?" he said.

She clicked the button, and the bulb emitted a blue light.

Nausea hit Ethan like a train, and the blue light washed over him, inexplicably wrapping around him. The world undulated beneath him, and he fell to his knees.

Melissa continued to hold down the button, pointing it at him, and the blue light filled his vision. He lifted his hand, eyeing what looked like a translucent hand, seeing the grass right through his palm.

"What—" He could barely breathe. Barely form words. "Are you—"

Then everything went dark.

He opened his eyes and saw blue.

A bird flew by, and he realized he was on his back, staring up at the sky. The ground beneath him was damp, and the grass tickled at his ears. Ethan groaned.

"God. It's about time," Melissa said.

He tried to sit up but fell back down. His head was still spinning. He tried again, slowly this time, bringing himself up on his elbows. "What happened?"

She sat on the corner of the stone wall, filing her nails. She shrugged. "You passed out. The weirdest thing. No explanation for it. Alright, get up. Let's go."

He propped himself up against a headstone and finally got a look at the surrounding cemetery. Several headstones also glowed the same blue glow.

"What's happening there?" he asked.

"Oh. That? Best to keep that between us. You passed your evaluation, by the way."

Ethan took in a few breaths. The nausea subsided. "No, seriously. Why is everything glowing blue?"

"Trick of the light? Swamp gas? Does it matter?" Melissa stood up and added, "Well, I don't want to tromp through those woods in the dark. Let's go."

In an attempt to stand, Ethan rolled onto his knees, then saw that his hands were glowing the same shade of blue. "Oh shit! I'm blue! What the fuck?"

"Oh. That. Yep. You're blue."

"Why in the fuck am I blue?" he demanded, flipping his hands over. He then pushed his sleeves back and saw his arms were glowing too. "Is it everywhere?"

"Well," Melissa scoffed. "I didn't check everywhere. I don't want you filing harassment on me. But everything visible is blue."

Ethan jumped to his feet, adrenaline superseding the remnants of nausea. He glared at Melissa and shouted, "What in the fuck, Melissa? What did that stupid remote do to me?"

"I'm sorry. Remote? I don't know what you are talking about," she said as she crawled over the wall.

"Oh, no you fucking don't!" he said, chasing after her. "You pointed a clicker at me. What did it do?"

Melissa laughed uncomfortably as she hurried back toward the car. "What? No. That's crazy. I would never."

"Don't lie to me! I'm fucking Grover! Why am I fucking Grover!"

She turned and raised his hands to him. "Fine. Okay. Fine. It's a new device from upper management. They instructed me to beta test it. Happy?" She turned and started back toward the car.

"No! I'm fucking blue!"

"Watch your tongue, mister! You are still under evaluation," she said as she walked.

"Fuck your stupid evaluation! Fuck! Why am I blue?" he screamed.

"Don't worry. It should probably wear off in a couple of days."

"Probably? Days? What do you mean, probably?"

"Well, you were bluer when it first happened. It's already fading."

He stopped in his tracks and said, "Wait. Hold on. How long was I unconscious?"

"I don't know. Like, an hour? I threw a couple things at you, and you just lay there. I even poked you a few times with a stick."

"Stop walking! Stop! Just stop!" he begged her.

She stopped, sighed, turned, and faced him.

He took a deep breath. "Just tell me what that stupid clicker did. Please?"

She rolled her eyes. "Fine. If you must know . . . it's a new device from upper management. It identifies spiritual remnants and abnormalities. Like the grave. There used to be a spirit there until NRDS sent it to the great beyond a few years ago. Clearly, there are remnants. Happy?"

"No. Obviously not. Why am I blue? Your little explanation failed to mention that."

Melissa grinned. "Well, that would be because you're a fucking psychic who doesn't need a badge. I suspected it, but the proof is in the pudding, and I have all I need to report you up the fucking chain." She turned and started tromping to the car again. "If you actually followed the manual, you'd have reported shit like that, by the way. I have all I need to take you and Buck down. Dumbass."

"Wait, take me down? Why? Why Buck?"

"For aiding and abetting a known psychic. I've been waiting for this damn moment to get that bastard off my team."

"Aw fuck," Ethan said, dread filling his chest as he tromped behind her.

Forty-One

A Visit from Dad

E THAN WALKED INTO THE office, sporting a torn shirt and holes in his suit pants. He held up two weather-worn briefcases and shouted, "Creepy twins in the woods have been caught!"

Buck followed in behind him, with an equally scuffed suit, and found Doris's desk. "We're going to need two uniform replacement forms."

River peered out from behind his desk, leaning back in his chair. "Aw man, I wanted in on that. Did they do any weird shit?"

Ethan nodded. "They possessed a murder of crows. And then they attacked us."

Something glinted in the corner of Ethan's eye. He turned, jumped, and saw Alexus inches from his face, holding a machete. "I would have cut them all down. Each and every crow."

Doris handed Buck the forms and sighed. "Finance isn't happy with all these uniform replacements. Soon enough, they are going to push back."

Ethan approached the case wall, catching Bryce's eye while he passed the corner desk. Ethan slid the cases into place and said, "Yet we have another two ghosts off the streets. Sounds like finance can deal with it."

Buck plopped down into his chair, looked over his mug of questionably old coffee and chugged it. "Don't get cocky, rookie. Finance will start penny pinching soon, then you can bet we'll all be in some oversized denim overalls that we have to turn in at the end of the week."

"That doesn't sound so bad," Alexus said, finding her chair and running her finger along the machete.

A laugh sounded from Melissa's office, lower than Melissa's usual squeal. Ethan raised an eyebrow. "Who's in there?"

River sat up and grinned. "Bryce's dad."

"Really?" Ethan said, trying to gauge Bryce's stone-faced expression.

"Came all the way from DC," River added.

Bryce rested his elbows on his desk and hid his face from the rest of the office.

"Is that a bad thing?" Ethan asked.

Doris cleared her throat. "Mr. Fillmore is here to review the evaluations with Melissa. She put in a formal request for him to come in person for the review about a week ago."

"Well, that can't be good." Buck said.

"Fuck," Ethan muttered.

The laughter in Melissa's office stopped for a moment, and the office fell into silence.

"What? Did you fuck up that bad on evaluations?" Alexus asked.

"No. It's just," Ethan started, then turned toward Buck, "She knows."

Buck let out a sigh and swiveled in his chair. "She knows what?"

"That I'm psychic."

River's eyes widened, and he nearly flipped out of his seat, looking back at Bryce. "Whoa! Don't know what you're saying there, kiddo. You're joking, right?"

Bryce closed the file on top of his desk and looked at River. "I know."

Trevor, who'd been staring at his phone screen since Ethan had come into the office, looked up and said, "Wait. Ethan's a psychic? First ghosts. Now you're telling me he can read my future?"

Doris rolled her eyes. "No, you idiot. He can just see ghosts without a badge."

Ethan frowned. "Wait. Doris, you know?"

She nodded and took a sip of her coffee. "You keep talking to Bob without your badge. If it was a secret, you weren't all that great at hiding it."

"Well, I didn't know," Trevor said, turning back to his phone.

Bryce grabbed his mug of coffee and rolled his seat over to the circle of agents. "And now Melissa knows?"

Ethan nodded. "She used one of those damn clickers on me. Turned me blue."

Buck crossed his arms and glared at Bryce. "Weren't you supplying Melissa with clickers?"

Bryce's face turned red, and a vein bulged out of his neck. "She used a clicker on you? That's—that's against regulation!"

"Well, my dude," River started, "what did you suspect was going to happen from a crazy megalomaniac? Pretty sure whatever you and her were doing with those clickers was only a matter of time before one of you thought to use it on a person."

Bryce's knuckles turned white on the mug as his gaze traced back to Melissa's office. "No, it was him."

"Him?" Alexus said.

"My dad. He supplied the clickers from R&D. She must have gone behind my back."

The door to Melissa's office opened and a portly man, who had Bryce's blond hair and blue eyes superimposed on an aging man who looked more like Bruce Willis and Danny DeVito had spawned a child, stepped out of the office behind Melissa.

"Bryce, my boy! Glad to see you made it into the office. You know, I have an opening back at headquarters if you are looking for—"

"No, Dad, I'm not."

Mr. Fillmore raised his hands and laughed. "Can't say I didn't try. Your mother's been nagging me to find you a position back home, but if you don't want it . . ."

"I don't." Bryce said.

Mr. Fillmore nodded at that and surveyed the office. "Then on to business. Melissa, why don't you introduce me to your team?"

Melissa jumped in front of him and pointed to Trevor and Doris. "These two cover the front desk. Trevor is Doris's assistant. The one I've been telling you about."

"Ah, yes." Mr. Fillmore nodded. "I suppose now is as good a time as any to tell you that your thirty-seventh request to remove Trevor has been declined." He shot a wink at Trevor, whose face had turned white.

Melissa winced, her smile faltering for a second before panning over to River. "And this is River and Alexus. You'll know from their evaluations that they are hanging on by a thread."

"As one does in the middle of nowhere. As I've told Melissa, the two of you have cased more spirits separately than my whole DC region combined. Keep up the good work."

Melissa huffed and waved her hand at Buck. "And you know Buck."

Mr. Fillmore let out a huge smile and held out a hand to Buck. "Agent Hampton, it is an honor to be in your presence. I hope you've been acclimating well up here."

"That I have, sir."

"And Gerry? I miss all those desserts he'd make for the office. Please tell me he is well?"

Buck cleared his throat. "On and off. He's had a few bad days recently, but he'll be up and cooking again in no time."

Mr. Fillmore patted Buck on the shoulder. "It will all turn out alright. Give Ger my regards." He then looked at Ethan and held out his hand. "And I take it you are Agent Malik?"

Ethan shook it and Melissa butted in, the grin on her face resuming in full force. "Yes. He's the one I told you about. The—"

"Psychic," Mr. Fillmore finished.

Ethan's face flushed, and his grip on Mr. Fillmore tightened.

"Firm grip you have there, son," Mr. Fillmore said.

Bryce cleared his throat. "Dad. I heard Melissa used the blue clicker on him. Did you authorize that?"

Mr. Fillmore shot Bryce a glare. "I thought I told you to keep that information private."

Bryce rolled his eyes. "They all know about the clickers. Melissa wasn't the greatest at keeping them hidden."

Melissa's face turned scarlet. "Neither were you! Did you tell him about your little red clicker escapade?"

"Enough," Mr. Fillmore said, "What is this about, Bryce?"

"You told me you'd stop testing the clickers on living things. Ever since—"

Mr. Fillmore nodded. "Mr. Banks was an unfortunate loss. But that was an early prototype. The risk of death is so low now."

"Risk of death?" Ethan blurted out.

"You blew up my pet rabbit!" Bryce shouted.

Ethan's eyes widened, and he looked at Melissa. "That thing could have blown me up?"

Melissa shrugged. "There was a minor risk."

Mr. Fillmore held up a hand. "The risk was well below minor. We've been testing the model for years now without barely any casualties."

"Casualties?!" Ethan said.

"Dad! What if Mom found out?" Bryce said.

Mr. Fillmore ignored him, his gaze locking on Ethan. "It's been a long time since NRDS has identified a psychic. Let alone one of their own agents."

Ethan tried to step away, but Mr. Fillmore gripped his hand tight.

Ethan stammered over his words. "I'm not. I mean. I don't think I'm—"

Mr. Fillmore grinned. "But you are. And NRDS regulations would have us bring you into custody at the central NRDS office."

Bryce stepped forward. "Dad! If you'd just—"

Mr. Fillmore pushed his son aside and looked at Ethan. "You've been identified, Mr. Malik. The FUCS office would have us turn you in immediately for up to one year in custody while they evaluate your risk to the population. However, I think upper management can keep them out of our hair while I bring you down to R&D."

Ethan shook his head. Up to a year? "Wait. But I don't want to—"

Mr. Fillmore smiled. "This isn't a choice for you, Mr. Malik. You've signed a contract with NRDS. Failure to accept your reassignment will be a failure to comply with federal law. NRDS can't protect you from FUCS if you don't comply. I'd rather not include any more departments than I need to."

Ethan stared at Buck, his mouth agape. "What do I? What can I?"

Buck looked down at the ground. "Not much you can do, rookie. They found you out."

Alexus glared at Mr. Fillmore, her grip tightening around the machete.

River pushed Melissa out of the way and knocked Mr. Fillmore's hands free from Ethan and gave Ethan a hug. He whispered in his ear, "If you decide to run, I've got a smoke bomb in my desk. Just say the word."

Ethan pushed him off and shook his head. "No. I. I don't want anyone else to get in trouble."

"Wise decision, Mr. Malik," Mr. Fillmore said.

Ethan nodded at Mr. Fillmore. "Fine, I'll go."

Bryce stepped in front of Ethan and stared down his father. "Dad. Will you listen to me?"

Mr. Fillmore rolled his eyes and focused on Bryce. "What?"

"You can't take Ethan. He needs to stay here. He has to take care of his grandmother. She's—"

"Doing fine," Melissa said. "Ethan's grandmother and sister will be fine without him."

Mr. Fillmore nodded. "That's settled then, good."

Bryce steadied himself in front of Ethan and said, "No. Ethan's. He's. We're dating. He's my boyfriend."

Mr. Fillmore took a step back and frowned. "But you said you were seeing someone named Eve?"

"Eve is Ethan, Dad. I just. I didn't know how to tell you. I wasn't sure how you'd . . ."

Mr. Fillmore looked between Ethan and Bryce. "Oh, I see."

Melissa took the opportunity to speak. "All the better to take him in then, right? Inter-office relations are a detriment to NRDS. Isn't that right Mr. Fillmore?"

Mr. Fillmore frowned and turned to Melissa. "You know that my wife is also in upper management?"

Melissa blinked and said, "Yes. Of course I do. I just mean inter-office romances for agents. It's never been good from my perspective. I always thought—"

"It would be best if you stopped talking," Mr. Fillmore said, his attention turning back to Bryce. Melissa huffed and crossed her arms. "So, do you love him?" Mr. Fillmore asked.

Bryce bit his lip and smiled. "I. I think so."

Mr. Fillmore nodded and looked at Ethan. "I can see why."

Melissa shook her head. "But he's a psychic. You are supposed to take him in. Assess him. Test him. And reassign him. I was supposed to—"

"Get the promotion of your dreams?" Mr. Fillmore rolled his eyes. "Looks like that is going to have to wait. It would seem Agent Malik's evaluation was lost in the system, but I can imagine you'd have a new one drafted up by this afternoon? One with the recommendation that he continue to serve this community accordingly?" He looked at Bryce and said, "I will send you an updated protocol for testing the limits of Agent Malik's abilities in the next few weeks. Both you and Melissa are to report on the progress. To me. Understood?"

"And my promotion?" Melissa said.

"Involvement in this study will look great on your resume. Better than what you were going to get without it."

Mr. Fillmore looked at his son. "Does this arrangement better suit your business needs here in New Richmond?"

Bryce smiled. "Yeah. It does. And you're okay with it?"

Mr. Fillmore smiled. "Your mother and I are more open-minded than you seem to think. We don't care who you love, as long as you're happy."

Tears welled up in Bryce's eyes, and he dove in for a hug. "I am. I am happy."

"Good, then it is settled." He looked at Ethan and smiled. "And don't think you're getting away scot-free. You're coming to dinner, boy. I need to know all about the boy who swept my son off his feet."

Forty-Two

No One Believes in Ghosts

"After you, my ladies," Ethan said as he held the door to New Richmond Middle School open for Granny Rosemary and Ellie.

"See Ellie? Chivalry is not dead," Granny said, stepping into the hallway.

Ellie, carrying a trifold poster that was almost the same size she was, eyed Ethan as she stepped into the school. "I wish you'd dressed like a normal person."

"What's that supposed to mean? It's a suit." He said, following them down the hall.

Rosemary ran her fingers along her cardigan and grinned at Ethan. "She means suits aren't hip. You're looking more like my dad when I was Ellie's age."

"You look like an IRS agent from a bad 80s movie in a suit that barely fits," Ellie added.

Ethan looked at his exposed ankles and ran his hand over his tie. "Hey, I look professional."

"Professionally stupid, nerd." Ellie said.

"You're both just jealous. I'm going to stand out as an upstanding, dapper gentleman. Plus, these looks are going to help your score, right? Having a real, professional NRDS agent standing next to your project to answer questions."

Ellie laughed. "What? No. People hate you."

Granny nodded. "She's right. I listened to Fran and June on the radio yesterday, and the number of callers complaining about your office took all the airtime."

Ethan pulled open the cafeteria door for them. "Well, great. Thanks for telling me."

Five long rows of tables filled the cafeteria. On either side of each table, students were setting up their trifold posters. Each one hoping to win the coveted blue ribbon, indicating they had created the most interesting project of the year. To sweeten the pot, a gift card for thirty dollars to Haus of Dairy Ice Cream Parlor accompanied the ribbon.

Ethan scoped out the competition as they found their way to Ellie's designated spot. Nearly everyone had a variation of baking soda volcanos, foam ball solar systems, and plants growing in cups displays. A few caught Ethan's eye, like the "How Many Candy Bars Can the Average Fourth Grader Put in Her Mouth" experiment or the heavily illustrated "Five Types of Poop" display; but overall, Ethan saw nothing as cool as what Ellie was presenting.

He leaned in and whispered in Ellie's ear. "Oh, you've totally got this."

"Oh, I know," she said as she opened up the trifold.

Ethan stared at the header on her trifold and read, "NRDS: Real or Fakers?" On the left panel there was a decorated list entitled, "Things NRDS Claim" and on the right panel, there was a two-column chart entitled "True or False."

Ethan crossed his arms and frowned. "Wait! I thought you were doing a presentation on ghosts? What is this?"

Ellie shrugged. "No one was going to vote for ghosts. This is more edgy, and I want to win."

Rosemary leaned in and nudged Ethan's arm. "She's right. No one believes in ghosts, sweetie."

Ethan's jaw fell open. "What are you talking about? That's literally my job. We talk about it all the time. You sent me to talk to your friend Mable!"

"We believe you, dear. But the public. They aren't ready for that." Rosemary said.

Ellie rolled her eyes. "I'm not going to win if everyone here gets mad at me. I need something they can relate to."

Ethan threw his hands up in the air. "So, you're throwing me under the bus?"

"You can handle it," Ellie said.

"Sweet girl and I talked about it," Granny explained. "And you have to admit that she has a better chance of winning if she goes with a more relevant topic."

"Wait. You're in on it? What?" Ethan stammered.

"People will like this one," Ellie said.

"People like ghosts! Ghosts are cool!" Ethan declared.

"Depressed millennials like ghosts," Ellie said before waving her arms out to the crowd. "Does this look like the right crowd?"

Ethan smoothed his tie and looked out to the crowd, noting that nearly everyone was older than him. He sighed and leaned in, reading the details on the two panels. "Please tell me you concluded we're real."

Ellie shrugged. "I left it up to the reader to decide."

"Come on! What is this? There are only four reasons for NRDS and eleven reasons against it!"

"That's what the research led me to. I had to stay true to the science," Ellie said.

Ethan looked at Rosemary. "And you let her do this? This isn't going to help."

Rosemary smiled at Ellie. "My granddaughter did her research. We can't dismiss her conclusions."

Ethan glared at Ellie. "You didn't even ask me. Half of these look made up. You're. You're just a lying liar face."

Ellie stuck her tongue out at him. "Be careful or I might add that your little secret club hires a bunch of dum dums."

Granny put her hand on Ethan's shoulder and pulled him from Ellie. "Why don't you see if you can find us some refreshments?"

"There are no refreshments at the science fair," Ethan said.

"It's code for 'go away', dum dum," Ellie said.

Granny shot Ellie a look and squeezed Ethan's shoulder. "Just go look for some."

Ethan shrugged her off and threw his hands up. "I see how it is. Well, maybe I'll find another kid to cheer on then."

He turned and stomped off, finding an empty chair near the other side of the cafeteria to sit and pout. "No one believes in ghosts," he mumbled to himself. "Maybe I'll just get a briefcase and show them."

He watched as a girl in Ellie's class set up a trifold at the end of a row that read, "What Music is Best for Studying?" Waving to her, Ethan called, "Great project! Hope you win!"

She gave him a nervous smile, looking around before saying, "Uh, thanks, mister."

"Great, and now I'm the creepy guy in the corner," Ethan said.

He stood and started walking down the tables, checking out the displays and trying to find anything remotely interesting to read. He paused as a chill ran down his spine, and a faint blue light caught in the corner of his eye.

He turned and strolled to the end row. Projects lined both sides, and children and parents chatted happily. A man with a mustache and clipboard, one of the middle school teachers that Ethan remembered as a child, took notes as he passed the trifold presentations. Everything seemed normal, yet the sensation in Ethan's gut told him something was off.

"Mom. Make it stop," a young boy said behind him.

Ethan spun around, seeing a model of a solar system spinning as a young boy tried to grab and steady the various planets.

"If you don't want it to spin, don't flick it," a woman, presumably his mother, said as she helped him steady it.

"But I didn't this time," the boy complained.

Ethan shook his head and took a deep breath. Nothing. Nothing was here. He just needed a vacation.

"Jamie. It's not time yet," a different parent further down the same aisle complained.

"But I didn't do anything," the child said, tears streaming down their face as colored foam erupted from a papier mâché volcano.

Blue light glinted in Ethan's vision, and he dashed to peer down the aisle. Nothing.

He waited, but nothing seemed out of the ordinary while Jamie's parent helped try to salvage the experiment.

He took a few steps back and leaned against the wall, watching the room.

"Why? Why did you wreck my plant?" a kid from the middle aisle yelled.

"I didn't do it!" another child replied.

Blue light glinted in Ethan's periphery again.

"Hey!" a kid another aisle over cried. "Don't poke me!"

"It wasn't me," another child responded.

"Can you get a hold of your daughter, please?" a parent shouted.

Another aisle over, the judge with the mustache crashed to the floor. Ethan looked down the aisle to see children giggling as the judge struggled with his shoelaces and demanded, "Alright! Who tied my shoes together!"

Ethan found a chair and stood on it, surveying over the tops of heads to get a better look at what was happening.

Scanning the aisle, he finally saw them. At the far end of the room.

Dylan snuck toward an unsuspecting child as Jean stood behind him, giggling. "What are they doing out of the cemetery?" Ethan whispered, jumping off his chair.

Not only that, but why were they tormenting everyone?

He shouldered through the crowd, muttering, "Oh, you don't believe in ghosts, Ellie? Wait till you see this."

He spotted Dylan as he grabbed a girl's ponytail and yanked it. The girl screamed and turned around, tears forming in her eyes as Jean laughed wildly.

Ethan took out his phone and dialed Buck. The other end of the line rang for a few seconds before a voice came over the line. "What do you want, rookie?"

Ethan kept his eyes on Dylan, creeping toward him. "I'm at the science fair. Dylan and Jean are here, and Dylan can interact with things now."

"Well shit," Buck said.

"What do I do?" Ethan asked as he watched Jean try and fail at knocking over a glass of water onto a student's project. Dylan stood behind her, rooting her on.

"Do you have a case?"

"No. And there's too many people. Everybody with a kid in town is here."

Using his entire hand, Dylan shoved the glass. It slid across the table, seconds from tipping onto a report before the student snatched it up, staring wide eyed at the glass.

"Then you have to reason. They need to get back to the cemetery. Pronto," Buck said.

"How? They're kids." Ethan asked, inching closer to them.

"Figure it out," Buck barked.

"Well, can I get a little help?" Ethan pleaded.

"No."

"Why not? Where are you?"

"I'm sitting on a beach in St. Lucia."

"But I saw you yesterday!"

"And now I'm here, reading a book on the beach."

"Seriously? What the hell am I supposed to do with this?"

"You'll figure it out."

"Thanks for nothing," Ethan said.

"You'll be fine. Just don't get anybody killed."

"Great. I'll try that," Ethan said sarcastically as he hung up the phone. He was within ten feet of Dylan now, who was standing next to a small boy in a blue and white striped shirt whose trifold read, "How Many Licks to Finish a Lollipop?" Dylan was grabbing at one lollipop glued to the boy's project.

"Dylan! Stop that right now!" Ethan commanded.

Dylan, Jean, and the boy in the white striped shirt all snapped to attention.

"Um. My name's Andy, mister," the boy said, concerned.

Dylan eyed Ethan while his hand continued pulling at the lollipop.

Ethan pointed his finger at the ghost. "Don't you touch that candy!"

"Mister, I don't even know you," Andy whined.

"What's going on here?" the judge with the mustache said, approaching.

"Nothing, I just need to, uh," Ethan said, his eyes still locked on Dylan.

"This man's yelling at me," Andy said to the judge.

Dylan stretched toward the lollipop.

"No! Get over here!" Ethan said, his hand outstretched.

A strange sensation overcame Ethan, and suddenly his hand glowed blue. Dylan's eyes widened as he clutched the lollipop and his feet lifted off the table toward Ethan.

The trifold slid across the table, flying toward Ethan as Dylan held on for dear life.

"What the hell?" the judge said, pulling Andy back away from Ethan.

Dylan finally let go as the trifold fell to the floor, and he flew to Ethan's hand like he was caught in some kind of vacuum.

Dylan flailed about, shouting, "Let go of me!"

"My project!" Andy cried.

Ethan stepped back, and the glow on his hand vanished, dropping Dylan.

"Sir, I. I don't know who you are. But I'm going to ask that you don't sabotage the presentations," the judge said.

Jean raced over to Dylan and pulled him back. "Come on, Dylan. Let's go."

Dylan shook his head. "No. I want candy."

Ethan glared at Dylan. "You touch that candy and I'll personally stuff you in a briefcase."

"Excuse me? Do I need to call the police?" the judge said, taking a step toward Ethan.

"Come on, Dylan," Jean said.

Dylan pulled free from Jean and jumped toward another project.

"Don't you dare!" Ethan shouted before Dylan set off another volcanic eruption, this time a mixture of soda and candy that sent a fountain into the air.

The eruption sprayed the judge, covering him in foaming soda.

"Sir! I don't know what you are playing, but this is highly improper! You need to leave!" the judge demanded.

Dylan stuck his tongue out at Ethan and yanked a lollipop free from the trifold on the floor. He then chucked it at Ethan, decking him in the head.

Ethan rubbed his head, feeling a welt forming. "That's it, you little shit!"

"Run for it!" Dylan screamed as he grabbed Jean.

"You two are headed to the graveyard, even if I have to drag you there myself!" Ethan shouted as he lunged forward.

His hands glowed blue again, and Dylan and Jean froze in mid-run.

Blue light washed over them, and they rose into the air.

Jean was the first to move, zipping through the air, phasing through the wall out of sight.

Dylan, however, writhed against it, flying about the room erratically.

Trifold presentations flew off tables as he twisted and turned through the air.

"You! Can't! Make! Me!" Dylan shouted as he whizzed left and right around the room.

Ethan did not know what was happening, but he knew he was behind it. "Get your ass back to the graveyard!" he shouted.

Tables flipped over, and people fell to the ground as Dylan flew across the room.

Then, in an instant, he vanished, phasing through the wall.

Ethan's hand stopped glowing, and he stared, awestruck, at the presentations floating down to the floor.

"What the hell was that?" Ethan muttered to himself.

All eyes turned toward him, children with tears in their eyes and parents with rage strewn across their faces.

Ethan spotted Ellie in the corner of his eye, scrawling a twelfth entry on the side against NRDS.

Forty-Three

A Ghost Walks into a Bar and Asks for Gin

E THAN STROLLED ALONG THE side of highway sixty-five, enjoying the brisk air, full moon, and gravel on his feet. He smiled as he peered out into the miles of cornfields, finally alone, just him and the breeze. Headlights shone up ahead, slowing down and coming to a stop just in front of him. Before the driver could step out, a blue figure phased through the car. Bob shouted. "What in the hell are you doing?"

Ethan covered the beams of light with his hands and squinted, spotting River stepping out of the car. He frowned and said, "I was enjoying a walk. Why?"

River reached into the back of his car and then approached Ethan. "'Cause Buck called me. Said you were supposed to check in an hour ago. To be clear, you do know that you're walking along a highway naked, right?"

Adrenaline hit Ethan, and he looked down. Sure enough, all he saw was skin from head to toe, illuminated by the headlights. Heat filled his face. "I. Uh."

"You 'uh' what, private?" Bob shouted.

River tossed Ethan a towel. "I'm guessing you haven't suddenly decided to live a life as a nudist?"

Ethan quickly wrapped the towel around himself. "No. I haven't. Thanks."

River sighed. "Shame. Elmore's farm would love to have some fresh meat. With the three of us, it would be a real sausage fest."

"Ha-ha. Hilarious." Ethan said.

Bob stomped his foot and glared at River. "We were sent on an important mission from the head honcho. This is serious!"

River rolled his eyes. "Calm down, Bob, we found him." He looked at Ethan and said, "So, why are you walking, dick out, in the middle of nowhere?"

"I. I don't know." He strained to remember, and flashes filled his mind. "I was. I was with Alexus."

River nodded. "Buck said Melissa assigned you two a case tonight, right? Do you remember where?"

"Some bar. I think? Sampson's, maybe?"

River looked down the road. "Well, that's about five miles down the road. Makes sense."

Ethan gathered his surroundings and looked down at his feet, noting how sore they were from walking on gravel barefoot. "What the fuck?"

River shrugged. "Well, come on, streaker. We need to save Alexus."

Bob laughed. "She's going to love that."

Ethan rubbed his head in the passenger seat as River pulled back onto the highway. "I don't get it. Everything was normal. It was a routine check. Barely anything ticked the boxes except a string of assaults. If anything, it should have been just a Class Three."

"And yet, you're wrapped in a towel in my car. So, guess not," River said.

As they reached the parking lot of Sampson's, Ethan spotted his clothes strewn about in a line leading up to the door. "Ghosts can't do that, can they? Command people to strip naked and take a hike?"

Bob leaned in and whispered in Ethan's ear. "Punch River in the face."

Ethan frowned.

"What the hell, Bob?" River asked.

Bob folded his arms in the backseat. "Worth a try."

River stared at the entrance to the bar. "I've never seen it myself, but I think there is a section on it in the manual. Class Fours and Fives get real weird. We just need to be quick, yeah? I've got a spare case in the trunk. If we both have one, we should be able to get it by surprise."

Ethan hopped out of the car and started pulling clothes back on. "Yeah, that should work."

River pulled the case from his trunk and carried Bob's bag in the other hand. They stood outside the doors, and River said, "On the count of three. One. Two."

The gravel felt great beneath his feet, and the moon shone bright on his face as he strolled along the road. Ethan smiled, not giving a single care to the world. He squeezed the warm hand he held, vaguely remembering that it was River's, and enjoyed the sight of miles of rolling cornfields.

A blue figure flitted in and out of vision, waving their arms in front of Ethan.

"Wake up, you motherfuckers!"

Ethan blinked and focused on Bob, inches from his face.

"Bob?" Ethan asked.

"Holy fucking shit! Finally! I've been shouting at your nekkid asses for the past mile. Do you know how embarrassing it is to watch you two stargazing while cars drive by?"

Ethan blinked a few times and looked down, noting he was naked again—and holding River's hand, who was equally naked and holding onto Bob's bag.

"Goddamn it!" Ethan shouted and let go of River's hand.

"What?" River asked, blinking a few times while his eyes gazed forward.

"River. We're naked, walking along a highway."

River looked down and laughed. "Well, that I am." He held up the bag and shook it. "Bob? You there?"

"Yes, you dumbass," Bob said.

River looked at Ethan and smirked. "I don't have my badge. Did he say anything?"

"You smartass motherfuck—"

Ethan nodded. "He pulled me out of it. Now he's mad at you."

"Aww. Don't be mad, man. Did you see anything?"

"Besides you two nekkid motherfuckers ignoring me for the last half hour?" Bob asked.

Ethan rolled his eyes. "We clearly didn't mean to. Did you see anything?"

"Yeah. The ghost in there is strong. Got to be a Class Five. You two walked in. River tried to do his usual stupid-ass River shit. It didn't want any of that. The thing sent you two out the moment it saw you had a case."

"What's he saying?" River asked.

Ethan held up his hand. "What about Alexus? Did you see her?"

Bob nodded. "Everyone else in the bar was dancing. No one looked too happy to be doing it."

River faced Ethan and rested his hands. "Well?"

Ethan did his best to avert his eyes, holding on to the threads of modesty that he could. "The ghost sent us away 'cause we had cases. Alexus is still in there, stuck . . . dancing?"

River started down the road. "Oh, I have to see that."

Ethan raced to keep up with him as they headed back toward the bar. "We need a new game plan. If the ghost is sending us away because of the cases, then maybe one of us can go in without one?"

"Then what? Get stuck inside with the rest of them?"

"Just don't send me back in there. That guy gives me the heebie-jeebies," Bob said.

Ethan frowned. "What? Why?"

Bob shrugged. "Something that can do all that to living people. What do you think it could do to me if it wanted?"

"Yeah, fair." Ethan rubbed the back of his head. "Well. I mean, maybe I could go in? But both you and Bob got me out of it. If I have you in my ear, that might wake me up?"

River shrugged. "Sure. Worth a shot."

"I've got a Bluetooth earpiece in my pants. If you stay near the door and get ready with a case, then I think I can figure something out."

River wrapped his arm around Ethan. "Sounds like a plan to me, rookie."

"Hey! You two break it up!" Bob yelled.

Ethan stared at Bob and smiled at the opportunity to make him cringe. He wrapped his arm around River and said, "What? A little PDA too much for you?"

Bob let out a huff and said, "No. You're. You're in a committed relationship, private. And he's. Well. He's a real homewrecker."

Ethan laughed and let go of River. "Noted, Bob." He straightened his shirt and put in his earpiece.

"Oh, get in there and blend in," River started.

"Do some recon, then relay back to base. We'll await orders to infiltrate," Bob said.

Ethan looked at River and nodded. "You two ready?"

They nodded, and Ethan took in a breath before stepping through the doors of the bar.

A wave of heat washed over him instantly, followed by the stench of sweat in the air. The dance floor was filled with people pressed up against each other, moving to the beat of a real twangy country song Ethan had never heard before.

He took another step into the bar, and everyone froze, stopping their dance to turn and look right at Ethan.

A man stepped out from the crowd wearing an all-white suit, aviators, and a mustache that he styled into fine points on either side of his face. "I see you finally decided against the briefcase. Good choice, my man."

Ethan took another step forward, his eyes scanning the frozen people in the crowd behind the man. "Well, I didn't want to miss out on the party."

His eyes found Alexus, sweat pouring down her face and her hair caked on her neck as her eyes dully stared at him.

The man clapped his hands together. His eyes glowed a faint blue, and he smiled. "Good, then let's get back to dancing."

"Earth to Ethan. You there?"

Ethan swayed on the dance floor, sweat forming on his brow.

"Paging Dr. Ethan."

The voice tickled at something in the back of Ethan's mind, but he couldn't be bothered by it. He'd rather dance.

"Yo Ethan. If you don't wake up, I might see if Bryce is looking for a little side piece."

Ethan blinked. "What?"

"Hey! You're awake."

Reality slowly poured back in, and Ethan found himself in the middle of the dance floor, in the middle of an undulating crowd of people with their eyes glazed over. "Yeah. I'm awake. What was that you said about Bryce?"

"Nothing. Eyes on the prize, buddy. What's going on in there?"

Ethan spotted the white-suited man at the bar, sitting back and watching the crowd. Ethan turned his back to the man and kept dancing with the crowd. "Creepy guy in a white suit seems to be the ringleader."

"Great, so possession and mind control. You two were in over your heads."

Ethan looked down at his hands. "I think I have an idea." He focused, and for a second he could see a faint flicker of blue on his fingertips. "Just be ready if you hear screaming."

"Screaming?" River said over the phone. "What?"

Ethan lifted his arm and held his palm out toward the man in white. It glowed as he took in a breath and shouted over the music, "Hey, asshole! Why don't you get out of that body?"

His fingertips tingled, and the man jumped out of his seat, his arms flailing and knocking over a bar stool. A blue silhouette shimmered around the man, and he let out a loud howl.

The dancers all jerked and bumped Ethan, and the glow on his hand flickered out.

The man regained his composure and straightened his suit, eyes glowing blue. "You're not going to take me that easy. Not until I have my fun. Now kneel."

A pressure built in Ethan's head, and the world blurred. Before he knew it, his knees were planted on the ground, and the man in white was approaching.

Forty-Four

Bartender Says, "Sorry We Don't Serve Spirits"

E THAN KNELT ON THE sticky bar floor, his eyes locked on the man in white. Around him, bar patrons danced, completely oblivious to the world around them as the possessed man continued to control them.

The man in white pulled a bottle of gin from behind the bar by the neck and swung it around a few times. "You know, I don't really like pigs showing up and crashin' my parties."

"Heyo, Earth to Ethan! Snap out of it." River's voice shouted over the Bluetooth headset in Ethan's ear.

The man in white approached, readying the bottle like it was a bat.

Ethan blinked a few times, River's voice pulling him out of the ghost's command.

"Pity you didn't just keep walking, piggy piggy," the man said, holding the bottle above his head.

The man brought down the bottle in the same second that clarity hit Ethan. Ethan dove out of the way, his mind still not in complete control over his body, so he just fell, hard, onto the ground. He shook off the last bit of numbness and jut up his hand, slamming his palm into the man's chest. His hand glowed a bright blue, and he shouted, "Get out!"

A blue light encompassed the man, and Ethan felt a rush of energy flow through him. With it, the sensation of snapping threads played in his mind. The man shouted as he jerked and twitched, blue light spilling out of him like he was smoking.

"What the fuck is going on?" Bar patrons started shouting behind Ethan.

"Why am I so thirsty?" and "I'm so tired," followed shortly after that.

"Ethan?" a voice shouted above the others.

"Over. Here." He struggled to shout as the man collapsed on top of him.

The expunged blue light coalesced, forming into a floating man dressed in a suit that looked straight out of the twenties. He looked down at his hands, then at the man in the white suit.

"No!" he shouted, his eyes staring at the dispersing crowd. "I can't let them leave!"

"Case the fucker!" Alexus shouted.

"I. Don't. Have. One," Ethan grunted.

"You've got to be shitting me," Alexus complained.

The ghost's eyes widened, and he dove back into the body. It shuttered and twitched in Ethan's arms.

"Oh shit," Ethan said.

Alexus broke through the crowd, reaching Ethan's side. She held up her badge, looking left and right, "Okay, where is he?"

"He's already—"

The man in white shoved off Ethan and stood. He straightened his suit and said in a low growl, "Restrain him."

"Oh, dammit," Ethan mumbled.

Alexus went completely rigid, her eyes glazing over before she rushed to Ethan and held his hands behind his back.

Ethan kicked his legs back, trying to catch her off guard, but she dodged everyone while she smiled. "Oh, come on!" Ethan said.

The man in white nodded at Alexus and looked past her to the remaining bar patrons.

Everyone else had already left the dance floor, some sitting down to catch their breath from the hours of dancing, while others were walking out the exit.

"No!" the man in white shouted. He pushed past Alexus and spread his arms, his voice booming over the music. "Why don't you all stay?" His voice traveled through the air, reverberating in Ethan's ears like some kind of melody.

As Alexus turned him around, Ethan saw the little, thin blue threads spreading out from his hands, wrapping around patrons like they were all puppets. Everyone froze, as if they were turned into statues. Some were resting in chairs, while others were partway in the process of donning a coat or stepping outside.

He continued, the little threads of blue pulsing light. "Why don't you all grab yourself a drink? Enjoy yourselves."

Smiles spread across all their faces, and those in the process of leaving turned. Laughter filled the air as the crowd converged on the bar. Several patrons hopped over, grabbing bottles and filling glasses.

"Why won't you just let them go?" Ethan said.

The man in white gave Ethan a smile. "I can't."

Ethan frowned. "You can't? What the hell does that mean? Of course you can. You just stop. Like. Right now. Just stop."

The man looked out the window. "They need to be here when Petey shows up. If he sees an empty bar again, then he's going to have my head."

"Petey? Who's Petey?" Ethan said.

The man shot a look at Alexus, and she squeezed Ethan's wrists, hard.

He let out a yelp, and the man in white smiled. "You pigs are all the same. Trying to shut us down. How much to pay you off? Twenty? Fifty?"

"What the hell are you talking about?" Ethan said.

The man in white shoved a finger in Ethan's chest. "You know exactly what I'm talking about. One of you feds was in here last week trying to shut us down too. You just can't leave hard-working people alone."

River's voice cracked over the Bluetooth headset. "Yo, Ethan. I don't think this guy knows he's a ghost."

"No shit," Ethan muttered.

"And now you're here to do the same. If this bar ain't kept at full capacity, then my head's on the chopping block. So you're gonna sit tight, right here, till Petey gets back."

An idea surfaced in Ethan's mind. "I. Uh. What if I cut you a deal? You tell me what's really going on here, and I keep the other feds away."

The man in white raised an eyebrow. "You want in? And you'd keep the fed off my back? What's the catch?"

"No catch," Ethan said. "How about you give me ten percent?"

"Five."

River laughed in the earpiece. "Five percent? Counter for seven. Don't go for it."

Ethan ignored him. "Fine, five percent. We got a deal?"

The man smiled. "I like it. How do I know you aren't pulling my leg?"

"Uh. You don't, but what better option do you have? Kill me? What happens when I go missing? You think the next feds are going to offer this?"

The man in white nodded. "Fine. I think we've got ourselves a deal."

He nodded to Alexus, and she released Ethan. He rubbed his wrists, feeling the blood flowing back into them.

The man held out his hand and helped Ethan to his feet. "Name's Johnny. Johnny Kincade. what's yours?"

"Ethan. Look, Johnny, I left my briefcase out in the car. Didn't want you thinking I was here to arrest you, but I think it might have something you're interested in."

The man in white flinched, and the lights above flickered. His voice changed, registering lower as he whispered. "No one leaves tonight, Johnny, got it? Keep the doors locked and wait until Petey comes."

River's voice sounded in Ethan's ear. "Johnny Kincade, 1923. The internet says this dude was supposedly responsible for locking thirty people in the basement of an underground prohibition bar in New Richmond. Bar caught fire that night while a Peter Reisman was unloading barrels of liquor and the feds caught him. Looks like it was a shootout."

Ethan held up his hands. "Okay, Johnny. I don't need to get it. We can just stay here."

"If you can pull him out again, I think I have a plan," River said.

Ethan took a step toward Johnny, but Alexus grabbed his shoulder. He looked back, seeing the dazed look on her face, and mouthed the words, "I'm sorry," before elbowing her in the gut.

She stumbled back, and Ethan aimed his hand at the man in white. "Get out!" he shouted, his hand flickering blue.

Johnny stumbled back, and a faint blue light encompassed him. His face blurred as the spirit of Johnny fell out of sync with the man's movements, as if he were some type of glitch. "You. Can't. Make. Me"

"Get out!" Ethan shouted.

Johnny looked at Alexus, and the thread between them flared a bright white. "Stop him!"

"Oh shit! River, Hurry!" Ethan said over the Bluetooth.

He looked back, spotting Alexus recovering from the gut punch and taking a step toward him. Her dull eyes locked on him.

River burst through the door, followed by Bob.

"Please don't beat me up for this," River said as he held up his briefcase like a shield and ran right into Alexus, knocking her to the ground.

Bob raced past Ethan and leaped into the air, running right into Johnny.

Blue light burst into the room, like a disco ball emitting from the man in white. Johnny detached from the man, and both he and Bob tumbled out of the body. The threads that attached Johnny to nearly everyone in the room vanished.

The man collapsed to the ground, unmoving.

Ethan lowered his hand, exhaustion rolling over him in waves.

"Get off me!" Alexus shouted, flailing underneath River.

"Are you still going to beat up Ethan?" River said.

"What? I'm going to beat both of your stupid asses!" She kicked her legs up, aiming for River's groin, but he was too quick, rolling off her and jumping to his feet.

"Well, she's back," River said.

"What the hell is going on?" a woman, standing up from the bar with a drink in hand, said.

The lights in the bar flickered, and Johnny let out a loud groan that bored into Ethan's bones. He shoved Bob off him with enough force to send him into the wall. The force of him hitting the wall sent a shockwave that shattered the window and knocked down a neon, "Miller Time" light. All the remaining patrons jumped. The daze from Johnny cleared away as they raced out the bar doors.

Johnny stood, his eyes glowing a brilliant white. "You let them leave."

Bottles, chairs, and tables lifted off the ground as if someone had shut off gravity.

River unclasped the case and raced forward. "Come here, you ghosty-ass motherfucker."

A bottle whizzed across the room and decked him in the head, knocking River out and sending the case reeling across the bar.

Johnny took a step toward Ethan. "You lied to me."

Alexus raced toward Johnny.

Another bottle flew, but she dodged it.

Johnny paused, his attention shifting to her. He sent a chair after her, but again, she dove out of the way before the chair could hit her.

"Ethan, get the case!" she yelled.

He sprang into action, racing across the floor, sliding the last few feet before grabbing the case.

A table flew through the air, catching Alexus in the stomach and pinning her against the wall.

Ethan scrambled to his feet, case in hand.

Johnny cocked his head, his eyes locked on Alexus, and said, "You'll do."

He glowed a bright blue, and fine tendrils wrapped around Alexus. She squirmed and shoved at the table, but it didn't budge.

She froze, her eyes glossed over as Johnny passed through the table and started merging with her.

Ethan flung the case across the floor. It stopped underneath the table and let out its own blue light.

Johnny froze, and all the floating objects in the bar fell to the ground.

"No!" he shouted, the tendrils that wrapped around Alexus fleeing.

In an instant, he vanished inside the case and Alexus slumped over on the table.

Ethan chased after the case, snapping it shut and looking around at the two unconscious NRDS agents and the carnage of broken bottles, chairs, and tables.

"Well, this is going to be fun to explain."

Forty-Five

Ethan's Face is a Thing of Beauty

"Look at this!" Ethan said, gritting his teeth as he gestured toward the giant banners hanging on either side of the stage.

The bright red, eight-foot-tall behemoths featured an enormous picture of Ethan's face with the words, "Public Enemy #1!" across the top and "Vote for Chax!" on the bottom. Surrounding Ethan's picture was the rest of the NRDS office, but Ethan's face was twice the size of everyone else's and sported a look like he had just smelt something horrific.

"I don't like it," he said to Bryce who stood next to him.

Bryce grinned and wrapped his arm around Ethan's shoulder. "Well, I think it's kind of cute."

Ethan gesticulated at one poster as he talked. "Cute! Look at me! I look like a moron!"

Alexus, who stood on Ethan's other side, said, "You look like someone threw your ice cream on the ground."

River laughed, cutting between Alexus and Ethan. "You look like someone just ripped one."

Alexus side-eyed River, then said, "You look like you just stepped barefoot in cold dog vomit."

"I get it, thanks," Ethan said.

"No, you look like you just walked in on two ghosts fucking. Remember that?" River countered back with a laugh.

Bryce squeezed Ethan and kissed him on the cheek. "Don't listen to them. You've got one of those cute, dumb faces. What do they call them? Himbos?"

Alexus snorted and repeated, "Himbo," between gasps of breath.

Ethan pulled Bryce's arm off him and eyed the scaffolding that framed the stage. "I think I could climb that and cut it down."

"Maybe you should, before I make #HimboEthan go viral," River said.

Alexus shook her head. "You can't cut it down."

"You don't think I can climb that high? I'm an excellent climber," Ethan shot back, flexing his biceps.

"That picture of you looks like you climbed a mountain looking for enlightenment only to find the gal you love—"

"Guy you love," Bryce corrected.

"Right. Thanks. The guy you love, entwined in an eight-some with those big ole ghosts from that speed date," River said.

Bryce tilted his head and looked over at River. "Do they have to be ghosts?"

Ethan huffed and looked up at the sky. "That's it. I'm taking it down."

Alexus grabbed his arm and glared. "I said no."

"But why?" Ethan asked, averting Alexus's stare.

"Do you see how I look in that pic? I look hot."

River nodded. "That leather jacket really brings everything out."

"Thank you," Alexus said.

"Too bad you have Himbo over here with a look like he took a swig from the bong water by mistake," River added with a smile.

"Where's Trevor?" Ethan said, looking around the room. "He'll back me up on this."

River took out a joint and lit it. "He's backstage." He took a long drag and then added, "He got a VIP pass because he's an influencer."

A portly woman in blue jeans two sizes too small and a T-shirt that read, "We Don't Need Ghostbusters!" glared at him and said, "Excuse me, you can't smoke in here."

"Nah lady, I've got a condition. Can't help it." River blew smoke toward her and laughed.

The woman pursed her lips, her face turning red as she stomped off.

"What condition is that?" Alexus asked.

River took another long drag. "I'm an asshole. Doctor says it's chronic."

"Yeah, I hear it's incurable, too," Bryce said.

"You should have seen my face when I found out," River said with a smirk.

Ethan glared at him. "Let me guess. You looked like me on the sign?"

"Oh. No way! I could never look like that. You look like you walked in on your high school crush going down on granny."

Ethan threw up his hands and stepped in front of River. "Woah! Leave Granny out of this."

"That's what he said when I suggested a threesome," River retorted.

Before Ethan could respond, the lights in the room dimmed while the lights on the stage came up. The crowd cheered, and Chax Tamish took the stage in a bright blue suit and an immaculate white smile. "Hello New Richmond! You are beautiful!" he yelled into the microphone.

The fifty people in attendance cheered in response.

"No seriously. I love each and every one of you!" Chax replied.

"Why does this guy have such a punchable face?" Alexus said, cracking her knuckles.

"We love you too, Chax!" a woman yelled from across the room.

"Thank you for coming tonight! You've all given me so much and I am so excited about where we are going!" Chax yelled.

"That's what your granny told me last night," River quipped.

"Keep my Granny out of your mouth!" Ethan demanded.

Bryce giggled. "That's what he said."

Ethan's mouth dropped open in shock. "You too? Oh, my God, I give up."

Alexus pointed at Ethan, her eyes wide. "Sweet Jesus! That's the look! Right there!"

River clapped Bryce on the back and they both laughed. "You're my new favorite person," River said, offering Bryce a hit of his joint.

Bryce looked at Ethan and shrugged. "I'm so sorry. I couldn't help it. It was perfect timing."

Chax's voice drowned them out. "And I'm excited to tell you that tonight you all have helped us raise forty thousand dollars for my campaign!"

The crowd clapped and cheered with excitement.

"Did we give him something to be here?" Alexus asked.

"Tickets were two-hundred a piece with a recommended additional donation," Bryce said.

River blew smoke into the air. "We paid this douche canoe eight hundred dollars?"

"A thousand dollars. I also paid for Trevor," Bryce said.

"Alright, Daddy Warbucks. Are you feeling spendy enough to take me out to dinner after?" River said, shifting his eyes between Ethan and Bryce.

"Damn, Ethan. I didn't know you were into sugar daddies," Alexus said.

"Now, now," Chax said over the microphone. "While that is exciting, that's not what's brought us together."

A hush fell over the crowd as they waited for his words.

As that happened, a tingling chill passed through Ethan, and the lights above him flickered. Ethan looked up, darting eyes between stage lights and ceiling lights, but neither the feeling nor the flicker happened again. "Did anyone else see that?"

River blew more smoke into the air. "See what?"

"The light flicker?" Alexus asked.

Ethan nodded.

Bryce pulled his badge from his pocket and looked up. "Probably nothing."

Chax yelled into the microphone, his voice coming across more like a pastor than a politician. "There is a great threat facing this community. One corrupting the very fabric of our lives. The NRDS!"

The crowd booed so wildly it caused Ethan to move closer to Bryce.

"That's right! These so-called federal agents are wasting your tax dollars! They claim to be protecting us while unleashing havoc like and terror. A few weeks ago, they tried to silence me with the Cleveland Cleaver stunt. There's no telling what else they might try!" Chax continued.

The crowd booed more and a fist-pumping chant of "No more nerds! No more nerds! No more nerds!" took hold.

"Seems that little stunt may have been ill-advised," Bryce commented.

"Not my best idea," River said.

"And they must think we're stupid! They think we're complete idiots! They want the people of New Richmond to believe in things like ghosts so they can control you. Well, I say, FAKE NEWS! I DON'T BELIEVE IN GHOSTS! Say it! Say it with me! I DON'T BELIEVE IN GHOSTS!"

The crowd cheered in response and began chanting, "We don't believe! We don't believe!"

Another chill hit Ethan, and one light above him grew bright and silently popped, followed by another, and another. He turned to the others and said, "Something in here."

"What is it?" Bryce asked, scanning the ceiling.

Ethan looked up and squinted. "I don't know. It's hiding in the lights, I think. I can feel it though. Just before it does something," Ethan said.

Chax continued his speech. "The NRDS are destroying our town! It's just a matter of time before they come after your children. You might think you're safe, but they've come for our churches, and even last week they attacked the pub outside of town. People were missing for hours, with barely a scrap of memory, but everyone was fatigued and many needed medical attention!"

"Boo!" and "No more nerds!" and "We don't believe!" screams came from the crowd.

The shiver ran through Ethan again, and he spotted a faint blue glow slip between wires. "There's a spirit in here. On the ceiling. Moving through the wires."

Alexus handed Bryce her keys and pulled her badge. "Alright, Bryce, grab the case in my car. Ethan, track it. River and I will keep an eye on the crowd. If it does anything funny, magic it," Alexus said.

"Magic? I don't use magic," Ethan said.

"Really? You're gonna argue on psychic semantics now?" River said with a laugh as he walked away.

Chax's voice boomed over the speakers. "I say no! Demand justice! They need to pay for what they did for the poor people in the bar. They deserved to be thrown in jail!"

The crowd responded with shouts of, "Lock them up! Lock them up! Lock them up!"

Ethan slowly waded through the crowd, keeping his eyes trained up, trying to follow the faint glow as it hopped wires.

"And if you elect me! I'll make sure that the NRDS ARE NO MORE!"

"No more nerds! No more nerds! No more nerds!" the crowd chanted.

He felt the chill again, this time boring deep into his bones. An anger came with it, and a scream that echoed in his head. The lights in the entire room flickered, and some people in the crowd took notice.

"No more nerds! No more nerds!" the crowd continued.

"That's right! A vote for Chax is a vote for no more nerds! We can finally put this stupid ghost hunt to rest!" Chax affirmed into the microphone.

The lights strobed on and off, and Ethan's mind was filled with rage as the blue light leaped from wire to wire. Then the blue light leaped into the rafters above Chax, swirling around a stage light.

It wobbled and swayed violently, wrenching free. Ethan's eyes trailed down, finding where the light would fall if it came loose. Chax stood directly below it, completely unaware of his impending doom.

Ethan shoved through the crowd and screamed, "Get out of my way!"

"Think about our lives once we put this behind us! Think about how safe and happy we will be once we can stop talking about ghosts and finally look at the bright future New Richmond has!" Chax said, completely oblivious to the lack of future he was about to have.

Ethan broke through the crowd and jumped onto the stage. "Watch out!" he shouted as a screw popped loose and landed near Chax's foot.

Chax didn't see it. Instead, he looked offstage, and his eyes wide as he shouted, "Help! They're trying to silence me!"

Another screw popped loose, and Ethan dropped his shoulder like he did when he played football. He raced forward and wrapped his arms about Chax, taking him with him as they both landed hard on the wooden floor.

Seconds later, the stage light crashed onto the stage, and the crowd let out a loud scream.

Chax stared at Ethan, wide-eyed.

"I saved you," Ethan whispered.

Something changed in Chax's face, and he screamed into his microphone, "Help! Help me!"

Police officers jumped on the stage and pulled Ethan off of Chax.

Chax stood, brushing off his suit before pointing a finger at Ethan. "Don't be fooled. This federal agent and his men are trying to silence me. I want him behind bars!" He looked back at the light fixture, smashed right where he had been standing. "He tried to kill me! You all saw it!"

The officers gripped onto Ethan's arms and pulled them behind his back. "You have the right to remain silent," they said as they clamped cuffs on them.

Ethan stared in disbelief as they pulled him offstage, his thoughts drowned out by the crowd shouting, "Lock him up! Lock him up! Lock him up!"

Forty-Six

Paranormal Paparazzi Problems

E THAN TURNED IN THE passenger seat for the seventh time and peered out the back window of Buck's Oldsmobile Cutlass.

"What do you keep looking at?" Buck asked.

Ethan bit his lip and turned around, his eyes still on the black van following them in the side mirror. "So, uh. Someone's following us."

"Huh," Buck grunted, keeping his eyes fixed on the road ahead of them.

"Doesn't that make you nervous?" Ethan turned around again.

The van kept a reasonable distance, but after they'd hit the country road out of New Richmond, it was clear they were following them.

"Nah," Buck said.

"But like, what if they do something to us? It could be that creepy 80s ghost again?"

"It's not her."

"How do you know? She could try to run us off the road."

"She doesn't chase me. I chase her."

"Okay." Ethan said, facing forward again. "Well, what if it's someone from upper management? Then what? What if they come and take our badges?"

"Then I'll retire, finally."

Ethan huffed and crossed his arms. "Well. Uh, what if . . . What if it's actually some kind of assassin squad coming to kill us? What if all these murders are being done by . . . um?"

"Can't think of anybody planning on killing the two of us, can you?"

Ethan leaned forward, his finger pointing up. "What if they are the Mexican drug cartel and they are laundering money in New Richmond? And now they're killing anyone who might get in the way, and we're next? Wouldn't that make you nervous?"

"No. Because that's the plot to Ozark."

Ethan rolled his eyes. "Dammit. I figured you'd still be stuck trying to use a VCR."

"Gerry made me watch it."

"Did you like it?"

"It was fine."

"Fine! Seriously? It's amazing! I mean, all the twists. There were so many times when I thought the plot was going to go left and it just went right."

"Breaking Bad did it better."

Ethan clutched his chest and gasped. "How dare you!"

Buck pulled into the brick entryway of the Oakland Cemetery and killed the engine. "That doesn't surprise me."

"What the hell does that mean?" Ethan asked, his eye on the black van as it pulled off onto the side of the road twenty yards behind them.

Buck grabbed the clipboard from the backseat and popped open the door.

Ethan grabbed his arm. "No, wait. What if we're in trouble?"

Buck cocked his head and adjusted the rearview mirror. "I mean, it could be . . . No. I haven't seen them in ages. It couldn't be."

Ethan's eyes grew big. "Couldn't be what?"

"Nothing. Forget I said anything," Buck said, waving him off.

Ethan grabbed Buck's arm and squeezed. "Buck. Seriously. If we're in danger, you have to tell me."

Buck shook his head. "No. I mean, it's crazy. They'd never come up here. I don't think."

"God! Buck! Who? Who is it?" Ethan screamed.

Buck took a deep breath and then said, "Vampires. It might be vampires."

"No way! Vampires? Are you fucking serious? They aren't in the manual. What do we do? Do we need to make some stakes or something? If I distract them, maybe you could find some branches in the bushes over there, right? What's the plan?"

Buck pushed open his car door and stepped into the street. "There's no plan. We just do our job."

Ethan threw his door open and hopped over the hood of the car, grabbing onto Buck's shoulder. "But what about the Vampires? You're going to get us killed!"

"There are no vampires, kid. I was just screwing with you."

"Wait? What?"

Buck shrugged Ethan off and started toward the cemetery with his clipboard in hand. "No Vampires. Just the ghosts of dead kids. Normal day at the office. Let's go."

Ethan stood next to the car and shouted, "Wait? Seriously? There really aren't any vampires? With all the weird stuff we see?"

"If there are, we don't deal with them, and I've never seen them. Just ghosts. Get a case and keep up, kid."

"Ugh, fine," Ethan said as he grabbed a case from the trunk and hurried behind Buck.

Ethan turned around to get another glimpse of the van but couldn't make out anyone through the front windshield. Instead, the van appeared to be shaking back and forth, as if someone were rummaging around . . . or . . . well . . . He laughed to himself and mumbled, "Drug Cartel."

He flipped his middle finger to the van, and as he did, the side door slid open.

Ethan jumped back and screamed.

"What is it now?" Buck said, turning back to his partner.

"They're. Uh. They're getting out!" Ethan shouted, pointing at the van.

"Goddamn it, Ethan. Can we just get this done? We've got to see that stupid clown next, and you know he's a talker."

"Wait. They're coming over here," Ethan said, backing up again.

Three college-aged men emerged from the van. The first, a good-looking kid with blond hair and dimples, marched toward them with a smile on his face. Behind him came a tall one carrying a boom mic that was attached by a black cord to the shoulder camera carried by the third larger boy.

"Ah, Fuck," Buck mumbled. He grabbed Ethan by the arm and pulled him toward the cemetery. "If we're quick, maybe we can get out of here before those little shits are ready."

"Excuse me! Pardon me!" The good-looking one called after them as the other two raced to keep up.

"Keep walking," Buck said, yanking Ethan.

"I said excuse me! We'd like a statement from you," the good-looking one called again.

Buck and Ethan passed through the line of trees and into the graveyard. The air turned colder, and Ethan grabbed his elbows as he shivered. "That's weird," he said.

Mable stood next to a grave, lips pursed and eyes on the three remaining children, Harold, Jean, and Dylan. They sat cross-legged on the ground, heads sagging down.

"Mable," Buck said. "Sorry we're late for our check-in."

Mable placed her hands on her hips and glared at the children. "Well, I hope you brought some cases with you, because I've got some very naughty children here."

Buck pulled a pen from his coat pocket and said, "Alright, well, what's going on?"

The camera crew broke through the trees at that moment, boom mic hovering above Buck's head. The good-looking man held up a mic and looked into the camera. "What's going on is we're here at Oakland Cemetery just outside of New Richmond, filming a documentary on fake government agencies siphoning city money away from citizens."

"He's not talking to you," Ethan said to the guy.

Mable huffed and gestured to the camera crew. "Now, what in God's creation is this?"

"Ignore them, please," Buck said.

"Oh, I will not be ignored, sir. Do you even know who I am? Chester Wainwright, an award-winning journalist from the University of Chicago." He paused, then when Buck didn't acknowledge him said, "And the people have a right to know what you and your sham agency are spending their money on."

Buck rolled his eyes. "Please, continue Mable."

"Well, little Dylan over here has encouraged the others to leave the cemetery whenever they want," Mable said.

Chester cleared his throat. "Well, I'm no Mable, but first question Mr. Hampton. What do you have to say about the ongoing issues from the concerned citizens about the NRDS?"

"You mean Agent Hampton," Ethan corrected.

"Sure it is." Chester laughed.

Buck made a note on the form. "Would you say that this has been going on every night?"

"I told them if they all continued, you'd be over here and start casing them," Mable said, looking down at Dylan.

Dylan slumped his shoulders and said, "I said I was sorry."

"You're sorry now that I'm making you sit here and face the consequences," Mable said.

Chester frowned and looked into the camera. "Okay, that wasn't really an answer. Here's another. Which one of you tried to kill Chax Tamish?"

"We tried to save him. Did no one see the light fall from the ceiling?" Ethan asked.

"Save him? If you call tackling him while he gave a heartfelt speech and dislocating his shoulder saving, then you and I have different definitions." Chester laughed.

"No. That's not how it went down at all," Ethan complained.

A shiver ran through Ethan as Dylan pointed at the camera crew. "I don't like them. I want them to leave," Dylan said.

Mable's eyes widened, and she looked at Buck. "This isn't good. Can you please get these idiots out of here?"

Buck checked his watch and turned back to his clipboard. "Just a few more questions. What have the children been doing when they leave?"

Chester stuck out the microphone to Buck. "Why exactly do you hate the town of New Richmond? What's your goal with this small, sweet town?"

Ethan butted in between them and pushed the microphone out of the way. "What? No. I grew up here. I love it here."

"No good. Mischief throughout. They've confessed to playing with the electricity for starters," Mable said.

"Was he at the rally two nights ago?" Buck asked.

"I don't like them," Dylan said again. "Make them leave."

"No. The three of them said nothing about a rally," Mable said.

"So you were the disgraced town superstar quarter back then?" Chester asked. "How does it feel to know you are now taking part in destroying the city you once loved?"

"Alright, I've had about enough of you," Ethan said.

"Oh no. What are you going to do? Will you tackle me too?" Chester mocked.

"Harold," Buck said. "Did you go to the political rally two nights ago?"

Harold picked at the grass. "We were at the school. That's the only place I go. Dylan and Jean were with me all night."

"We were just walking around the hallways of the school. It was pretty empty," Jean piped in.

"Can you please comment on the fact that the entire town now hates you?" Chester asked Ethan.

"People don't hate me," Ethan said.

A spark shot out of the camera, and Dylan screamed, "I mean it! I want the camera to leave! I don't like it!"

"What the hell?" Chester said.

Buck glared at Dylan and scribbled some notes before looking at the other ghost boy. "Harold, this is important. If you are hiding anything, then we'll need to case you and your friends. You're endangering people."

"Can you? Can you two just cut whatever this is out? Stop pretending like you are talking to nothing. We're not just going to leave you alone," Chester said.

The hair on Ethan's arms stood on end, and he looked back at Dylan. Something about him emanated an energy that made Ethan's stomach turn into knots. "Look. Chester, right? You can't see them, but we're in the middle of something, and if you don't want a ghost possessing your ass, you should just go."

"Oh. Invisible possessing ghosts? I'm so scared," Chester said, mocking Ethan.

"I hate this!" Dylan said. Energy rippled through the air, and the college-aged kid holding the boom mic flew back, landing on his ass several feet back.

"Calm down, okay?" Jean said, rubbing his back.

"Ethan, get the case ready," Buck said.

"Please! Please don't case us," Harold pleaded.

"What the hell is going on?" Chester said, feeling the air in front of them. "What. Do you have wires somewhere? If there are ghosts, why can you see them and not me?"

"Well, we have badges," Ethan started, but a banshee-like scream coming from Dylan cut him short.

"Where's the case!?" Buck yelled as Dylan levitated off the ground. Wind picked up, and trees swayed as a gust of wind slammed into Ethan.

Electricity sparked off Dylan, and he glowed a bright blue.

"What . . . the?" Chester started, staring up at a very visible Dylan.

"Get out! Get out! Get out!" Dylan screamed.

Chester screeched several octaves higher than Ethan expected. "It's real! It's real!" He stumbled over his cameraman as the three of them stumbled back.

Buck dropped his clipboard and snatched the briefcase from Ethan's hand. "Dylan. If you can't get a grip, you are going in the case."

"They'll ruin everything!" Dylan said, as the ground below Ethan shook.

Ethan stepped forward, holding his hands out. "Dylan! Listen to me, please. Focus. Think. The cameras are here for us. Not you. Please, just come back down here."

"They'll ruin everything!" Dylan shouted again.

"You'll ruin your chance to stop them if you don't calm down. Do you want that? Do you want to be in a case?" Ethan shouted.

The light around Dylan dimmed, and he shook his head. "I don't like them."

"I don't like them either," Ethan said. "But hurting them will only bring more. Why don't you let me deal with them, and you just come down here?"

Dylan nodded and slowly descended, his feet landing back on the ground. He yawned and looked at Mable. "I'm tired."

Buck picked up his clipboard and looked back toward the camera crew, who were racing back to their van. "We'll do our best to keep them away. Let's keep this escalation off the record for now."

Mable nodded and stared off toward the camera crew. She frowned, thinking something over before she spoke slowly, "You should still focus on getting these children crossed over, but let's just say I'm not surprised if something looms over the Tamish family." With that, she grabbed Dylan by the shoulder and turned, heading back toward his plot.

"Wait," Ethan said. "What's that supposed to mean?"

Forty-Seven

I Brought a Jell-O Mold

E THAN DOUBLE-CHECKED HIS PHONE, confirming the address on Creekwood Drive once again. From where he stood, the house looked like any other two-story among a sea of white sides and gray roofs. He stepped across the front yard, unlatching the fence to the backyard while contemplating what he'd do if this wasn't the right house.

Color filled his eyes the moment he stepped into Gerry and Buck's backyard. Pink peonies lined the fence, each bush filled with flowers in full bloom. Daylilies, in random assortments of orange, yellow, and blue, were planted in front of the peonies, adding to the burst of color. Throughout the middle of the yard, connected by winding white stone paths, were Adirondack chairs arranged around two small fire pits that were already burning.

Ethan looked to the porch stemming from the house and saw multiple long tables filled with small sandwiches, fruits, vegetables, and one covered with a variety of bottles that Ethan assumed Gerry had selected with precise care.

Gerry stepped out from a pair of sliding glass doors, wearing a pair of aviators, a slimming pair of navy slacks, and a blue and pink vertically striped button up with the top four buttons unbuttoned, revealing a patch of graying chest hair. If Father Christmas had a summer brother, Gerry would fit the bill.

"Ethan, you made it!" Gerry said, setting down a charcuterie board filled with meats and cheeses on the table.

"Wow, Gerry!" Ethan said, the plastic Jell-O mold Gerry had instructed him to bring tucked firmly under his arm. "This is. I mean. Wow!"

"We're happy you are here! Both Doris and Trevor called last minute and canceled, so I was worried no one would show," Gerry called. He turned to face the table of alcohol, selected a bottle, poured a deep red liquid into a small glass.

Buck stepped out from inside carrying a half-finished beer and wearing tan slacks and a striped white and brown shirt that matched Gerry's shirt.

Ethan looked down at his own attire, jeans and a white shirt, and said, "I feel underdressed."

Gerry waved a hand at him. "You're wearing *the* jeans. You're dressed just fine."

Ethan laughed and held out the plastic container. "I brought the Jell-O mold you told me to bring."

Buck chuckled and took a swig of beer. "Where's the Jell-O?"

Ethan's breath caught in his throat. "Wait? What?"

Buck grinned.

Handing Ethan a glass, Gerry said, "Here, I'll trade you."

Ethan handed the Jell-O mold over and said, "I'm sorry. I didn't . . . I mean, I thought you wanted the mold."

Gerry laughed. "I suppose I could have been more specific."

Ethan looked down. "Granny told me I should actually make something, but I told her you just said a Jell-O mold."

"Sounds about right," Buck grunted.

"It's a lovely mold. I'll have to have you over to show off my famous peaches and cream Jell-O," Gerry smiled.

"I hope I didn't ruin the party."

Gerry put his hand on Ethan's shoulder. "Oh, sweetie. If my party depended on your Jell-O mold, it wouldn't be much of a party at all, now would it?"

Ethan looked up and smiled.

"Now, drink," Gerry said, motioning to Ethan's glass. "And let's find a place to sit."

Ethan sipped from the wineglass, and his nostrils filled with the aroma of plums and chocolate. All the anxiety cleared in an instant. "Wow. What is this?" he asked.

"2016 Dews Port. I opened it just for you," Gerry said, taking a seat in a chair and laying the empty mold on the ground.

"I love it," Ethan said.

"I knew you would." Gerry grinned. He winked and said, "I've got everyone's names on a Post-it on their curated beverage."

Ethan took another sip.

"Drink it slow, big boy. It's got a kick," Buck warned.

"Now, where's Rosemary and Ellie? I heard they couldn't make it," Gerry asked.

"Ellie's girl scout troop does a big thing every fourth," Ethan said. "They go to the troop leader's house and make candy together. It's a big deal."

"You're bringing that candy to the office, right?" Buck asked.

"I'd have to pry it from Ellie's kung-fu-death-grip first," Ethan laughed.

"And Bryce was called away as well?" Gerry asked.

"He's back in New York for the month." A gnawing feeling in Ethan's gut surprised him. He wondered how it was possible that, even though they'd been together for a few months, he felt like part of himself was missing when Bryce was gone.

Buck gave him one look and laughed. "Jesus, kid. He's only gone for a few weeks."

Gerry pushed Buck's arm. "Leave him alone. It's sweet."

Buck took another drink and said, "I can't have him moping around work."

"I won't," Ethan pouted.

"Be nice," Gerry warned Buck.

The gate to the fence swung open and Alexus, carrying a cake container, entered the backyard. Ethan gasped at the white sundress she wore. It occurred then that he'd worked with her for ten months and he'd never seen her wear anything but jeans. She did, however, wear her leather jacket, something he assumed she'd rather die than take off.

Gerry rushed toward her with his arms open. "Alexus! I see you're wearing my gift. How's the fit?"

Alexus's usual glare of apathy softened into something that was almost a smile as she hugged Gerry. "I love it. Totally my style."

"She hugs people?" Ethan asked Buck.

"Only Gerry," he replied.

Gerry took the cake container from Alexus and rushed to the kitchen while Alexus joined Buck and Ethan at the firepit.

Ethan stood and held out his hands for a hug. "Um, hey. Nice. Um. Nice dress."

"Hug me and I'll cut out your intestines, loop it around your head, and tie it into a pretty Christmas bow on top of your head," she said, taking a seat next to Buck.

Ethan dropped his arms and sat back down. "Did you bring a cake?"

Alexus crossed her arms and glared. "Yeah, why?"

Ethan laughed at the idea of Alexus baking in her leather jacket. "And you made it yourself?"

"I did," she replied, her glare intensifying.

"What kind is it?" Ethan fought to get his mind around Alexus's baking.

"It's a sour cream vanilla cake with lemon rosemary buttercream icing, adorned in a berry glaze, and decorated with strawberries and blueberries. And it's fucking delicious," she said, leaning forward in her chair.

Ethan held his hands up. "Oh. Holy shit. That sounds amazing."

"Ethan brought a Jell-O mold," Buck said.

Alexus sat back and nodded. "I fucking love Jell-O. What kind?"

Ethan's heart sank.

"He just brought the mold," Buck said, motioning to the plastic container on the ground next to Gerry's chair.

"You fucking moron," Alexus said.

Ethan collapsed in on himself and took another sip of his wine.

Rejoining them, Gerry handed Alexus a black and pink beer can and said, "We picked this doozy of a stout up in Iowa. I noticed it last week and thought of you."

Alexus took a sip and nodded. "Thank you."

"Thanks for inviting us over, Gerry. Your backyard is gorgeous," Ethan said, hoping to shift the conversation away from his absent Jell-O.

Alexus shook her head. "Where's Fillmore? I like you better with Fillmore around."

"Wow, thanks for that." He took another sip of his wine and said, "He's in New York. Seeing family."

Buck grinned. "Are you nervous he's going to meet someone else?"

Ethan's hands grew icy, and his heart raced. He hadn't considered that Bryce might go home to see someone else. "Wait. Do you think he has another boyfriend in New York?"

"The rookie is jealous," Alexus said.

"No, I'm not," Ethan said.

"Oh. That's sweet," Gerry said.

Ethan felt heavy with the weight of everyone's eyes on him. "I'm not jealous," he said. "Bryce is just on vacation with his family. That's all."

Before Buck and Alexus could get another dig, the gate opened again and Melissa, wearing a bright blue muumuu, stumbled through it. "Alright. I found it. I'm here," she said, gasping for breath like she'd just run a marathon.

Rushing to her side, Gerry said, "Are you alright?"

Waving behind her, she gasped, "This is the fourth house I tried. Didn't know so many of your neighbors had dogs. It was a whole thing. I brought the donuts you wanted." She held up a bag.

"Donuts?" Gerry said, taking the bag.

"I don't know," she said, waving him off and stomping over to the table of booze. "I forgot what you said to bring, so I got donuts."

"Well, these look wonderful," Gerry said, peering inside the bag.

Ethan eyed Buck. "With everything going on, you invited her? She's out to get us all fired."

Buck raised his glass to Melissa and muttered for Ethan to hear, "Keep your enemies close."

Melissa snatched a bottle of white wine and held it up to examine it. "Hey! How'd you know this was my favorite? You even put my name on it," she added, ripping the Post-it note with her name on it off the bottle, crumpling it up, and throwing it over her shoulder.

"The entire bottle is for you. I uncorked it earlier to let it breathe," Gerry said, picking up the paper and heading into the house with the donuts.

"What was she supposed to bring?" Alexus asked Buck while Melissa grabbed a handful of meats and cheeses from the table.

"Her charming personality," Buck grinned.

Ethan laughed, and Alexus cut him off. "You don't get to smile. Who brings a fucking empty Jell-O mold?"

Ethan dropped his head, the alcohol already hitting him. "Sorry."

Melissa arrived at the chairs and realized there wasn't a space for her. "Hold on," she said, considering the bottle of wine and her handful of food before handing Ethan the handful of cheese and dried meats.

She grabbed her bottle of wine and chugged while grabbing a chair from the adjacent fire circle. She dragged it across the lawn, digging up dirt while she brought the chair between Buck and Gerry's spot. "There," she said, plopping down into her seat.

"Happy Fourth of July," Ethan said, handing Melissa back her handful of food.

Melissa waved him off and held out her hand to Buck and said, "Give it."

Ethan slowly lowered his hand to his side and dropped the food beneath his chair.

"Give what?" Buck challenged.

Melissa snapped her fingers. "You know what."

Alexus sat forward and held out her hand. "Yeah. Me too. Fork it over."

Buck shook his head. "Fine," he said, reaching below his chair and pulling out three Churchill-sized cigars. Snipping the ends off of them, he passed one to Melissa and one to Alexus.

"Light me," Melissa demanded.

Buck took a lighter from his pocket and lit her cigar, doing the same for Alexus before lighting his own.

Melissa took a long swig of her wine and said, "Ah, that's good stuff." She then took a drag from the cigar, blew the smoke into the air, and asked Ethan, "Where's your sugar daddy?"

Ethan sipped his wine. "He's visiting family."

Buck blew smoke into the air and said, "He's nervous Fillmore has another man in New York."

"No, I'm not," Ethan insisted.

Melissa took another long swig from her wine. "You never know with those upper management types. They have an ass in every port, if you know what I mean. Bunch of sleaze balls."

"I thought you wanted to be upper management," Alexus said.

"And?" Melissa said, taking another long drag on her cigar. "Regardless, if I got promoted, I'd make some big changes. That's for sure."

"What changes?" Gerry asked as he found his way back to his chair.

"Well, for one," Melissa said, pausing to swig from the white wine bottle. "No more waiting around for spirits to figure out what they need. They either move on or get cased. Period."

"But helping them find out what's keeping them is the fun part," Ethan said.

"Yeah. Okay, rookie," Melissa laughed. "You spend as much time at this job as Buck and me, and then get back to us. Right, Buck?"

"Agree to disagree," Buck said.

"Okay. But you know what I'm saying," Melissa said, taking another swig.

Gerry popped up from his seat as the gate swung open again. River, wearing a tie-dyed shirt and massive flowing harem pants, stepped into the backyard carrying a tray of brownies. Looking over his rose-colored sunglasses, he said, "Whoa. Nice place, Ger."

"It's my place too," Buck mumbled.

Alexus snorted. "Yeah. Okay."

Following behind River, Ethan saw Bob step into the backyard. "Reporting for duty," he said, saluting the yard.

"Why'd you bring Bob?" Ethan shouted.

"So we can book it before the cops come. What's a better lookout than a ghost, right?" River shouted back.

"Goddamn it. I didn't bring my badge. That damn ghost has it out for me, I swear," Melissa said.

"Oh, River! Are these what I think they are?" Gerry asked as he gave River a hug.

"Yep. River specials." River grinned. "Already had one, so hurry and get on my level."

Gerry held up the tin and looked to the fire pit. "The party has now officially begun!" He motioned for everyone to follow as he headed inside.

Alexus stood, took another drag from her cigar, and asked, "Can the cigars come with us?"

"Afraid not. No smoking in the house," Buck replied.

"Well, shit," Melissa said, taking a final long puff on hers.

Ethan stood, the booze filling his head as he stared at his colleagues. A big smile stretched across his face, and a warmth spread through him. One he hadn't experienced since he was on the football team. "Hey guys, I just wanted to say that—"

"Oh, fuck no," Alexus said, marching away with her beer.

Melissa hoisted herself up out of her chair and raced after Alexus. "Yeah. Keep that sentimental shit to yourself."

Buck patted Ethan's back and tapped his bottle of beer against Ethan's glass. "Happy Fourth, rookie."

Ethan smiled back, downed the rest of this wine, and said, "Thanks, Buck."

Forty-Eight

It's Our Fault He's Dead

E THAN SLAMMED HIS FOOT down on the gas, and the black Mustang surged down the road.

"Hey, relax or I'm throwing you in the trunk next time," Alexus said, patting her dashboard and muttering, "It's going to be okay."

"I can't. This is it. I finally figured it out," Ethan said, a grin stretched across his face.

"Just like the time you thought the dog was going to send that one kid back," Alexus said.

"Hey, that was different. That was my first time." Ethan made a hard right, screeching the tires beneath them as they drifted onto the county road. "Rude bringing that up, by the way."

She peeled herself from the door and said, "And it's rude of you to wreck my fucking car. I gave you the keys because I thought you'd show Rosie the Reaper some fucking respect. If you put a scratch on my baby, no agent is going to find the case I bury you in."

Ethan kept his eyes on the road and pressed his foot on the gas. "You don't get it. We're almost out of time. One more outburst and upper management will have us case these kids. I can't. I won't do that."

Alexus sighed. "Okay, fine. Why is this time different?"

"Stephenson's journal."

JP RINDFLEISCH IX & JEFF ELKINS

"Fuck no. You woke me up to come get you so you could wreck my tires because of that old bastard?"

"Woke you up? It's three in the afternoon?"

"Do I complain about your sleep schedule?"

"Um, no?" Ethan frowned.

"Then shut the fuck up."

"Look, everything in the journal's been right so far," Ethan shot back.

Alexus rolled her eyes. "He's a lying dickwad. I thought I taught you better than this."

"Yeah. He's an asshole to us. But his journal was his record keeping. He didn't lie to himself."

"That old piece of shit lies to everyone. Especially himself."

"Okay, fine. But that journal hasn't been wrong yet." Ethan took a hard right, throwing Alexus into his side of the car. As she pushed off of him, he said, "There is a passage about Harold's dad. It took some digging, but I confirmed it. He was an inventor. I shit you not. He was working on something that looks a hell of a lot like solar panels. He also taught chemistry at the middle school, but they fired him."

"So what? Lots of dads get fired. That isn't enough to keep a kid around?"

Ethan smiled. He saw Alexus lean forward, intrigued, and that made him drive even faster. "Well, turns out their house was ransacked, too. They stole everything. All his work. Everything."

"Okay, that's weird. Still not connecting the dots."

"Well, I went to the library—"

She laughed, cutting him off. "Nerd."

He rolled his eyes. "I went to the library and found out that Harold died in a house fire. I'm thinking someone was trying to silence Harold's dad. Stop him from making a breakthrough. I bet he kept at it, day and night in the basement of their house, then that *someone* caught wind, locked the family inside, and lit the place up."

Alexus shook her head and laughed. "Wait. We're racing to the cemetery because you concocted some kind of conspiracy theory? Where's the fucking proof, Nancy Drew?"

Ethan gripped the wheel and spoke through gritted teeth, "You sound just like Buck."

"I fucking wonder why," Alexus said, smacking the dashboard. "Even your partner, the goddamn genius of this agency, told you this was a crock of shit."

"No, he didn't. He wanted more evidence before I had the plaque made."

"There's a fucking plaque involved in this nonsense bullshit?"

"Of course there's a plaque," Ethan said.

"What the fuck do you mean 'of course there's a plaque?'"

"Can't you see? That's what Harold wants. Someone did his dad wrong, and he wants people to know what he did. So, I made a plaque, and we are going to put it in the trophy case. Then Harold can cross over."

Alexus threw her hands up. "Goddamn it. I was having a pleasant fucking day off. Then you abducted me over this bullshit?"

Ethan pulled the car in front of the brick entrance to Oakland Cemetery and slammed on the brakes. They both jerked forward, and Ethan unblocked his seat belt. "I need backup in case I'm wrong and the poor kid escalates, okay?"

"Oh. Great. I'm the muscle in case your fucking nonsense theory is fucking nonsense?" She pushed open her car door and stepped out, rounding to the trunk. "I just wanted one normal day."

Ethan jumped out and joined her at the back of the car. "What are you doing?"

"Keys!" she said, holding out her hand.

Ethan took a step back. "No. Come on. This will work."

She pointed a finger in his face. "Give me my fucking keys."

Ethan sighed and held up the keys. "Not until you absolutely have to."
She reached for the keys, and he pulled them back. "Promise me."

She glared at him and held out her hand. "Fine."

"Say you promise," he said, holding the keys away.

"Give me the keys or I'm going to punch you in the fucking throat."

"Good enough," he said, passing over the keys.

Alexus opened the trunk and pulled a fresh briefcase from inside. "Let's
go," she said as she marched toward the entrance.

Ethan's heart raced as they arrived at the graves. Mable stood looking
up at the sky, her eyes wide. Dylan and Jean hid behind her skirt, looking
sheepish.

"What is it? What happened?" Ethan asked.

Mable looked down and shook her head. "I've lost Harold."

"What does that mean?" Alexus barked at her.

Ethan held up a hand to her and glared. Looking at Mable, he said, "Tell
us what happened."

Mable took in a breath and said, "His temper got the best of him."

"He was furious," Jean added.

"He started turning blue," Mable said.

"It was scary. He was more mad than I was. It wasn't fun anymore,"
Dylan chimed in.

"And then, well. He flew off," Mable said.

Alexus frowned. "He flew off?"

"Yeah. Like this," Dylan demonstrated, jumping abnormally high into
the air before landing gently beside Jean. "But, higher. And he didn't come
back."

Alexus grabbed Ethan's arm so hard he thought it might break. "You know what this means, right? This kid's gone nuclear, and we need to put him down."

Ethan glared back at her again. "You promised!" Turning back to the children, he said, "Do you have any idea where he was going?"

"He always wants to go to the middle school," Dylan said with a shrug.

"Alright. Let's get this over with," Alexus said, turning and marching back to the car.

"Come on. Everyone with us. Field trip," Ethan said, motioning for the ghosts to follow.

Alexus spun on her heal and said, "Fuck, no."

"We might need them," Ethan said. "They're all well past Class One at this point. Except maybe Mable."

Mable looked away from Ethan. "I can travel."

Ethan's eyes widened. "When were you going to tell me?"

She shrugged. "Someone needed to keep an eye on the children."

Alexus groaned. "You're insane. Think of the risk."

Ethan stood his ground. "You need to trust me. If they see him cross over, then it might motivate them to do it too."

"That's not how this is going to end." Alexus said, holding up her briefcase.

"Fine. Then it will scare them straight." Ethan said, crossing his arms.

Alexus looked at Mable and the children, rolled her eyes, and said, "Get in the back."

Alexus drove them to the middle school, driving with the same speed as Ethan, but with the finesse and care that he didn't have. Not once did the tires screech, nor was Ethan lurched into the car door as she turned.

They pulled into the school parking lot, and Ethan saw the clouds forming above the school, glowing a bright blue as they blocked out the sun.

"Cool!" Dylan said, exiting the vehicle without opening a door.

"Oh, Harold. What has gotten into you?" Mable muttered.

Ethan stumbled out of the car, gawking at the clouds, blue lightning dancing within them.

"I'm calling backup. Grab the case," Alexus said, tossing him the keys.

Ethan tore his gaze away and sighed. Before opening the trunk, he reached into the backseat and grabbed the small plaque he'd had made. He held it up, admiring the craftsmanship. Gold lettering read, "James Wagner. Distinguished Inventor and Renowned Teacher of New Richmond."

Plaque in one hand, briefcase in the other, he led the way through the front doors of New Richmond Middle School.

It was empty and quiet. Had they not seen the looming clouds overhead, he would have thought this was like any other school after hours.

"Should it be this empty?" Alexus whispered.

"No. Summer school let out only a half hour ago," Ethan said. "There should still be teachers around, I think."

Mable crept forward, peering down the halls. "At least the children are gone."

"Maybe," Alexus retorted.

They proceeded to the cafeteria and opened the doors, finding it completely empty. Same for the offices and art room. Everywhere they went, they found no sign of life, or Harold.

"If we keep going room to room like this, we'll be here for hours," Alexus complained.

"I. I might know where he is," Jean offered, sheepishly.

Alexus turned to her. "Speak."

Jean cowered in response.

Mable stood by her side and rested a hand on her shoulder. "Go ahead and share with us. You're not in trouble, dear."

"The basement. He always wants to go down there when we're here," Jean said.

"Of course it's in the basement," Alexus complained.

"He told us his dad's lab used to be down there," Jean continued.

"I knew it!" Ethan said with a fist pump.

Alexus glared at Ethan before nodding to Jean. "Lead the way, kid."

They traveled down a locker-filled hallway with a black door in a corner. Ethan eased the door open, and it creaked, echoing loudly down the hall.

"That's not ominous," Alexus said.

Blue light spilled into the hallway, light glowing from beyond the stone steps that led down into the basement. Dust hovered in the stale air as they descended into the cold underbelly of the school. To their right was a boiler room, covered in cobwebs and old newspaper. Down a hall to the left was another black door with the word "Storage" on it. The source of the blue light illuminated from the small window at the top of the door.

"That's where he wanted to go," Jean whispered.

A chill ran up Ethan's spine as he peered through the window.

Harold floated in the center of the room, blue threads pooling out of his eyes and mouth, hooking into the arms and legs of about twenty adults he recognized as teachers.

Blue, ethereal chalkboards stood in front of each of them, and their arms jerked and twisted as they scrawled across them.

"AGAIN!" he yelled, and the words on the boards vanished and the teachers started over again, writing, "It's our fault he's dead. It's our fault he's dead. It's our fault he's dead."

Alexus pushed Ethan aside and looked through the window. Stepping back, she pinched her nose with her fingers. "Okay. Here's the plan. I'm going in first. He'll probably take control of me. I'm the distraction while you come behind me and case him."

"No. You promised," Ethan said, holding up the plaque.

Alexus pursed her lips, and a vein popped out of her neck while she spoke slowly, "Listen, rookie. You can't win them all."

Ethan looked at his shoes and then at the plaque. "Just. Just let me try. Please?"

"Fine. You can be the bait. But when the rest of the team shows up, we're coming in and casing him. Got it?"

Ethan nodded. "Fine. Got it."

Alexus stepped away from the door, and Ethan set the briefcase on the floor. He held the plaque tightly in one hand and gripped the handle of the door with the other. "Wish me luck."

"Good luck, dumbass." Alexus said.

Harold stared right at him the moment he entered the room. Tears welled up in Ethan's eyes, and an agony that wasn't his tore at his insides. He held up his hands and said, "Harold. It's me. It's Ethan."

A force grabbed onto Ethan and dragged him into the room. A chalkboard materialized in front of him, and Harold yelled, "WRITE!"

Ethan's arm moved against his will, and every letter he wrote was another tear at his heart. He pushed against it, and pleaded, "Harold. No. You don't understand."

"WRITE! WRITE UNTIL YOU KNOW WHAT YOU DID!" Harold screamed.

Ethan's body spun around against his will, and he wrote, "It's our fault he's dead."

He felt the plaque in his other hand and thought if he could just—

From the corner of his eye, he saw Buck peering through the window of the door. He worked his jaw, tears streaming down his face while he mouthed, "No. Not. Yet."

Buck glared through the other side of the window.

"AGAIN!" Harold screamed, and Ethan's attention was yanked back to the ghostly board in front of him.

Forty-Nine

Write Until You Die

E THAN'S FEET HOVERED AN inch off the ground. He was caught in Harold's trap, along with the other teachers in the basement storage room. His hand ached, moving of its own accord, clutching glowing blue chalk and scribbling on the ghostly chalkboard. "It's our fault he's dead. It's our fault he's dead. It's our fault he's dead."

His focus was on his other hand, clutching a plaque, willing his arm to raise.

"KEEP WRITING! WRITE!" Harold screamed from the center of the room as a teacher slumped over from exhaustion. They let out a scream as their body twitched and their arm jerked across the board.

Ethan bit his lip. He was already exhausted; the energy sapping from him to Harold, and he'd only been there a few minutes. There was no telling how long the teachers were down here, or how much longer they would last.

A rattle sounded behind him. The door. Ethan knew Buck, River, Bob, and Alexus were on the other side, ready to break in and case Harold before Ethan had a chance to stop it.

He pushed against the energy holding him in place. A snapping sensation, like strings breaking from too much tension, rippled through him and he turned his jaw. Tears streamed down his face from the agony, but he moved enough to catch Alexus's eye in the window. "No. No Please. Not yet," he mouthed.

Alexus slowly shook her head and then held up her middle finger into the window. "You fucked up," she mouthed back.

"AGAIN! WRITE IT AGAIN!" Harold screamed. Ethan's face snapped back to the board, which was now completely erased, and his hand flew up to the corner of the board. The motion was too quick, and his grip loosened on the plaque. It fell, clattering to the ground next to him.

He pushed against Harold's will again and pleaded, "Harold. Please! It's me! It's Ethan!"

"NO TALKING! WRITE!" Harold screamed.

His power reverberated in the room like electricity, and everyone screamed as they wrote faster, their fingers scraping against the boards.

The door behind him burst open, followed by the sound of things skidding across the floor. "No!" Ethan cried.

He knew that sound. *Briefcases.* They'd moved on to Plan B without him and threw open briefcases into the room.

It would suck Harold into the blue light any second, trapped in a storage sub-basement in New Jersey for decades to come. Alone. Stuck in his anger. He could have saved him. He should have saved them all.

He wished there was something he could do to stop it. Something that would . . .

A force billowed out from his gut, twisting his stomach in knots as the threads Harold used against him ripped apart.

The force reverberated out, and Ethan heard a crash behind him as he crumpled to the floor.

"Shit!" Buck screamed.

"What the hell was that?" Alexus shouted.

Ethan lifted his head and saw the other teachers slumped to the ground, three briefcases thrown against the wall behind him, and Harold laying dazed on the floor.

"Quick! Bob!!" Buck shouted.

"On it, Honcho!" Bob yelled, racing into the room. "This little motherfucker is in some deep kimchi."

Bob took one step closer and froze.

Blue electricity sparked off Harold, and he levitated into the air. His eyes glowed blue, and tendrils emanated out of him.

"Oh fuck," was all that Bob could muster.

Tendrils wrapped around everyone in the room, and in an instant, Ethan flew back into the air as Harold screamed, "WRITE!"

Buck and Alexus hovered in the air next to Ethan, their arms wildly writing, "It's my fault he's dead. It's my fault he's dead. It's my fault he's dead."

"Hey," Ethan said to Buck.

"You're a fucking moron, rookie," Alexus complained.

"If he could just see what I made him," Ethan said.

"He's too gone, rookie. You should have cased him on the spot. Have I taught you anything?" Buck said.

Ethan kept his eyes on the board, too afraid to see Buck's disappointment. "Is anyone left?"

"Hey, you son of a bitch. You can't hold me for long." Bob screamed from across the room.

"Well, he got Bob," Alexus grumbled.

"WRITE!" Harold screamed, forcing everyone to pick up their pace again.

"Rookie!" Bob shouted. "I'm going to beat your ass for fucking with the cases!" Bob screamed in reply.

"Where the fuck is River?" Alexus screamed.

"He stayed in the hall," Buck said.

"We have one. That's good, right?" Ethan yelled.

"One fucking coward!" Bob screamed. "Where'd you learn loyalty? The academy of spineless defector motherfuckers? I know children with a bigger fucking spine than you!"

"River!" Buck yelled.

"Yep, still in the hall!" River called back.

"If you step into this room, he'll have you," Buck yelled, his hand scribbling at an inhuman pace.

"Jesus! Please! Make it stop!" a teacher yelled.

"Yeah, I got that. So, what do I do?" River called back.

"I've got a shovel and some gasoline in my car. Dig up his body and light it up!" Alexus screamed.

"Wait," Ethan started, "Why do you have that in your car?"

"No, too much time. The teachers won't make it," Buck said.

"The clown ghost!" Bob screamed. "Go get that fucking clown ghost! Everyone's afraid of that fucking clown ghost!"

"Only you're afraid of Bingo Bango," Ethan yelled.

"Shut the fuck up, rookie!" Alexus screamed.

"Get Melissa on the phone! We need backup!" Buck yelled.

"WRITE! WRITE! WRITE!" Harold screamed.

Ethan's finger scraped along the board, and a smear of blood drew across the board.

"Wait, I think I have an idea." River chuckled from beyond the door.

"If it doesn't involve calling Melissa, fucking forget it!" Alexus screamed.

"No. No. I think it will work," River called.

"River! Call Melissa!" Buck screamed.

"She won't help. I got this," River said.

He cleared his throat and spoke in a deep and authoritative voice. "Harold. Harold Wagner. This is your father. Put these nice people down right now, you hear?"

Energy crackled in the air, and the door flew off its hinges.

"WRITE!" Harold screamed.

River appeared at his own ghostly board between Ethan and Alexus. "Well, you were right," he said as his hand began scribbling the phrase, "It's my fault he's dead."

"Idiots. I'm going to die with a bunch of idiots," Alexus complained.

Ethan's muscles were so tired, and his fingers hurt from the scrapes that had opened wounds. He wanted to cry, but he'd run out of tears. "What do we do, Buck?" he pleaded.

"We hang here until we die," Buck said, in a calm voice.

"Goddamn it," Alexus said.

"Hey!" Bob shouted.

"We could all try to fight it at the same time?" Ethan offered.

"What do you think we're doing? You're the only one who was able to do anything," Buck said.

"I was supposed to die in a sex orgy. Not like this," River said.

"Yeah, I thought I'd go out with a machete in one hand," Alexus said.

"If you bastards die and leave me here," Bob screamed. "I'm going to make your afterlife a living hell!"

"Um. Mister, Ethan?" A voice said from beside him.

Ethan fought to look down, barely catching Jean in his peripheral vision. "Jean! You're not writing!"

"Dylan left. He was scared," Jean said.

"What. What about Mable?" Ethan forced out.

"I'm here," Mable called from the door. "But I can feel him pulling me in."

"Then don't come in," Buck said.

"Mister Ethan, you dropped this," Jean said, holding up the plaque that had fallen out of Ethan's hand.

"You can hold it?" He said, eyes wide.

Jean nodded. "Harold taught me."

"Listen. Jean," Ethan said. "Take that over to Harold. Show him. Show him what it says."

"But. But what if he hurts me? Dylan said he was going to hurt us," Jean replied.

Every muscle in Ethan's body screamed with pain. "I don't. I don't think he will," Ethan said. "If he. Wanted to. He'd have already done it."

"Okay. I'll, um. I'll try," Jean said.

Ethan couldn't turn to watch, but he could feel her moving away. He bit his bottom lip. This had to work.

"Hey. Um. Harold? It's me. It's Jean."

Ethan braced for Harold to scream and the pace of his writing to pick up again, but nothing came.

"You look sad," Jean said.

A rush of cold air filled the room, and Harold spoke in a soft tone. "They took him from me. They. They need to know. I. I want him back."

"But that was a long time ago. They didn't do it," Jean said, pointing to the teachers.

Harold sniffed. "They're all dead. My whole family is gone, and I'm all alone."

"But I'm here. We're family," Jean said.

Harold didn't reply, but everyone in the room stopped writing. Ethan's hand slumped to his side, and a silence filled the air.

"So, um. Mr. Ethan has something for you," Jean said.

"Wait. That's . . . That's my dad's name!" Harold said.

Ethan felt his toes touching the floor, and the board in front of him vanished.

"We could put it upstairs. In the trophy case if you want. That way, they can remember him. What do you think?" Jean asked.

"I don't know," Harold said.

"I think your dad would like it," Jean offered.

"Yeah. I think he would," Harold said, leading Jean out of the storage room.

The energy that held everyone up vanished, and everyone collapsed to the floor. Pain shot up Ethan's legs and back, and exhaustion beckoned him to sleep.

"Good job, kid," Buck whispered, staring up at the ceiling.

Alexus and River wobbled to their feet and backed up toward the exit.

"Alexus!" Buck barked as he strained to stand. "Call 911, then Melissa. Have her report this up. Bob, go with Alexus. Ethan and River. Grab two cases and come with me."

"No, come on," Ethan said.

"Grab the goddamn case, kid," Buck said.

"Fine," Ethan said as he could feel his legs work again. He stood, stumble-jogging toward the other side of the room. One case was completely broken, but the other two were still intact. He handed one to River, and they headed out of the room and back up the stairs.

"Look, River. You can't case him. I still have a shot at getting him to cross over. I can feel it," Ethan said as they raced back down the school's hallways toward the trophy case.

"Ten seconds, bro," River said, running behind him. "If I see his eyes glow, in the case he goes."

Harold, Jean, and Mable stood in front of the trophy case, their eyes on a newly placed plaque.

Ethan swallowed and took a step forward.

Harold turned to look at him, and an icy chill surged through Ethan's body. "Hey, Harold. How are you feeling?"

"I'm sorry I made you write that stuff," Harold said.

"It's okay. You're sad. I get it," Ethan replied. He nodded to the plaque. "But now they'll all know. They'll know that your father was a good man."

Harold nodded, then frowned at something behind Ethan.

Ethan looked behind him, spotting River a few feet away. "What is it?"

"There's um. There's a light behind you," Harold said, nodding toward Ethan.

"I think it's here for you, buddy," Ethan said.

Harold looked up at Mable, and she smiled, nodding at him while he gave her a hug. Jean joined in and said, "You'll have to show me around when I make it over, okay?"

Harold let go and nodded. "Okay."

He stepped up to Ethan and held out a hand. Ethan grabbed it, feeling a cold air tingling around his palm. "Are you ready?"

"I think so, I just—" He paused. Peering at something Ethan couldn't see. Tears fell from his face. "Dad?"

Harold took another step forward, and his ghostly form dissipated, leaving behind a faint chill on Ethan's hand. "Goodbye, big guy."

Fifty

Ducks Have Needs Too

HEADLIGHTS TURNED OFF THE county road and beamed onto a large white barn and matching white horse stables far off down a dirt driveway. All but the massive wooden barn quilt, painted with pinks and greens, hanging above the barn door, was white, including what appeared to be an abandoned white Dodge parked on the other side of the gate to the road with the driver's door wide open. Nothing else was around for miles, just pitch-black empty fields and little copses of trees lurking in the dark.

Ethan leaned forward from the backseat between Buck, who was driving, and River, who blew a mass of smoke out the window. Buck came to a stop at the gate, his car jostling from the deep rivets in the muddy driveway as he stared at the chained lock.

"This looks like some sketchy bullshit, man," River said, taking another drag from his joint.

"Everything always looks like sketchy bullshit," Buck grunted.

"No, seriously. Like, where's the woman that called us?" River asked.

"Well, there's her truck. Maybe she ran away?" Ethan suggested.

River blew smoke out the window. "I dunno man, if it was your barn and you called us, wouldn't you stick around to let us in?"

Ethan unbuckled and popped the door open before smiling. "Well, it took us a while to get here."

"Yes, it did," Buck agreed, killing the engine and joining Ethan outside.

"Look, I told you, I have a condition," River said, rolling up the window.

"Asshole-ee-o-philia," Buck grumbled.

"No. No. This is serious," River said.

"Bullshit," Buck grunted.

Turning to face him, River complained, "Anxiety is no joking matter, man. It's a serious medical condition."

"You said it was glaucoma," Ethan said.

River pushed open the door and frowned. "Well, that too. But can't I have both?"

"You made us stop to see your drug dealer," Buck replied, popping open the trunk and pulling out a briefcase.

River took another long drag of the joint. "I have a prescription. Okay?"

"Let me see it," Buck said.

"Why? So you can narc? It's not my fault they moved me to a back-asswards state that makes me buy my medication on the street."

Buck snorted a laugh. "You're full of shit. Gerry has a card. Do you think he's getting his supply on the street?"

"Well, Gerry has connections, man," River said.

Ethan grabbed his case and peered out toward the barn, his eyes drifting out of focus for a moment. "It's weird, right? I don't see anything. But where is she?"

"I don't know. Maybe her friends picked her up?" River offered, swiping a case from the trunk before Buck closed it.

"And she left her door open?" Buck asked.

He reached the gate and wedged himself through a small opening, waving for River and Ethan to follow through.

"Yeah, why not?" River said, motioning with his hands as he gyrated through the gap in the fence. "Maybe she's the super-hot type who drops everything and goes to the bars. Bet she's got an amazing ass that you just want to . . . " He smacked the fence, and a metallic ring sounded through the air.

"Well, I wouldn't know what to do with a woman's ass," Buck said with a perfect deadpan.

River laughed. "Hold up, Buck. Was that a fucking joke? Did you just make your first funny? I'm so proud."

Ethan wedged through the gate and frowned up at the barn. "But seriously. Could a ghost have called us? What if this is a trap or something?"

River turned back and stumbled into one of the tire tracks in the driveway. "Trap? Who do you think is going to trap us?"

"It has to be vampires. Ethan thinks they're real," Buck said, grinning.

"Vampires? Seriously, rookie? I thought you read the fucking manual." River laughed.

"Okay, whatever, but maybe it's upper management or something coming to arrest us," Ethan said.

"You think upper management cares enough to come out to fucking-no-where-Midwest to arrest us?" River said.

"I dunno. With all that's happened. And me, and—"

"Gentlemen," Buck said, swinging his case around to glare at them. "It's late. I'm tired. Let's get this over with." He turned and marched toward the barn at double his previous pace.

River and Ethan sped to keep up, trudging through mud and high grass. Ethan looked down, running the dry-cleaning numbers through his head as the mud caked onto the sides of his suit pants. Why couldn't they just wear jeans for once? Suits were so impractical.

River's shoes squelched as he walked. "So, we're in the middle of fuck all. Did anyone look this place up? I mean, if this is some Yellowstone bullshit and cowboys roll up on us with AR-15s, I vote we give them the rookie and make a run for it."

"Good plan," Buck affirmed.

"Hey!" Ethan said.

"Seriously though. This must be the biggest fucking ranch in New Richmond. I mean, there was nothing driving up here," River grumbled.

"Oh. That's because we came past a waterfowl protection area," Ethan said.

River jumped over a puddle. "A what the fuck who now?"

"A waterfowl protection area? It's federal land. Where, like, ducks and geese and crap live."

"Really? That's a thing?" River said, laughing.

"Yeah, it's a thing. There's a couple 'round here."

River took another drag of his joint and then said, "There are federal duck orgy zones? Like a duck-fuck resort? Where fucking ducks go to fuck ducks?"

"Um. Yeah. I mean, I've never heard it described like that," Ethan said.

River smiled and nodded. "Did you know ducks have corkscrew dicks? And the ladies, well sometimes they have—"

"River," Buck grumbled as he stepped over a large puddle, "Can you be half the moron you usually are?"

"Why you gotta hate on my duck dick fuck facts?" River groaned.

"Cut it out. Focus on the job," Buck said.

Thrusting his hips as he walked, River grumbled, "Sounds to me like someone's jealous of the duck-fuck resort. Maybe they need a Buck-fu—"

"Alright," Ethan said. "I agree with Buck. No more duck fuck facts."

"Ducks have needs too, you heartless bastards!" River shouted.

"That's it. No more talking until we reach the barn," Buck barked.

River mumbled something unintelligible under his breath and trudged on.

They walked the last fifty yards in silence, and Ethan pulled out his phone, seeing the last message he got from Bryce, forty-five minutes ago:

They're keeping me here another few days. Can't wait to come back and see you!

Ethan hated how much Bryce traveled. And a pit in his stomach kept growing the more he thought about it. He'd never had a long-term relationship, let alone a long distance one. Could they keep this going? What if Bryce found someone else, and Ethan was just—

They stopped in front of the side door to the large barn, which was cracked open, adding to the ominousness of the moment.

River took one last drag of his joint before flicking it away and said, "Welp, I'm not going first, so one of you step the fuck up."

Ethan took a deep breath and pushed his thoughts back down. He squeezed his briefcase and stepped forward. "I've got it."

He reached for the door, his hand shaking slightly as he gripped the steel doorknob. It was ice cold, and he wondered if that meant anything. He felt Buck right behind him, and he took in a breath and threw open the door.

Ethan darted into the space, claiming the left side while Buck followed in and took to the right and River followed in behind. They stood in the silence, watching and waiting.

Farming equipment cluttered the space, looming high above them in massive dark shadows and sharp edges. Ethan peered into the dark, making out a second floor and what looked to be a line of office windows looking down on them. Nothing in the room seemed out of the ordinary, and the silence ebbed at his ears.

"Hey!" Buck yelled.

"What the fuck?" River yelled, jumping back toward the door.

Their echoes traveled through the barn and died. There was no response. Buck looked at Ethan and shrugged.

River stepped halfway out the door and said, "Well, looks like a bust. Guess we can go."

"Could have been a prank call," Ethan said.

"Ow, fuck!" River screamed, as the door behind him slammed and caught his leg in the frame.

He pulled it free, and the door slammed shut with a loud bang. Falling to the ground, he cradled his leg and whimpered, "I'm too young to die."

"What was that?" Ethan asked, trying to slow his racing pulse.

"Don't know," Buck said. "Stay alert. River, get up."

River tested his foot and found it to be suitable to stand on. He looked to the floor and said, "What? I thought it was broken."

They moved along the wall, Ethan holding up his phone's flashlight as they looked over the tools hanging on the walls.

"What if it's one of those spider spirits with like ten legs that crawl on the ceiling?" River asked.

"Wait. What the fuck. Is that a thing?" Ethan asked, imagining a mass of arms and legs crawling above him.

"No, rookie," Buck said, but the inflection in his voice gave away that he wasn't telling the truth.

Green light filled the room, and River let out another scream. He jumped behind Buck and whispered, "I told you it was ghost spiders."

Ethan focused near the light, squinting. "I still don't see anything. This is weird."

"What's your spider sense tell you?" Buck asked.

"Spider sense?" Ethan asked.

"The psychic thing. What do you feel?"

Ethan shrugged. "Nothing."

The green light suddenly vanished, and they were consumed by darkness once again.

River stepped out from behind Buck and shouted, "Come on, you bastard! Show yourself!"

"Weren't you curled up in a ball back there a few seconds ago?" Buck asked.

"That was when I thought it was right behind me. I can outrun it if I know where it is."

"Outrun? A spider ghost with ten legs?" Ethan challenged.

"I just have to outrun you and Buck. And don't think I won't trip one of you guys either."

"Nice teamwork," Buck scoffed.

"Well, Ethan's stupid ideas had me writing lines last week. I'm not getting strapped to some ghost tractor this week to till the ground, okay? No way."

Ethan frowned. "I haven't even had any ideas yet."

"It was your idea to come in here," River whined.

"Technically," Buck said, stepping toward the tractors. "That was my idea."

Before Buck could get more than a few feet further into the room, two tractors roared to life.

"Nope!" River screamed as he ran for the door.

Ethan braced himself, but the tractor never moved. It just sat there, idling.

"Fuck!" River screamed from behind them.

Ethan turned back to see River pulling at the door with all his might. After a few seconds, he let go and yelled, "We're locked in!"

Two more tractors roared to life, and the room smelled of exhaust. Green lights started flashing in strobes around the room, and then bangs sounded throughout the barn.

"This ghost is fucking weird," Ethan said.

"Yeah," Buck said, peering past the tractors.

A deep and gravelly voice filled the room. It had a buzz to it, as if it were being electronically amplified. "NRDS! Confess or die!"

"Fuck you, stupid ghost!" River screamed. "Show yourself, and we will give you the old one if you let us go!"

"Really, River?" Ethan said.

"What? Want me to offer you up?" River replied.

"Confess your sins, NRDS!" the voice said again, echoing through the space. "Confess your sins and we'll let you live."

Ethan huddled close to Buck and River, whispering, "How does it know who we are? And why does it want us to confess? I'm so confused."

"Keep it busy," Buck said as he stepped backward into the shadows.

"On it," River said back. He stepped forward and yelled, "Okay, confession! Last night, Bob was being an asshole, and I was a little drunk, so I left him in a potpourri shop."

Ethan laughed. "Oh, my God, you are an asshole."

River continued yelling to the voice, "And then, before that, I was at a bar. And there was this super-hot girl there. Everyone wanted her. But she chose me. Because I'm a sex magnet."

"Uh, is that really a confession?" Ethan asked.

More tractors roared to life, and the green light flashed on and off. "No!" the voice screamed. "Not those sins! Confess your NRDS sins! Or you will die!"

"But I think you're going to like this one!" River screamed, trying to drown out the sound of the tractors. "Picture me, this hot girl, seven spoons, and a vacuum cleaner that isn't being used according to industry standards, if you know what I mean!"

"Confess what you have done to this town!" the voice yelled.

"I'm trying, dammit!" River screamed. "I'll tell you what I've done to every person in this burg! And I've done some stuff! You should get comfy!"

"No! No! Tell us your real sins! Or you will—Hey! How did you—AHHHH!"

The voice cut out and a bang sounded loud in the air.

Ethan frowned. "What the hell was that?"

River smiled back at him. "Buck got em!"

The tractors powered down, the green lights turned off, and the screech of feedback filled the room, and then Buck's voice came over the loudspeaker. "Come on up, boys. I got 'em."

Ethan looked up to the second floor, seeing the light spilling out from the office windows.

River patted Ethan's shoulder and pushed him toward the stairs. "See, rookie? Nothing to be scared of."

"Wait. What? I wasn't scared. You were," Ethan said.

"Sure, man. Whatever you say."

Fifty-One

NRDS Debunked

E THAN'S EYES LOCKED ON to the light pouring out from the windows as he and River ascended the stairs to the offices in the barn. Sweat formed on his palms, and he strained to keep his voice steady. "So, who do you think is up there?"

River pulled a joint from inside his suit coat and lit it. "It's probably upper management."

"Wait? What? Really?" Ethan asked, pausing on the stairs.

"Yeah. It's all a test. They show up, put us under some pressure, and see which one of us cracks."

"Really?"

River stopped at the top of the stairs and eyed Ethan. "Did you really read the manual?"

"Yeah. Why?"

"Article 52. Internal Audits and Unannounced Inspections. It's all in there. This is textbook stuff."

Ethan bit his lip. "Oh, yeah. Article 52. I read that."

"No, you didn't. There is no Article 52. Audits are in Article 37."

"Well. Uh—I skimmed it. Okay? I didn't read the whole thing."

River let out a laugh. "I fucking knew it, you little liar!"

"Fine. Whatever. What about this inspection, though?"

"Well, if you don't get higher than a C grade, they cut you."

Ethan stumbled on the last step before reaching the second-floor platform. His heart pounded in his chest. "Do you think any of us got a C? What do I need to do to get a C?"

River looked at his fingernails and smiled. "It's all about meeting expectations. They have a profile on you already. That's why I act scared, and Buck was all stoic. I'm guessing your profile says you're the athletic type, so you probably failed." River nodded to the door up ahead. "Well, it's been nice working with you."

Sweat dripped down Ethan's brow, and he frowned. "No. Wait? Really? How is that fair? How can you act like a chicken, and I get fired?"

River took a drag from his joint and shrugged. "You gotta meet expectations, man."

"Wait. No, fuck you. You're messing with me."

River let out a laugh. "Finally, he gets it. Fucking with you is too easy."

"Wait. Is there really an article 37?" Ethan asked.

"Dude. Read the fucking manual," River said, heading toward the door.

Ethan raced to keep up. "Yeah. Sure. I knew you were kidding, anyway."

They entered the room and found three college-aged guys sitting back-to-back on the floor, tied up with a microphone cord.

"Hold up! These are the guys from the cemetery!" Ethan exclaimed.

Blowing smoke into the air, River said, "Buck, who are these douchebags?"

Buck stepped out from the shadows and swatted at the head of the nearest tied up guy. "We've run into these yahoos before trying to film us. Ethan thought they were vampires."

Ethan's eyes widened. "What? No, I didn't."

"There's no such thing as vampires, bro," River said.

"I know! Stop reminding me."

The blond guy with a pair of well-placed dimples shouted, "You can't hold us here like this! You know that, right? This is kidnapping!"

"We're federal agents, dumbass. We can do whatever we want," River shot back.

"Oh. That's great. Mind repeating that on camera for me?" the blond one said again. "The corrupt fake agent claims he can do corrupt things. Real shocker there!"

The taller of the three kids rolled his eyes as the heavier one said, "Hey. Uh, Buck right? I'm just doing this for a class. I don't even know these two all that well. Can you let me go?"

"Way to throw us under the bus, Ricky," the blond one said.

Ethan crossed his arms. "Oh really? Doing this for school? Then, what class?"

The tall one rolled his eyes. "It's advanced documentary filmmaking. Our senior thesis."

The blond one jerked his head and hit Ricky's shoulder. "Shut up! This isn't about the grade. This story is going to bring you fuckers down! We're award-winning journalists!"

Buck laughed. "Oh yeah? What award did you win, punk?"

River's eyes grew ten sizes, and he held up his hands like he was framing Buck. "Hold up. Did you fucknuts hear that? Was that a Clint Eastwood impersonation?"

"Stop distracting my prisoners," Buck growled.

"Say, 'Do you feel lucky, punk,'" River said in his best Eastwood impersonation. He stepped closer to Buck, his hands outstretched and one eye closed.

"So, what award did you win?" Ethan asked.

The tall one perked up and grinned. "Best student project last year. We exposed a pyramid scheme that was taking over campus. We got on the Dean's list at the University of Chicago for it."

"Oh, nice. I bet that felt good. You guys should be proud," Ethan said with a smile.

"Stop inflating my prisoners' egos," Buck said.

"Buck. Hey Buck," River said, trying to get Buck's attention. Doing his Eastwood voice again, he said, "Say, 'Everyone wants results. But no one wants to do what they have to do to get things done.'"

"Enough," Buck barked. He looked at his prisoners and said, "Ignore those two. Focus on me if you want to get out of here."

"You're all going down for this. We won't stop until everyone knows how full of shit NRDS is," the blond one said again.

"Your name's Chester? Right?" Ethan said, looking at the student and trying to remember his name.

"Chester Wainwright," the bigger one said.

"So what? Yeah, I'm Chester," the blond student said. "And you are all going behind bars. When this film hits the shelves, the American people are going to know that bullshit you've been up to. And you're all going to be left answering for your crimes."

"What do you think our crimes are?" Buck asked, cocking his head with interest.

"Spending taxpayer money to spy on us, dig up bodies, and prey on those of us in mourning. You're the definition of government waste," Chester shot back.

"Waste? Oh. You shouldn't have said that," River laughed. Nudging Buck, he said, "Tell him, Buck. Say, 'Get three coffins ready.' Go ahead. Tell him in that Eastwood voice."

"Kid, I'm going to give you one more chance," Buck said.

"Look, man. You can keep Chester. Just let me go. I'll go back to Chicago and forget all about this," the big one said.

"Traitor!" Chester shouted.

"Dude. Chill the fuck out," the tall one said.

"Where's your journalistic integrity? I knew I should have brought Becky!" Chester shot back.

"Becky doesn't want anything to do with you, dumbass," Ricky said.

"He seems a little high-strung," Ethan said to the tall one.

"You've got no idea. And he doesn't help with any of the post edits," the tall one answered.

"I am the face of this documentary. That should be enough," Chester said.

"Well, the face of this documentary is going to have a fucking black eye when I get out of these cords," Ricky said.

Ethan looked out the window and frowned. "Hold on. How'd you guys get the tractors to start on their own? And the lights?"

"Remotes. We nicked a few from the robotics lab and set up before you got here," the big one said.

"Wasn't all that hard," Ricky said.

"Dudes, shut up," Chester said. "They're the enemy. Don't talk to them."

Buck crossed his arms. "Alright. Look, kid. We can do this the easy way or the hard way. But either way, you're going to tell us who put you up to this."

"We're here because you are a blight on American democracy," Chester declared.

"You're telling me a bunch of college kids from Chicago lugged a ton of camera equipment up here, in the middle of nowhere, to expose NRDS? Why wouldn't you stalk the Chicago units? They're expanding their offices now as we speak. Or better yet, why wouldn't you go to DC and film the offices for your narrative? I'm not buying it."

"Chicago is getting a bigger office? I want a bigger office," Ethan said to River.

River nodded. "Yeah. And they have their own Starbucks in the lobby."

"Aw man. Fuck Chicago," Ethan said.

Chester writhed against the cords. "We came to expose you all. The people need to know."

Ethan looked around the room and frowned. "Where is the camera, anyway?"

Ricky nodded behind Ethan and said, "Over there."

Ethan turned to see the camera sitting on a table behind them. The red light beamed back at him. "Um, guys? The camera is on."

"Seriously?" River said. He picked it up and propped it up on his shoulders. Impersonating David Attenborough, he pointed the camera at the three guys and said, "And here we have the supposedly famed *Duumasus journalus* in their natural environment. These creatures spend all day scavenging and brushing too close with better, more refined animals."

"Please be careful with that. It's on loan," Ricky said.

"This is pretty cool," River said, looking through the viewfinder.

"That's right, it is cool. And you know what else is cool? The automatic feed uploads onto our cloud server. You are all so fucked," Chester said.

Pointing the camera at him, River shot back, "Mr. Chester-man. What happened to you to make you such a douchebag?"

"Becky dumped him," Ricky said with a snicker.

"I'm exposing the injustice of the American system," Chester said into the camera.

Buck grabbed a chair from a desk near him and sat down in front of Chester. "Look, kid. You and I both know you're being paid to be here. Tell us who it is, and I'll let you out of here. Then you can go back to school and apologize to Becky for whatever shitty thing you did."

Chester smiled. "We've got everything on camera, old man. I've got him rolling around like a coward, and I've got you tying us up and threatening us. You're going down."

"River. Smash the camera," Buck said.

Chester sat up, his face flushed. "It's all in the cloud. Smashing won't do anything."

Buck looked at his fingernails. "You said it was on loan, right?"

River smiled and held the camera over his head. "Say when."

"No! Stop!" Ricky yelled. "It's that mayor, dude. Chax Tamish. He gave us each five hundred to come and video you. Please, they'll have my head if that camera is smashed."

River put the camera back on his shoulder and pointed it at Ricky. "I take it all the footage goes to you, and you'll delete it?"

Ricky nodded. "Whatever you want, just don't break it."

Ethan put his hands on his hips. "Fucking Chax Tamish. I'm sick of that asshole."

Buck shook his head. "Why would he send a film crew after us? He's trying to shut us down, yeah, but he's bound to get a ghost on film if he keeps digging."

"He said you tried to kill him," the tall one said. "He wants to make your lives hell."

"We didn't try to kill anyone," Ethan shot back.

"Oh, sure. So that light that almost took him out just fell by happenstance?" Chester shot back.

"That was a ghost," Ethan said.

Chester let out a laugh.

"We didn't do that, kid. But we're investigating who, or what, did," Buck said. Standing, he looked at River and said, "Alright. Put the camera down. Let's get out of here."

"But what about us?" the tall college student said.

"You'll figure it out," Buck said, stepping out of the room. "Ethan, untie them."

"Oh. Sure. Okay," Ethan jumped to action, searching the cord for the knot Buck had tied.

River set the camera down and tapped on his chin. "You know, if you guys are looking for a good documentary idea about government waste, did you know that the land all around us is a federal park created so ducks will have a place to fuck?"

Ethan pulled at the knot. "It's a waterfowl protection area," he explained.

"Yeah. Uncle Sam is paying to keep orgy areas for ducks. I mean, that's a documentary I'd watch. Ducks fucking? Come on. The story tells itself."

Ricky pulled the cord off himself and stood, stretching. "Sounds interesting. Better than the Three Stooges footage we have on you."

Ethan pulled on the cords around Chester and said, "Or better yet. Why don't you look into all the housing development in this area? Last week a whole retirement home was evicted by some stupid multimillion housing corp. There has to be corruption there."

"We didn't hear about that," the tall one said.

"Yeah. I only know about it because my gran knows some people who got kicked out. The news has said nothing," Ethan said.

Chester shoved off the cords and grabbed the camera, giving it a once over. "You're not talking us out of the actual story. You'll be sharing a cell with that old guy in no time."

River sighed and nodded. "I've done that. Not fun." Before walking out of the door, he turned, saluted, and said, "Gentlemen, it's been a blast."

Ethan sighed and followed behind River, "See you around, then."

As Ethan left the room, he overheard Ricky. "Why are you such a fucking dick? No wonder Becky dumped your ass."

"She'll see. They'll all see," Chester muttered.

Fifty-Two

Ghostly Grievances

E THAN SQUEEZED BRYCE'S HAND and rubbed his thumb against Bryce's smooth, uncalloused skin. It was the hand of a New York elite, someone who never had to pick up side gigs at restaurants or construction jobs. A hand vastly different from his own, but Ethan couldn't let go . . . didn't want to let go since Bryce's return to Ethan's insignificant blip of a town.

Bryce brought the coffee cup to his lips and took a sip, considering it for a moment before smiling. "You're right. It's unexpectedly good."

Ethan traced his smile, following the curve of his lips and the dimple on his cheek. Ethan grinned in return and sipped his own coffee. "I know, right? Who knew a little gas station at the edge of town had it in them, but Ms. Grace roasts on site. Still, probably nothing like what they've got in New York."

"Bodega coffee is hit or miss," Bryce said with a shrug.

"What's a bodega?"

Bryce slowed his pace up the stairs. "It's like a gas station with no gas. They're all over New York."

"Huh," Ethan said with a nod.

"When you come to New York with me, I'll take you to all my favorites."

Ethan stopped on the stairs, his heart fluttering in his chest. "Wait. Go to New York? When? Seriously?"

Bryce turned around and smiled down at Ethan. "I was thinking a few months from now. You've got to meet the family sometime. They're opening an office there now too. I'm sure I could pull a few strings if you wanted."

Thoughts raced through Ethan's mind. He couldn't leave, could he? Before another thought could worm its way into his head, he blurted out, "Yes. I. I'd love to."

Bryce pushed open the office door and said, "Good. It's settled then."

Ethan raced up the last few steps, a grin stretching across his face as he gave a peck on Bryce's cheek.

"Donut?" Doris asked from behind her desk as they stepped in. She held up a tray of fluffy pastries, from red jelly-filled to maple frosting and pecan and everything in between.

"No, I'm good," Bryce said, patting his stomach. "Someone made me fill up on gas station food this morning."

Ethan's mouth watered, and he reached toward the box. "I'll take one."

"No! NO DONUT FOR THAT DUMBASS!" Melissa shouted, bursting from her office.

Trevor, who kept his eyes trained on the floor, followed her out of her office.

Ethan frowned and looked up at the rest of the office. River sat at his desk, glaring at Melissa while Buck continued typing on his computer. Neither Alexus nor Bob, were in the office, which was out of place for both of them.

Ethan locked eyes with Melissa and inched his hand closer to the donuts.

She stuck a finger out at him and said, "Do it, and so help me Jesus, I will cut your hand off. And we're not talking about the sweet, kind Jesus. I'm talking Jesus riding in on the black unicorn with wings made of fire with an AR-15 in each hand, like the one on the flags those idiots carry at those political marches. Go ahead, try me. Touch that donut and GI Jesus and me will kick your ass!"

Doris gave Ethan a shrug and turned back to her computer, but she didn't pull back the box of donuts.

Bryce adjusted glasses. "What is going on?"

Melissa shot Bryce a glare. "Oh, I don't need your upper management sugar daddy interference with this one. He's stepped in some royal shit and there's no helping him. He and these two yahoos are in so much deep shit it's way up past their knees, and there's no way they'll get it out. This shit is so deep, it's—"

Ethan waved his arm and cut her off. "Okay, I think we get the analogy, but I haven't done anything."

"None of us have done anything," River said.

Melissa snapped her fingers. "Trevor! Pass me the evidence!"

Trevor frowned. "I sent it to your computer like you asked."

She snapped her fingers again. "Hand over your phone."

He rolled his eyes and handed over the phone. "Fine. Here."

"Oh, this is a lot of excitement for a Monday morning," Doris said, pushing the box of donuts closer to Ethan.

Melissa fumbled with the phone for a few minutes before tossing it back at him. "No, this won't work. No one can see it. Go get my laptop."

Trevor let out a loud sigh and scurried back into her office.

Melissa glowered at the office and added, "All your asses are mine now. The phrase fireable offense comes to mind."

Buck laughed to himself from his computer.

"Oh, what's that Agent Hampton? You think you're too famous to fire? Not after this PR disaster."

Doris shot another glance at Melissa before nudging the box of donuts toward Ethan again.

"Wait. Is this about the thing that happened at the farm?" Ethan asked, grabbing one of the maple-frosted donuts before heading to his desk.

Melissa's face turned red as he took a bite of the donut, and she mocked him in a whiny child-like voice, "Is this about what happened at the farm?"

"I'm sorry, guys," Trevor said, returning from Melissa's office with her laptop in hand. "She caught me watching it this morning. I didn't mean to rat you out."

"Rat us out? What did you record, you sneaky bastard?" River said, leaning forward in his chair. "You didn't follow me into the fucking feed store, did you? I was off the clock! That was my personal time!"

Trever frowned. "Um, no?"

Buck looked up from his computer and said, "What did you do?"

"Nothing! I didn't do anything. And if this fuck caught it on camera, then it's a complete lie!" River barked back.

"I don't know what the fuck you are talking about. But you know the feed store has security cams, right?" Trevor said defensively.

"Whatever it is, it's a deep fake!" River declared, standing and pointing at Trevor. "This Fake-News-Deep-Faking-Sneaky-Asshole is a liar!"

"Hold up. We're friends, you asshole," Trevor said.

"Objection! I don't know this man!" River yelled.

"Oh my," Doris said, grabbing a blueberry donut and tearing off a piece, popping it into her mouth like popcorn.

"Enough, you paranoid dumbass," Buck said to River.

Crashing down into his chair, River folded his arms over his chest. "I'm innocent until proven guilty by something other than his sneaky asshole's lying videos."

"What is this video?" Buck asked Melissa, then pointed at River. "And we're going to have a conversation about what you did at the feed store later."

Bryce finished his coffee and said, "Can we hurry this along?"

Melissa turned her laptop around and said, "Get a load of this."

On the screen was a TikTok of the blond college film maker, Chester Wainwright.

"I knew this was about the barn," Ethan said with a proud nod.

Melissa hit the spacebar on her computer and Chester Wainwright came to life.

He stood in front of their offices, pointing to the NRDS sign. "Nationally Recently Deceased Services? Helpful government agency or just another corrupt law enforcement division that wastes our hard-earned taxpayer dollars? You decide."

A video of Buck, Ethan, and River in the barn filled the screen. Green flashed, and River lay on the ground, whimpering, "I'm too young to die!"

Chester reappeared on the screen and said, "If ghosts were real, then would these so-called agents face them with integrity?"

Buck appeared on the screen, wrapping them up in a black cord.

"Corruption," the voiceover said.

River loomed over the tied-up college students. "We're federal agents, dumbass. We can do whatever we want."

"Intimidation," the voiceover stated.

"Focus on me if you want to get out of here," Buck growled into the camera.

The video changed, and Buck growled, "Alright. Look, kid. We can do this the easy way or the hard way."

The voice over declared, "Destruction of Personal Property!"

Buck pointed at the screen. "River. Smash the camera."

Chester reappeared on the screen. "Why were we beaten and detained for no reason? Because they want to kill a local official who dares to stand against them, and we called them out."

Ethan appeared on the video, his hands on his hips. "Fucking Chax Tamish. I'm so sick of that asshole."

The screen froze on Ethan's face and the voiceover said, "Like, share, and follow! More to come!"

Melissa let out a laugh as she closed the laptop. "I've got you now, assholes."

"Well, the cinematography was nice," Doris said, popping the last of her donut in her mouth.

Buck turned back to his computer.

"Come on. You believe that? They set us up," Ethan complained.

"Doesn't matter. You're on camera threatening a public official," Melissa said.

"Technically, he didn't threaten anyone. He said he was sick of Chax," Bryce said.

Melissa pointed her finger at Bryce. "You stay out of this. The report is going right above your head because of your relations."

Bryce grabbed a donut and shook his head, taking a seat next to Ethan. "Whatever you say, Melissa."

Buck loudly clicked return on his keyboard and swiveled in his chair, smiling. "I filed the report on the farm event. You'll find that everything has been included, in detail, including my decision to detain the students. I filed an audit against our actions, including a self-assessment with disciplinary recommendations. Any further punitive action regarding this event against any team member involved will need a 7-80d form filed."

"You motherfucker," Melissa complained.

"What's a 7-80d?" Ethan asked Bryce.

Bryce laughed and whispered. "It's a forty-seven-page form that requests action on an already filed official report."

Melissa stood up and shoved her laptop under her arm. "This isn't over, old timer."

She left without another word, slamming her office door behind her.

Trevor sulked back to his desk near the door and muttered, "I'm sorry, guys."

Ethan shrugged. "She would have found out one way or another. Good thing it hasn't gone viral yet."

Trevor flipped open his phone. "Well, it already has over ten million views."

"Oh, shit! We're famous!" River said, blowing a cloud of smoke toward the ceiling of the office. "No smoking in the office. Put it out," Buck barked.

River hopped out of his chair and looked at the clock. "Well, look at that! Smoke break!"

As River headed toward the door, Buck said, "And we're talking about what happened at the feed store. Whatever you did is going in a report."

"Yeah, yeah," River said, reaching for the door.

Before he pulled it open, the door burst open and sent him staggering back.

Alexus stood in the doorway, her hands clutching onto a small cloth bag and her eyes glowing blue.

"Morning Alexus. Donut?" Doris asked.

Alexus ignored her, eyes locked on River.

He held his hands up. "No. Wait. I can explain."

Before he could say another word, Alexus crossed the room. Her eyes flared a bright blue, and her fist met his jaw, sending him reeling to the ground.

"Damn!" Trevor said, holding up his camera to stream the episode.

"Hey!" Buck yelled, holding up his badge.

Alexus rested a foot on River's chest, and a man's voice came out of her. "Stay down there, you motherfucker!"

"What in the hell is going on?" Melissa said, bursting from her office.

Alexus shook her head and cleared her throat. "Alright, Bob, get out."

She frowned, then her eyes dimmed, and Ethan watched as Bob stepped out of Alexus.

"Oh, Bob's back?" Doris asked, fishing around in her drawer before she pulled out a badge.

"I think you broke my nose," River complained from the ground.

"That's what you get, maggot," Bob said.

"Someone needs to start talking," Melissa demanded.

Bob smiled and stood over River with a grin on his face. "Didn't think I'd figure out how to get out of there, did you?"

"Bob, stand down. Alexus, talk," Buck demanded.

"This asshole left Bob in a potpourri store. For a week," Alexus growled.

River let out a giggle, and Alexus kicked at his side, causing him to let out a groan.

Alexus continued, "Bob possessed the owner so he could call me to come get him. You made him escalate."

Ethan grimaced. "Oh, not cool, man."

"Very not cool. Bob will need to be evaluated and cleared for duty," Bryce said to Buck.

Interrupting, Buck said, "I know. Dammit, River." He looked at Melissa. "We'll need to file a 14-32f."

"And a d80-1 to cover Bob," Bryce added.

Melissa nodded. "Alexus, let him up."

Alexus dug her boot in once more before taking a step back.

"River, two-week suspension, no pay. This is a real fuck-up," Melissa said, her face without a single sign of emotion or her usual grin.

"Two weeks?" River complained.

"Bob, you're eligible for reassignment after you file a grievance to HR, if you'd like. Ethan, help him with the paperwork," Buck said.

Ethan's eyes widened. "Um. I don't know which forms are—"

Bryce rested a hand on Ethan's and said, "I'll show you."

Bob nodded, back turned to River.

"Leave your badge on my desk and get out," Melissa said, arms crossed.

River looked at Buck, who turned back to his computer. His face turned red. "Fine!" he shouted and stomped into Melissa's office, tossed down his badge, and stomped to the exit. "Bye, losers. Hope you're happy you won't have to see my face."

"You're lucky you aren't fired. Go think about what you did," Buck said.

River shot an eye at the donuts and made a beeline for them, but Doris pulled them off her desk. He left without another word.

"Buck, get started on all those forms you rattled off," Melissa said with a dismissive wave as she went back into her office.

Ethan looked up at Bob and said, "Sorry, man. We didn't know where you went. You want to start on that form?"

Bob bit his lip and nodded. "Affirmative, rookie."

Ethan turned back to his computer screen and leaned toward Bryce. "Okay, where do I go?"

Bryce nudged Ethan's hand off the mouse and inched closer to Ethan. He started clicking through the files and said, "I'll give you this. Your office is never dull. You sure you'd want to join me in New York? It's not as action-packed."

Ethan looked into Bryce's eyes and smiled. "I'm sure."

Fifty-Three

Lost in the Library

"THIS IS FUCKING HOPELESS!" Ethan said, slamming the large bound volume of old Hudson Star newspapers. His fingers rubbed his temples as he took in slow, labored breaths before heaving the book atop the pile of the other twelve volumes he'd already worked through. He stood and marched through the empty library toward the stairs.

Joan peered over her glasses from the circulation desk. "Going for more?"

"Yep," Ethan shot back as he yanked the basement door leading down to the archives open.

"I'm sure you'll find what you're looking for soon," she called from behind him as he stomped down the stairs.

"Yeah, right," he muttered.

He flipped the switch and the old dusty room, packed with metal shelving, filled with light. Marching to the back right corner of the room, he hefted the next three volumes off the shelf. Each massive book contained three hundred sixty-five newspapers, a year in the life of Saint Croix County. Not only were they oversized, but they were frustratingly heavy and three was all he could carry up the stairs at once.

His arms ached from the strain as he let them drop on the table with a loud crash. He shot a glance over at Joan, who only pursed her lips at the noise before returning to her computer.

He sat flipping open the first volume and leafing through it. Articles on local boys who'd gone off to war in Vietnam, news stories about local protests, opinion pieces on Johnson not seeking another term, headlines mourning the assassinations of both King and Kennedy, articles on the race between Nixon and Humphrey, Nixon's victory, and finally the first United States astronauts to orbit the moon.

Ethan flipped through the major headlines, homing in on the local events. Football, basketball, and hockey announcements, festivals coming and going around the county, and most importantly, the obituaries. Each day, page after page of people's lives ending. As the events of the world unfolded, the daily grind of Saint Croix County chugged along.

He scribbled names and dates in a little notebook off to his left, his hand cramping as the only writing utensil he could get his hands on was one of those half-sized pencils. Half his notes were gibberish at this point, all the information streaming over him without a single blip that signified what he was looking for.

He tossed the 1968 volume aside and picked up 1967. Before he could crack it open, he heard a familiar voice echoing in the library.

"You are looking radiant Joan, how's your uncle doing?" Bryce said, approaching the circulation desk in a well-tailored powder-blue suit and brown suede shoes.

"Not well. The new nursing home has them all packed in three to a suite. I'm at the point where I might have him move in with me and hire someone to care for him." Joan said.

"Oh, I'm sorry about that. Well, if there's anything I can do to help . . ."

Joan waved her hand. "You've helped enough. It's just this damn city not caring for their elderly."

"I hear ya," Bryce said, staring off at Ethan. "Well, if anything changes, keep me posted."

Ethan buried his nose back in the volume, forcing the flutter in his chest down from the sight of Bryce. He skimmed headlines about James Bedford's attempt to freeze himself for preservation and Green Bay winning the super bowl before brown suede shoes entered his vision.

"How's it going?" Bryce asked.

Ethan kept his head buried, flipping to the next page. "It's fine."

Bryce placed a white bag and a Styrofoam cup in front of him. "Brought you some lunch."

"Cool, thanks," Ethan said as jotted down a note.

Bryce walked around the table, pulled out a chair, and took a seat next to him. "Buck said you've been here since six this morning."

Ethan sighed sharply, trying his hardest to focus on the papers. "Sounds about right." He turned the page and scanned the obits. Nothing stood out, so he moved on to the next day.

Bryce pulled out some fries from the white bag and ate a few. "He said he told you he didn't think this would work, but that you were a 'man on a mission.'"

"That is how that conversation went."

Bryce pushed the bag toward him. "Rosemary said this was your favorite deli."

The scent of herbs, bread, and meat hit his nose, and Ethan's mouth watered. His stomach let out a growl, but he kept his eyes on the newspapers.

"It's roast beef. With horseradish, pickled onions, mayo, and Swiss. That's your favorite, right? They called it 'The Ethan' when I ordered it, which was cool. Except, I wonder if this is the sandwich you want named after yourself."

Ethan bit his lip and surrendered, snatching the bag and reaching inside. He unwrapped the sandwich, and the pungent odor of Swiss, horseradish, and vinegar filled his senses. He took a bite and leaned back, enjoying the acidity of the onions, the tang of the horseradish, the sweetness of the Swiss, and the creaminess of the mayo that brought it all together.

"Thank you," he mumbled with his mouth full.

"You've got to be starving. Have you been here all day?"

"What time is it?" Ethan said as he took another bite.

"Three-thirty."

Ethan sighed and looked back at the book. The words all blurred together and his eyes watered.

"Why don't you call it quits for now? Let's go out. Do something fun," Bryce said as he rubbed Ethan's back.

Ethan shrugged it off and shook his head. "I've got to keep going." He took another bite of the sandwich and stared back down at the page, forcing his eyes to focus on the text.

Bryce picked up a volume Ethan had already looked at and flipped through the pages as Ethan skimmed an article about a man named Richard Speck being sentenced to death for killing eight nurses.

"Have you gone through all of these?" Bryce asked, putting the volume he'd looked at back on the stack.

"Yep," Ethan said as he scanned a new batch of obituaries.

"You know, most of this has been digitized. We might be able to just Google it."

Ethan shook his head, his nose still buried in the volume. "They only digitized the Star back to 1979. I started there. When I didn't find anything, I moved to paper copies."

"Huh," Bryce responded, picking up another volume and flipping through it. "How many more do you have to go through?"

"The paper started in the 1860s. So, about a hundred more."

Bryce laughed. "Ethan. Come on."

"What?" Ethan snapped, looking up from his volume and locking eyes with Bryce. An anger he couldn't quite place washed over him, rushing through his veins.

Bryce gave a patient smile. "You can't read a hundred years of news in a day. It's not possible."

Looking back down at his volume, Ethan said, "Watch me."

Bryce sighed. "I can help. Can you at least tell me what you are looking for?"

Ethan took a deep breath, hoping it would calm him, instead it made him tired. "You can't help."

"I don't know," Bryce said, flipping through a few pages. "I know I may look like a neanderthal, but I promise you I was quite the book nerd in my youth."

Ethan stifled a laugh, his frustration out-competing with any humor Bryce might have. He chewed the last bite of his sandwich and looked back down at the book in front of him. "You can't help because I don't know what I'm looking for."

Bryce cocked his head to the right. "What does that mean?"

Ethan could feel the tears threatening to crawl out of his eyes. He pushed them down. "I don't know what I'm looking for. Clues, I guess? But if I knew what they were, I wouldn't need to look for them."

Bryce smiled again. "Clues to what?"

Ethan gritted his teeth. Bryce didn't understand. No one did. He threw his arms in the air. "I don't know! Clues to everything! Clues to anything!"

Bryce held his hands up defensively. "Okay. Take a breath."

"I can't! I can't take a breath, because if I do, I'm going to look up and it's all going to be gone!"

"I feel like there is a story happening here that I've somehow missed."

A wild laugh escaped from Ethan's lips. "Oh? You've missed it? I've missed it!"

Bryce stared at Ethan for a long moment, then asked, "Did you visit any of the cemeteries today before coming here?"

Ethan tossed the book on the table, pushed his chair back, stood, and pointed at Bryce. "Nope. No. Don't do that."

Bryce laughed in disbelief. "Don't do what?"

"I'm not possessed. This isn't some kind of supernatural mania. This is just me losing my shit because everything is falling the fuck apart. Okay? That's all this is. Just normal, everyday desperation."

Bryce nodded. "I'm not here to fight with you. I'm here to help."

"Don't you think I want that? I would love for you to help . . ." A tear slipped past his wall, and he wiped it from his cheek with the back of his hand.

"Help me. Let me know what's going on?" Bryce said, reaching out for Ethan's hand.

Ethan jerked his hand back. "You want to know what's going on? Well, let me just tell you. Everything is falling apart. Old folks are losing their homes, I've got two escalating ghost kids, and a murdered ex-teacher of mine I haven't been able to help because she needs to watch said kids."

"I get that. It's a lot for one person to handle." Bryce said.

"I'm not even done! There's also a murdered assistant who can't remember fucking anything, my boss has these weird clickers she's been testing on us for fuck knows why, someone tried to murder the next douche mayor, there's a fucking film crew trying to shut us down, one of my team was just suspended, and our BOB is possessing people. Oh! And there's a goddamn clown ghost who goes by Bingo Fucking Bango! We don't even know his fucking name. He's just a clown!"

Ethan slumped in his chair, head in hands as he laughed uncontrollably. "He's a fucking clown!"

"It's going to be okay," Bryce said, resting a hand on Ethan's shoulder.

Ethan wiped away tears and glared at Bryce. "Maybe for all of you. Maybe for everyone else. But if this all falls apart, I'm fucked. You get to go back to New York. Buck? The legend? He just goes back to Chicago. The rising star Alexus could go anywhere she wants because she's fucking awesome. Bob will get reassigned. River clearly can't get fired no matter how much he fucks up, so he'll be fine. But me? What's gonna happen to me? Do you know what I was doing a year ago today? Do you?"

"I can't say I do," Bryce said.

"I was stocking shelves at Walmart." Ethan laughed. "Fucking Walmart." More tears ran down his cheeks. "Do you know how fucked it is to be stocking soup cans while people remind you all about your glory days in high school every day? It fucking sucks."

Bryce leaned in and held Ethan. "That's not your life. Not anymore."

"It will be if I can't fix this. If I can't find at least one goddamn clue, then it all goes away. If the field office fails, everyone goes back to their old lives. I can't go back. I won't. If I have to read every one of these goddamn books to figure out what the fuck is happening in this town, then I'm going to do it. I'm going to sit here as long as it takes and I'm going to fucking figure it out. Because I have to. Because . . . I can't lose everything."

Bryce squeezed Ethan one more time before grabbing an unopened volume. "You won't lose me."

Ethan glanced over, his tears uncontrollably streaming down his face. "Really? You'd stay after that?"

"We all have our moments. Besides, a hundred years of history in a night sounds like a perfect date. I don't want to pass it up," Bryce said with a grin.

A knot in Ethan's chest unfurled, and the words spilled out of his mouth before he could stop them. "I. I love you."

Bryce pulled Ethan in for a kiss. "I love you too."

Fifty-Four

Animal House

E THAN FROWNED AS HE stared up at a bold red house with two green pitched roofs, noting how out of place the house looked compared to the others on the street. The place looked like someone had plucked it right out of some German fairytale where someone might have stumbled upon it up in snow-covered mountains. Not quite the bland beige and whites of New Richmond.

"I swear I've never seen this house before," he said to Alexus and Bob.

"Aw, is the little baby-waby agent scared?" Bob teased.

"Well, unless it fell from the sky, it's here now," Alexus said, pulling two briefcases from the trunk of her car and handing one to Ethan.

"We've got company." He nodded to the van parked down the street, an unmarked white van that was clearly filled with a camera crew watching their every move. They might as well have just spray painted "film crew" on the side of the van, as Ethan could clearly see the passenger holding up a camera to them.

"Don't worry, candy ass. I'll go ape on these fuckers!" Bob shouted, racing off toward the van.

Ethan laughed. "He's eager today."

"He's just happy not to be with River anymore."

Ethan watched as Bob slipped through the side of the van. "I always thought they had like a big brother-little brother thing going."

Bob emerged, a grin on his face.

"From what I heard, it was more like torturer and tortured," Alexus said.

Rejoining them at the curb, Bob said, "Problem neutralized."

Ethan's eyes widened. "Wait. Did you kill them? Tell me you didn't kill them."

Alexus snorted a laugh.

"What if I did, rookie? Are you going to question a senior officer?" Bob stuck a finger in Ethan's chest.

As Ethan searched for words, Bob continued, "Have you ever tried to bring charges against an officer? It's my word against yours. Whose word do you think they are going to believe?"

"Nice," Alexus said, giving Bob the approximation of a fist bump.

Ethan stammered. "I don't . . . charges? What are you talking about?"

Alexus rolled her eyes. "It's from a movie, dumbass."

"Um, okay," Ethan said.

"*Paths of Glory*. Excellent film," Bob said with a smile.

"We've started on the Kubrick catalog," Alexus said.

"Cool. Cool," Ethan said, nodding along and hoping they wouldn't expect him to know what they were talking about.

"So, Colonel Dax, they still in the van?" Alexus said.

"Affirmative. They were trying to decide when to infiltrate, but those crater-faced sons of bitches won't be coming out any time soon."

Ethan raised an eyebrow. "What'd you do?"

"I possessed one of the little shits and made him meow like a deranged alley cat," Bob said.

Alexus laughed again. "Well played."

Ethan took a step back. "Bob, that's against protocol." He shot a glare at Alexus and added, "And you shouldn't encourage it."

"Okay, grandma. Don't get your pantyhose in a knot. I just wanted to scare the Subterraneans."

"Lighten up. He's just having some fun," Alexus said.

Ethan shook his head. "He'll escalate even more if he keeps possessing people." He shot a glare at Bob. "Do you want to end up in a case?"

"Lay off, dickweed," Alexus said. "Trust Bob to keep it under control. He can do more than River led us to believe."

"That's right, maggot," Bob said with a smug smile. "Now that I have someone who actually listens to me, I can do the shit I was doing when your mommy was wiping your little ass."

"Easy, big guy. We're a team, remember?" Alexus said.

"Noted," Bob replied.

Alexus looked up at the house. "What are we looking at?"

Ethan pulled out his phone and opened his email. "The file says a single man, Wallace Jenkins, in his nineties, has not been seen for three weeks. Neighbors called when the house changed colors, and they reported seeing strange animals in the windows."

"Projections, maybe?" Alexus wondered.

"Class Five?" Bob said, rubbing his hands together.

Ethan thought back to the manual, remembering a section he'd actually read which depicted Class Fives, the highest ranking for spirits. They were not only the most dangerous but able to craft projections that could take on mass and interact with the world.

He scratched his head. "Have either of you ever had to deal with this before?"

"Negative, Ghost Rider," Bob said.

Ethan looked at him and raised an eyebrow.

"*Top Gun*, shit stain," Bob replied.

"Yeah. I got that one." Ethan said. "What about you?" he asked Alexus.

"Nope. Like most things here, this is new to me."

"You want me on advanced recon?" Bob asked.

"If they're projections, that might stir them up," Ethan said.

Alexus smiled. "I like you better now that you've read the manual. We need to find the source. Bob, go in through the garage door. Ethan and I will go through the front. We'll clear the first floor. Bob, clear the garage and meet us before going upstairs."

"What are we looking for?" Ethan asked.

"The body. You said he's been missing for a few weeks. Straightforward case and dash before the cops come."

"Why wouldn't we talk him down?" Ethan asked.

Alexus shook her head. "He's too far along. I don't want to risk it." She rolled her neck and shoulders. "Ready?"

Bob started toward the garage. "Remember, boys. There are no points for second place. Losers have to use the ladies' room."

Alexus shouted after him. "Do I need to put on the sensitivity training again?"

He ignored her, slipping in through the garage door.

Ethan and Alexus crossed the lawn and leaned up against the front door. The house was silent.

"Bob seems a lot happier with you," Ethan whispered, testing the doorknob. It was locked.

Alexus took a step back from the door. "Funny how treating someone like a human can do wonders." She rocked back on her heel and kicked the door down as Ethan stumbled back.

"What the fuck? Warn me next time," he shouted.

They raced inside, slipping into the living room. It was beautifully cared for, without a speck of dust on an array of animal prints upholstered to the furniture, wooden masks and taxidermy on the wall, and even the massive giant rhino glaring at them in the middle of the room.

"Oh, shit!" Ethan exclaimed, turning to catch Alexus's eye.

The rhino scraped its hoof against the hardwood floor and snorted.

Alexus raised her hands and took a small step back. "Back out slowly."

Ethan's heart pounded in his ears as his eyes made contact with its weathered horn. The tusk was chipped in places, and all he could think about was the pain if that thing tore through him.

"Remember, it's not real," Alexus whispered reassuringly.

"It looks pretty fucking real to me!" Ethan whispered back.

They both took a step backward.

The rhino let out a low growl and took a step forward.

"Fuck!" Alexus shouted as the rhino lunged forward.

Ethan shoved Alexus to the right, pushing her out of the way. The rhino lowered its tusk, and Ethan squeezed his eyes shut, ready to be stuck like a kebab.

Seconds passed like hours, and he thought of Ellie and his grandmother making pancakes in the kitchen. Then he was in the library, holding Bryce's hand. "I love you," fell from his lips. Then he was in the office watching Buck type. The old man looked up and smiled as a torrent of icy wind passed through him.

He opened his eyes and patted his chest. Everything was intact. He spun around to see wisps of blue smoke vanishing in the air, and shouted, "They're not real! They're just ghosts! I'm alive. I'm a-fucking-live!"

Alexus pushed herself up off the floor and punched him in the arm. "You dick. Don't you ever fucking do that again."

He rubbed his arm and pouted. "Sorry. Jesus."

"And thank you, I guess. That was . . . nice."

Bob peeked his head out into the hallway that led into the kitchen and shouted, "First floor and garage, clear! Lion projection is in the study! Moving up the stairs."

"We're on your six," Alexus said, grabbing onto her briefcase.

A hippo with seaweed dangling from its mouth roared at them as they came to the top of the stairs.

Ethan brushed past Alexus and Bob and waved. "Hello, mister ghost hippo. Just gonna scoot right by ya."

He ducked into the first room bedroom and then the second one as Bob and Alexus came up behind him. "First two are clear," he called as he ran down the hall.

"Octopus in the tub, otherwise, bathroom's clear," Alexus called.

"Third bedroom, clear," Bob called.

Ethan pushed open the door to the last bedroom. It was clear, aside from a small pack of macaque monkeys standing on the bed. "Hey. Come check out these cute monkeys," Ethan called down the hall.

"Stay focused! Find the body," Alexus yelled back.

Moving closer to the bed, Ethan said, "Hey there, little guys. How are my little ghost monkeys?"

The monkey in the center of the pack bared its teeth at Ethan.

"Well, that's rude," he said, giving it a stern look. He turned away and shouted, "Guys! Seriously! You'll never get this close to one in a zoo. You've got to check this out!"

Then the monkey jumped up from the bed and slapped Ethan's face, leaving behind a sharp sting as it screamed in his face.

He stumbled back and out the door, slamming it shut. He raced down the stairs, shouting, "Those were real! The monkeys are real!"

"Dumb ass rookie. Have you looked at the walls?" Bob laughed.

Ethan paused, taking in all the portraits of macaques lined up the stairs, dressed in little outfits. "Oh. Well, shit."

"Both of you shut up. He's got to be in the basement," Alexus said.

"How do you know?" Ethan asked.

"Smell," Alexus said, holding open the door to the basement.

Ethan leaned forward and took a whiff, instantly gagging.

"Don't you fucking vomit in here," Alexus said.

Ethan took in a slow and steady breath. His throat burned as he said, "Don't worry. I swallowed it."

Bob laughed and shook his head. "Fucking rookie."

"Let's move," Alexus said, creeping down the stairs.

Ethan followed, holding his breath as much as he could as the smell intensified.

At the bottom of the stairs was a carpeted basement with a pool table and neon tiki bar signs lining the walls.

A flickering light streamed in from a cracked door on the other side of the room. Ethan stepped forward, pushing open the door and finding a beautiful television room filled with squashy leather couches and chairs. Toys and coloring books lined the wall, leading up to a massive TV airing images of animals in the African Sahara.

He brought his attention to the sofas, and right in the middle sat a corpse, bloated and covered in flies.

Ethan covered his nose and stepped back out into the poolroom. "Found it."

"Excuse me, young man. Can I help you?" an old voice called from behind him. Ethan spun around and came face to face with a ghostly version of the dead man.

Alexus slipped into the room, cracking the clasps on her briefcase open.

Ethan held up a hand to her and mouthed, "Just wait." He brought his attention to the ghost. "Mister Jenkins?"

The man nodded. "Yes? Can I help you?"

"I'm Ethan. I'm here to help."

"Help? My family's picking me up any minute. Can you make this quick? It's my grandkid's birthday. We're off to the zoo," he said with a smile. "Little Annie loves her animals."

Ethan bit his lip, pain ringing in his heart. "That sounds really nice."

"So, what is this about?" the old man asked.

"I need to show you something. Do you mind? It's in here," Ethan said, motioning to the television room.

"Yes. Yes. We just need to hurry. They'll be here soon," the old man said, following Ethan into the room.

Upon seeing his corpse, Wallace Jenkins didn't need any more convincing. He passed easily into the light after Ethan agreed to call his grandchildren and let them know he was sorry he was going to miss the trip.

Later, back in the office, Ethan would discover that the man had been suffering from dementia, and the trip to the zoo had occurred almost fifteen years ago. Annie, who was now a veterinarian outside of Cleveland, told Ethan she still remembered that day as she spoke to him over the phone.

Alexus clapped Ethan's back as they left the house. "You're getting pretty good at this, rookie. Keep it up and they might have to rewrite the manual."

Ethan felt his cheeks flush. "Thanks," he said with a shrug.

A second later, Chester Wainwright and his camera crew rushed out from the bushes, cameras in their faces.

"Stop right there!" Chester declared. Turning to the camera, he said, "We're streaming live in New Richmond where we've caught these monsters breaking and entering again! What did you assholes steal? Why are you terrorizing us?"

Alexus pushed past the camera and waved her hand. "Bob? You got this?"

Bob rubbed his hands together. "On it!"

"Wait. I don't think—" Ethan started.

Before he could finish, Bob jumped into Chester.

His eyes glowed blue, and he looked into the camera. "I can't believe all you stupid sheep. You know I'm being paid to film this, right? I'm a stupid college student who just wants to get rich off you dumb fucks! Don't you get it? Meeeooow."

Bob continued meowing into the camera through Chester as he puppeteered him to jump around. Ethan joined Alexus and hopped into the car, peering back at Chester. "Are you sure this is a good idea?" Ethan asked, eyeing the poor, confused college students who seemed to have no idea what was happening to their leader.

"Meh. We'll see. At least he's having fun," Alexus said as she started the engine.

Fifty-Five

Voted off Ghost Island

E THAN PEERED OUT AT the rows and rows of graves as he leaned up against a headstone in Oakland cemetery. One day, he'd be like them, buried six feet under in a place filled with experiences and memories lost to the living. Well, almost all the living.

He looked up at Mable. The elderly ghost stood still, her fists clenched and her eyes pinched shut. "It's alright," Ethan said to her. "It was just an idea."

"Quiet. Give me another second. Hold on, I almost have it," Mable said as she strained.

"She looks like she's gonna explode," Dylan, the young ghost sitting to the right of Ethan, said.

"Please don't pop, Ms. Mable," Jean, the last of the ghost children, said as she jumped up.

"I know this is hard and risky, but something in my gut tells me you have an answer locked up in there somewhere," Ethan said. He knew Buck would be pissed if he found out what they were doing. Mable had to attend to the children, and she couldn't if she crossed over. Yet, something inside Ethan told him that the night Mable died might hold some answers. Answers that might finally put the puzzle of New Richmond together.

Mable held the tension for another minute before relaxing. She sighed and crossed her arms. "Where do you get this idea again?"

"Stephenson's journal," he said with a shrug. "It said something about being able to retrieve memories with concentration."

Mable rested against the headstone and stared up at the sky. "Well, I guess I'm just not capable of that level of concentration."

"I don't believe that," Jean said with a smile.

"You had to watch over Harold and me. If you can do that, you can do anything," Dylan added.

"It was a long shot. Just keep trying, every day. Maybe you'll get something," Ethan said.

"I wish I could tell you more," Mable said.

A man cleared his throat and shouted. "Hey, um, so, like, are you going to do anything else today?"

Ethan looked over and spotted Ricky, the larger cameraman. He and his taller boom-mic-toting friend stood ten yards away, their camera pointed at Ethan.

"Maybe we are trying to concentrate in the wrong way," Ethan said, standing up and facing Mable. "Maybe we should try yoga? Like, a more relaxing, clear-your-mind thing?"

"Are you going to answer the big man with the camera?" Jean asked.

"Yeah. Ms. Mable says it's not nice to ignore people when they talk to you," Dylan said.

"It's also not nice to sneak away from the graveyard, and you two don't seem to care about that," Ethan said.

"Ethan," Mable said, wagging a finger at him.

He lowered his head and mumbled, "Sorry, Ms. Mable."

"Dylan is right. You should answer those poor boys. They've been standing over there for twenty minutes. Why don't you invite them to come and sit down with us? It's such a nice day," she said.

"Yeah. You should ask them to come over," Jean said.

"I could make them come over," Dylan offered with a grin.

"Absolutely not," Ethan said, pointing his finger at Dylan.

"Speaking of people being rude," Mable said, glaring down at Dylan.

Ricky let out a sigh. "Come on, man. Seriously? Chester said we can't leave until we have something good. Can you just run around like an idiot or something?"

"Where is the blond one? He's usually with these two, right?" Mable asked.

"True," Ethan said. Looking up at the camera crew, he called, "Hey. Where is Chester?"

The tall one called, "He's doing an interview."

"Greg, shut up. He said not to tell," Ricky said.

"What, am I supposed to care?" Greg asked.

"Look, man. I just want to go back home and watch some *Love Island*, alright? So, maybe just make one of those faces you make or something?" Ricky called over.

Jean frowned at Ethan. "You make faces?"

"No," Ethan said.

"He does. Like this," Dylan said, letting his jaw drop open and his eyes get big.

Ethan widened his eyes, his mouth readying to drop open before he caught himself. "I do not."

"Or remember when we were playing hide and seek and he said he was the master hider and then he did this," Jean said as she knit her eyebrows together and pursed her lips.

"Or remember the first time he came here with Agent Buck," Mable said. She looked at the ground and stuck out her bottom lip as if she were a baby about to cry.

"Hey, why are you joining in? None of that is true," Ethan said, pointing at all of them, but the ghosts just laughed in response.

"Wait, I have a question," Dylan said with a laugh.

"Yes, dear?" Mable asked.

"What's *Love Island*?"

"Yeah. Yeah. What's *Love Island*?" Jean asked.

"Well. Um," Ethan said as he struggled to find the words to explain the TV show to the children. "So, these really pretty people go to live on this island together."

"Why do they have to be pretty? Mable said not to judge people on looks. It's not nice." Jean said.

"That's a good point," Ethan said.

"What do they do on the island?" Dylan asked.

"Well, the pretty people go to the island and they all date each other," Ethan started again.

"They all date each other? Do they . . . kiss each other?" Jean asked.

"Well. No. Yes. I mean. They don't date each other. They take turns dating one another and then they . . . I don't know. Some of them get voted off the island if they can't get a date."

"Oh, that's sad. I don't like it," Jean said.

"That's mean. You shouldn't do that to people," Dylan said.

"He's right," Mable agreed.

"Well, don't look at me. I didn't do it," Ethan said.

"What if I was dating, like, three people and I got voted off an island? Would I see them again?" Jean asked.

Ethan shrugged. "I don't know what happens."

"We don't vote each other out of the cemetery," Dylan said, brimming with pride at the place where he lived.

"And if a new ghost comes? We're going to what?" Mable asked.

"Be nice and helpful," both children said with a smile.

"That's right," Mable said.

"Not like the people on Agent Ethan's horrible island," Jean said, eyeing Ethan with a glare.

"It's not my island. It's his island," Ethan said, motioning to Ricky.

"Why does he like to watch people be mean to each other?" Dylan asked.

Ethan called over to Ricky, "Hey, the ghosts want to know why you have such shitty taste in television."

"Screw you, man. Those people are hot," Ricky said.

"Super hot!" Greg added.

"Hot means pretty," Dylan said to Jean, who nodded.

"Okay. Let's focus," Ethan said, turning back to Mable. "I don't want to know about the night you were killed. I just want to know about your house. Before you died, did anyone come and ask about it? Did anyone make an offer? Anything at all? If I could just get to the bottom of it, I think I could stop some of the insanity going on around here."

"Well," she said, thinking. "I don't think so. I'm sorry. You know, I just didn't think about any of that. I went to get coffee with your granny on Monday, we had hamburgers on Tuesday, we played bridge on Thursday, and I went to church on Sunday. That was pretty much my life. I didn't really think about anything else. I just figured it would work itself out."

"That sounds fun," Dylan said, picking at a piece of grass with his ghostly fingers.

Jean fell back on the grass and stared up at the sky. "I want a burger."

"Dude! Come on! You're seriously killing me!" Ricky yelled. "Do something! Anything!"

Ethan smiled and looked at Mable. "Thanks for trying. I appreciate it."

"Can I take him over and make him dance around like a monkey? Please?" Dylan begged, eying Ricky.

"Hey," Ethan called. "One of them offered to possess you. Like with Chester? Would that make you leave me alone?"

Ricky pulled a large gold cross hanging on an oversized chain out from under his collar and yelled, "Try it, motherfucker! We've got protection now."

"What does he think that's going to do?" Jean asked with genuine curiosity.

"Nothing, dear. We're not vampires. The man is just being silly," Mable said.

Ethan whipped his head around. "Wait, vampires? Do you know if they're real? Are they real?"

Mable waved her hand at him. "I'm not at liberty to say."

"Maybe it shoots lasers," Dylan said with a smile. Making finger guns, he pointed at Ethan and said, "Pew pew pew."

Jean giggled and joined in. "Pew pew pew!"

Ethan kept an eye on Mable but grabbed his chest, pretending like they had shot him. He fell over, tongue sticking out.

"Quick!" Dylan said, jumping up. "We need to take him to Love Island!"

"To Love Island!" Jean said, jumping up. The two young ghosts stuck their arms out in the air as if they were wings and pretended to be planes. They chased each other through the graveyard, yelling about how they were voting each other off the island.

Ethan sat up and brushed off the grass. "Well, they seem to be doing better."

JP RINDFLEISCH IX & JEFF ELKINS

"Seeing Harold cross over was good for them. They needed to see him as their friend again and not what he was becoming," Mable said with a smile.

Ethan nodded. He was proud that he'd helped two of the four children move on. "Two down. Two to go," he said.

"Soon enough, they will all be together again," Mable said with a smile.

"Ms. Mable! Ms. Mable!" Dylan yelled, running toward them. "She's back! She's back!"

Mable and Ethan both stood and looked toward the entrance to find Jean, frozen in her tracks, staring down the pathway. The playfulness was gone from her face and had been replaced with fear.

Mable nodded to Dylan. "Thank you, sweetie." Looking at Ethan, she said, "You need to get that camera out of here. I'll get Jean."

"On it," Ethan said as he turned and jogged toward the camera.

At the sight of Ethan suddenly running at them, Ricky and Greg both backed up, eyes wide as they fumbled with their crosses.

"Stay back, motherfucker. I'll get Jesus all over your ass! Stay the fuck back!" Greg shouted.

Ethan slowed his pace and held his hands up. "Look, guys. A mourner is here. We need to get out of sight."

Not listening and certain his cross had worked, Ricky stepped forward and declared, "That's right, demon boy! I knew this shit would work." Glancing over his shoulder, he said to Greg, "See, bitch! I told you. I told you they were demons." Looking back at Ethan, still inching forward, he declared, "The power of Christ compels you, bitch. Back the fuck up."

Ethan snatched the plastic cross from Ricky's hands and yanked it from his neck.

"Ow! Shit!" Ricky yelled, grabbing his neck with one hand.

Throwing the cross into the grass, Ethan pointed at the two college students and channeled his inner Buck. "Now you two fuckers listen up. There's someone coming here to mourn, and you need to get out of sight. Right fucking now."

"Okay, man. Okay," Greg said, his hands up in the air.

Ethan pointed to a large above-ground tomb twenty yards away. "Over there. Follow me," he demanded.

"There's no fucking way I'm going inside there," Ricky said.

"Not inside it. Behind it, dumbass," Ethan said as he ushered the two students off toward the hiding place.

Ethan peered out at the graveyard from behind the tomb. He found Mable and Dylan with their arms wrapped around Jean, guiding her through a small grove of trees at the edge of the cemetery.

His heart raced as he wondered if this was the answer he'd been looking for that would help Jean cross over. He'd never seen anyone visit her before, and Mable had never mentioned anyone, but Jean had been here much longer than Mable.

A tug came at Ethan's pant leg, and he looked down to see Ricky lying in the grass with his camera. "Move, man, your leg is in my shot."

Ethan moved his leg even more to block the view. "Dude, cut it out. What's wrong with you? Film me all you want, but leave other people out of it."

Ricky sighed and pulled back his camera, standing behind Ethan. "Sorry man, you're right."

They all watched as a thin, stately woman emerged into the cemetery. Ethan immediately recognized her. Joan from the library.

He watched as she made her way to Jean's headstone and rested one white and one pink rose on top of her grave.

"How did I not see that connection?" Ethan whispered.

"Who's that?" Ricky whispered in Ethan's ear.

"Joan, the head librarian in town. I. I think Jean's her sister," Ethan said.

She stood at Jean's headstone for a long while before resting a small book next to the flowers. Breathing a sigh of relief, Ethan said to himself, "Finally. A lead."

"Fuck yeah, man," Greg said, clapping him on the back.

Fifty-Six

NRDS Go Camping

"WHO WAS THAT AGAIN?" Ethan asked as Bryce pulled up behind Buck's old clunker on the side of the road and killed his engine.

"The Tems. They're good, aren't they?" Bryce said.

"Yeah. Really good. Like everything you introduce me to. Could you send me that playlist?"

Bryce leaned over and planted a kiss on Ethan's cheek. "You're so cute."

Ethan's heart fluttered, and a shiver jolted up his spine. He turned and pulled in Bryce for another kiss. He could sit in this moment forever, savoring the simplistic beauty of the moment and Bryce's soft lips against his.

Bryce let out a laugh and backed away. "You ready?"

Ethan sighed and looked out the window, spotting the dirt trail that led off into the woods. "I don't know. Maybe we shouldn't even go. I mean, Melissa said it was optional."

"Ah, but team building is important. How else are adults supposed to make friends?" Bryce asked with a wry smile on his face.

Ethan rolled his eyes. "Oh, shut up. The last thing we need is more team building. Sometimes I think we're too close. The other day, Alexus went into great detail about her recent conquest. I. I didn't even know people were that flexible."

Bryce laughed as he pushed his door open and stepped out. "Alexus doesn't count. She has no filter."

Ethan hopped out of the car and looked over the roof of the car. "Okay. But let's think about this. They are going to be pissed when they find out. They don't have to know. Are you sure you want to deal with all that drama?"

Bryce chuckled. "I don't think Gerry has ever been pissed about anything in his entire life."

"Okay. Fair. But Alexus? She might stab us. Like, literally stab us. You know she carries an entire arsenal in there," Ethan said, pointing across the street to where Alexus's car was parked. "She had a shotgun strapped under the car. I saw it the other day."

"Yeah, yeah. Come on. Let's get this over with," Bryce said as he started down the path toward the campsite.

Ethan followed like a puppy on a leash being led to the vet. They walked through the woods together for five minutes until they came upon a clearing. A fire pit sat in the center of the clearing with nine chairs around it. Gerry, Buck, Alexus, Bob, and Doris were already occupying chairs with alcoholic beverages in hand.

"Gentlemen! Welcome!" Gerry called, jumping up from his chair and almost spilling his martini. He gave them both a hug and wrapped an arm around Ethan. "Come over and have a seat."

The knot in Ethan's chest loosened as Gerry led them to two seats next to Doris. She held a massive mug with a bright pink straw protruding out of it. "What are you drinking?" Ethan asked.

She pulled the drink away from her and eyed it. "Well, you know. I'm not sure. Gerry gave it to me, and I can't put the thing down."

Bryce waved at Doris as he sat. "So, how is everyone's site coming along?"

"Buck helped me with mine," Doris said, her words slurring together as she motioned behind her to the simple green tent some ways behind her. "He even got my cot up."

"And we got here early to set up," Gerry said, motioning to the other side of the clearing where a circular tent that resembled a mini circus tent was standing open. Through the tent opening, Ethan could see a fluffy looking bed with a checkered bedspread, a red Persian-looking rug, and several decorative baskets of pillows. There were twinkle lights hanging inside the tent, illuminating the space, and a small refrigerator stationed next to the door.

"Wow. That's an impressive setup. We should've talked to them," Bryce said, nudging Ethan.

"Well, if Buck had his way, we'd spend the night in sleeping bags in tiny army tents, but I told him when we started dating that if I had to spend an evening outside, I was going to do it in style. You know they named the term 'glamping' after me, right?"

"Still think my old army tent would be just fine," Buck grunted as he sipped a bourbon.

"Tell that to your chiropractor, dear," Gerry said with a wave of his hand.

"Where are you at?" Ethan asked Alexus.

"Bob and I are over there," Alexus said, using her beer to motion behind her.

Ethan squinted into the darkness and finally made out a shabby-looking hammock hanging between two trees. "Is that it? Just a hammock?"

"Now, that's real camping," Buck said, toasting Alexus with his beer.

"Bob's here?" Bryce asked.

Bob nodded, a smile across his face. Ethan was shocked. He'd been so used to him hurling insults at everyone, he'd forgotten or maybe never experienced a relaxed Bob. "He's next to Alexus. Just . . . smiling," he told Bryce.

"Oh, Bob's here? That's so nice. Cheers to you, Bob," Doris said in a dreamy voice as she took another sip of her drink.

"What'd you give her?" Bryce asked with a laugh.

Tapping the side of his nose, Gerry said, "It's my secret. Made it special for her."

"And it's wonderful," Doris said.

"Mother-bastard-asshole!" A shout sounded from behind Ethan. Turning in his chair, he noticed Melissa for the first time in a corner of the clearing behind him. The fabric of her tent was twisted into a strange X. Above her head, she held two giant tent poles that were bent at angles they were clearly not intended to be.

"Does she need help?" Bryce asked.

"Hey, Melissa. You want help yet?" Buck called with a grin.

"Go fuck a gorilla, you old dried-up turd!" she yelled back, twisting the poles in a different direction and getting herself further tangled in the tent. "A big gorilla. Go fuck a five-hundred-pound gorilla, you nosy old fart."

Bob laughed. "That one was pretty good."

"How long has she been at that?" Ethan asked.

"At least an hour," Gerry said, frowning. "We keep offering to help, and she keeps telling us no."

"Usually with a fantastic string of profanities," Alexus said.

"Oh, my! I almost forgot! Your drinks!" Gerry said, and he rushed away to his tent.

Motioning to the tent, Bryce asked, "I don't hear a generator."

"We used to have one," Buck said. "But we snagged a battery and some panels a few years back. It's a lot quieter and does the trick."

"God, you two are literally the coolest couple," Ethan said.

"That's true," Doris chimed in, slurring her words slightly. "I find myself asking 'what would Gerry or Buck do' all the time. Two weeks ago, I was at the grocery store about to get my regular box of wine when I asked what Buck and Gerry would do. I got myself a fine bottle of pinot and drank the whole thing." She took a big sip of her drink and winked at Buck.

"Maybe you should slow down," Buck suggested.

Clutching the mug, she glared at Buck and said, "If you try to take this from me, I will murder you right here in these woods." She stroked the side of her mug and added, "This is all I've ever wanted in the entire world."

"Bitch-ass whore of a tent!" Melissa yelled. Ethan turned just in time to see her scream, "Motherfucker!" and throw one of the tent poles javelin-style into the woods.

Alexus clapped and called, "8.2. Good distance. Poor form!"

"You can't pitch the tent without that," Buck yelled without looking at her.

"Well. Shit," Melissa said before tromping through the underbrush after it.

"Who the fuck invited you?" Alexus shouted behind Ethan.

Ethan turned, finding River standing at the entrance of the clearing with a duffel bag under one arm.

River winced and gave a half smile. "Hey guys."

"I invited him," Gerry said, stepping out of the tent with two cocktails in hand. "His suspension lifts next week, and you all need to work out some stuff before then."

Bob glowed a bright blue, and Alexus stood up.

As his mouth moved, so did Alexus's. "The fuck I do."

"This probably wasn't a good idea, dear," Buck said.

River waved his hand at Bob, badge in hand. "Hey Bob. I. I was such a dick. I'm sorry."

Bob frowned, his glow dimmed, and Alexus shook her head before knocking back her beer and plopping down in her seat. "Leave me out of this, Bob."

"You've never said sorry before," Bob said.

River shrugged and looked down at the dirt. "I didn't treat you right. I let that get to my head."

"You left me in a potpourri store!"

"I know. Things got out of hand, and that's on me. I don't expect you to forgive me. I just hope you're happier with Alexus."

Bob nodded, "I am."

"Then I won't take that from you."

The tension in the air lifted. "Good," Bob said.

River dropped his bags and headed toward an empty seat.

Doris let out a sigh and took another big gulp of her drink. "Well, seeing as nothing is flying, can we get the drinks flowing? I need everyone on my level."

Alexus stuck out her hand as River passed. "Gimme what I want, and we're all good."

River pulled out a joint from his pocket and handed it to her. "Freshly rolled, just for you."

Alexus fist bumped him and pulled a lighter from her pocket.

Gerry smiled. "Well, that's settled." He handed Bryce a frosty dark concoction. "A black velvet for you." He handed Ethan an amber colored liquid with ice in it, "And a dark and stormy for you."

Ethan took a sip and immediately tasted rum and ginger. His eyes widened, and he took another sip. "This is amazing."

"Planned it just for you," Gerry said with a smile. "Now, River, I've got something special for you. Anyone else need a top off while I'm up?"

"I'll have another," Alexus called.

"Me too," Buck nodded.

"You are a beautiful man. Just a beautiful man," Doris said.

"Melissa? Can we help you now, dear?" Gerry called to Melissa as she emerged from the woods with her tent pole in hand.

Pointing the pole at him, she yelled, "I don't want to say mean things to you. Because I like you." Pointing the pole at Buck, she yelled, "Stop smiling at me, you old, wrinkly ball sack!"

"I wish I had someone taking notes. These are golden," Bob said with a grin.

"'Old, wrinkly ball sack'," River said as he typed on his phone. "I got you, bud."

"Well, this ball sack is here when you're ready to give up and let me help you," Buck said, toasting her with his beer.

"I'd rather this pole get shoved through my eye than get help from you!" she screamed.

Doris laughed. "That reminds me of the last time I camped. Now, don't tell anyone, but Ben and I went to this swingers camp, and some bitch named Carol stole my bra. She apparently was hell bent on making a tent entirely made from bras. Could you imagine?"

Ethan stared at Doris in horror. Flashbacks of the undulating ghosts raced through his mind as he tried to forget what Doris told him.

She shrugged. "What? Do you think I'm just some old boring lady?"

"I knew you had a wild side." Bryce grinned.

"When we're ready," Gerry said from his seat. "I've prepared a delightful build-your-own shish kabob bar for dinner. We'll be able to roast the food over the open fire."

Ethan looked at the faces around the circle, and a wave of guilt surged in his stomach. Gerry had worked so hard to make this a beautiful evening, and he was about to ruin it. He took a sip of his drink and then said, "I have a confession to make."

"You're not camping with us," Alexus said.

Ethan's mouth fell open. "How'd you know?"

"No tent," Buck said.

"No bags," Alexus added.

"And you're a general pansy-ass who's probably scared of bugs, you fucking sissy," Bob said with a grin.

"We got a hotel room up the road," Bryce said.

Looking down at the ground, Ethan explained, "I don't like sleeping outside. My granny made me do Boy Scouts as a kid. I swore I'd never camp again." Looking up at Gerry, he said, "But this is really nice, and I feel terrible that we aren't staying the night."

"As long as you stay for the s'mores, then I'll consider this a success," Gerry said.

"I mean, who would miss the s'mores?" Ethan said.

Stomping into the circle, Melissa went to the two empty chairs next to Alexus. There were small twigs protruding from her hair, and her blue track suit was covered in grass stains. "Which one is the asshole in?" Bob laughed as Alexus nodded to him. Melissa took the chair next to him and said, "Gerry! Drink me!"

"Absolutely. I'll be right back," Gerry said, jumping up from his chair and heading back to his tent.

"You give up yet?" Buck asked.

"Fuck you," she said. She swiped the joint out of Alexus's hand and took a drag, sitting back in her chair and closing her eyes. "I was just thinking that I probably don't need a tent. I'll just sleep here tonight."

"Excuse me, everyone," Buck said, as he got up from his chair and headed to Melissa's tent.

Returning, Gerry handed Melissa a large stout beer. The mug appeared to be frosted. She accepted it and took a long sip. Leaning back again, she said, "You are my favorite person tonight."

Gerry grinned and took his seat. "This is nice, everyone. There is no better way to spend a holiday than with people you love." Raising his martini glass for a toast, he said, "Here's to you. The most wonderful civil servants in the Midwest."

"Merry Christmas!" Doris proclaimed, proudly holding up her mug.

"And happy Labor Day," Bryce said with a grin, returning the toast.

"Happy Labor Day," everyone else replied.

Fifty-Seven

I Dream of Bingo

E THAN LOOKED AROUND THE huddle. The sweat and breath of the eleven exhausted and muddy guys in the circle with him created a cloud of heat. He could see more tops of helmets than eyes and his heart sank, knowing they were on the verge of giving up.

He glanced at the scoreboard. 27 to 21 with 15 seconds on the clock. This was it. Their last chance. He shook his shoulders and nodded. "Alright, we're not giving up, guys. All eyes on me." Everyone in the circle met his gaze. "This is it. Last play. Last chance. For us seniors, this is the moment we decide if we ride home as champions or almost-weres. I-Formation. Forty-Eight Option-Right. Twenty-two yards to glory, guys. What are we?"

"Champions!" the others shouted.

"What are we?" Ethan shouted back.

"Champions!" the huddle roared back at him.

The energy vibrated through him, and newfound life lit up in his teammates' eyes. "Let's bring it home!" his running back yelled, and the huddle erupted in clapping and yelling.

Ethan stepped back and yelled, "Let's show these guys why we're New Richmond Champions! On three! One. Two. Three! Break!"

The huddle scattered and moved to the line. His five linemen and two tight ends made a line in front of him. His wide receiver jogged out to the far right. He stepped up behind his center as the two running backs aligned behind him.

Time slowed as he looked at the stands. Everyone he loved was there. His grandmother sat with her arm around Ellie, and next to them sat the ghostly forms of his parents. In front of his grandmother were Buck and Gerry. Next to them were Alexus, Doris, Trevor, River, and Bob. On the other side of his grandmother was Bryce. He smiled and Ethan smiled back, knowing that everything would be alright.

Ethan leaned forward, putting his hands under his center. He looked left down the line and then right, locking eyes with the three linebackers: Chax Tamish, Melissa, and Mayor Davies. They were locked on him, glaring, ready to rush in on him and rob him of his destiny.

"Hut! Hut!" Ethan screamed, and he saw Chax twitch forward. Ethan eyed the goal, twenty yards away, and smiled. Nothing could stop him.

"Hike!" he screamed, and the field erupted into action as the ball came into his hands. Pivoting on his left foot, he spun and headed right. Meeting the first running back at the four hole between the guard and tackle, he glanced left and saw Melissa rushing to fill the gap. Ethan let the back pass through without giving him the ball and felt the collision between him and Melissa. Rushing forward, he came to the end of the line and turned up field. He saw, out of the right side of his helmet, his second running back tracking a step behind him, ready for the pitch.

Ethan's heart raced as he turned up field. His heart pounded in his ears. Mayor Davies was there, waiting for him, and Ethan knew he had to force the man to decide. Locking eyes with the threat in front of him, he jab-stepped to the right. Mayor Davies committed and dove to block the pitch that Ethan didn't throw.

Racing forward, Ethan felt the yards passing under his feet. A faceless cornerback dove for his legs, but he hurdled over the defender. Another bared down on him from the left, but he spun to the right, away from the attacker's attempt to bring him down. With five yards left, he could see out of the left side of his helmet Chax Tamish taking an angle on him. The linebacker charged. Rather than pitching, Ethan picked up speed. With his eyes on the goal line, he lowered his shoulder and collided with Chax. Pumping his legs, Ethan erupted through the attacker, knocking Chax off his feet as they both crossed the goal line.

He crashed into the ground, and the stadium erupted in cheers. The band burst into song and his team was on him, piling on top of him, banging on his helmet and screaming at the top of their lungs.

As the mass cleared, one of his teammates held out a white-gloved hand and helped pull him to his feet. "Agent. Agent Malik," his teammate said.

Ethan faced the roaring stands and held up the ball. Everyone cheered, waving their arms high in the air. He was a champion. He'd done it. His team would be remembered as the ones who'd brought honor and glory to New Richmond.

His teammate grabbed his left arm again. Ethan looked down at the player's oversized shoes as he heard, "Agent Malik. Agent Malik. We need you."

Ethan pushed him off and mumbled, "Go away." He looked back at the stands and locked eyes with Bryce. He pointed the football at him, and Bryce smiled and clapped. Ethan's cheeks hurt from grinning, and he thought his heart might burst from his chest.

His teammate grabbed his left arm again. "Agent Malik. Please. Wake up."

Ethan pushed him off again and raced toward the stands. He jumped the fence and raced up the stands. Cold air hit his face as he pulled off his chin strap and yanked off his helmet, feeling the icy sweat drip down from his head. Each step he took seemed to stretch the distance between him and Bryce instead of shrinking it.

Bryce stepped down the stairs toward him, his white button down tucked perfectly into his blue slacks. Ethan wanted nothing more than to take him into his arms. Yet, with each step Bryce took, another two steps seemed to separate them.

A hand wrapped around his left arm again, and he turned. Terror filled his chest at the sight of a clown in full makeup, red nose, and rainbow wig standing inches from his face. Ethan pulled away, but the clown moved closer. "Wakey, wakey, eggs and bakey!" The clown laughed.

Ethan slipped on the stands and fell, his stomach twisting and turning as the world melted before his eyes. Adrenaline filled his veins, and he lurched up in bed.

He gripped the sheets with both hands, trying to catch his breath. He looked over at Bryce on his right, still fast asleep, his hair tousled and his mouth opened slightly.

As Ethan caught his breath, he glared at Bryce, irritated by the fact that he could be so attractive even early in the morning as he lay here fast asleep.

His breathing slowed, and he looked around the room. Things were as they were supposed to be. No murderous clowns were waiting for him. He was safe.

He lay back down, nestling into the pillow and pulling the sheets back over him as he closed his eyes.

"Wakey, wakey, Agent Malik," a strange voice said in Ethan's ear.

Ethan screamed and jerked up. Terror rushed through his body once again. He peered into the dark and made out the ghostly shape of a clown to his left. He screamed again.

"No, no, no. Wait, wait," the clown said.

"What the fuck!" Ethan yelled as he grasped for his badge on the nightstand to his left.

"What's happening?" Bryce said, sitting up and rubbing his eyes.

"Agent! No! It's me!" the clown said, holding up a flower.

"Fuck off!" Ethan screamed as he thrust his badge into the clown's chest. The spirit flew across the room, flying through the bedroom wall. Ethan jumped up, pulling on a pair of sweatpants and looking in all directions.

"What in the hell is going on?" Bryce asked.

"We're under attack," Ethan said through gritted teeth.

Bryce rubbed his eyes and grabbed his glasses from the nightstand. "Under attack by what?"

"A fucking ghost clown," Ethan said.

Bryce let out a laugh and shook his head. "Are you sure it wasn't just a bad dream? Come back to bed."

Ethan squinted his eyes and looked left and right, examining each shadow for the intruder. "It was a good dream. Until that bastard tried to kill me in my sleep."

Bryce looked at the clock next to him. "It's three-thirty in the morning."

"Yeah. I know," Ethan said, inching toward the door.

Hands materializing through the wall, followed by the clown. "I surrender."

"Got you, you bastard!" Ethan yelled as he hit the clown with his badge again. This time, the clown crashed to the ground.

"No! No! Wait!" the clown said.

"Bryce! There's a case under my bed. Grab it!" Ethan said as he held the badge over the ghost.

"Wait! Agent Malik! It's me! Bingo Bango," the clown pleaded with a smile.

"Why do you have a case under your bed?" Bryce asked.

"Just hand it over. I'm going to case this bastard clown and then we can go back to bed."

"What? No. You've got it wrong," the clown said with a nervous laugh.

"Agent Malik. Please," a new voice said from the other side of the room. Ethan whipped his head around to see Lester Buchalter, Chax Tamish's murdered assistant, emerge from the shadows. Dressed in his sleek blue suit and thick black glasses, he said, "We came here to alert you, not to hurt you."

"Oh! Is it time to rhyme?" Bingo asked. "Bingo Bango thinks on a dime, which really is sublime, as long as entertainment isn't a crime, but he would happily take the fine."

"It's too early for that shit. And that last one didn't even rhyme," Ethan barked.

"Please. Agent," Lester begged. "We didn't mean to scare you. I'm so sorry. We need your help."

Bryce held up the briefcase and shook it. "Can you please tell me what is going on?"

Ethan tossed the badge to Bryce. "Here. Take this."

"Snake hiss. Fake bliss. Make piss. Cake mix," Bingo chimed to himself.

Bryce picked the badge up from where it landed on the bed, looked up, and said, "Oh. Hello."

Lester nodded and Bingo giggled out, "Hello, mellow bed fellow."

"Alright," Ethan said, his pulse finally calming. "Tell me what in the fuck would make you two think it was a good idea to break into my house in the middle of the night."

"We had to shake the Agent awake because there was a lot at stake."

Ethan shoved a finger in Bingo's face. "I mean it. Cut that shit out."

Bingo shrugged and gave an uncomfortable smile. "Fit trout. Hit bout. Get doubt."

The door creaked behind him, and Ethan's heart raced. His muscles flexed as he prepared to launch himself at another intruder, but it was only Ellie. "What's going on?" she asked, rubbing her eyes.

"Clear here we're queer, so stay near," Bingo mumbled.

Ellie frowned, her sleepy eyes gazing at Bingo.

Grinding his foot through Bingo's face, Ethan smiled at his sister and said, "Go back to sleep, El. It's nothing."

She rubbed her eyes again and looked through the darkness. "Hey, Bryce."

"Hi Ellie," he said with a nod.

"Are you staying to make me pancakes again in the morning?" she asked.

Bryce smiled. "With blueberry compote?"

She yawned and nodded.

"Of course. But first, you need to get some more sleep," he said.

"Okay," she waved, closing the door behind her.

"Smo-kay, No-kay," Bingo started, but Ethan pointed down at him with a stern finger.

"One more word and I'll case you. I mean it," he growled.

Lester stepped forward. "Look. I'm sorry we barged in. It's just, there's something happening, and we didn't know where else to go."

"What's happening?" Bryce asked.

"It's this house. It's. Well. It's pulling all the spirits around from their graveyards and drawing them to it," Lester said.

Bryce frowned. "That doesn't seem right. Vortexes aren't strong enough to do that."

"Yet tonight, we fight the vortex plight even though its pull is might. So we might shed light on Agent's sights," Bingo said with a proud smile.

"Give me the case," Ethan said to Bryce, holding his hand out.

Bryce held the case out. "Why is this thing under your bed?"

"Once the kids started traveling, Buck said it was a good idea to always be prepared," Ethan said.

"Look. We don't have time for this," Lester said, crossing the room. "You can see it out the window," he said, pointing to the closed shades.

Ethan walked over to the window and pulled the blinds back. His mouth fell open when he looked out into the night. About a mile away, he could make out a large blue light shooting up into the sky. The source of the light was blocked by rows and rows of houses, but he could tell it was coming from the middle of a nearby neighborhood. Joining him, Bryce looked over his shoulder and asked, "What is that?"

"We need to move," Ethan said.

Bryce snapped into action, pulling on a pair of sweatpants from on top of the dresser. "We're going to need more than the case under your bed. Call Buck. Get the team moving."

"On it," Ethan said as gripped the case and pulled his phone off the dresser.

Fifty-Eight

Beam Me Up

E THAN, BRYCE, LESTER, AND Bingo Bango pulled up to a 1980s style suburban house that matched nearly every other house on the street, complete with a two-car garage with an attached basketball hoop, a pink tricycle discarded in the front yard, a tall cedar tree that dominated the right side of the lawn with a plastic swing hanging from one of its branches, and a clean brick path leading up to the front door.

This house was lived in, and from what little details Ethan had, he could tell it was a happy family. Even the mailbox, which contrasted the simple brick mailboxes of the neighborhood, was a custom-carved wooden cardinal, complete with a little door that read, "The Anthonys."

As he stepped out of the car, he imagined his life in this house. Coming home from college with a sack of laundry over his shoulder and sauntering in through the garage, passing his mother in the kitchen while she was making dinner, tossing his month's worth of dirty clothes in the laundry room, and finding his dad in the living room with the game on the TV and a book in his hand. Ellie would stop whatever dubious plan she was concocting in her room and come running down the stairs when his mom yelled, "Ethan's home!" and wrap her arms around his neck. Then she'd dive into a slew of updates about her friends and the wild adventures she'd had without him.

He'd have no inkling of a different world. One where his parents were no longer there, and he had to drop out of college and pick up the first job he could to help cover the bills for his grandmother as he and his sister upended her life. He'd never known a life that led him here, standing in front of a brilliant blue beam shooting into the sky and a crowd of translucent spirits staring up at the light.

"This is . . . I've never seen anything like it. There are no words," Bryce said, stepping beside Ethan.

Lester phased through the car. "You see now why it was so important that we had to wake you up?"

Bingo cartwheeled through the car and held his hands up to the sky as his feet lifted off the ground. "It's like a tractor beam from outer space sucking all the ghosts to the mothership. Beam me up, Scotty!"

Ethan opened his mouth to ask Bingo how he could levitate but shut his mouth, knowing the clown wouldn't give a straight answer. Instead, he stared at the beam of light. All his worries seemed to melt away. All he wanted to do was stare.

"What do you think?" Bryce asked.

Ethan pulled his attention away from the light of the vortex and focused on the spirits swirling around it. Some were dressed in bathrobes, others in suits, and a myriad of both age and decade of death. Nearly all their faces were blank and trained within the house, at the unseen source of light.

"I don't know," Ethan said. "Looks like all the ghosts are in a trance or something."

"Alright, which one of you fuckups did this?" Alexus said, her voice in Ethan's ear.

Ethan jumped and fell on the grass in front of him. "Jesus Christ! Stop doing that!"

Alexus held out a hand and pulled Ethan back up to his feet. "Then don't fucking call me at o'dark-thirty in the morning for this kind of shit."

"There's like a thousand ghosts out here. What was I supposed to do?" Ethan asked.

"Put on your big boy pants and clean up your own messes," Alexus said.

"Oooh. I like this one," Bingo said, bending forward to see Alexus. Holding out a deck of ghostly cards, he said, "Pick a card. Any card."

Alexus smiled. "So this is the reason Bob won't get out of the car. I'm gonna case him."

"No! Wait! You can't!" Lester yelled, stepping between Alexus and Bingo.

"Oh, glory goggins!!" Bingo yelled. The weird expression he used made Ethan hate him more.

"Maybe a case will do him some good," Ethan said, grinning at Alexus and knowing full well she had no intention of following through.

"No! We helped! We brought you here!" Lester screamed.

"Morning!" someone shouted from down the street.

Ethan turned and saw Buck. Relief washed over him, certain Buck would know what to do.

Buck held out a carrier with four coffee cups in it. "Gerry got a new pour over and insisted I bring some samples of his autumn spice oat milk lattes."

"I love your husband," Bryce said, taking a cup.

"Don't mind if I do. Is this from that Ethiopian farm he was talking about?"

Buck nodded and frowned. "Where's River?"

Ethan shrugged. "He never answered his phone."

"Coffee! Just what the doctor ordered," Bingo said, picking up a cup from the container. He lifted it to his mouth, and a stream of tan liquid splashed onto the pavement at his feet.

Buck ignored Bingo completely and handed Ethan the last coffee.

Ethan eyed Bingo and the now empty floating cup. "You know you're not funny, right? You just make me nervous."

Bingo's face transformed, his features growing sharp. He smiled, opened a mouth full of pointed teeth. "Do I frighten you in your nethers? Do I make your balls knock in your knockers?"

"I really want to case him," Alexus said.

"We all do, but he knows something," Bryce replied, shaking his head. Pointing to the house, he said, "and we've got bigger issues to manage right now. Buck, have you ever seen anything like this?"

"I saw one out in Arizona, but that grabbed a handful of ghosts. This thing is ten times bigger than that."

Bryce frowned, staring up at the sky before saying, "Hold on. You were at the '87 Sedona outbreak?"

"Yep. Back when ten ghosts was an all hands on deck issue. Called out of Chicago on assist."

Bryce gave Buck a nod. "How'd you shut the vortex down?"

"We didn't. It was naturally occurring. Something about the spiritual energy of the place coming to a head."

"You think this is that?" Ethan asked.

"Well, the Sedona one had been there forever. This one just started tonight," Buck said.

Alexus sipped her coffee and said, "We'd need a hundred cases to get all these locked up."

"I've never seen so many in one place before. Even in Sedona, there were only fifty max," Buck said. The concern in his voice sent a chill down Ethan's spine. If Buck was scared, then this was bad.

"What do we do?" Ethan asked.

"Has anyone checked on the family yet? The . . ." Buck leaned to peer at the fancy mailbox. "The Anthonys?"

They all shook their heads.

"Where's Bob?" Buck asked.

"He's being a chicken shit in the car," Alexus said. "But he might get caught in the beam, anyway."

"It appears the answer to all your problems is the magic of Bingo Bango!" the clown announced, throwing his hands in the air, ghostly sparks shooting from his fingers.

"Do that shit again, and I'll case you. I mean it," Alexus said, pointing at him.

Ethan took a deep breath. "No. I'll do it."

Bryce shook his head. "Wait? Hold on. You don't know what's in there? What if this is being caused by some kind of supercharged spirit?"

Ethan handed his briefcase to Buck. "This is something weird which has an impact on most ghosts. I'm the weirdo with psychic abilities. It has to be me."

"Bingo and Agent Ethan! A crime fighting duo that the world has never seen!" Bingo proclaimed, materializing next to Ethan wearing sweatpants and a T-shirt that matched exactly what Ethan had on.

"You better fuck right off, right now," Ethan said.

"We could send in this one," Bryce said, motioning to Lester.

"Can't trust him. He might have caused it," Buck said.

"I did not," Lester replied.

"Yet you still won't tell us who killed you," Alexus said.

"Well, I just . . . I can't. Not yet. It would put you all in danger," Lester replied, his eyes on the ground.

"Explain," Buck demanded.

"I can't. Not right now." Lester took off his ghostly glasses and cleaned them. "Besides. Don't we have more pressing matters at hand?" Lester asked, motioning toward the giant beacon.

"Fine, but you can't dodge the case for long. Either we get answers, or you better get used to confined spaces," Buck said with a sneer.

"Alright," Ethan said, rolling his neck like he used to before going into a football game. "Let's do this."

"How are you getting inside?" Buck asked.

"The door?" Ethan asked.

Buck shook his head. "Ten bucks it's locked."

"I got you," Alexus said as she turned and jogged to her car. She returned with a metal baseball bat and pointed it at the house. "Pick a window."

"So, we aren't going to try the door?" Ethan asked.

"You're wasting time," Buck said.

Ethan met Buck's gaze and shrugged. "Uh, I guess let's do the big one over there," he said, pointing at a set of windows that likely led into the living room and went almost to the ground. He wished he could see in them, but everything inside the house was swallowed in the blue blur of the light.

"When you're ready," Alexus said.

Ethan passed Bryce his coffee and gave him a peck on the cheek. "Hold this for me. I'll be right back." Looking at Alexus, he said, "Now."

They raced through the crowd of ghosts, Ethan's body temperature dropping as he slipped through their icy silhouettes. They stomped over the flowerbed and Alexus held up the bat, ramming it through the window in one hit. She cleared the remaining shards of glass in one circular motion and nodded to Ethan before backing away, her lips already turning blue.

Ethan held his breath, diving into the house headfirst.

He landed on the carpet and jumped to his feet. A loud beeping sound came from a room deeper in the house, and the glare of the beacon was so bright it took a few moments for his eyes to adjust. Spirits packed the room, shoulder to shoulder, all staring off toward the source of light.

He closed his eyes and focused on his time practicing with Bob. They'd made it a weekly schedule to test the limits of Ethan's abilities. He imagined a bubble around him, something blue that functioned as a sort of shield. As he did, the ghosts closest to him shifted, clearing a path ahead.

The room was freezing as it was, with so many spirits in one place, absorbing every ounce of energy to stay anchored to the earth. He was glad the bubble worked, preventing him from outright collapsing from hypothermia.

Ethan pushed forward, wading through the crowd and into the dining room, where the light was so overwhelming he had to cover his eyes.

The beeping sound was louder here too, and as he waved his arms around in front of him, his arm slammed into something, knocking it onto the ground.

The room went dark in an instant, and Ethan blinked, resetting his vision as the surrounding ghosts shuffled and shouted.

He covered his ears as the spirits screamed. "Where am I?", "What's happening?", and "How do I get home?"

Someone wrapped an arm around him and pulled him to his feet, pulling him down a hallway and out the front door.

He fell onto the front porch and caught his breath, the voices clearing out of his mind. He looked up at a large woman in a black tracksuit and sunglasses with a large box tucked under one arm. "Melissa?"

She looked down at him with her arms crossed. "Good thing I showed up when I did."

The rest of the team raced toward him. Bryce pulled him up and away from the house as he asked, "Are you okay?"

"Yeah. I'm fine. I'm fine," Ethan said.

"Where in the fuck did you come from?" Alexus asked, pointing her bat at Melissa.

"I came from my fucking house when Buck here didn't answer his phone. I've been getting calls for the past hour from two states over about this blue fucking vortex. You know that window is coming out of your paycheck, right? Did any of you fuckwads think to check if the back door was unlocked?" She pulled off her shades and pointed them at Buck. "But the real question is, why did it take you so long to get here?"

"What's with the box?" Buck asked, nodding toward the toaster-sized black box Melissa had tucked under one arm.

She tucked her shades away and held the box up, turning it over. "The source of that fucking beam. I'm taking it in. Maybe R&D can shed some light on it."

Alexus frowned and pointed her bat at Melissa. "Since when do you go on field missions?"

"Since I have corporate up my fucking ass and my team doesn't pick up the damn phone." She stuffed the box under her arm and pointed a finger at Alexus. "I don't like your tone, Agent. Maybe some time down in Mexico will do you good. Let's see how your leather jacket looks in a hundred-degree heat."

Alexus rested the bat on her shoulder and shrugged. "My bikini game is pretty spot on too."

Melissa pushed through them and headed to a car parked up the street. "Just be glad you are all still employed. Two points to me for saving the day, and Ethan's stupid ass."

"And the family? Are they okay?" Buck called.

Melissa turned around and rolled her eyes at him. "They're on vacation. Happy?"

As she walked away, Ethan rubbed his head and asked, "How does she know they're on vacation?"

"Good question, kid," Buck said.

Fifty-Nine

Jean Bean

RIVER PUT THE CAR into park across from the library, looked at Ethan in the passenger seat and then the child ghost in the backseat. He frowned and gripped the steering wheel. "You two are sure this is going to work?"

Ethan looked out his window and nodded. "If Jean says it's going to work, then it'll work."

Jean sniffled in the backseat and wiped at her cheek. "It's the last thing on the list. I'm ready."

"Well, let's make it quick," River said, eyeing the clock on the dashboard. The time flipped to noon, and his leg shook up and down.

"You okay, dude?" Ethan asked. "You're never in a rush. Where's the fire?"

"It's nothing. Everything's fine. I'm good."

"You don't sound good, Mr. Agent River," Jean said. "She's not that bad. You don't need to be scared. She'll be nice. I promise."

"What? No. I'm not scared," River replied, shaking his head and leaning back in his seat.

Ethan smirked back at Jean and said, "It's okay, man. Ghosts are scary."

Jean let out a giggle.

"You can fuck right off," River said, jamming a finger in Ethan's face. He glanced at the clock again. "I said I was fine. Everything is fine. Alright? It's fine."

"You said 'fine' three times. I think that means you aren't fine," Jean said.

"She's very intuitive for her age," Ethan said with a grin.

"Hey!" Jean shouted. "I'm older than both of you!"

"Good, then fuck you too," River said, pointing at Jean. "I felt bad cussing out a kid, but fuck you." He turned back to Ethan and said, "And fuck you again. I've got somewhere to be, alright Nancy Drew? Is that a sin? Is it against some rule in the manual I haven't read? Oh. What's that? That's right. You wouldn't fucking know because you've barely read it."

Ethan laughed and raised his hands. "Alright, calm down. I'm sorry. You just never have anywhere to be. Is it a date?"

Jean leaned forward, her eyes wide. "A date? With who? Who are you dating?"

River rolled his eyes. "You two caught me. Yep, it's a date. With a hot babe. We've got an early afternoon date at the strip mall, and right after that we're gonna have a shotgun wedding and make babies. We might even get a dog with a waggy tail."

Jean rested her chin in her hands. "Aw, that sounds nice. Maybe you can get a white picket fence to go around your trailer together."

"Oh, fuck off, Casper," River yelled as he got out of the car.

Ethan hopped out of his seat and met River at the trunk, both grabbing their briefcases before heading toward the library.

Ethan felt a surge of energy run through his chest and he stood up straight. Today was a good day. He could feel it. Some days he got attacked by monkeys, some days he had to run into a house of murderous rednecks, and some days he had to battle German ghosts in Christmas stores, but today he was going to help Jean cross over, and that made everything else worth it.

They pushed open the doors of the library and, as usual, the only person in the building in the middle of the week was the head librarian, Joan, standing behind the circulation desk with her nose buried in a book.

"Hey Joan, what are you reading today?" Ethan asked.

Joan looked up from her book and turned it over. "A young adult paranormal novel by a local author."

Ethan nodded. "Is it any good?"

Joan shrugged. "I'd like to think so. Young female heroine against an insurmountable foe. What's not to like?"

River tapped his foot and looked up at the clock.

Joan raised an eyebrow. "But I take it that is not why you two are here. Need access to the newspapers again?"

Jean peaked out from behind Ethan and gasped. "Wow. She's so old. What happened to my little sister?"

Ethan looked down at Jean and took in a breath. "I found this book in Oakland Cemetery." He held up a copy of *The Beginner's Goodbye* by Anne Tyler. "It was stamped as a library book, and I figured you'd want it back."

Joan took the book from him and ran a hand along the cover. "I left it there, on my sister's grave." She took off her glasses and started cleaning them haphazardly with a cloth. "It was our favorite, and I thought she might like it."

Ethan nodded slowly. "Well, that was nice of you."

Joan shook her head. "No, it was foolish. She's gone. I just hadn't been out there in so long. I felt like I needed to do something."

Jean brushed past Ethan and rested a hand on the book. "It's okay. I didn't need you to come and see me."

Ethan grabbed onto Joan's hand and squeezed. "You had a life to live, Joan. I'm sure your sister wouldn't have wanted you pulled down by her memory."

Joan nodded and muttered a soft, "Thank you."

River sighed and rolled his eyes. "Okay, can we move this along? Joan, I'm sorry. We brought you your book back, and now we—"

"We need to go in the basement, ma'am," Ethan cut River off, holding up his briefcase. "Official business today."

Joan glared at River, then pulled open a drawer and handed Ethan the keys to the basement. "Please take care of the books down there."

"Of course," Ethan said as River marched off to the basement stairs. Ethan smiled apologetically. "I'm sorry. He's been acting weird all day. We'll be right back."

Ethan followed River down into the dark and musty basement. Reaching up, he flipped the switch and the rows of steel shelves filled with dusty boxes of books were illuminated. The two agents stood and waited, but nothing happened.

"How'd you find the spirit down here last time?" River asked.

"I started looking through boxes and stuff." With one hand, River picked up a box from the nearest shelf and let it slam on the floor. They both waited in silence for the ghost to appear, but nothing happened. River tried again. This time, he swept his arm across a shelf and knocked three boxes to the ground. They waited again. Still, there was nothing. "This is bullshit," River complained.

"Hey, Jean. We could use some help," Ethan said into the air. The young ghost appeared next to him, making him flinch with surprise. "Anyway, you think you can pull him out?"

"Well, mom was always the loud one. Dad kind of hid behind her. If she was the ghost you met down here earlier, he's probably hiding in here somewhere."

"Well, I don't fucking see anything," River said.

"Dad? Are you here? It's me. Jean," Jean called into the storage space. There was rustling in the back corner of the room, and they all turned their attention in that direction. "Dad?" Jean called again as she moved toward the noise.

A mousy voice from the back replied, "Jean Bean? Is that you?"

"Hi, Dad," Jean said. "It's okay. You can come out. It's just me." From behind the stacks, a small man with round glasses peeked out from behind one of the shelves. "Hi, Daddy," Jean said with a wave.

The man stepped into the open. He was wearing a brown tweed jacket with patches on the elbows and blue slacks with round glasses. He straightened his tie, cleared his throat, and said, "Now, Jean Bean. Where have you been? Your mother and I have been worried sick."

"I was at my grave, Daddy."

"Well, that's no excuse. When your mother gets back, she's going to be quite angry with you, I assure you. She's not going to like that you were out this long. Not at all. You'll need to apologize, little lady. And likely do extra chores."

"Daddy, Mommy is gone."

Removing his glasses, he cleaned them with a handkerchief just like Ethan had seen Joan do. "Now, don't you talk back to me. I know she is out right now. But when she comes home, well. You know how she can get."

Jean looked at the floor. "I'm sorry, Daddy. I didn't mean to worry you."

"It's no worry, Jean Bean. Now, go upstairs and get Joan Bug. We'll wash up for supper before your mother returns."

Leaning close to Ethan, River whispered, "I'm gonna case him."

"Not yet," Ethan whispered back through gritted teeth.

"That's what I wanted to talk to you about, Daddy. You need to let Joan go. You need to move on."

Shaking his head, her father responded, "No. No. I can't do that. Your mother won't have it."

"Daddy. You are hurting her. She's stuck because you won't let go."

Her father shook his head with increased vigor. "No. No. Now Jean Bean, we don't want to upset your mother. You need to do as I say now."

"Mom is gone, Dad."

"No. No. She'll be back. Any second now. And when she comes back, she's going to be very angry that we aren't ready for dinner."

Jean took a step toward him. "Dad. Mom was a monster. And now she's gone."

"Careful, Jean," Ethan said. He could feel the energy building in her father. The tingle it gave his soul told him it was coming to some sort of breaking point.

"Let's just fucking case him and get out of here," River complained again.

Ethan glared at him. "Not yet. Give her a chance."

Taking another step toward him, Jean said, "Dad. Please. You have to listen to me. Mom is gone. I'm gone. We're all dead. And we need to let Joan Bug go. She needs to live her own life."

Her father wrung his hands together and shook his head with even more fervor. "No. No. Jean Bean. Now, you do as I say. I'm telling you to go and get your sister. Your mother is going to come home. And when she does, you are going to be sorry. I'm going to tell her about all of this. And you are going to be sorry for speaking to me like this."

Jean stomped her foot. "Dad! Stop it! No more!"

Blue energy began to radiate from her father. He looked up at her with rage-filled eyes. As he spoke, he began to levitate off the ground. "Jean Bean! I told you to get your sister!" The boxes on the shelves began to shake from the energy coming off of him. "Obey your father! And get your sister! Right now!" he screamed.

"Can I case his ass now?" River asked.

"Absolutely," Ethan said. Calling up to Jean, he said, "Jean. Get out of the way."

"Daddy! Please!" Jean cried. "Please just come with me!"

A box flew from a shelf and across the room. If River hadn't of ducked, it would have taken off his head. "No! Jean Bean! Listen to me!" her father screamed. The blue light radiating from him grew hotter and brighter with each word. It was almost as if all the rage he'd held all his life was now bursting from him like lava from a volcano.

"Jean! Move!" Ethan yelled as more boxes flew from the shelves in all directions. Ethan knew that if this continued to build, they would be caught in a tornado of boxes and books. He had to act.

"Daddy," Jean pleaded.

"Ethan! We are out of fucking time!" River screamed, shielding his face from the heat coming off Jean's father.

Knowing he had to act, Ethan raced forward. He shivered from the cold he felt as he ran through Jean. Cracking open the case as soon as he passed through her, he dove to dodge an oncoming box and dropped the case beneath her father. The blue light from the case grabbed at the ghost and pulled him into it. Jean too slid forward toward the case, but Ethan reached out for her with his free hand, using all of his psychic energy to hold her back.

"Ethan! Help!" she yelled as she slid closer toward the open case.

"Just hold on!" he yelled, focusing all his energy toward her. As the last bit of her father's energy slid into the case, Ethan slammed it closed and the room went quiet again.

"Thank you," Jean said, pushing herself up off the floor. She frowned at the closed case. "He wasn't himself. It's like he wasn't my dad anymore."

"He'll get the help he needs. I'm sorry you had to see that," Ethan said.

"Jean? Is that? Is that you?" Joan said. She pulled herself up off the stairs, holding on to the railing tight as she stared right at her deceased sister.

"Oh no," River said.

Jean stood, brushed herself off, and approached Joan. "Hi sis."

"How? How is this?" Joan asked, looking up at Ethan.

He stared at the bump forming on Joan's head. He rushed to his feet and stood by her side. "I think you might have a concussion."

"I'm sorry you had to see that." Jean said. "But you're free now. Dad's gone. Soon enough he'll cross over just like Mommy."

"Dad? What do you mean?"

Ethan helped Joan sit down on the bottom step. "Jean wasn't ready to cross over. Not until she made sure you were safe."

Jean nodded. "I didn't know where Dad ended up. Not until Ethan told me about the haunting in the basement. You're safe now, little sis." A bright light shone behind Jean. She turned, her eyes wide. "I think that's for me."

"But," Joan called out. "No. I. I don't want to let you go."

Jean shook her head. "I'm letting *you* go, silly. I'm sorry it took so long."

"But . . ." Joan reached out a hand.

"But nothing," Jean said. "I will be on the other side when you're ready. Until then, go have fun for once."

Jean turned toward the light, paused, and looked back at Ethan. "Will you tell Mable and Dylan that I love them? And that I'll see them soon?"

A knot formed in Ethan's throat, but he pushed it down and nodded. "Of course. Goodbye, Jean."

She smiled, turned, and stepped into the light.

"Bye, sis," Joan said, a tear rolling down her cheek.

"Jesus," River said as the light faded away. "That took for-fucking-ever. Let's go. I've only got ten minutes to get across town," River complained as he headed toward the stairs.

Ethan eyed the bump on Joan's head as he helped her stand. "Well, you're gonna be late then, since your first stop is the hospital."

Sixty

Dangerous Debate

E THAN WALKED SLOWLY BEHIND Gerry, careful not to bump into anyone else who stood in the street. He kept close to Gerry's wake, trying everything in his power to not stumble or fall behind as they made their way back to the rest of the NRDS team.

"Hey, everybody," Ethan said with a big, dopey smile on his face. "Are we? Are we having fun yet?"

Alexus, Buck, Bob, and Melissa turned, held up their fingers, and shushed him in unison.

Buck eyed Ethan for a moment, then looked at his husband. "Gerry, what did you do?"

"What? He was anxious about tonight, so I thought it would be smart to help the poor kid take the edge off."

Ethan found his balance by leaning on Gerry as he stared out into the crowd. A platform had been erected in the middle of the street, in the same spot Santa's tent had been during the winter festival. On the left side of the stage stood Kamila Gorski, reporter for FOX 47 News and moderator of tonight's debate. On the right side of the stage, kitty-cornered to face the audience, were two podiums.

Behind the first was Chax Tamish in a crisp blue suit that looked like it had been perfectly tailored to accentuate everything about the man. Chax stared patiently as the man behind the other podium spoke. That man was Mayor Davies, whose small stature was not helped by the plain blue button-up and red tie his re-election team had dressed him in.

"Agent Malik," Trevor said, pointing his phone in Ethan's face. "Tell all our followers who you think is going to win tonight's debate?"

Ethan closed one eye to maintain his balance and flashed the camera a look that was intended to be a suave smile, but he would later realize looked more like an old man pooping. "Well, I think this debate is one of the more important ones, and I just hope they don't talk about NRDS, or me, again." His face fell into a pout, and he said, "I just don't like it when he tries to blame me. I did nothing wrong. Why does he hate me?"

Gerry pulled Ethan away from the camera and held up his hand to Trevor. "I think that's enough Insta for this one."

Melissa put her hands on her hips and glared at Ethan. "This behavior is extremely unprofessional. I hope you know this will be recorded in your review."

Ethan's eyes widened. "But. But he's gonna say something mean again. I just know it. You can't—"

"Don't be a hardass. He's off the clock," Gerry whispered.

"Yeah. What he said. I'm off the clock," Ethan said.

Bob passed a hand through Ethan's head, causing Ethan's teeth to chatter. "Pull your head out of your ass, private. We're here to represent," Bob barked.

"You got it, captain," Ethan said, stumbling as he attempted a salute. He caught himself before falling into Alexus, and leaned in to whisper, "Bob's not being very nice."

Alexus crossed her arms and glared at him. "If you puke on me, I'm going to punch you in the throat. You understand me?"

"Please. No. I don't want that," Ethan said.

Gerry rested a hand on Ethan and whispered to Buck, "What did we miss?"

"Nothing worth repeating," Buck said.

"We haven't come up yet, which is always good," Melissa added.

Trevor attached his phone to a selfie stick and maneuvered into the center of the NRDS team. "Hey followers, that's right, the gang's all here. As you know, we've been the punching bag for almost all the debates, but today there hasn't been a single mention of us. Not yet, at least."

Ethan scanned the crowd. It wasn't as heavily attended as the last one. A loyal group of about twenty Chax Tamish fans filled the front with collapsible chairs, while another sixty or so stood crowded around the platform. Most listened, while others talked quietly among themselves as Mayor Davis spoke. He'd been in the middle of answering a question about the area's tax code as Chax Tamish rolled his eyes and smiled at the crowd.

Ethan sighed and looked around. "Where's Doris? I need a muffin?"

"She said it was too chilly, so she's watching from home," Buck said.

"Wait, that was an option?" Ethan asked.

"Not for you, you poster child for problematic NRDS agents," Melissa said.

Ethan looked past Melissa and spoke as if he hadn't just heard her. "Then where's River? He's got to have a brownie or two on him."

Gerry patted Ethan's back. "I don't think you need any of River's brownies. Maybe water will do you well? Let me see if I can find something."

Kamila's voice cut through the speakers. "Thank you, Mister Mayor, for that exciting explanation of the tax code."

"You know, I had a crush on her in high school," Ethan said to Alexus, nudging her with his elbow. "But I'm so happy I'm with Bryce now. He's super hot. Way hotter than Kamila."

Alexus pushed him back. "Elbow me again, and you lose the elbow."

Bob glowed a bright blue and pushed Ethan back, away from Alexus. "Goddamn it, soldier! You're an embarrassment. You're an embarrassment to me, to us, to your momma, to your momma's momma, and to all the mommas in your godforsaken generational line."

Ethan stuck his tongue out at Bob. "Well, my momma's momma loves me. She made me pancakes this morning. So you're wrong."

"Look here, shit for brains!" Bob started, but Buck leaned forward and cut him off.

Alexus grabbed her badge and spoke with a stern voice. "Bob. Stop fucking trying to protect me."

Bob's blue glow faded, and he stepped back. "Fine. But this asshat deserved it."

"For our last topic of the evening," Kamila continued on stage. "Federal overreach in New Richmond. The federal agency, the National Recently Deceased Services, is a topic you've both taken firm stances on. While some think they might be helpful, most believe they are a sign of the federal government impacting local government and businesses."

"Here we go," Buck said.

Ethan sighed. "She was mean like that in high school, too. Straight to the point. Knife in the heart."

"She looks like a cheerleader," Alexus said.

"Head cheerleader," Ethan replied.

"I hate cheerleaders," Alexus said through gritted teeth.

"Now children, let's not blame the woman for doing her job," Gerry said, returning to the group with bottled waters.

Ethan grabbed a bottle and nearly chugged the whole thing, not realizing how thirsty he was until the liquid hit his tongue.

Kamila continued. "What steps will you take to curb government overreach in our town? Mayor Davis, it's your turn to answer first."

Ethan scanned the crowd as the mayor shuffled his notes and muttered to himself. He'd already checked to see if Dylan had been wandering around, but he still suspected the kid was hiding somewhere among the crowd. He searched for that feeling inside him, that electric feeling in his gut that told him when his psychic abilities were working. Still, the only ghost he saw was Bob.

"Well, I think," Mayor Davis finally started. "I think we need to really investigate why they are here, and why now? From my count, there are seven full-time salaries being paid, not to mention rent on an office in the middle of town. Why didn't more of those jobs go to our current citizens? Only three were filled locally while they outsourced the rest."

Ethan grabbed Trevor's hand and pointed the camera at himself. "He's talking about me and Trevor."

"Everyone knows," Buck grunted.

Alexus groaned. "I really hate drunk Ethan. I feel like I'm losing brain cells."

"If the federal government actually wants to help our town, why not give more jobs to locals?" the mayor continued. "Or, what about focusing on all the crimes that have been overwhelming our police departments? Why not send an agency who could actually help our town, like the FBI, for example? These NRDS aren't helping us bring down our spike in murders. They're not helping with anything, actually. They're just federally funded ghost chasers wasting air."

"Oh, ghost chasers. That would be a pretty cool TV show. Don't you think so?" Ethan said. "You could have me and Alexus, like, the nice one and the mean one. We could film in some abandoned hospital, and you could be there too, Buck."

"Gerry's gonna pay for whatever he did to you," Alexus said.

"I'm with her," Melissa said. "Do we have to babysit this asshole all night? Where's his fancy boyfriend?"

"New York," Buck grunted.

Gerry waved his hand. "Don't listen to them, Ethan. They're all just bitter that I didn't offer them any special calming snacks."

Taking back the reins, Kamila said, "Thank you, Mister Mayor. Mister Tamish, your response?"

"Thank you, Miss Gorski," Chax said with a smile.

"God. He's so charming," Ethan said.

"While my opponent thinks more federal interference is the answer, I argue that the amazing people of New Richmond have all they need. We don't need outsiders coming into this beautiful city, taking our resources and threatening our way of life." There was a murmur of agreement in the crowd.

A twinge in Ethan's gut pulled his attention away from the crowd. It didn't feel like Dylan, but he followed the sensation until his eyes fell on someone familiar.

"Hey look," he said, pointing across the crowd to a car parked twenty yards away from the right side of the stage. Inside was a man with a big mess of curly hair. "There's River."

Alexus squinted. "What's that shitbag up to?"

"You want me to go find out?" Bob asked.

"He's looking at something," Buck said. "I think he has binoculars."

Ethan followed River's eyeline, landing on a muscular man in a tight black T-shirt. His military haircut and straight posture gave Ethan pause. He pointed to the man and said, "My spider sense says he's watching that guy."

"If this leads to him getting arrested again, I don't care what management says. He's getting canned," Melissa complained.

Buck shook his head. "This looks different from his normal antics."

"Our next mayor needs to look at the corruption of the federal government and tell them, 'No more!'" Chax continued from the stage. "No more wasted money! No more outsiders! No more lies about ghosts! No more!"

Ethan's gut pulled at him again, compelling him to turn around. He spun slowly and looked at the empty street behind them. "That's weird," he mumbled.

"I'm serious, Ethan. If you puke near me, I will cut you," Alexus said.

"Shh, wait. My spidey sense is tingling," Ethan said.

"Say it with me, everyone!" Chax said from the stage, stepping out from behind his podium. "No more! No more! No more!" The crowd responded halfheartedly, the enthusiasm from his previous rallies tempered by the chill in the evening air.

Ethan's gut pulled his eye line up. He searched the windows of the surrounding buildings but saw nothing out of the ordinary. The spark still pulled on him, and his eyes traced up to the roofs.

A shimmer caught his eye, followed by a blue light. He pointed up to the top of the building and said, "Hey, what's that?"

Melissa squinted up at the roofs. "I don't see anything."

Buck pulled his badge out of his pocket. "I see it. I just can't make it out."

Ethan closed his eyes and tried to focus. Opening them again, he looked harder, and the shimmer took shape. "It looks like a spirit. In a hoodie. With a rifle. Is that a scope?"

"Fuck," Alexus said.

"Bob! You and Alexus on the shooter!" Buck yelled as he raced toward the stage.

Ethan chased after Buck as Alexus and Bob ran toward the building. Adrenaline cleared his head, and he glanced to the side of the platform and saw River leave his car, his eyes trained on the military man.

Buck hopped onto the stage as Chax continued trying to get the crowd to chant, "No more!" with him.

"There's a shooter on the roof! Get down!" Buck shouted.

Kamila and the Mayor's eyes grew wide as they both raced from the stage, but Chax paid Buck no mind and continued to chant.

Ethan stumbled onto the stage and stood next to Buck. "Did you hear him? Get down! You have to get down!"

"Do you see what they are doing here? People of New Richmond! Open your eyes! The minute we try to call them out, this is how they respond!" Chax yelled into the microphone. The surrounding crowd looked left and right, frowns on their faces as they looked for the supposed danger.

A gun shot rang out, echoing through the night. That was the crowd's cue to scatter, leaving behind their chairs as they fled.

Ethan looked up at the building and saw Bob grappling with the shooter. Bob glowed a bright blue, and the rifle flew up into the air. Alexus appeared beside Bob and swung a fist into the ghost's face.

The hooded ghost toppled from the roof, landing hard on the ground.

Had it been a ghost, it should have sprung right back up. Instead, the hooded figure lay still for a moment. Then a blue haze glowed around them, and their appendages twitched and bent at strange angles. They stood up as if they were a marionette on strings and dashed away into the dark before anyone could reach them.

Ethan turned to Chax and held out a hand. "Mister Tamish. You need to get down, please. For your own safety."

Chax glared at Ethan and Buck, his face turning red. "This stunt will not go unanswered. You'll both pay for this. When I win the election, you're done. You're both done!"

Sixty-One

Stakeout Surprise

E THAN'S HEAD POUNDED AS he closed one eye and looked up at Chax Tamish. The mayoral candidate glared down at him and Buck from the stage and shouted, "This is all we needed. No one's going to support you now! It's over! You're done!"

Chax turned and marched off as Ethan braced himself against the stage. The world spun as Gerry's special cocktail went into full effect.

Ethan caught sight of a black sedan as it pulled up beside the stage. He was fairly certain the driver was the same muscular man he'd previously seen in the audience. Chax pulled open the back door and hopped in.

"Agent Malik! Will you comment on why the NRDS has a hit out for candidate Tamish? What will you do now that your second attempt failed?"

Ethan jumped and turned, finding the three college students from Chicago in front of him. Chester held a microphone in his face while the other two, whose names failed to surface, handled the camera and lighting.

"What? No," Ethan said, waving the microphone off. "That's not. No, that's not it." His words slurred, and his tongue felt like it stuck to the roof of his mouth. He looked around, his eyes wide as he realized Buck was no longer beside him.

Chester pushed the microphone back at Ethan. "And what if I told you we have evidence proving your involvement with the shooter?"

"What?" the tall one handling the lighting said. "We don't have anything."

"Shut the fuck up, Greg!" Chester shot back.

"Did you see where my partner went?" Ethan asked, looking out at the dispersing crowd. No one was by Chax's sedan, which still idled behind the stage, nor was he by Melissa, Gerry, and Trevor, who were all passing around a flask. Ethan's stomach rumbled, and he propped an elbow up against the stage.

"This is your one and only chance, Agent Malik. Confess now and control the narrative," Chester said.

Hot air intermixed with bile filled Ethan's mouth as he burped right into the microphone. "I. I need to find Buck."

The heavyset one peered from behind the camera. "He ran off into the alley that dude who jumped went into."

"Ricky, you piece of shit! I'm trying to do something here!" Chester complained.

Ethan pushed himself off the stage and gave a bow. "Thank you kindly, sir." He then promptly stumbled into Chester. "Oh. No. I'm sorry."

Chester grabbed Ethan's shoulder, digging his thumb in. "Does your current state of intoxication have anything to do with your guilt for hiring a hitman to assassinate a political candidate?"

Ethan grabbed Chester's hand and pulled it off his shoulder. "No. I was anxious about being used as a scapegoat again. But here I am. I should have had more of the red ones Gerry had." He burped again, and this time, the bile lingered much longer in his mouth.

"Stop keeping secrets from us. If you let it all out now, we can help save you from the fallout," Chester offered, maneuvering Ethan to face the camera.

Ethan looked into the camera, and a wave of cold washed over him. He hunched over and the entire contents of his stomach erupted from his mouth like a geyser, right onto Chester's white sneakers.

"What the fuck?" Chester shouted.

"I. I guess I let it out," Ethan smirked, wiping his mouth with the back of his hand.

"You asshole! I meant your confession!" Chester screamed as he kicked the vomit from his shoes.

"This is the best footage we've gotten in days," Ricky said.

"We could post this tonight." Greg laughed.

"You better fucking not!" Chester screamed. "Oh, my God, it's in my shoes."

Ethan closed one eye, then the other, as he looked out toward the alley. He saw Buck walking out, phone in hand, with Alexus and Bob walking behind him. Ethan took a step forward but failed to balance himself and fell backward.

Chester hovered over Ethan as he struggled to stand. "Enough! Tell me why you are trying to kill Chax Tamish?"

"It's a fucking ghost, you asshole. It possessed the shooter. Who, by the looks of it, left the body in the alley." Ethan pushed himself up and spotted Buck speaking with the police as they taped off the area.

"A likely story!" Chester countered.

Greg frowned. "Dude, you're going to deny possession now?"

"Shut up, Greg!" Chester barked.

Ethan heard an engine rev behind him, and he turned to see the sedan pulling away. Then, to his surprise, ten yards behind the sedan, River's clunker rolled quietly behind with its headlights off.

"What the hell?" Ethan muttered to himself.

Ricky let out a sigh. "Yo, Chester. Are we done here?"

"Yeah, man. I want to go home," Greg added.

"No. We don't have our climax yet," Chester shot back.

Ricky elbowed Greg and whispered, "Yeah, I bet that's what Becky said."

"Shut the fuck up, you dick," Chester said.

Something pulled at Ethan's gut as he watched River's car roll behind the sedan. Something that told him he needed to follow right now. "Uh, hey. You want your climax?"

"Yeah, we fuckin' do," Chester said.

"Where's your van?" Ethan asked.

Chester frowned. "Why?"

"One of my partners is tailing Chax as we speak, and I don't know why."

Greg lowered the camera. "So we tail the guy tailing the mayor? That doesn't sound very safe."

Chax's sedan stopped at a red light. If they waited any longer, they would lose him. "You want answers, right? Well, so do I. Come with me and get your award-winning scoop or stay here and keep asking questions that no one can answer."

Chester looked at his two friends. Both Greg and Ricky nodded. "Fine. Come on," Chester said as he motioned toward the van.

They crossed the street, Ethan stumbling as he followed them behind the stage and to their van. The inside of the plain Chevy wasn't as impressive as Ethan imagined. Instead of piles of equipment and screens, it was mainly empty, with haphazard duffel bags of dirty clothes and crumpled up fast food garbage scattered everywhere.

He climbed into the back and used one duffel as a pillow, ignoring the scent of dirty socks. "Just follow River. Wake me when he stops."

The next thing he knew, he woke up on his back, staring up at the van ceiling. His head pounded, and his eyes took a moment to adjust. He found both Chester and Greg fast asleep next to him and Ricky sitting in the driver's seat.

Ethan pulled out his phone and instantly noticed the twenty-two missed calls. It was just after midnight, which meant he'd lost five hours. The calls were all from Buck, Gerry, Alexus, and even Trevor. He added them to a group message and typed, "I'm fine. Chasing a lead."

He carefully climbed over the sleeping film crew and took the passenger seat.

Ricky nodded and peered out into the dark. Ethan could see that they were parked down the road from a strip mall on the other side of town. The black sedan was the only car in the small parking lot, and River's car was parked on the street thirty yards ahead of them. Ethan could make out a small orange spark of what he assumed was a joint in River's front seat.

"Where are we?" he asked Ricky.

"We're at Chax Tamish's campaign headquarters," Ricky said. "Your boy River followed them here and has been waiting ever since."

"And Chax and that big dude are inside?" Ethan asked.

"Yep. His name's Tomas. He doesn't talk much, but he's like Chax's bodyguard or something."

Ethan's phone buzzed, and a message from Alexus appeared on the screen. "Answer your fucking phone next time or I'm implanting a chip into you."

Ethan texted back, "Sorry. Followed River to Chax HQ. Scoping the place out." He looked up at Ricky and said, "So nothing has happened for five hours?"

Ricky nodded. "Nope. We're used to it. It's Chester's shift in about thirty minutes. One time, we sat outside your office for almost thirty-six hours."

Ethan laughed. "Why?"

"We were tailing the old guy. Buck? But he just spent both days sitting at his computer."

"He loves his paperwork."

"Total waste of time, especially when we had our answers."

Ethan frowned, then a lightbulb went off in his head. "Wait a minute!" he said, louder than he intended. He glanced back, seeing the other two still asleep. He whispered, "You were the ones who broke into the office!"

"Which time?"

"What do you mean, which time?"

Ricky smiled. "Your building isn't all that secure. My seven-year-old little sister could pick that lock."

Ethan's mouth hung open. "What did you assholes find?"

"Nothing useful, except those creepy briefcases, and we don't touch those."

"Smart," Ethan said.

"I think Tomas went in and trashed the place once too. Also, your pothead boy up there constantly breaks in when he forgets his keys. We have it on camera. Kinda funny cause he never tries the door."

"Sounds about right."

Ricky shifted in his seat and pulled out a smaller video camera and pointed it at the building. "Oh, shit. Here we go."

"Wait. What?" Ethan said, peering into the darkness.

"Tomas is coming out the back," Ricky said, pointing at the side of the building.

"How'd you see that?" Ethan asked, squinting his eyes as he found the muscular man coming out from behind a dumpster.

Ricky followed Tomas on camera and whispered, "Told you, bro. We do this all the time. We had eyes on you weeks before you knew."

Ethan shivered at the thought. "That's creepy."

Ricky shrugged. "That's journalism."

Ethan kept his eyes on Tomas as he walked away from the building, staying parallel to the road and keeping out from under the streetlights. He was quick, darting in and out of shadows faster than a man that buff should be able to.

Ethan's heart raced as he watched. It was like seeing some large predator hunting, and it made him even more uncomfortable. "Wait, you don't think he's coming for us?"

"Nope. He's locked on your boy," Ricky said.

Tomas closed in on River, approaching his blind spot. Ethan reached for the door handle. "Shit, I've got to warn him."

Ricky grabbed his arm. "No, man. I wouldn't."

Tomas pulled something from his side, and Ethan's heart sank. He knew what it was, and bile rose back up in Ethan's throat as Tomas attached a silencer to the end.

"He's going to fucking kill him!" Ethan said as he pushed Ricky out of the way and leaned on the van's horn.

The blaring horn set chaos in motion.

"Get off!" Ricky screamed.

Both college students in the back jumped to life. "What the fuck?" Chester shouted.

Tomas turned and pointed his gun at the van before running toward them.

"Shit!" Ricky screamed, dropping the camera and starting the engine.

A burst of light flashed from the tip of the gun. Ethan didn't hear the gunfire, but he heard the crunch of metal, and steam shot up from the hood of the van. Tomas fired another shot, and the van tilted to the passenger side as they lost a tire.

"Go! Go! Go!" Chester screamed from the back, pounding on Ricky's seat.

"What about River?" Ethan yelled.

Ricky slammed on the gas, and the van barreled toward Tomas. Ethan stared down the barrel of the gun, pointed directly at him, and time slowed. Bryce surfaced to mind. A love he'd never get to fully experience. Then his sister and grandmother, all the family he had left. His heart beat heavily, and he swore he could hear the click of the pistol. But before the pistol fired, Tomas jerked to the side as a mass of curly red hair rammed into him.

"Stop the van!" Ethan screamed.

"Fuck you!" Ricky screamed back.

"Drive! Get the fuck out of here!" Chester yelled.

Without a second thought, Ethan yanked open the passenger door and threw himself out of the moving van. His shoulder connected with the pavement as he rolled thrice over before splaying out on the road.

He wobbled as he pushed himself up and saw River and Tomas swinging punches on the ground several feet from him. The muscular man finally locked himself on top of River as the van squealed away.

Ethan jumped to his feet and ran. With every ounce of energy he could find, he rushed the man. Tomas held River down with one hand while he looked around, clearly looking for his gun. Ethan lowered his shoulder, remembering all the times he'd tackled bigger opponents in high school. He picked up speed and focused past the man. This wasn't high school anymore. He needed to pound straight through the man.

Tomas turned at the last second and held out an arm, leveling Ethan in an instant and taking every ounce of air out of his lungs as he tumbled forward. His face connected with the pavement and scraped across the ground.

Ethan's jaw was on fire as he rolled over and saw River still pinned by the man. Ethan pushed himself up, steadying on one knee as he readied for a second attack.

"Run, Ethan!" River screamed as Tomas reached out and found his gun on the pavement.

Ethan tried to move forward, but his legs shook with pain and didn't respond.

Tomas turned and held the gun out. Ethan looked down the barrel again. His heart stopped. Tomas smiled. There was nowhere to go. The bodyguard had him.

"Stop! Tomas, no!" a voice commanded from behind Ethan. Before Ethan could turn to see who was behind him, the barrel of a second gun pressed into the back of his head. "Not in front of the office, you dolt. In the back, where we can clean it up." Ethan didn't need to look to know the voice of Chax Tamish.

"You won't get away with this," Ethan said through gritted teeth.

"Get him up," Chax said to Tomas. Pressing the gun into the back of Ethan's head, he said, "Stand and walk."

Ethan rose, his knee still shaking with pain. Tomas pulled River up to his feet and pushed him next to Ethan.

"What the fuck are you doing here?" River muttered.

"What about, 'thanks for trying to save me, Ethan?'"

"You clearly did a good job at that, asshole," River complained.

"Enough. Walk. Behind the building," Chax demanded.

Tomas shoved Ethan and River forward, toward the back of the building, and toward certain death.

Sixty-Two

Meddling

T HE BARREL OF A gun prodded Ethan's back as he looked for an escape. It was too open, standing out in front of a dimly lit parking lot with the alley just up ahead.

"This is just fucking great," River complained as he walked. "Not only will they be pissed I got shot, but they're for sure going to blame me for your stupid ass too."

"I was just trying to help," Ethan said. His phone vibrated in his pocket. Instinctively, he reached for it.

"Stop," Tomas said, squeezing his shoulder hard.

Ethan froze, and Tomas slipped his hand into Ethan's pocket. "Sorry, I didn't—"

Tomas threw the phone over his shoulder, shoved Ethan forward, and said, "Little Alexus can't help you now."

"Move faster," Chax commanded, jabbing his gun into River's back.

"You can take your 'trying to help' and fuck right off with it," River complained.

They stepped into the parking lot, and Ethan peered out at the building. They were about forty yards from the front of the building and another seventy yards from the back of the building. Beyond that was woods. If he and River got to the tree line without being shot, they might make it. He wondered if Tomas could catch them. The bodyguard had been more limber than he'd expected, but could he run? Or maybe the questions Ethan should ponder were more about Tomas's marksmanship in the dark.

Ethan started dragging his feet, attempting to give him and River more time to think. "You're the one who went running off on your own. Who does that? We're supposed to be a team, man."

River sighed and looked up at the sky. "And what would have happened if I brought my half-baked suspicion to the team?"

"We would help you."

"Bullshit! Buck would've loaded me down with paperwork after telling me it wasn't our business. Alexus would have fucking punched me. And you would have demanded we call the cops, who are probably on this asshole's payroll."

"You don't know that. We might have helped."

"Love the tenacity, but sorry dude, I had to lone wolf this one. There were too many unanswered questions, and I couldn't trust everyone at the office."

Tomas nudged Ethan with the back of his gun and said in a gravelly voice, "Quit dragging your feet."

"Ow, fuck. I'm not, you asshole," Ethan complained, slowing down even more.

"Idiots until the end, the both of you," Chax said from behind them.

"Hey, we're not idiots. You're the idiot. We caught you," Ethan said.

"You caught me? With what? What do the NRDS honestly think they've found?" Chax asked.

"Uh," Ethan stammered. He didn't know. Not really, and now they were in front of the building, and he was running out of real estate. His heart pounded in his ears. He needed to do something.

River turned around, facing Chax's gun. "We know you're behind the murders. You killed your assistant. You've been killing off people in this town who stand in your way."

Cold sweat formed on Ethan's brow as all the pieces started snapping together. He turned around, ignoring Tomas, and glared at Chax. "You killed Mable!"

Tomas put the barrel of his gun in Ethan's chest and pushed him so hard, he almost lost his footing. "Keep moving."

Ethan pressed back on the gun with his chest. "Not until I get some answers! Mable was my grandma's friend. Why'd you do it? Why murder an old lady?" He scanned the street, looking for any sign of salvation, but there was nothing.

Chax sighed. "You honestly do not know what you've gotten yourself into, do you?"

River sighed. "It's about real estate, am I right? The same realty group owns all the property of everyone murdered in this town for the past few decades."

Ethan stepped back. "It was all a land grab? The nursing home too? Why? There's nothing here."

"Government duck sex parks," River said with a shrug.

Chax rolled his eyes and laughed. "Like I'd ever tell you two assholes. You're so far down the chain. Even if I gave you the names, you wouldn't even know who they are."

"Gave us names?" Ethan asked. Then another lightbulb went off in his mind. "Oh shit!"

"He's slow, but he's getting there," River said. He reached into his pocket, and Chax lifted the gun to his head. "Woah there, Chaxie boy. Mind if I grab one last hit?"

Chax looked down at River's pocket, then nodded.

River lit up and took a drag. "Keep going, rookie. You're almost there."

"You're working with upper management, aren't you? That's why we wouldn't know their names," Ethan said.

"Congratulations. Alright, turn around. Let's finish this," Chax said, pushing on River's head with his gun. Tomas mimicked him, holding his gun to Ethan's forehead and giving a hard push.

Ethan held up his hands and turned. "You're involved with those devices too. That means Melissa's in on it. But why?" Ethan asked.

"Think about it. What do the devices do?" River asked, taking another long drag from his joint.

"Keep walking!" Chax yelled, shoving River forward.

"They ramp up ghosts?" Ethan guessed.

"The first one did," River agreed.

"And they gather ghosts," Ethan said with a nod.

"It's a fucking Build-A-Walking-Dead-Horde. Pull all the spirits together and then make them all crazy." River took another drag and blew it into the air. "Boom. Ghost army."

Chax scoffed and spoke through gritted teeth. "You dumbass NRDS literally have a whole dead army at your disposal and do nothing about it. Nothing! The world continues to go to shit. War, famine, whole-ass plagues, and you dumbasses spend all fucking day listening to some dead and gone piece of shit talk about their stupid problems. Your whole department cares more about them than they do the living."

Ethan frowned. "So, what? New Richmond is your training ground? Factory? Boot Camp for the dead?"

"Something like that," Chax said. "And once I'm mayor, I'll be able to clear the way for all that newly available land to be picked up by eminent domain. Upper management will claim it, and Fort Richmond will be the first of its kind."

Ethan nodded. "Does that mean Melissa works for you?"

"She's upper management's pawn, who forgot her place until I gave her a firm reminder," Chax said.

"And you work with or for the people in upper management?" Ethan asked.

Chax let out a groan. "They all work for me, happy?"

"But why your assistant? Why kill him?" River asked.

"Because he wanted a promotion. Ghost general seemed like a fitting position," Chax said with a shrug.

"And who in upper management is in on this? I want names!" Ethan demanded.

"Um. No," Chax said.

"No? Come on! I need to know!" Ethan said, turning his head to look at Chax.

"Aw, are you worried your little boyfriend is in on it?" Chax grinned.

Ethan's fingertips grew numb. He hadn't thought of that, but now he did. Bryce had known about the devices. He'd been working with Melissa at first. Was he in on this? No, he couldn't be.

River took another hit from his joint. "Well, it sounds like you've got this all wrapped up in a nice little bow."

"I do. Thank you very much," Chax said.

River held up his joint and stopped in his tracks. "But like the Scooby-Doo Villain you are, you forgot about one thing."

Chax scoffed. "Oh really? What's that?"

"Us meddling kids!" River screamed as he spun around and jabbed the end of his joint right in Tomas's eye. As Tomas stumbled back, River grabbed for Chax's gun.

Ethan's heart skipped a beat, but he turned and jumped into action, grabbing on to Tomas's gun as he flailed and screamed. Ethan pulled, but the bodyguard's iron grip held firm. With his free hand, Tomas connected a stinging left cross to Ethan's jaw that felt like a sledgehammer. Ethan let go of the gun and crumpled to the ground. A second later, River fell next to Ethan, his nose gushing with blood.

"Enough of this shit!" Chax screamed, holding out his gun again. "Kill them here, and we will set a fire to cover it."

"You sure, boss?" Tomas asked, regaining composure with one closed eye.

"Yes. I'm fucking sure. Just do it," Chax said.

Tomas held up his gun. All Ethan could do was stare at the end of the barrel. At least he knew there was an afterlife, even if he wasn't ready for it.

Then headlights beamed from behind Tomas, and an engine roared. A black muscle car jumped over the curb and into the parking lot, racing straight for them.

Tomas turned around, firing a shot into the night before Alexus's car reached him. She didn't stop. Instead, she drove right into both Tomas and Chax.

Both of them flew over the top of her car, landing hard on the asphalt. Alexus screeched to a halt and hopped out of her car, baseball bat in hand. Without hesitation, she walked over to Tomas as he struggled to stand and swung, connecting hard with his ribs. "Stay down!" she screamed, pushing his head into the pavement.

Buck hopped out from the passenger side door and raced over, collecting both guns from where they had fallen. "You good?" he asked Alexus.

"Good," she said, shoving Tomas's head into the pavement again.

Buck looked over at Ethan and River. "You guys alright?"

Reality hit Ethan. He was going to live. He stared wide-eyed at Chax and nodded. "We're alright."

Chax cradled his arm and produced a sound between a laugh and a whimper. "You're all so fucked. Do you know what's going to happen now? After everyone believed you tried to kill me before? You hit me with a car. You're all going to jail!"

"Shut the fuck up," Alexus demanded.

Ethan looked around. Even if it were four NRDS against Chax, he'd blame them. He'd pay his way to ensure that they'd never taste freedom. Dread filled Ethan's chest.

"How about we kill you and start that fire you were going to start anyway?" River called.

"No!" Buck yelled. "No one is killing anyone."

"You are all screwed." Chax laughed painfully. "When the chief of police gets here, he's going to arrest all of you."

"Well, uh, sir. They're not," a voice came from behind Ethan. He turned around and found Ricky and Chester coming out from the shadows in the alley, camera pointed right at Chax.

"We got everything," Chester said.

"Fuck, yes," River said with a laugh. "Meddling kids. Every fucking time."

Buck pulled his phone from his pocket and smiled. "Perfect. I wonder what your chief will have to say now that we have proof."

Ethan frowned, looking up and down the parking lot. "How did you guys get over there?"

Ricky smiled. "We parked around back and came in through the woods."

A thought struck Ethan. "Wait. Were you going to film us getting shot?"

Chester reached for Ethan and held out a hand while he shrugged.

"You were going to let us die?" Ethan shouted.

"We're journalists!" Chester said. "We document. We don't get involved."

River laughed, but Ethan glared at Chester, his fist clenching. "Oh, fuck you guys."

"Just be thankful you have friends, rookie," Alexus said.

"Yeah. I need an ambulance and the police at campaign headquarters for Chax Tamish. Oh, um. Hold on." Cupping his phone, Buck called, "Does anyone know the address of this shithole?"

Sixty-Three

Pass the Buck

W HILE CARRYING A COFFEE in one hand and a chocolate chip muffin in the other, Ethan hummed as he walked up the stairs. After the arrest of Chax and Tomas, things moved quickly. Buck advised they bring Bryce into the fold, and he took the news to his superiors. Shortly after, Bryce got the approval to remove Melissa from the New Richmond office.

Ethan arrived at the office an hour later than usual to avoid Melissa's escort from the building, per Bryce's advice. He pushed the knob down with his elbow and backed the door open, spotting Trevor perched in his usual spot near the door.

"Hey, man," Trevor said.

"Oh, good. Ethan's here too," Doris said, looking down at her hands.

Ethan looked around, noting the strange, somber tension in the air. Then a scream pierced through the air, and he jumped.

Melissa's office was still closed, and a second shout filled the air from behind the door. "This is my fucking highlighter, and I'm fucking taking it and there's nothing you can fucking do about it! Fucker-fuckhead!"

"Oh, great. She's not gone yet?" Ethan asked, crossing the room and finding his desk.

"Nice of you to join us. We've only been tormented by this banshee for the past hour," River said from his desk.

"Just put your head down and finish up your report on the Tamish case," Buck grunted from his computer. He had his reading glasses on, which Ethan knew meant he wasn't planning on leaving his desk soon.

Another scream burst from the office. "And this! This is my goddamn box of paperclips. I bought this with my own goddamn money, you goddamn spoiled candy-ass wannabe goddamn nobody!"

"Oh, my. She doesn't need to use so much language," Doris muttered to herself.

"Did you notice she keeps getting stuck on one curse word at a time? You don't think she's stroking out on us, do you?" Trevor said.

"No, don't be insensitive. The poor woman is losing her career," Doris said.

Ethan sat down at his desk and sipped on his coffee. "Where's Alexus and Bob?"

"Dispatched to a graveyard in Deer Park that was registering some activity," Buck grunted.

"Lucky," Ethan mumbled as he took a bite out of his muffin.

Buck looked over his computer screen at Ethan and said, "Good things come to those who come to work on time."

"And this chair! This shit-ass chair is mine! I bought it from my own shit home! And it's going right back there, you shit-face with your shitty stupid bow tie and your shitty glasses and your shitty expensive-looking brown shoes and your shitty suspenders."

"I think her tantrum is losing steam," Trevor said.

"I hope so," Doris said.

"I like his suspenders. She's just being mean," Ethan asked.

"Your lover boy looked exceptionally nerdy today." River laughed.

"Hey! I helped pick some of it out," Ethan said.

"And this stapler! This is my stapler, you bastard! You keep your grubby little bastard fingers off it! You. You. Little bastard man."

"Should we, I don't know, help him or something?" Ethan asked.

"This is why he gets paid the big bucks," Buck said.

The door to Melissa's office swung open, and Bryce stepped out. He gave a smile to Ethan but gracefully said nothing, stepping aside to allow space for Melissa to come out of her office.

Melissa pushed a black leather chair out in front of her, which held three boxes overfilled with office supplies and various power cords Melissa had evidently claimed. Her face was red and puffy as she glared at everyone in the office.

"Well, you shit-eating assholes, you've finally done it. Ding dong, your fucking witch is dead. Way to go." She clapped loudly and slowly, in much the same way someone might clap for someone who'd just spilled the contents of a cooler carrying a fresh heart to an awaiting transplant. "I hope you are all just so fucking proud of yourselves. Great job."

"Melissa. It's time," Bryce said as gently as he could.

"No. Hold on. I should be allowed to say goodbye to these backstabbing traitor bastards." Motioning to Trevor, who had captured everything with his phone, she continued, "Like you. Always fucking filming everything. How do you still work here? What have you contributed besides taking up space?"

He smiled and kept the camera on her. "I'm streaming this live on Instagram."

"Of course you fucking are," Melissa said. Turning to River, she said, "And you? Have you smoked out the last two remaining brain cells yet, you dumb stupid turnip of a human? A kindergartner's art project has more worth than you."

JP RINDFLEISCH IX & JEFF ELKINS

River grinned and shrugged. "And yet I caught you in your shit."

"Catch me in what, dumbass? Following fucking orders? You realized this is all just politics, right? Blame the poor woman at the bottom of the totem pole while poor little Bryce's daddy and friends line their pockets. If you had a brain cell, you would have seen that." She turned to Buck, and said, "And you. Happy I'm out of the way, Captain Hampton? That's what you want, right? You've been pining for my job since the first day you got here."

Buck laughed and kept his eyes on his computer. "If I wanted your job, I wouldn't have turned it down before they gave it to you."

Melissa's face turned a new shade of red, and every muscle in her body clenched like she might explode at any moment. "Oh! What? No! Fuck you! Fuck you right to hell!"

"Whatever makes you happy," Buck said to her without looking away from his computer screen.

"I'm coming back for your ass! Mark my words. As soon as this all gets cleared up in DC, you're the first on my list, you old fucker."

Melissa huffed, and Ethan looked up from his desk. She caught his eye, and her lips pursed. "And you! Your betrayal hurts me the most. I brought you in. Mentored you! You wouldn't be here if it wasn't for me."

Ethan frowned and looked over at Buck. "Uh, Buck mentored me."

"You didn't do shit," River confirmed. "We all know you were too busy licking your boss's boots to care about us."

"Don't fucking interrupt my moment! God! You're all such assholes!" she yelled. Finally, turning to Doris, she said, "Except you, Doris. We might have had our moments, but you always came in with a smile and baked goods. You were the only one I could depend on."

Doris smiled and said, "Why, thank you? That's very sweet of—"

"So, this is it," she said, cutting off Doris and turning to the room. "I know where your loyalties all lie. When I'm back, and don't think I won't be back, hell is coming with me. Fire and fury, bitches."

"Is that from *Tombstone*?" Ethan asked.

"I think she's mixing *Tombstone* and *Reagan*," River said.

"The commenters are saying it wasn't *Reagan*," Trevor said.

Throwing her hands up, Melissa said, "Oh, all of you fuck off. Jesus. I can't even give a moving goodbye speech without you traitors trying to catch me in something."

"I think we're done here. Can I help you to your car?" Bryce asked.

She jabbed a finger in his face and pushed her chair toward the door. "Don't touch my shit, sellout. I'm getting your ass transferred to middle of fuck-all Arkansas the minute I get to DC. You better get packing! With my connections, not even your big bad daddy will protect you!"

Melissa reached the door and attempted to pull it open while maneuvering her chair before looking at Trevor. "Do you mind? Maybe you can actually do something for once."

He smiled and walked over, pulling open the door. "Happy to see you out."

She shoved her chair into the hall, and as the doors closed, she shouted, "You haven't heard the last of me! I'll be back!" Then the door slammed behind her, followed by the muffled sounds of, "How the hell am I going to get this down the stairs?"

Bryce let out a sigh and rested his hands on his hips. "Well, that's done. Apologies that you all had to witness that. I hoped to have it done before you arrived this morning."

"What's going to happen to her?" Doris asked, staring down at her lap.

"Trevor. Do you mind?" Bryce said.

Trevor put his phone down. "Sorry. Bad habit."

"Paperwork for Melissa's probation was approved this morning until an internal investigation regarding Chax Tamish's claims is complete," Bryce explained. "She's reporting back to the DC office while they review her role at NRDS. Regardless of the outcome, she will not be dispatched back to the New Richmond office, since there would be understandable friction if she were here."

"So, what? We get a new boss now? Who is it?" River asked.

"Well, Buck will be your interim chief. They won't make anything official until the investigation is complete," Bryce said.

"Woah! Way to go, Buck!" Ethan said.

Buck tapped away on his keyboard and mumbled, "Don't get excited. I'll expect you to actually do your paperwork now."

"An investigation sounds serious," Doris said as she fidgeted in her chair. "Will they question us? Are they going to take us downtown to the station? I've never been arrested before."

Bryce shook his head. "Nope. Upper management might come to the office for a few questions, but really, the investigation they conduct will go mostly unnoticed."

"Oh, good," Doris said.

"However, you all still have a part to play," Bryce said. "The assassin is still on the loose."

"Whoever was trying to kill Chax," Ethan agreed.

"This will still be an open case until we can tie up that loose end," Bryce said.

"We're on it," Buck said.

"I know you are, and I know you'll find them," Bryce said. He cleared his throat and looked at Ethan. "Hey. Um. Could I see you in Melissa's old office for a second?"

Ethan's heart raced in his chest, and a sudden flashback of him in school getting called to the principal's office crossed his mind. "Oh. Uh. Sure."

He followed Bryce into the office and closed the door behind him. His hands were sweaty, and he tried wiping them on his pants without Bryce noticing. "What's up?" he asked.

Bryce took a deep breath, took off his glasses, and started cleaning them. Ethan knew it was what he did when he was anxious, and that made it worse. "Well. They asked me to spearhead the investigation."

"What?" Ethan asked, a smile spreading across his face as he rested his hands on Bryce's shoulders. "That's good news, right? I mean, why wouldn't it be good news?"

Bryce grimaced. "It is a big honor. But—"

"But what?" Ethan asked, his thumb tracing Bryce's clavicle.

"It's in DC."

Ethan let Bryce go. "Oh, no. I. Uh. Does that mean we—" He couldn't finish the question. He couldn't ask Bryce if this meant they were over.

"Well," Bryce started, grabbing Ethan's hand. "I know this is sudden. But. I get to pick my team. Would you come with me?"

Ethan's eyes grew wide, and relief washed over him. "I thought you were about to dump me."

Bryce chuckled and squeezed Ethan's hand. "Nope. The opposite, actually. I couldn't imagine anyone else I'd want to spend time with."

Ethan looked away and bit his lip. "I can't just move to DC. Can I? What about my sister? And Granny?"

Bryce looked down. "It's a lot, I know. But it's a temporary assignment. We just need to map out who Melissa was working with and turn it in. Then we'll be back here. Who knows, the investigation might even bring us back here a couple of times."

Ethan stared at the window shades for a long moment, considering his options. "I'm in," he said.

"Really?" Bryce asked.

"Really," he said, grabbing Bryce at the waist and pulling him in for a kiss. "I don't want to pass up the chance to be with you."

Bryce kissed him back, then pulled away and cleared his throat. "Great. Yeah, great. Well, I'll file the paperwork then. But you all still need to catch that assassin. And you'll need to wrap up any cases or hand them to someone else."

"Of course. I'll get right on it."

Bryce stared at Ethan and bit his lip. "You know, we could get an apartment together. Save on rent and all."

"Bryce Fillmore, are you asking me to move in with you?"

Bryce smiled and nodded.

"I couldn't imagine a more perfect assignment," Ethan said, a grin spread across his face.

Bryce reached for the door and said, "You're going to love DC. And you'll finally get to see the mother ship in action."

Sixty-Four

Staring Down that Hill

"HOW ARE WE GOING to do this?" Ethan asked as he tapped his foot so rapidly it shook the car.

Buck was parked at the top of the hill leading down into the cemetery of St. Patrick's Episcopal Church. Ethan, sitting in the passenger seat, had a direct line of sight down the hill, where he could see vague outlines of Bingo Bango and Lester milling about.

"What the hell do you mean?" Alexus asked from the backseat. "We're walking down there and casing their asses."

"I'm not walking down there," Bob said.

"Wait, what? Why?" Ethan asked as he watched Bingo transform into a rotting zombie and shamble after Lester.

Bob shook his head and raised his hands. "I don't fuck with clowns."

"Why can't you grow a pair and do your job?" Alexus asked.

Folding his arms over his chest, Bob said, "I can't grow a pair of anything, thank you very much. And. I. Don't. Fuck. With. Clowns."

Alexus laughed. "Weren't you some badass marine drill sergeant? Now you're telling me you're afraid of some dude in makeup?"

"I was a mechanic. And it's not some dude in makeup. It's a fucking clown," Bob said.

"Come on. This is serious. We need a plan," Ethan said.

Buck killed the engine and looked out Ethan's window. "He's right. This one is different."

"What about Ronald McDonald? Are you afraid of Ronald McDonald?" Alexus asked.

"No. He's not a clown. He's a mascot," Bob replied.

"He's a clown mascot."

"It's different," Bob said, looking out his window.

Ethan cut in and said, "What if we go in pairs? Buck and I take the right. Alexus and Bob go left. We charge down the hill as fast as we can. We'll get them by surprise, and they won't know what to do."

"What are you, seven?" Alexus quipped. "I bet you want us to yell and wave our hands while we run down the hill too?"

"Yeah, that plan is no good," Buck said.

Ethan shrugged. "Yelling could disorient them."

"What about the Joker?" Alexus asked Bob.

"From Batman?"

"Yeah."

Bob paused and tilted his head from side to side. "Nope. I'd kick his ass."

Alexus frowned. "But he's a clown."

"No. He's a supervillain. It's different," Bob nodded.

Ethan groaned as he watched the two spirits hang out. "Okay, new plan. We get three cases out of the trunk and walk down the hill with them open. Whatever gets sucked up gets sucked up."

"And, in this brilliant plan of yours, when they see us open the cases a whole football field away, what keeps them from just running?" Buck asked.

"Okay. I get what you are saying. But it will work because the blue light will distract them," Ethan said, nodding.

"That's not how that works," Buck said.

"What about It?" Alexus asked.

"Like from the Stephen King novel?" Bob asked.

"Yeah."

"Nah," Bob said, shaking his head.

"Because he's really a giant spider alien thing?" Alexus asked.

Bob nodded. "Not scary."

"But like, Emmett Kelly?" Alexus asked.

"The old hobo clown that used to sweep the spotlight up?" Bob clarified.

"Yeah. That guy."

Bob shivered. "Scary as fuck. Keep that fucker as far away from me as possible."

"What happened to you as a child that made you like this?" Alexus asked with another laugh.

"You don't get it yet, but you will," Bob said. "Clowns are Satan's messengers, with their weird makeup and their big painted-on smiles. They'll take your soul when you're not looking."

"Okay then," Ethan said, turning to Buck. "No running down the hill. We drive down that hill. Just floor it. As fast as we can. Then drop an open case out of the door as we drive by." Wiping his hands together like he was dusting something off his palms, he added, "Bingo, bango, bongo, it's down."

"Bingo, bango, bongo, huh?" asked Buck.

"Yep. Clean. Easy. No one has to deal with Bingo Bango making weird things appear or Lester possessing anyone. No casualties."

"What about all the gravestones we'd have to plow through to get to them?" Buck asked.

Ethan let out a sigh and looked at the car ceiling. "I didn't think about the gravestones."

"Are we sure they both need to be cased?" Alexus asked. "I mean, they couldn't both have possessed the shooter at the debate. Shouldn't we try to figure out which one of them did it?"

"Oh, it was the fucking clown," Bob said. "No doubt about it. Satan's fucking general. You've got to case that motherfucker."

"I mean, the nerdy assistant has a motive. What motive does the clown have?" Alexus asked.

"Who knows? We don't have any files on him," Ethan added. "We don't even know his real name."

"He's a fucking clown. That's all you need to know," Bob retorted.

"She's right. We don't know that they are both involved," Buck said.

Ethan looked down the hill again, noting that there was only one ghost in his line of sight now. "Hey, um. So," he started to say.

Buck cut him off and said, "We've got to go by the book and talk to them. Maybe now that Chax is behind bars, one of them will plead guilty."

"Or the clown is going to peel off his face and show his true colors while he murders your asses!" Bob declared.

"Why the face peeling? That doesn't make sense," Alexus asked.

"Guys. Seriously. I think we lost one of them," Ethan said, still searching the graveyard.

Bob rolled his eyes. "Oh, sure. Make jokes. When he starts pulling poisoned balloon animals out of your ass and then choking you with them, you won't be laughing then."

"Are they poisoned because they are coming out of my ass? Or are they coming out of my ass because they are poisoned? Or is the poison irrelevant to my ass altogether?" Alexus asked.

"If you're so scared of him, why did you get in the car?" Buck asked.

Bob grunted and pointed to Alexus. "It's not like I had a fucking choice. I wanted you all to leave my bag at the office, but no. You assholes grabbed me and dragged me along. Dammit. I hate being tied to that thing."

"Yeah. My bad," Alexus nodded. "I wasn't paying attention."

"Hey! Will you finally pay attention to me?" Ethan demanded.

"Okay, Queen," Alexus said with a grin. "What does needy-neederson need now?"

"I've been trying to tell you that one of them is missing," Ethan said, pointing out his window down the hill.

"One of who?" Bingo Bango asked as he materialized in the rear middle seat between Alexus and Bob.

"Shit!" Alexus screamed.

"Dammit!" Ethan yelled.

"Oh absofuckinglutely not!" Bob screamed as he leaped through the car door and into the street.

"What's up with Captain Buzzkill?" Bingo said as he morphed his clothes into Bob's uniform. "You'd think he saw a ghost!" He pulled a horn from his sleeve and honked it three times. It rang loud inside the car, forcing Ethan to clamp his ears shut.

Leaning to Alexus, Bingo said, "Funny, right? Because I'm a ghost? You get it? Because I said, what'd he see, a ghost? Get it? Funny."

"Yeah, real funny," Alexus replied, cracking her knuckles.

Leaning forward toward Ethan's ear, Bingo said, "The best jokes always need a little explaining. Because they're so complex. And my audience can be pretty . . . dense. You know? I like to just lay it out for them. Here's the joke that I said. And here's what it means."

"I don't think—" Ethan started to say, but Bingo Bango interrupted him.

"Just make it clear. Really, the longer the explanation, the funnier it gets. The key is to really dig deep into that explanation, just to make sure everyone knows I made the joke because I'm the ghost in the scenario. And don't let it go, no matter how confused they look. Just. Keep. Explaining."

"Alright!" Buck yelled. "Everyone out of the car!"

Buck, Ethan, Alexus, and Bingo all exited the car. Buck rounded to the back and popped open the trunk, pulling out the briefcases. Bingo positioned himself between Alexus and Ethan, so it looked like they were standing in a line. Snapping his fingers, he transformed his clothing into a worn and wrinkled gray suit that matched the one Ethan was wearing.

"If you were alive, I'd knock you out with Betty," Alexus said.

"Who's Betty?" Bingo asked. "Your girlfriend?"

"Her baseball bat," Ethan said.

Bingo gave Alexus a broad smile and moved his eyebrows up and down in reply.

"I think he's funny sometimes," Ethan said.

"You would," Alexus replied.

Buck handed Ethan and Alexus both a briefcase and ignored Bingo's outstretched hand. "Everyone, follow me. We need Lester for this conversation too," he barked as he headed down the hill.

"Leave my bag! Hey! Leave my bag here!" Bob yelled from the other side of the street.

"Fine, chicken," Alexus called back as she untied the bag from the loop in her jeans and left it on the ground. "If someone steals your ass, it's not my fault."

"I'll take my chances," Bob yelled back.

As they marched down the hill, Bingo said, "I'm glad you came out today. Lester's been a bit depressed. It'll be good to have some visitors. Denise came by, but she's all business. No fun at all."

Buck spun on his heels at the mention of his jump-suit clad ghost nemesis, and asked, "Denise came by?"

"Yep. She came by to hang out. She stops by every once in a while. We're besties."

"Besties?" Buck grunted.

"Yeah. You know. We have cool club rings and everything," Bingo said, holding out his hand to display an unseemly large diamond ring on his finger, which disappeared when he pulled his hand back.

Buck pointed a finger in the clown's face and said, "Now you listen here, stay away from her. She's bad news."

Still in his NRDS suit, Bingo Bango said, "Sir, yes, sir," as he clapped his heels together, stood up straight, and saluted.

"I mean it," Buck reiterated.

"As do I, sir," Bingo nodded.

"Good. Let's go," Buck said as they headed back down the hill.

Sixty-Five

Case Closed

L ESTER, STILL DRESSED IN his sleek blue suit and thick-rimmed glasses, leaned against a grave as Buck, Ethan, Alexus, and Bingo Bango approached. He looked up for a moment before staring down at his nails without a word.

"Well, Lester and Bingo. We've got some good news for you two," Buck said.

Bingo disappeared from their side and reappeared next to his friend. "Good news or bad news?"

"A little of both, maybe," Buck said.

"Hmm. Bad news would call for tissues," Bingo said, pulling a box of ghostly tissues from behind the grave Lester was leaning on, "but good news calls for celebration," he said, pulling two cigars from behind the grave with his other hand. He took a drag from one cigar, the end lighting as he breathed in. "I'll hold on to both. For now."

"This is serious," Ethan said.

Bingo nudged Lester and said, "This is so exciting. I'm dying to know this potentially good or potentially bad news. Aren't you excited?"

"Riveted," Lester replied in a monotone voice.

"Lester, your old boss, Chax Tamish, has been arrested," Buck said.

For a second, Bingo's clothes transformed into a tight black pantsuit, and his hair turned into a gray bob as he pointed to Buck with a pair of glasses, impersonating Miranda Priestly, "You buried the lede, darling. This is a celebration."

The tissue box exploded into confetti and balloons. Bingo handed a newly lit cigar to Lester.

"They charged him with multiple counts of murder. Yours included," Buck added.

Lester took a drag from the cigar and smiled. "I appreciate you telling me."

Ethan looked around the cemetery, expecting to see a light appear and for Lester to step in. They wouldn't need to case anyone if that happened, but no light appeared.

Buck continued, "We recorded his confession and handed it over to the authorities. It'll be an open and shut case."

Lester took another drag of his cigar. "That is good news."

"We figured that's what you were waiting for," Buck said.

Ethan looked down at Buck's hand, which was repositioning the briefcase he held to make it easier to open.

Lester blew a smoke ring into the air. "Maybe I was. Maybe not."

Bingo Bango blew smoke into the air as well, but instead of a blue ghostly haze, his took the shape of a middle finger, aimed up at the sky. "Take that, you bag of shit Chax Tamish. Don't worry friend, sometimes it takes a while to see the light at the end of the tunnel. I mean, look at me. I've been here . . . I don't even know how long. But I still hold out hope. That light is coming for me any minute."

Suddenly, a beam of light shone directly onto Bingo.

Ethan frowned and stepped back, looking for the door to the other side.

Bingo struck a pose, and a bouquet appeared in his hand as he wept. "The time is finally here. Thank you all. Except you," he pointed to Buck. "You were useless."

Ethan looked at Alexus and Buck. "I don't see a door. Do either of you?"

The light flickered out, and the bouquet wilted into nothingness. Bingo slumped his shoulders. "Never mind. False alarm."

Buck cleared his throat, gripping his case. "You know, sometimes spirits don't cross over when we come with news because it wasn't new news to them," Buck suggested.

"That feels like victim blaming," Bingo said, crossing his arms and giving Buck a wide-eyed look.

Lester blew more smoke into the air and stared at his cigar. "If there's something you need to get off your chest. Why don't you just say it?"

Alexus stepped forward, flipping open the clasp of her briefcase. "You're the ghost I pushed off the roof. The one trying to shoot Chax in that poor guy's body. He's dead, you know."

Bingo took a step forward and held his hands up. "Hang on a second. Why don't we all just calm down?"

"And I suspect you were the one loosening the lights at Chax's political rallies," Buck said, moving his free hand to the clasp of his case.

Ethan's heart raced as a bead of sweat ran down his cheek. He unclasped his briefcase and locked eyes with Bingo. It was clear they were after Lester, but Bingo was a wild card he couldn't ignore.

"Bingo, step aside," Buck said.

"Now, listen. Things happened. He made mistakes. But stuffing him in one of your little boxes isn't going to help," Bingo said.

"Just let it go, agents. Move on and close the case." Lester took a long drag from his ghost cigar, which oddly didn't get smaller as he smoked it.

"Bingo, if you stand in our way, we'll case you too," Ethan said. "Just step aside. Lester's coming with us."

Bingo slipped between Lester and the three agents, holding up his hands. "Look, agents. I would love to quote Billy Joel's "I Go to Extremes" here, but I've heard he's incredibly litigious, and who could afford a lawsuit in this day and age? Am I right? I mean, lawyers? Scum. Right, Lester?"

"You know, I'm a lawyer," Lester said.

"What did I tell you about inside voice and outside voice? Jesus, Lester. Don't tell the ghost-rent-a-cops that you stole their watches." Bingo held up his hand to show he was wearing a ghost version of Buck's watch.

"Last chance," Buck said, as he flipped open the latch to his case. Alexus and Ethan both followed suit.

Bingo's eyes flared blue, and cold air rippled across Ethan's body. One second Ethan was standing next to Buck and Alexus, and the next he was levitating off the ground.

"What the fuck? What the fuck? Put me down!" Ethan shouted, arms flailing as he dropped his case.

Bingo held up his hand, and Ethan floated straight to him. Cold clown fingers wrapped around his neck, holding him off to the side, and squeezed. "Now look here, agents," Bingo said, his voice amplified as if it were coming out of a megaphone. "You holster those pistols or the kid gets it, see?"

"Put him down, clown," Alexus sneered.

Bingo pointed with his other hand. "I'm not messing around here, copper. I'll blow his brains all over these tombstones, see?"

Bingo's free hand transformed into a gun, and cold metal pressed up against Ethan's head.

Ethan squeezed his eyes shut, images of Bryce, Rosemary, and Ellie flashing through his mind.

"I suggest you all leave," Lester remarked.

"We can't do that, Lester," Buck said, his hand holding the case from opening.

Bingo spoke from the side of his mouth. "Lester, buddy ol' pal. You're not helping. I've got this. Just walk away. Vamoose."

"I'm not walking away, Bingo," Lester said. "They can either leave now or get buried six feet under."

Alexus laughed. "You're coming with us one way or another."

Lester smirked and flicked his cigar off to the side. It vanished in an instant. "That's where you're wrong." He lunged forward, shooting past Bingo and Ethan and into Alexus. Her body radiated a bright blue light for a second, then she collapsed to her knees.

"Alexus?" Buck asked.

Alexus looked up at him with bright blue eyes, then leaped up and threw a fast right hook. Buck jumped back at the last second, stepping out of the way of her swing.

"Oh, shit!" Bingo screamed.

"Let. Me. Go!" Ethan croaked, trying to will his limbs to move.

Alexus growled and took another swing at Buck, then another, both of which Buck sidestepped. "You're not putting me in one of those boxes!" she screamed.

Buck was good on his feet, but Ethan knew it was only a matter of time before Lester connected with a punch or two. He also knew that Buck would never hit back, as he'd actually be hitting Alexus. Desperately, Ethan searched for an answer, but he felt completely powerless. As Buck continued to dodge Alexus's advances, Ethan pleaded, "Bingo. Please. This isn't what you want. Let me go."

"No can do, chief. In for a penny, in for a pound," Bingo said, squeezing tighter around Ethan's neck.

Ethan closed his eyes. He couldn't move physically, but that didn't rule out the other things he could do. He focused on that lingering feeling inside his gut, pulling at all the energy he could muster to make something happen.

"Wait! What are you doing? Stop that!" Bingo yelled in his ear.

Sidestepping another swing, Buck used his case to deflect Alexus's jab, but the power of the impact sent him stumbling backward. Losing his footing, he tripped and fell on his back.

"Last chance," Ethan whispered to Bingo. He could feel the spiritual energy humming in his brain. Every muscle fiber in his body tingled with the power his mind had gathered.

"No!" Bingo yelled, gripping Ethan tighter.

Lester landed a powerful kick to Buck's ribs, causing the old man to scream in pain as he covered his midsection with both hands.

The cold was gone from the back of Ethan's throat. The energy he'd gathered had pushed him beyond tangible things. His mind expanded, and his vision grew beyond the limits of his eyes. He sensed his own energy, bright and full of life, held up by a mere shadow in comparison. He could sense Lester's rage, Alexus's confinement, Buck's pain, and Bingo's fear. It was all around him.

Alexus kicked Buck again and laughed. "You'll never get me in that box! I'll kill all of you first!" Kicking Buck with each word, he screamed, "Every! Single! One! Of! You!"

Ethan took in a quick breath and focused on Lester. He could see the little puppet strings he had on Alexus, and one by one, Ethan pulled them away.

Lester's head tore away from Alexus's, and he screamed, "What the fuck?"

The rest of him peeled away, and Alexus stumbled forward.

Ethan grabbed Bingo's hand and peeled it away like it was nothing. He slowly descended back onto the ground, his eyes locked on Lester. Ethan raised a hand, and Lester froze in midair.

Alexus grabbed her case and flung it open, swinging it underneath Lester's feet. "Case it is, asshole."

Lester let out a loud moan as the light from the case pulled him down into its depths. In an instant, he was gone, and the case latched shut.

All eyes turned to Bingo, who held his hands up in surrender. "Listen. Gang. That was cool, right? I mean, wow! Did you even know you could do that?" Clapping, he said, "I mean, bravo. Ethan. Your parents would be so proud. Excellent work."

Still sensing the surrounding energy, Ethan held out a hand toward Bingo. Blue lights encased the clown, and Ethan waved his hand toward the case. It flipped open, and Bingo slipped right inside, his always-smiling face now changed into a frown.

Ethan teetered over, exhaustion filling his bones. He looked over at Buck, who lay looking up at the sky, holding his ribs.

"Good job, kid," Buck said with a wheeze.

Ethan lay down on the grass, finding comfort on solid ground. "We did it," he mumbled as the world faded to black.

Sixty-Six

See Ya Later, Alligator

E THAN LEANED ON THE tombstone, overlooking the graves of Oakland Cemetery. This was where it all started, nearly a year ago, when his grandmother asked him to check on her recently deceased friend. Little did she know the path it would take him and the rest of the NRDS.

Mable was the first murder victim they'd met. And Dylan had pulled them into the orbit of the mayoral race. They could have discovered both things anyway, but it didn't change that this was where they all started. And now look at him. He wasn't the Walmart employee he was over a year ago. Now he was Agent Malik, leaving for an investigation in DC.

He kicked at the dirt. If someone had told him then that in a year he'd start wearing a baggy Goodwill suit, carrying briefcases, and talking to ghosts, he wouldn't have believed a single word of it.

Ethan took in a breath and looked up at Buck and smiled. Buck was now Captain of New Richmond, the man who showed Ethan everything he needed to know. And now Ethan had a job to do.

He turned to Dylan and Mable and said, "Alright, let's go over this again." He scanned the list on his clipboard, checking off as he spoke. "We checked on your dog, and he's fine. We talked to your friend Joey, and he's okay. Your mom is sad, but we agreed she is going to be okay. Your dad is mayor for another term, and they are not going to sell your house anytime soon. Can you think of anything else that might keep you here?"

Dylan shrugged and looked at the ground. "I don't know. I'm sorry."

"There is nothing to be sorry for," Mable said, putting her arm around him.

"But I'm still stuck here while all the other kids are gone," he said.

"It's not unusual. Sometimes it takes a while," Buck said.

Dylan sighed and looked up at Mable. "But you can't go until I go. And that's not fair."

"Oh, Dylan, you aren't keeping me anywhere. I choose to be here. I would stay for an eternity just to keep you company."

"But it's not fair. You have to have someone on the other side you want to see."

"They will be there when the time comes. And as for being fair, nothing in my life or yours has been fair. You think it was fair that they murdered me and that you died so young? You should have had another fifty years to make all kinds of mistakes." She bent down, raised his chin with her finger, and looked him in the eyes. "Your death was unfair."

Dylan shrugged again.

A thought suddenly hit Ethan. "What if we're going about this the wrong way?"

Buck raised an eyebrow. "What do you mean?"

"Dylan, I think we're asking the wrong questions. We've been trying to figure out what was left undone. Mable wanted to know why she was murdered, and she wanted to keep all you kids safe, so she hung on," Ethan explained. "She lived a full life and needed only a few things to be straightened out before letting go."

Buck nodded along, catching on to where Ethan was going. "Smart, kid."

"But you," Ethan continued, smiling at Dylan. "Your whole life is unfinished business. It isn't one or two details. It's all the details. You never rode your first roller coaster, or won your first big game, or had your first kiss, or your first job. Even the other kids were spirits long enough, even for decades, for them to fill in the gaps they'd missed. But you've only had a year."

A ghostly tear ran down Dylan's cheek before he sat down in the grass and wiped his nose on his sleeve.

"Oh, dear," Mable said. Sitting next to him, she wrapped an arm around his shoulder.

"Your whole life is unfinished," Ethan said.

Dylan leaned into Mable. "Yeah, that's it," he said as more tears ran down his cheeks. "But I don't know how to fix that."

Buck rested his hands on his hips. "I've got an idea."

"Really?" Dylan asked, looking up with wide eyes.

"How would you like to become a BOB, Dylan?" Buck asked.

Ethan snapped his fingers. "Oh, that's perfect!"

"What's a BOB?" Dylan asked.

"A not-so-nice nickname we give our spirit agents we employ at the National Recently Deceased Services," Buck said.

"An agent? You mean, like you guys? Do I get to wear a suit and stuff?" Dylan asked, a slight smile forming on his face.

"You'd help people cross over, just like Ethan and I do. It'll be hard work, and you'll have to go through training, but—"

"I want to do it," Dylan cut him off, pushing himself up off the ground. "I want to be an agent."

"We'll have to excavate your grave. And you'll have to leave New Richmond. But, in a few months, you'll be partnered with someone like Ethan or I." Buck said.

Dylan nodded. "Yes. I want to be an agent. Please make me an agent, Mr. Buck."

"That's a wonderful solution," Mable said.

"It might take a few weeks to process the paperwork. Are you okay with hanging on for a bit longer?" Buck asked Mable.

"I'll stay here as long as he needs me to," she said. "The afterlife isn't going anywhere."

"Then it's settled. Thank you, Mable," Ethan said.

"Of course, Ethan dear. And you better enjoy yourself in DC, you hear?"

"I hope this is the last time we talk, Mable," Ethan said with a grin, turning with Buck to head back to his car.

"Me too. Me too," she called after him.

Ethan slipped into Buck's car, and Buck drove off toward his home. The drive was silent while Ethan watched the town he'd known his entire life pass by. He bit his lip, trying not to get sentimental as he pictured himself on the other side of the country, away from all this.

He chanced a glance at Buck. As always, the old man had both hands on the steering wheel at ten and two, which made Ethan laugh. He'd never admit it, but Buck had been more of a father to him in this last year than he'd had since his own father died. He'd learned so much from him and could say without hesitation that he would love nothing more than to become him some day.

"Hey," Buck said, breaking the silence. The sound of his voice made Ethan jump.

"Uh, yeah?" he asked.

"Stop getting all misty-eyed over there." he said, not taking his eyes off the road. "No one's fucking dying. Cut it out."

"I'm not getting misty-eyed," Ethan said, wiping his eyes.

"Bullshit."

"Well, fine. What if I am? I'm leaving you guys, and I'm leaving home for the first time."

"So?"

"So, it matters, okay? I'm allowed to have feelings."

"Fuck your feelings."

Ethan laughed. "Did you just tell me to fuck my feelings?"

"Sure did," Buck replied, still not taking his eyes off the road.

"Well, then. Fuck your feelings too."

"I don't have feelings."

"Liar," Ethan scoffed. "You're pulling the tough act so you don't get all misty-eyed too. Admit it. You're going to miss me."

"Oh please. I might actually get some paperwork finally done without you around yacking my ear off all day."

Ethan smiled. "I'll miss you too."

"Goddamn it. Cut it out or I'll pull this car over and kick your ass right now."

"Ha! I'm not some drunk guy in a bar, old timer. I've got moves," Ethan said with a grin.

"Sure, kid. How about you don't test me," Buck growled.

Ethan held up his hands in surrender. "Aw, don't be so touchy. If you could catch me, you'd absolutely kick my ass."

Buck laughed to himself. "Gerry would be pissed, though, if you showed up to the party with a black eye."

"He'd punish you for weeks."

"He'd probably stop getting me food."

"And scotch. You'd be miserable."

"Yeah. Not worth it."

Buck pulled into his driveway and killed the engine. "I need to have a serious conversation with you now. Before you leave us."

Ethan looked over at Buck, and his heart skipped a beat. The way Buck was staring at him forced him to shift in his seat. He slouched a little, his gaze turning to Buck's house. "Uh, sure," he said, trying to cover up his nervousness. "What's up?"

"DC won't be a walk in the park, kid. You can't treat it like some fucking vacation."

Ethan swallowed nervously. "What do you mean? I'm not—"

"You're not there to see the sights. There are some big names you and Bryce are investigating. Big names that have no problems skirting through paperwork to see you and countless New Richmond locals dead. It's a mission. And I need you back here in one piece."

Ethan looked at his mentor. He could see Buck's brow was furrowed, and his eyes were focused somewhere far off in the distance. He was scared. And that meant Ethan should be too. "Message received, boss," he said with a nod.

Buck cleared his throat and looked down at the floorboard. "I'm sending River with you two. Bryce agreed that his connections, mixed with Bryce's, should be able to keep all of you safe. Trust each other. You're going to need it."

"We'll be okay," Ethan said.

Buck shook his head. "If I could, I'd go. But someone needs to manage all the cases still happening here, and I don't trust anyone else."

"Please. Like anyone else could do the job better than you?" Ethan asked with a smile.

Buck looked at him again. "You remember what I've taught you? Keep your head down. Do the work. Keep good notes. You'll figure it out."

"And I've read the manual. So, I've got that going for me," Ethan said with a grin.

"And don't trust any of those corporate fuckers. They'll drown you all in paperwork if they sense you coming."

"I'll be careful."

Buck grabbed his arm and squeezed it gently. Ethan knew this was the closest he'd ever got to a hug from the old oak. He held on to the moment as long as he could, saving it away in his memories.

Buck looked Ethan in the eye and said, "You come back alive. You hear me?"

Ethan nodded. "Yes, sir."

"You're an excellent agent, Ethan Malik. I want you back on my team when this is all over. Remember your training, and kick some ass for me," Buck said with a smile.

"Thanks, Captain Hampton," Ethan replied.

Buck let go of Ethan's arm and stepped out of the car. "Alright. Let's get inside before Gerry has a fit. You know he's already got a cocktail waiting for you."

"I wouldn't have it any other way," Ethan said, pulling open the car door. He smiled, reflecting on all that had happened this past year, letting the pride overwhelm him. He was proud to have a man like Buck in his life, and proud that Buck felt he'd grown enough to trust him with something so dangerous.

"Stop sitting there grinning and get the fuck out of the car," Buck yelled as he walked toward the party.

"Yeah, yeah. I'm coming, old man!" Ethan yelled back as he trailed behind Buck.

Don't Ghost Us Just Yet!

T HANK YOU FOR READING season one of NRDS. There's more
where that comes from, so buckle up.

Here's the deal, we're independent authors, and reviews are the best way
to help spread the word and reach new readers.

If you could spare a few seconds, would you please consider leaving an
honest review on this book's Amazon, Goodreads, Storygraph, or other
pages?

Your support helps keep the lights on at NRDS, and we all know they
need all the support they can get.

Scare you later,
JP Rindfleisch IX & Jeff Elkins

The NRDS Return In Season Two

Want to catch up on NRDS episodes as they are released? Check out season two and beyond on Kindle Vella. Season two picks up on Episode 67.

http://bit.ly/nrds_agent

About the Authors

JP Rindfleisch is the curator of things dark, strange, and queer. They are the author of the LGBT Cozy Suburban Fantasy called Mandrake Manor and the co-author to the Dark Urban Fantasy project called the Leah Ackerman series. To follow JP's work and find their other books, go to www.jprindfleischix.com.

Jeff Elkins writes stories about outsiders searching for community who fight for the rejected and forgotten. He's the author of ten novels and too many short stories to count. You can find more of his work at www.JeffElkinsWriter.com.

Milton Keynes UK
Ingram Content Group UK Ltd.
UKHW010749010324
438477UK00001B/16